DEADMAN SWITCH

Trembley's arms were moving forward now, reaching out toward the black Deadman Switch panel. For a moment they hesitated, as if unsure of themselves. Then the hands stirred, the fingers curved over, and the arms lowered to the Mjollnir switch. One hand groped for position ... paused ... touched it—

And abruptly, gravity returned. We were on Mjollnir drive again, on our way through the Cloud.

With a dead man at the controls.

TIMOTHY ZAHN

DEADMAN SWITCH

BAEN BOOKS

DEADMAN SWITCH

Copyright © 1988 by Timothy Zahn

Excerpts from the *New Jerusalem Bible*, © 1985 by Darton, Longman & Todd, Ltd., and Doubleday, a division of Bantam, Doubleday, Dell Publishing Group, Inc., reprinted by permission of the publisher.

A Baen Books Original

Baen Publishing Enterprises
260 Fifth Avenue
New York, N.Y. 10001

First printing, October 1988

ISBN: 0-671-69784-6

Cover art by David Mattingly

Printed in the United States of America

Distributed by
SIMON & SCHUSTER
1230 Avenue of the Americas
New York, N.Y. 10020

CHAPTER 1

I'd been sitting at the window of my small cubicle for nearly an hour, listening to a Joussein symphonaria and watching the intricate drift of sunlight and shadow across the city from a hundred twenty stories up, when the call I'd been expecting all morning finally came. "Gilead? You in there?"

"Yes, sir," I replied, turning off the music with a wave of my control stick and standing up. The Carillon Building's intercom speakers were very good, and I had no trouble discerning the excitement and anticipation in my employer's voice. With Lord Kelsey-Ramos, that could mean only one thing. "I take it the raid is nearly finished?"

He snorted, just loudly enough for me to hear. "Is it that obvious?"

"It is to me," I said simply.

He snorted again. "Well, you're right. Come on in."

"Yes, sir." Stepping across the starkly plain room— kept so by my own request—I set the control stick down by the player and crossed to the second of the room's two doors. "Gilead Raca Benedar," I told it, speaking distinctly. The voicelock was a slightly ridiculous precaution, here in what amounted to Carillon's inner sanctum, but I'd long since stopped feeling annoyed by it. Paranoia, in one form or another, was one of the many burdens of wealth.

The door opened; and from my cubicle I entered Lord Kelsey-Ramos's office.

Lord Kelsey-Ramos himself had once likened the contrast of the two rooms to that between midnight and noon; but for me that comparison fell far short. From the dark at the bottom of a mine shaft to noon, perhaps; or even to the searing brightness outside a sunskimmer's slingshot pass by a star. For a pair of heartbeats I paused there on the threshold, senses struggling as they adjusted from the peace of my undecorated room and quiet music to the flamboyant luxury laid out before me.

To the luxury, and even more to the shrewdly engineered contradictions embedded within it. The milky-white living carpet, the shimmering Vedant woodling panels and camocarvings, the massive gemrock desk—the sense of the room reaching my eyes was one of extreme wealth, calm and stable. At the same time, the subtle yet distinctive sounds of the InWeb news/data analyzer and Wall Street Interactive machine gave off a totally opposite sense, that of frantic haste and unrest. It created just enough emotional confusion that first-time visitors were invariably thrown slightly off stride, though few of them realized on a conscious level just what it was that was bothering them.

And in the midst of it all, as much a study in contrasts as the office itself, sat Lord Kelsey-Ramos.

Seated straight-backed at his desk, gazing almost disinterestedly at the displays facing him, he blended quite well with the calm decor . . . but as I stepped closer, the lines around his eyes and the play of his facial muscles radiated the message I'd already learned from his voice. Somewhere out there, on some ethereal battlefield of paper and computer memory, a war was raging. A quiet, civilized war, fought by opposing sums of money . . . for no more purpose than the acquisition of even more of that same money.

The love of money is the root of all evils, I quoted to myself. But it was an automatic, almost ritual thought these days. Once, I'd thought in my pride that my mere presence might be enough to influence the way Lord Kelsey-Ramos handled his wealth; now, years later, I could barely consider myself lucky that that part of my own conscience hadn't become uselessly numb. *Pride goes before destruction, a haughty spirit before a fall* . . . Another ritual thought, and one that always included the reminder that destruction came in many forms. Including stagnation.

After eight long years, I still didn't fit in here. And most everyone knew it.

Lord Kelsey-Ramos shifted in his chair, the faint squeak of embroidered cloth on camileather reminding me I wasn't here just to indulge myself in self-pity. Over the familiar scents of the room's woodling and living carpet I caught a whiff of *Marisee Tinge,* the executive secretary's perfume; beneath that, I could smell the very human odor of Lord Kelsey-Ramos's tension. The images, sounds, scents—all of it blended together into the all too familiar sense of civilized warfare that I'd felt upon entering. I'd seen it many times before in my time at Carillon . . . but this time something about it was different. This time, there was something more than just money at stake. Something far more important . . .

And at that moment, it was abruptly over. The tension lines left Lord Kelsey-Ramos's face, and his eyes softened, and he looked up at me. "Congratulate me, Gilead," he said, his voice rich with overtones of satisfaction. "After ten years of trying, I've finally done it."

"Congratulations, sir," I said. "What is it you've finally done?"

Amusement lines replaced those of the earlier tension, and the sense of his satisfaction deepened. "I've obtained the Carillon Group a transport license for Solitaire."

My stomach tightened. "I see," I managed.

He peered up at me. "Bothers you that much, does it?"

I looked him straight in the eye. "It's the paying of a blood offering in exchange for wealth," I said bluntly.

His lip twitched, and some of the satisfaction left his face. But not very much. "I'm sorry you feel that way." Reaching to his desktop, he snagged his control stick and began punching buttons, my opinion already dismissed from his thoughts. "If it helps your conscience any, Carillon won't actually be handling flights in and out of Solitaire system, at least not directly. What I've done is simply to buy up a controlling share of HTI Transport, the company with this particular license. I thought it might be interesting to call up HTI's chief exec and see how he reacts to the news."

Which was why he'd sent for me, of course. "Anything in particular you want me to watch for?"

"Signs of resistance, mostly. HTI's always been stiffnecked jealous about its autonomy, and I want to know how badly they're going to resent being swallowed up. Ah—"

A decorative young woman had appeared on his desk's center display. "HTI Transport; Mr. O'Rielly's office," she said pleasantly.

"Lord Kelsey-Ramos of the Carillon Group," Lord Kelsey-Ramos identified himself. "Mr. O'Rielly will want to speak to me."

A flicker of uncertainty touched the secretary's face, but she was obviously knowledgeable in the names of Portslava's business elite and she put the screen into hold without argument. A moment later it cleared to reveal a middle-aged man wearing an expensive business capelet. "Lord Kelsey-Ramos," he nodded in greeting. "What can I do for you, sir?"

"He doesn't know yet," I murmured from just outside the phone's range.

Lord Kelsey-Ramos's eyelids dipped briefly in acknowledgment. "Good morning, Mr. O'Rielly," he said.

"I just wanted to call and personally welcome you into the Carillon Group."

O'Rielly's face went the whole gamut—shock, disbelief, more shock, outrage—all in the space of a second and a half. Behind him, the out-of-focus background shifted as the camera tracked his lunge forward, and through the stunned silence I could hear the faint click of nervous fingers on control keys. One look was really all he needed. "Spike you, anyway, Kelsey-Ramos," he snarled. "You putrid, smert-headed—"

"Thank you, but I've heard it all before," Lord Kelsey-Ramos interjected calmly. "I'll leave it to you to inform the HTI board of this, and I'll want a meeting scheduled to discuss any changes that'll need to be made. In the meantime, do you have anything besides insults you'd like to say? On or off the record, of course?"

Some of the pure fury was fading from O'Rielly's face, to be replaced by an icy bitterness and more than a little discomfort. "What, off the record with your little pet lie detector Benedar there somewhere?" he sneered, eyes darting around as he searched the limits of his screen for some sign of me. The sarcasm wasn't nearly strong enough to cover his discomfort. "Or did you think I didn't know about him?"

Lord Kelsey-Ramos had indeed thought that, but only I caught his annoyance. "I take it that means you'll save your statement for the board meeting, then," he told O'Rielly. "Equally fine. Have your secretary call mine when you've scheduled the meeting. Oh, and we'll be wanting to send a rep to Solitaire to check on your locals there. I'd appreciate it if you'd send word to Whitecliff to expect him."

O'Rielly's lip twisted. "You're really enjoying this, aren't you? You've been trying to get your sticky little fingers on a Solitaire license for, what, eight years now?"

"Closer to ten," Lord Kelsey-Ramos said coolly. "Not that it matters. I'll be sending a courier over to your office within the hour; kindly have copies of all your

records and documents ready by then. Good morning
to you, Mr. O'Rielly."

He waved his control stick, and the display blanked.
"And *that* is *that*," he commented, dropping the stick
on his desk and looking up at me again. Some of the
thrill and triumph was draining out of him now, leaving
a measure of tiredness behind. "A very profitable day's
work, I'd say."

I nodded, a neutral enough response. "You'll be going
out to Solitaire yourself, I take it?"

He smiled. "Is it that—?" Abruptly, the smile vanished. "Is it that obvious?" he asked cautiously.

The paranoia of the wealthy. "It is to me."

A muscle in his cheek tightened. "Could it have been
obvious to O'Rielly, too?" he asked.

I thought back, trying to remember every nuance of
the man. "It might have been," I agreed. "The shock of
it all was wearing off at the end, and he wasn't ready
yet to give up. Once he stops to think about it he may
be able to guess at least that much."

Lord Kelsey-Ramos pursed his lips. "Tell me everything else you got."

I went back through the conversation for him, giving
as best I could the sense I'd had of O'Rielly at each
juncture. "Do you think he'll put up a fight over this?"
he asked when I'd finished.

"Yes."

"A legal fight, or otherwise?"

I shrugged. The sense of the man on that point had
been abundantly clear. "He'll fight to the limits of
either his abilities or his conscience. I don't know where
either limit lies."

Lord Kelsey-Ramos gnawed the inside of his cheek.
"I have a pretty good idea of both limits," he growled.
"Unfortunately. So. You think he'll figure me to go
charging off to Solitaire to personally stick Carillon's
flag into the dirt, eh?" Gently, under his breath, he
swore. "You know, Gilead, I've waited for this moment
for ten years now. Petitioned and maneuvered to get
the Patri to grant new transport licenses, pushed and

prodded at companies who already had them—" he glared up at me, discomfort flicking across his face— "*and* put considerable money into trying to find a substitute for the Deadman Switch. I've *earned* the right to be the first man to ride a Carillon ship to Solitaire, vlast it."

He broke off, took a deep breath. "And now I've got to stay here and duel with O'Rielly and the HTI board instead. Thanks to you."

"You could ignore my advice," I reminded him. "You've done so before."

A touch of dark humor came back into his face, as I'd expected it would. "And usually wished I hadn't," he pointed out wryly. "Besides which, what's the point of hiring a Watcher in the first place if I'm not going to listen to him?"

"People have done stranger things to themselves, sir. Often even willingly."

His eyes flicked past me, to the door of my—to his mind—painfully plain cubicle. "And more often done those strange things to others. Not willingly."

Punishing the parents' fault in the children and in the grandchildren to the third and fourth generation . . . "The training really hasn't been a burden, Lord Kelsey-Ramos," I assured him quietly. "There's a great deal of beauty in God's universe—beauty that you may never even notice, let alone be able to appreciate."

"Does that beauty make up for all the ugliness that's also there?" he asked pointedly. "Does it make up for the fact that you have to strip a room practically bare to get a little relief from sensory overload?"

To one he gave five talents, to another two, to a third one . . . "I do what I can with what I've been given," I said simply. "In that way, at least, I'm no different than you."

He pursed his lips. "Perhaps. Someday you'll have to tell me—to *really* tell me—what it's like to be a Watcher."

"Yes, sir." I never would, of course. He didn't really want to know. "If that'll be all . . . ?"

"Not quite." His face tightened slightly, his sense that of a man preparing to deliver unwanted news. "I concede that you're right, that I can't afford to traipse off to Solitaire right now. But *someone* ought to go, if for no other reason than to let them know Carillon will be taking things firmly in rein. It seems to me that the obvious person for that job is Randon."

He clearly expected a negative reaction, but I had none to offer. At twenty-five, Lord Kelsey-Ramos's son still had a lot to learn about life, but he knew enough about how to handle people—his own and others—to make a reasonable ambassador to a conquered firm. "I presume you'll be sending a financial expert along with him?" I asked. "In case their records need looking over?"

"Oh, I'll send a whole slate of experts along with him—don't worry about that. Still, even experts often miss important details . . . which is why you'll be going, too."

I took a careful breath, feeling my heartbeat increase. "Sir, if it's all the same with you—"

"It isn't," he said firmly, "and I'm afraid I insist. I want you there with Randon." He hesitated. "I realize the whole idea of the Deadman Switch bothers you, but I'm sure you can handle it this once."

Solitaire . . . and the Deadman Switch. For a moment I nearly told him no, that this time the price was too high. But even as I opened my mouth, the quiet reminder of why I was working for him in the first place drained the defiance away.

As it always seemed to do. *Punishing the parents' fault in the children and in the grandchildren to the third and fourth generation . . .* "All right, sir," I told him instead. "I'll do my best."

CHAPTER 2

The Carillon Group numbered several small courier ships among its modest fleet, and I naturally expected our group would ride one or more of those to Whitecliff, transferring at that point to one of HTI's freighters. But Lord Kelsey-Ramos would have none of that. This was his personal triumph, and he had no intention of having us ride someone else's ship into Solitaire like hitchhikers or afterthought cargo.

Which consideration made it almost inevitable that he would saddle us with the *Bellwether*.

From his point of view, it was a generous favor, of course. His own personal craft, the *Bellwether* was a genuine superyacht, with all the luxury and heavy-duty status that that implied. Unfortunately, the size and sleek lines carried their own hidden costs: the size meant the *Bellwether* could do only eighteen hours at a stretch on Mjollnir drive before having to go space-normal to dump its excess heat; and the sleek lines meant it then took up to six hours to cool down enough to continue on.

Which meant that instead of the twenty-three-plus light-years per day a heavily radiation-finned courier ship could cover, we stodgered along at barely eighteen. Which meant the hundred-odd light-years to Whitecliff took us nearly six days to cover, instead of a courier's four and a half.

Which meant HTI's representatives in Alabaster City were primed, ready, and waiting when we arrived.

I'd half expected them to try and hide their preparation, but they apparently knew better than to try and play stupid. Instead, they'd opted for the opposite response: laying the honey on with a sealant spreader.

It started practically before we'd even gotten our feet on the ground, with the spaceport director himself greeting us at the *Bellwether*'s gatelock as we disembarked. He bubbled a message of greeting tinged with nervous awe, led us through an artificially brief customs ritual, and then escorted us across the terminal to the connecting hotel. The three best suites, we found, had already been reserved for us, as had the most secure meeting/privacy room on the lobby level. Randon left a message with the hotel registrar to be transmitted to the local HTI office, and we retired to our rooms.

Even then, the HTI people showed their expertise in such matters, giving us a half-hour to relax and readjust to groundfall before arriving at the hotel.

They were sitting at one end of the polished gemrock table as we entered the privacy room: two men, one dark and almost too young, with a slightly overformal black and burgundy capelet draped carefully over his tunic; the other older and graying, with a sense of long tiredness hanging on his shoulders as visibly as his physician's white capelet. On the table before the younger man sat an open computer, humming faintly. "Good day to you," Randon nodded as they rose to their feet at our approach. "I'm Randon Kelsey-Ramos of the Carillon Group; you must be our HTI hosts."

"Good day to you as well, sir," the younger man said with a nod that was as formal as his capelet. His dark eyes flicked to me, the sense of him shifting from stiff and grudging politeness to animosity as he did so. "I'm Sahm Aikman—HTI legal affairs department," he continued, eyes shifting back to Randon. "This is my colleague, Dr. Kurt DeMont—" he gestured, the muscles of his hand as taut as the rest of him— "who handles the various medical aspects of the Solitaire run."

DeMont's eyes came back to Randon from their uneasy study of me and he nodded his own greeting. "Mr. Kelsey-Ramos," he said gravely. His eyes shifted again to me, and I sensed a surge of boldness peek through, as if he were considering speaking to me directly. But caution and protocol prevailed, the boldness withered, and he remained silent.

All of which would have been abundant proof, if I'd needed any, that the message O'Rielly had sent here had included the fact that Randon might be bringing his father's Watcher along. But they weren't quite sure yet . . .

"Pleased to meet you," Randon said, nodding acknowledgment of the introductions. He, too, had picked up on their interest in me; equally clear was the fact that he intended to draw out their uncertainties as far as he could. "May I say, first of all, that I appreciate your getting all the accommodations trivia out of the way—it certainly made life easier for my aides." He waved vaguely in my direction; like magic, both sets of eyes shifted to me. The gesture shifted smoothly, Randon's hand ending up pointing at the computer sitting on the table. "You've brought me copies of your records?"

"Uh, yes, sir," Aikman said, shifting gears with visible effort, his attention lingering on me for a second after his eyes had gone back to Randon. Standard business etiquette said that entourages like me were to be ignored in direct address until and unless they were formally introduced, and Randon's deliberate failure to do so was beginning to irritate him. "I thought we could take a few minutes to go through them now, if you're willing."

"You have *all* HTI's records here?" Randon asked.

"Oh, no—just those involving shipment through Whitecliff," Aikman said. "The complete records are of course kept only in the Solitaire office."

"Ah," Randon nodded. "Well, then, I think I'll pass. Not much sense in spending time studying one corner of the painting when I'll get to see the whole thing in a couple of days, is there?"

A flicker of surprise touched both men, followed immediately by annoyance in different degrees. I gathered the local HTI office had gone to some effort to gather the records into easily digested form, and Aikman in particular was clearly put out at Randon's casual dismissal of all that work. "As you wish, Mr. Kelsey-Ramos," he said, managing to keep his voice civil. "In that case—"

"What I'd rather do," Randon interrupted him, "is see what kind of night life Whitecliff has. I presume it *does* have some?"

Another flicker of surprise. DeMont recovered first. "Oh, certainly," he said. "Nothing like what you're used to on Portslava, I don't suppose, but enjoyable in its own way. Here in Alabaster City, particularly, we have a wide mix of different entertainments."

"Yes, port cities tend to be that way," Randon nodded. "Though I certainly wouldn't like to think I'm too much of a snob to enjoy something new. You'll both be my guests, of course?"

Aikman and DeMont exchanged glances. Clearly, Randon wasn't fitting into their expectations, and they weren't entirely sure how to handle him. "We'd be honored to serve as your guides, Mr. Kelsey-Ramos," Aikman said diplomatically.

"Excellent," Randon said with a smile. "I'll have to bring a couple of my shields along, too, of course. Company policy, I'm afraid."

"Understandable," Aikman nodded. "Well, then, whenever you're ready—"

"Oh, and Mr. Benedar will be coming, too," Randon said blandly, gesturing a hand toward me. "I'm sorry;

I've been remiss, haven't I? Mr. Aikman, Dr. DeMont—Gilead Raca Benedar."

It was a game on Randon's part, of course—nothing more or less than a way to suddenly spring my name and Watcher status on them and force a reaction. Certainly he had no interest in trying to carouse through Alabaster City's night life with someone he considered a religious fanatic hovering disdainfully in the background. My own interest in playing that role was equally microscopic.

But Aikman and DeMont didn't know that. "Mr. Benedar," Aikman said in acknowledgment, his formal stiffness turning abruptly rigid. "Mr. Kelsey-Ramos . . . with due respect for your position, I'd like to suggest that it would be best if your associate remains behind."

"Oh?" Randon asked, almost innocently. "Is there a problem, Mr. Aikman?"

Aikman locked eyes with him. "To put it bluntly, sir, Watchers aren't especially welcome in Alabaster City."

Randon met his gaze steadily. "I understood the Watchers have a settlement here on Whitecliff."

"I'm sure he'd be welcome there," Aikman countered. "But not anywhere else on the planet."

For a long moment the room was silent; silent with heavy discomfort from DeMont, with almost calm calculation from Randon, with black hatred from Aikman. *I lie surrounded by lions, greedy for human prey . . .*

An icy shiver ran up my back. I'd encountered hatred before—Watchers who left their settlements couldn't avoid running into it these days. We'd been barely tolerated before Aaron Balaam darMaupine and his followers had come on the scene; now, two decades later, feeling against us was still running high. There was hatred everywhere—unthinking hatred, frightened hatred, even inherited hatred. But Aikman's hatred was different. Cold, almost intellectual, it had far less actual emotion simmering beneath it than it ought to have had.

God had given mankind intellect, one of my teachers had once said, and the Fall had given him prejudice;

and there was no human force more dangerous than a combination of the two.

Randon broke the brittle silence first. "I seem to remember, Mr. Aikman," he said, choosing his words deliberately, "that one of the chief cornerstones of the original Patri Articles was the banning of religious discrimination in the Patri and in all future colony worlds. I was unaware that policy had been repealed."

The words were indignant enough; the emotions beneath them far less so. Randon's father, I knew, would have felt automatic anger at such a brazen display of discrimination, but Randon's own world view wasn't set up that way. To him, I was less a human being than a tool with useful properties. But that didn't prevent him from using my humanity to score a few points in this psychological trapshoot he had needled Aikman into playing.

Not that Aikman needed much prodding. "We have a fair number of emigres from Bridgeway," he countered harshly. "They haven't forgotten what darMaupine nearly did there. Neither have the rest of us."

"That was over twenty years ago," Randon pointed out coolly. "Mr. Benedar was all of eleven years old when darMaupine's experiment in theocracy was brought down."

"I'm not responsible for his age," Aikman said, the first hint of caution beginning to break through the anger as he abruptly seemed to remember who this young man was he was arguing with. "I'm also not responsible for the concept of guilt by association. I merely state the relevant facts."

"Then I take it you've not forgotten the most relevant of those facts, Mr. Aikman," Randon shot back. "I'm in charge of this man . . . and the Carillon Group is in charge of HTI. Which means *I* make the decisions on this trip."

Behind his lips, Aikman clenched his teeth, and for a second some of his hatred for me shifted to Randon . . .

"Excuse me, Mr. Kelsey-Ramos," I spoke up, before Aikman could find a response he might later regret. "If you wouldn't mind too much, I'd rather stay here this evening. I'd appreciate the opportunity to get a good night's sleep in real gravity."

Randon turned to eye me, the sense of him one of approval. He'd made his point—had boldfaced his authority for the others—and now was perfectly ready for me to make my excuses and back out. "Yes, I remember you never slept very well aboard ship," he commented. "All right, then, you're excused." He shifted his attention back to Aikman and DeMont, who were looking as if we'd just pulled the rug out from under them. As we had, of course, just done . . . and even though I knew I shouldn't, I couldn't help enjoying their discomfiture just a little bit. "My apologies, gentlemen," Randon continued briskly, "but it appears it'll just be you two and me after all. Well, then. Give me a few minutes to change into something more appropriate and I'll be back. Oh, and I *will* take those records, I guess—my financial expert may find himself bored tonight."

Tight-lipped, Aikman reached down and pulled a cyl from the computer. His hand was shaking noticeably with emotion as he did so. "We'll see you in a few minutes, Mr. Kelsey-Ramos," he said, his voice fighting hard to remain civil as he handed the cyl over.

Randon nodded and we left. In the elevator, several floors from the lobby level, he finally turned to me. "Quite a show, Benedar, eh?" he said with a smile.

I swallowed. "Indeed, sir. I really don't think it was a good idea to bait them the way you did, though."

He dismissed the comment with a wave of his hand. "The fastest way to get through a corporate mask is to give the person wearing it a good, hard push," he told me off-handedly. "I'm sorry if you felt offended in there, but you have to admit you're a very convenient lever to push with."

A tool with useful properties. "I'm also reasonably capable of reading people without the need to push them," I reminded him, annoyed despite myself. "The whole purpose of me being here—"

"Is to use your wonderful powers of observation to spot things that I miss," Randon cut me off with a patient sigh. "Yes, I know. I've heard my father go on and on about your vaunted Watcher mind-reading tricks."

"It's not mind-reading—"

"So then let's have it, eh? What did you see down there that I missed?"

I clenched my teeth. "They don't like you," I told him. "They aren't sure yet whether you're a clever manipulator or a pompous fool, but they're prepared to dislike you either way."

"*That* one's pretty obvious," Randon snorted. "Also obvious is that Aikman, especially, dislikes you even more than he dislikes me. I was thinking more along the lines of something a bit more subtle. Are these really the full records for the Whitecliff shipping route, for instance?" He waved the cyl.

I thought back over the conversation, over the shifting senses of the two men during it. "There was no lie in either of them," I told Randon. "Whatever you have there, it was given in good faith."

"I'm sure it was," he shrugged. "Also self-evident, I'll point out. Falsifying records isn't a job given to middle-levelers like those two. Not if the corporation's smart, anyway."

"How do you know they're middle-levelers?"

"You don't think HTI would waste any of their high-level people running back and forth playing zombi escort, do you?" he snorted. "Come on, Benedar—that's simple logic."

My stomach tightened. Zombi. Dehumanizing with a label. "Yes, sir."

He gave me a hard look. "You're not going to go all queasy on me when we reach the Cloud, are you?"

"I'll be all right by the time we reach Solitaire," I assured him.

I hadn't exactly answered his question. He noticed, but let it pass. "I hope so," he said instead. "If HTI's going to try and obstruct us, it'll be the people running the Solitaire office who'll be behind it. I'll want you running at full power by the time we face them."

I gave a neutral nod, hearing the anticipation in his voice. *He grew into a young lion; he learned to tear his prey; he became a man-eater. The nations came to hear of him; he was caught in their pit; they dragged him away with hooks to Egypt . . .* "Yes, sir," I murmured. "I'll be ready by then."

I learned the next morning that Randon's baiting of Aikman and DeMont hadn't ended with my departure, but had merely changed its form. From the bleary eyes of the two shields he'd taken along I gathered that they'd returned to the hotel considerably after local midnight; from the fact that Aikman and DeMont dragged their way to the *Bellwether* nearly an hour after we'd arrived I gathered that Randon had employed one of his father's old gambits. Lord Kelsey-Ramos had been notorious in his youth for the technique of celebrating his opponents into a frazzled mess, and it was clear that Randon had inherited both the stamina and vodkya tolerance required to play such a game.

A dangerous and rather childish game, to my way of thinking . . . and yet, in retrospect I can't help wondering if perhaps there was more behind it than Randon's grim determination to be in control. Because if Aikman and DeMont hadn't been late—if I hadn't already been in my stateroom preparing for departure when they arrived—I almost certainly would have been right there at the gatelock when they and the spaceport authorities arrived.

They, the authorities . . . and the two human sacrifices they delivered to the ship. Our two zombis.

CHAPTER 3

It was the middle of ship's afternoon two days later, and I was playing singleton chess in a corner of the crew lounge, when we reached the Cloud.

Without warning, oddly enough, though the effect sphere's edge was supposed to be both stationary and well established. But reach it without warning we did. From the rear of the *Bellwether* came the faint *thunggk* of massive circuit breakers firing as the Mjollnir drive spontaneously kicked out, followed an instant later by a round of curses from the others in the lounge as the ultra-high-frequency electric current in the deck lost its Mjollnir-space identity of a pseudograv generator and crewers and drinks went scattering every which way.

And then, abruptly, there was silence. A dark silence, as suddenly everyone seemed to remember what was about to happen.

A rook was drifting in front of my eyes, spiraling slowly about its long axis. Carefully, I reached out and plucked it from the air, feeling a sudden chill in my heart. We were at the edge of the Cloud, ten light-years out from Solitaire . . . and in a few minutes, up on the bridge, someone was going to die.

18

*For in honor of their gods they have done everything
detestable that God hates; yes, in honor of their gods,
they even burn their own sons and daughters as
sacrifices—*

A tone from the intercom broke into my thoughts.
"Sorry about that," Captain Jose Bartholomy said. Behind his carefully cultivated Starlit accent his voice was
trying to be as unruffled as usual . . . but I don't think
anyone aboard the *Bellwether* was really fooled. "Space-
normal, for anyone who hasn't figured it out already.
Approximately fifteen minutes to Mjollnir again; stand
ready." He paused, and I heard him take a deep breath.
"Mr. Benedar, please report to the bridge."

I didn't have to look to know that all eyes in the
lounge had turned to me. Carefully, I eased out of my
seat, hanging onto the arm until I'd adjusted adequately
to the weightlessness and then giving myself a push
toward the door. My movement seemed to break the
others out of their paralysis—two of the crewers headed
to the lockers for handvacs, while the rest suddenly
seemed to remember there were glasses and floating
snacks that needed to be collected and got to it. In the
brisk and uncomfortable flurry of activity, I reached the
door and left.

Randon was waiting for me just outside the bridge.
"Benedar," he nodded, both voice and face tighter than
he probably wanted them to be.

"Why?" I asked quietly, knowing he would understand what I meant.

He did, but chose to ignore the question. "Come in
here," he said instead, waving at the door release and
grabbing the jamb handle as the panel slid open.

"I'd rather not," I said.

"Come in here," he repeated. His voice made it clear
he meant it.

Swallowing hard, I gave myself a slight push and
obeyed.

There is a unique smell that accompanies death. I
don't mean the actual, physical odor of decomposing
flesh, but a wider scent that extends somehow to all the

other senses as well. I'd smelled it twice before: once at my grandfather's deathbed, where all the hospital disinfectants in the air were unable to disguise it; once at the scene of an accident where the victim was conscious to the end. Both times, for hours afterward, I had tried to separate out the sensations I had felt into pieces that I could understand . . . and both times I had failed. There was a fear of the unknown involved, certainly, combined with a sense of the profound mystery surrounding the departure of a human soul from this world. But there was more to it than that, and neither my own intellect nor those Watcher elders I took it to could ever totally solve the puzzle.

Randon and I entered the bridge . . . and for the third time in my life I found the smell of death.

Captain Bartholomy and First Officer Gielincki were there, of course: Gielincki because it was technically her shift as bridge officer, Bartholomy because he wasn't the type of man to foist a duty like this off on his subordinates. Standing beside them on the gripcarpet were Aikman and DeMont, the former with a small recorder hanging loosely from his hand, the latter with a medical kit gripped tightly in his. Flanking the helm chair to their right were two of Randon's shields, Daiv and Duge Ifversn, just beginning to move back . . . and in the chair itself sat a man.

The *Bellwether*'s sacrifice.

I couldn't see anything of him but one hand, strapped to the left chair arm, and the back of his head, similarly bound to the headrest. I didn't want to see anything more, either—not of him, not of anything else that was about to happen up here. But Randon was looking back at me . . .

The days of my life are few enough: turn your eyes away, leave me a little joy, before I go to the place of no return, to the land of darkness and shadow dark as death . . .

Taking a deep breath, I set my feet into the gripcarpet and moved forward.

Daiv Ifversn had been heading toward Aikman as we

entered; now, instead, he turned toward us. "The prisoner is secured, sir, as per orders," he told Randon, his face and voice making it clear he didn't care for this duty at all. "Further orders?"

Randon shook his head. "You two may leave."

"Yes, sir." Daiv caught his brother's eye, and the two of them headed for the door.

And all was ready. Taking a step toward the man in the chair, Aikman set his recorder down on one of the panel's grips, positioning it where it could take in the entire room. "Robern Roxbury Trembley," he said, his voice as coldly official as the atmosphere surrounding us, "you have been charged, tried, and convicted of the crimes of murder and high treason, said crimes having been committed on the world of Miland under the jurisdiction of the laws of the Four Worlds Of The Patri."

From my position next to Randon and Captain Bartholomy, I could now see the man in profile. His chest was fluttering rapidly with short, shallow breaths, his face drawn and pale with the scent of death heavy on it . . . but through it all came the distinct sense that he was indeed guilty of the crimes for which he was about to die.

It came as little comfort.

"You have therefore," Aikman continued impassively, "been sentenced to death, by a duly authorized judiciary of your peers, under the laws of the Four Worlds Of The Patri and their colonies. Said execution is to be carried out by lethal injection aboard this ship, the *Bellwether*, registered from the Patri world of Portslava, under the direction of Dr. Kurt DeMont, authorized by the governor of Solitaire.

"Robern Roxbury Trembley, do you have any last words?"

Trembley started to shake his head, discovered the headband prevented that. "No," he whispered, voice cracking slightly with the strain.

Aikman half turned, nodded at DeMont. Lips pressed tightly together, the doctor stepped forward, moving around the back of the helm chair to Trembley's right arm. Opening his medical kit, he withdrew a small hypo, already prepared. Trembley closed his eyes, face taut with fear and the approach of death . . . and DeMont touched the hypo nozzle to his arm.

Trembley jerked, inhaling sharply. "Connye," he whispered, lower jaw trembling as he exhaled a long, ragged breath.

His eyes never opened again . . . and a minute later he was dead.

DeMont gazed at the readouts in his kit for another minute before he confirmed it officially. "Execution carried out as ordered," he said, his voice both tired and grim. "Time: fifteen hundred twenty-seven hours, ship's chrono, Anno Patri date 14 Octyab 422." He raised his eyes to Bartholomy. "He's ready, Captain."

Bartholomy nodded, visibly steeled himself, and moved forward. Unstrapping Trembley's arms, he reached gingerly past the body to a black keyboard that had been plugged into the main helm panel. It came alive with indicator lights and prompts at his touch, and he set it down onto the main panel's front grip, positioning it over the main helm controls and directly in front of the chair. "Do I need to do anything else?" he asked Aikman, his voice almost a whisper.

"No," Aikman shook his head. He threw a glance at me, and I could sense the malicious satisfaction there at my presence. The big pious Watcher, forced to watch a man being executed. "No, from here on in it's just sit back and enjoy the ride."

Bartholomy snorted, a flash of dislike flickering out toward Aikman as he moved away from the body.

And as if on cue, the body stirred.

I knew what to expect; but even so, the sight of it was shattering. Trembley was *dead*—everything about him, every cue my Watcher training could detect told me he was dead . . . and to see his arms lift slowly away from the chair sent a horrible chill straight to the center of my being. And yet, at the same time, I couldn't force my eyes to turn away. There was an almost hypnotic fascination to the scene that held my intellect even while it repelled my emotions.

Trembley's arms were moving forward now, reaching out toward the black Deadman Switch panel. For a moment they hesitated, as if unsure of themselves. Then the hands stirred, the fingers curved over, and the arms lowered to the Mjollnir switch. One hand groped for position . . . paused . . . touched it—

And abruptly, gravity returned. We were on Mjollnir drive again, on our way through the Cloud.

With a dead man at the controls.

"Why?" I asked Randon again.

"Because you're the first Watcher to travel to Solitaire," he said. The words were directed to me; but his eyes remained on Trembley. The morbid fascination I'd felt still had Randon in its grip. "Hard to believe, isn't it?" he continued, his voice distant. "Seventy years after the discovery of the Deadman Switch and there still hasn't been a Watcher who's taken the trip in."

I shivered, my skin crawling. The Deadman Switch had hardly been "discovered"—the first ship to get to Solitaire had done so on pure idiot luck . . . if *luck* was the proper word. A university's scientific expedition had been nosing around the edge of the Cloud for days, trying to figure out why a Mjollnir drive couldn't operate within that region of space, when the drive had suddenly and impossibly kicked in, sending them off on the ten-hour trip inward to the Solitaire system. Busy with their readings and instruments, no one on board realized until they reached the system that the man operating the helm was dead—had, in fact, died of a stroke just before they'd entered the Cloud.

By the time they came to the correct conclusion, they'd been trapped in the system for nearly two months. Friendships, under such conditions, often grow rapidly. I wondered what it had been like, drawing lots to see who would die so that the rest could get home . . .

I shivered, violently. "The Watchers consider the Deadman Switch to be a form of human sacrifice," I told him.

Randon threw me a patient glance . . . but beneath the slightly amused sophistication there, I could tell he wasn't entirely comfortable with the ethics of it either. "I didn't bring you here to argue public morals with me," he said tartly. "I brought you here because—" he pursed his lips briefly— "because I thought you might be able to settle the question of whether or not the Cloud is really alive."

It was as if all the buried fears of my childhood had suddenly risen again from their half-forgotten shadows. To deliberately try and detect the presence of an entity that had coldly taken control of a dead human body . . .

"No," I managed to say.

Randon frowned. "No what? No, it isn't alive?"

Trembley's dead hands moved, changing the *Bellwether*'s course a few degrees down the twisting and ever-changing path to Solitaire . . . and suddenly I felt very ill. "I mean, no, I can't do it."

A slight frown creased Randon's forehead. "Look, Benedar, I'm not expecting miracles—"

"I can't *do* it," I snapped at him.

All heads on the bridge turned to me. Even Randon seemed taken aback. *Even were I to walk in a ravine as dark as death I should fear no danger, for You are at my side* . . . Taking a deep breath, I forced calmness into my mind. "Mr. Kelsey-Ramos, the man there is dead. He's *dead*."

"He was a condemned traitor," Aikman put in, malicious enjoyment at my discomfort coloring his tone. "He was responsible for the deaths of over twenty people on Miland. You feel sorry for him?"

I met his eyes, but didn't bother to speak. He couldn't understand—wouldn't want to even if he could—how much more grisly the zombi was for me than it could ever be for him. To sense overwhelmingly the fact that he was dead; and at the same time to see evidence of life . . .

"Who was Connye?" Randon asked.

Aikman shifted his attention to him. "Who?"

"Trembley mentioned a Connye, just as Dr. DeMont

injected him," Randon said. Annoyed though he might be at me for refusing his order, he still had no intention of letting an outsider like Aikman take free shots at me. "Was she one of the people he killed?"

Aikman shook his head. "She was one of his accomplices." His eyes went back to me. "She was executed on an earlier flight into Solitaire, incidently."

I clenched my teeth. "Mr. Kelsey-Ramos . . . with your permission, I'd like to leave."

He studied me a moment, then nodded. "Yes, all right. Perhaps on the trip back you'll be better able to handle it."

I nodded, acknowledging his statement without necessarily agreeing with it. "I'll be in my stateroom if you need me," I told him.

"You might take a minute to stop by the other zombi's cell first," Aikman added as I turned to go.

I paused, looking back at him. Again the hatred of me . . . but this time combined with something else. Something very much like gloating. "Oh?" I asked.

"Or not," he said, studiously off-handed. "It's entirely up to you." Deliberately, he turned his back to me and pretended to be watching Trembley.

I glanced at Randon, saw my puzzlement mirrored there, and silently left the bridge.

Aikman was playing some sort of game, of course. Unfortunately, we both knew I knew it, which meant his ultimate goal could equally well be to goad me into visiting the *Bellwether*'s other prisoner or else to make sure I avoided the cell completely.

But I wasn't going to play his game . . . and not playing his game meant doing whatever I did for *my* reasons, not his. And in this case . . .

In this case I didn't want to face the prisoner. Didn't want to see someone who had committed a crime worthy of death.

Didn't want to risk feeling any empathy for someone with whom I had no business, and who would regardless be dying in no more than two weeks.

But a Samaritan traveller who came on him was moved with compassion when he saw him . . .

There were times, I reflected bitterly, when religious duty was more trouble than it was worth. With a sigh, I changed direction and headed for the prisoner's cell.

The "cell" was really nothing but a specially prepared stateroom, cleared of anything that could be used for escape and equipped with an outside lock. A guard would be posted outside, of course; but as I came down the corridor I saw that at least that worry had been for nothing. Mikha Kutzko, Lord Kelsey-Ramos's own favorite shield chief and one of the few people aboard who neither treated me as a vaguely amusing fanatic nor walked on eggshells in my presence, was himself standing guard by the door.

He watched my approach, a genuinely friendly grin on his face even as his hand drifted a few centimeters closer to the needler belted to his thigh. An unconscious reflex, I knew, one that had probably helped keep him alive all these years. "Gilead," he nodded in greeting, eyes twinkling behind the tinted lenses of his visorcomp. "Welcome to the *Bellwether*'s dungeon. What brings you here?"

"I'd heard there was a miracle taking place," I said with a straight face. "That you were actually up here walking the drawbridge yourself."

The smile became a grin. "And you said, 'I must go across and see this strange sight'?" he suggested wryly.

. . . and why the bush is not being burned up, I automatically completed the reference. Kutzko's knowledge of scripture was generally limited to those with novelty value, but it was still nice to hear even that being used in public. "Of course," I agreed. "You have to admit it's been a year or two since you had to pull straight guard duty."

Some of the amusement went out of his eyes. "It's been even longer since any of my shields had to guard a death cell," he said quietly. "It's blazing depressing having to stand around here thinking about it."

I nodded. Until we reached Solitaire Kutzko didn't

have any real shield coordination work to do . . . and like Captain Bartholomy, he wasn't the type to push unpleasant duty off his own back onto his subordinates'. Lord Kelsey-Ramos had a knack for attracting people like that. "I don't suppose it is," I agreed. "What can you tell me about him?"

"Her," he corrected. "It's a woman from Outbound. Convicted multiple murderess."

My stomach knotted. Outbound. I'd grown up there, on the Watcher settlement. "Any idea," I asked carefully, "just where on Outbound it happened?"

He frowned. "No. Why?"

"A few minutes ago Aikman suggested I might find it instructive to come here and see her," I said. With Kutzko, I could be honest. "I wonder . . ."

"If she could be someone you know?" Kutzko tapped the temple of his visorcomp. "Identity card: *Bellwether* outzombi."

I grimaced at the word. Braced myself . . .

"Name's Calandra Paquin," Kutzko reported, reading from the visorcomp's head-up display. "Sound familiar?"

I shook my head, the knot in my stomach easing fractionally. "No."

"Um. Let's see . . . originally from Bridgeway . . . murders occurred in the Outbound capital of Transit City."

Some of the Watchers from Cana settlement did occasional business in Transit City. Could her killings have included someone I knew? "Do you have the names of her victims there?" I asked Kutzko.

"No. Sorry." His eyes focused on me again. "That's right—you're from Outbound, too, aren't you?"

"I grew up there." I hesitated . . . but if the ship's records didn't have that information, there was only one other person besides Aikman himself who might. And I would rather talk to a murderess than ask Aikman for such a favor. "Do you suppose I could go in and talk to her?"

Kutzko studied me. "Why?"

"I'm not entirely sure," I admitted. "I just feel like I should, that's all."

"Well . . . by the book, you know, only my shields and the HTI people are supposed to have anything to do with her." He scratched his cheek thoughtfully. "On the other hand, I *was* going to check on her soon anyway; and if you just *happened* to wander in to keep me company . . ." He raised his eyebrows questioningly.

I nodded. "I owe you."

"Forget it." Turning, he busied himself with the lock. "I'll go first," he instructed me as the mechanism tripped. "Stay out until I give you an all-clear."

Rapping twice on the door, he pressed the release. The knock was typical, I thought as the panel slid open—for someone in his particular line of work, Kutzko was unusually polite. A man, I'd sometimes thought, who would apologize for the inconvenience as he broke your neck.

For a moment his back blocked my view of the room beyond. Then, taking a step forward, he moved off to the side. "All right," he said over his shoulder. "You can come in."

But for that first moment, I couldn't move. Beyond him, the woman—the murderess—was seated in front of the stateroom's reader, her face turned questioningly to Kutzko. Her eyes met mine . . . and in those eyes, in that face, in that whole presence, there could be no mistake.

Calandra Paquin was a Watcher.

CHAPTER 4

Slowly, I stepped into the room. The woman watched me, and I could tell that she too had recognized our common heritage. "Mikha," I said carefully, "I'd like to speak to Ms. Paquin alone for a moment, if I may."

He half turned to frown at me. "May I remind you —?"

"It'll be all right," I cut him off. My knees were beginning to tremble with a tangle of contradictory emotions. "Please."

Kutzko looked at Calandra, back at me. "All right. But just for a minute." Slipping past me, he left the room. The door slid halfway closed, and I heard him move to the opposite side of the corridor, where he could see but not really hear us.

I took a deep breath. "Gilead Raca Benedar," I introduced myself. "Cana settlement, Outbound."

Her face might have flickered at the mention of Outbound. "Calandra Mara Paquin," she nodded in return. "From . . . ?"

"I was raised in the Bethel settlement on Bridgeway. If it's any of your business."

I felt cold. Bridgeway: Aaron Balaam darMaupine's world. For a brief, unnerving second I wondered if she

might actually have been involved in that perversion
. . . but another second and I realized how unlikely
that was. Calandra was only about thirty-eight—five
years older than me—which meant she'd have been
barely sixteen when darMaupine's grab for temporal
power was finally overthrown. "We're both Watchers,"
I reminded her. "Committed to God and to each other.
That makes our lives each other's business."

She snorted gently. "Sorry, but I gave up commit-
ments like that a long time ago."

I felt a vague stirring of anger. I was trying as hard as
I could to forget her crime and accept her as an equal,
and all she was doing was rubbing salt on my patience.
"Maybe the rest of us haven't given up on you," I
gritted. "Just because you ran out on your people when
they needed you—"

"Oh, you think I ran out because of what Aaron
Balaam darMaupine did to us with his insane vision?"

"You wouldn't have been the first," I told her, fighting doggedly to give her the benefit of the doubt.
"With all the animosity that mess generated—"

"Animosity?" she cut me off. "Is *that* what you got on
Outbound? *Animosity*?"

I pursed my lips. *Others fell among thorns, and the
thorns grew up and choked them* . . . "I'm sure it was
a lot worse on Bridgeway. Especially for a teenager."

She glared at me. "I doubt you could even imagine
it. Certainly not from such a lofty and protected place
as the Carillon Group. Oh, don't look so surprised—I
know whose ship I'm on. I haven't been living in a hole
all these years. Or in a Watcher colony." She cocked
her head slightly to the side. "And before you start
talking about deserting the faith, you might remember
that you aren't exactly living at *your* settlement, either.
Haven't for quite a few years, as a matter of fact."

Anger stirred within me . . . anger, and a painful
feeling of helplessness. Of course she would have picked
that up: my speech patterns, my body language, a
thousand other cues—they all pointed to my long ab-

sence from a Watcher settlement as clearly as a space-port skysign.

And in those eleven years I'd been away from home, I was suddenly learning, I'd forgotten what it was like to be with another Watcher. How profoundly naked it felt to stand beneath that all-seeing gaze.

I nearly turned around and walked out right then and there. But I didn't. *Blessed are the merciful: they shall have mercy shown them . . .* Perhaps it was a desire to prove that I knew the actions as well as the words. "I'd like to ask you a few questions about your crime," I managed.

"Why?" she retorted. "Have the elders added some form of ritual last rites to the repertoire?"

I ignored the jibe, all I could think of to do. "I just want to talk. To hear your side of . . . what happened."

She studied me, and I felt my discomfort grow stronger. "No Watchers died. Not from your Cana settlement, or from anywhere else. Is that what you wanted to know?"

"Partly," I admitted, my sense of nakedness growing stronger. Here I was, trying my best to mask my emotions from her; and not only was she reading them like a book, she was just as casually picking up my thoughts, too. It made me feel like a child again. "I also wanted to know why you did it."

She looked me straight in the eye. "I didn't."

For three heartbeats I thought I'd heard her wrong. "I—you—?"

"You heard me right. I didn't do it."

For a long minute I looked at her. "I don't . . . " I began; but the words faded into silence. She was hiding a great deal of herself from me—that much was clear. But she couldn't hide everything . . . and the sense of her was definitely that she was telling the truth.

"Don't believe me?" she finished my sentence. "I can't say I'm surprised. No one else did, either."

"But—I mean—" I broke off, trying to get my tongue under control.

"I was set up," she said softly. "Set up in a very

professional manner. Most of the evidence pointed very neatly to me."

"What about the parts that didn't?" I persisted. "Weren't there any counterwitnesses? Odd physical evidence? Your own pravdrug testimony, for heaven's sake?"

She looked at me. "Most of the evidence fit neatly," she repeated. "The parts that didn't . . . they ignored." She shook her head, dropping her gaze from my face.

I took a deep breath; but before I could speak there was a rustle of movement behind me, and I turned to see Kutzko in the doorway. "Daiv just called in—says Aikman's headed this direction," he reported. "You'd better get out before he finds you and goes blazing off to Mr. Kelsey-Ramos."

"All right." I turned back to Calandra, my heart aching in sympathy. Framed for a crime she didn't commit . . . and sentenced as a result to be sacrificed to the great god Profit. "Don't worry, Calandra," I told her quietly. "I'll get this thing turned around."

A flash of surprise crossed her sense. "Wait a minute, I don't want you to get involved—"

"I'm already involved," I said, backing out of the room. "I'm a Watcher."

The door closed on her, and Kutzko cocked an eyebrow at me. "You really believe her?"

I nodded, feeling my muscles trembling. The confrontation had been more of a drain than I'd realized. "Yes," I said. "I'm a Watcher, aren't I?"

He thought about pointing out Calandra was one, too, thought better of it. "So what now?" he asked instead.

"I go hit Mr. Kelsey-Ramos with it, of course," I said, starting down the corridor.

"He won't like it," Kutzko warned.

"I can't help that," I called back. "See you later."

I found Randon in his stateroom, going over the Whitecliff numbers with Dapper Schock, one of Lord Kelsey-Ramos's top financial experts. "Can it wait?" he asked with a touch of annoyance as I came in. His full attention was on the report, and he clearly wanted to keep it that way.

"The details can, sir, if necessary," I told him. "But I think you ought to hear the high points right now. I have reason to believe that Calandra Mara Paquin, our . . . outzombi . . . didn't commit the crime she was condemned for."

The financial data was abruptly forgotten. "Oh, really?" Randon frowned, leaning back in his seat. "What makes you think that?"

I raised my eyebrows, and he half smiled. "Yes, of course," he conceded wryly. "Foolish question."

Schock cleared his throat. "Calandra *Mara*, did you say? Isn't that a Watcher-style middle name?"

"Humility name, yes," I corrected him. "Does that make a difference?"

"Well . . . " He glanced at Randon. "It's a general rule, Benedar, that a professional magician, say, can easily blaze out another magician's tricks, simply because he knows how all of them are done."

"My observational skills aren't tricks," I told him. "Certainly not in that sense. It's a matter of having been trained since childhood to really *see* God's universe."

"We're aware of that," Randon cut in, a little uncomfortable at even so tame a religious reference. "I think Schock's point was that a Watcher who knows what you're looking for might be able to mislead you. Bury the appropriate signals, maybe, or distract you at just the right moment."

"I understand," I nodded. "I don't think she could misdirect me *that* completely, but I suppose it's theoretically possible. Let me turn it around, then. If she *is* lying about it, what can she hope to gain?"

"A stay of execution?" Schock suggested. Clearing the display of financial data, he busied himself with the keys.

Randon shook his head. "Hardly seems worth the effort. The best she could hope to get would be a few more weeks."

Schock was peering at his computer screen. "Here's the record," he said. "Uh . . . she was convicted of throwing a bomb into a street crowd from a window in the Outbound HQ of Melgaard Industries. Seen by witnesses . . . caught when she tried to leave the building."

I chewed the back of my lip. "Any extenuating circumstances?"

He looked at me in astonishment. "For a *bombing?*"

I couldn't think of one, either. "How about possible mistaken identity, then?" I asked. "How would she have gotten *into* the Melgaard building, for starters?"

"She was employed there," Schock said, scanning the display again. "She'd been working as a reception/converser for the previous two months."

"Nice cushy job for a Watcher," Randon grunted. He considered for a moment. "What was the track record on the trial itself?"

"Uh . . . " Schock flipped through a few pages. "From what we've got here it looks pretty standard."

"No extraordinary measures? No indications they did any psychological reconstructions or anything else of that sort?"

"No, sir. Just a standard trial and the requisite double appeal. It's not even clear anyone asked for pravdrug questioning."

Randon looked up at me, shook his head. "Sorry, Benedar, but if Melgaard wasn't willing to put any money or influence into her trial, they must have been convinced she was guilty."

"Or at least convinced she was someone they didn't want around?" I asked pointedly.

Randon gave me a hard look. "I'll admit to the existence of prejudice in the Patri and the colonies," he said steadily. "I won't listen to specific accusations without proof."

A reasonable enough caution under most circumstances. Here, in the privacy of his own ship and stateroom, it made for a weak argument, and he knew it. "All right, then," I said. "Let's just talk theoretical.

Assume for a moment that Calandra *was*, in fact, framed; and further assume it wasn't an isolated incident."

"Grand conspiracy?" Randon said with an amused half smile. "Oh, come *on*. What would anyone have to gain by dropping Watchers one by one down the chute?"

"Who says we're just talking Watchers?" I countered. "There are any number of minorities out there, religious and otherwise, that could be targeted."

"To what end?" Schock asked.

I gestured to his computer. "Check and see if Melgaard Industries has a transport license for Solitaire, will you?"

He turned to the instrument; but Randon spoke up first. "No, they haven't," he said. "They've been trying to get one at least as long as Carillon has." His eyes were on me, no longer amused. "What's your point?"

"That they may have abandoned Calandra for reasons other than guilt."

"Such as internal pressure?" Schock hazarded. "Melgaard's home office hoping to get in good with the Patri by not putting up a fuss over the creation of new zombis?"

The creation of new zombis. Somewhere in the back of my mind I marveled at how neat and sanitized euphemisms could make death sound. "Yes, except that the pressure may not have all been internal. Some could have come from outside Melgaard."

Schock cocked a thoughtful eyebrow. "As in from the Patri themselves?"

"Why not? As long as the Solitaire ring mines are operating as profitably as they are, they have to keep finding people to die."

"Hold it right there," Randon growled. "If you're suggesting the Patri are putting pressure on the judiciary —*and* that the judiciary is knuckling under to that pressure—then you're skating dangerously close to slander and possibly even treason."

Schock and I exchanged glances. "It's not a matter of slander, Mr. Kelsey-Ramos," I said. "Any reasonable person has to acknowledge the pressure exists. The Patri *have* to keep up the supply of zombis, and they have to do it against a long history of public inertia against death penalty overuse."

"And it's going to get even worse," Schock murmured. "As soon as they get that fourth Rockhound 606 into full-stream operation out there, they're going to outstrip the licensed transport capability again. Either the Patri will have to up the numbers even more—which means more zombis—or else find a variation of Mjollnir drive that can handle bigger freighters."

I nodded agreement. "As I said, the pressure exists. The only question is whether the Patri and the judiciary are yielding to that pressure."

For a minute the room was silent. A brief and almost undetectable shift in the pseudogravity told me the *Bellwether* had altered course again. Dimly, I wondered what would happen if rigor mortis paralyzed the body at the helm before the ten-hour trip through the Cloud could be completed. Though presumably after seventy years Dr. DeMont and the other high priests of this sacrifice had found a way around that particular problem.

"Well," Randon broke the silence at last. "I suppose there's no harm in taking a look into this." He seemed to brace himself as he looked up at me. "Unfortunately, as far as Paquin's particular case goes . . . " He shrugged uncomfortably.

I looked him straight in the eye. "Mr. Kelsey-Ramos, she's *innocent*."

"Maybe. Maybe not. Either way, what do you expect me to do about it?"

"Grant her a stay of execution, of course, until her story can be checked. It's the only thing you *can* do."

The instant I said it I knew I'd made a mistake. Abruptly, Randon's sympathetic interest tarnished as he perceived himself being pressed too hard by a sub-ordinate. Lord Kelsey-Ramos would have understood my insistence as merely an excess of strong feeling; Randon was still too young to risk even the appearance of weakness, certainly not in the presence of a third party. "May I remind you," he bit out, "that if I do that the *Bellwether* winds up trapped in Solitaire system?"

"We could send a message out on another ship," I pointed out doggedly. Backing out now would do nothing but give Randon's emotional opposition time to solidify. I had no choice but to keep pressing him, to keep his thoughts and feelings fluid until I could find a formula that would allow him to save face while still keeping Calandra alive. "A courier ship could make the trip to Outbound and back in, what, twelve days?"

"Closer to ten," Schock offered.

"Okay; ten days," I said. "We could request the full transcript of Calandra's trial and have the whole thing reviewed before you were planning on leaving Solitaire anyway."

"Except that there may not be any couriers heading for Outbound right at the moment," Randon countered. "*And* the judiciary on Outbound is under no obligation to release their records to us, anyway."

"But—"

"*And*," he cut me off, "suppose you're right? Suppose we *do* find something that warrants a new trial?"

"Well, then—" I stopped in midsentence.

Randon nodded grimly. "Right. If we decide to take her back to Outbound, how do we get the *Bellwether* back through the Cloud?"

I looked at Schock. Somehow, I hadn't gotten around to thinking that far ahead. "Well . . . we could send another message to Whitecliff at the same time, couldn't we? Ask them to send us another felon to take Calandra's place?"

"They won't do it." There was a positiveness in Randon's tone, a clear sense that this one wasn't just a theoretical position for argument's sake. "The authorities won't allow more than two zombis to a ship, except under *extremely* unusual circumstances. You would have to be able to prove that Paquin was innocent before they would even consider sending us a substitute."

"How can we prove anything like that until we have

the trial records?" I growled. "It's a storage loop argument."

"Yes, it is," Randon agreed. Not apologetic, not really angry: just agreeing. "I'm sorry, but the system simply isn't set up to allow convicted felons to slide through the net at this stage."

Or in other words, Calandra's life wasn't worth enough to him to buck established channels. Lord Kelsey-Ramos would have had the courage to do that—

But Lord Kelsey-Ramos wasn't in charge here. Randon was.

I took a deep breath. Rarely had righteous anger hit me with such a surge of emotion, and I had to fight to try and think through the haze. "All right," I said at last. "If I can . . . if I can find us a substitute zombi before we're ready to leave, will you, as master of this ship, grant Calandra a temporary stay of execution?"

Randon eyed me thoughtfully. "One life worth more than another? Hardly what I'd have expected of you."

Hardly what I would have expected of myself. I said nothing, and after a moment he nodded. "All right, Benedar, you've got yourself a deal." He hesitated. "I don't have to remind you that you have to remain within legal bounds in obtaining this zombi for us, do I?"

The warning felt surprisingly like an insult. But perhaps the knife twist in my stomach was coming entirely from my own conscience. If I could offer a life in trade for Calandra's, was it so big a step to trading a life for profits? "I understand, sir," I said, my mouth dry. "Thank you, sir."

I turned to go. "Benedar?" he called after me.

Steeling myself, I looked back. "Yes?"

His gaze was almost physical in its intensity. "You'd better be right about this."

I swallowed. *Truth? said Pilate. What is that?* "Yes, sir," I told him quietly, and left.

CHAPTER 5

It took me a long time to fall asleep that night. So long, in fact, that I was still awake at one-thirty when the Mjollnir drive kicked off and the *Bellwether* was once again space-normal.

There was something eerie about lying alone in the still of the night, I'd long ago learned; something that turned even the most ordinary of daytime noises into something darkly ominous . . . and the distant *thunggk* of the Mjollnir circuit breakers was hardly an ordinary noise.

For a long minute I just lay in the darkness, suddenly weightless, listening to my heart pounding in my throat and straining to hear anything more. If there was something wrong—if somehow we'd lost our path through the Cloud and been brought out too early . . .

From the rear of the ship a faint drone became audible, increasing gradually in volume and pitch, and beneath my bed I could feel the faint answering tremor as the living-ceramic deck of my stateroom angled to keep itself perpendicular to the acceleration vector. A measure of effective weight returned, and increased, and it was clear that the *Bellwether*'s voyage was progressing normally.

If such a word as "normal" could be used about a voyage piloted by a dead man.

I gritted my teeth and swung my legs out of bed. I knew myself far too well to let this slide. In my mind's eye still lingered a dark, irrational terror: the *Bell-wether*, helpless, stranded somewhere out in deep space, light-years from Solitaire.

You will come to know the truth, and the truth will set you free . . .

Fortunately, in this case truth was easy to obtain. Padding the two steps to my lounge desk, I picked up my control stick and flopped down into the contour couch. "Wall: front view," I called, activating the computer. Ahead of me, the pastel blue stateroom wall faded into the black of space—

I took a deep breath, the knots in stomach and psyche dissolving. Off to the left, blazing an artificially muted light against the scattering of stars, was Solitaire's sun.

I watched it for a moment, then turned my attention to the rest of the skyscape, searching for Solitaire itself. It was easy to find: a small crescent, just below and to the right of center, with an identical crescent a few degrees away. We'd come space-normal practically on top of it, astronomically speaking. Incredible precision, especially coming from a possessed dead man—

I shook the thought away. "Wall: grid," I called. The faint red grid lines appeared— "Wall: section fifty-six: magnification one thousand."

The picture jumped, enlarging to fill the wall with the two crescents. Solitaire and Spall, all right—the one known exception to the usual rule that double planets were terrible real estate for humans to dig into. Vaguely, I remembered reading somewhere that both of these worlds were habitable, though the specific reasons why Solitaire had been chosen over Spall eluded me. For the moment, though, I didn't care. The crisis was over, we'd made it through the Cloud, and with luck I could finally relax enough to get to sleep. I started to ease out of the couch—

And paused. As long as I was up anyway . . . "Wall: locate Collet," I ordered. "Magnification, quarter-fill."

There was a brief pause as the computer searched for the gas giant and calculated the magnification needed to make the image the size I'd asked for. Then the twin crescents disappeared . . . and despite knowing what to expect I very nearly gasped out loud.

Not at the planet itself, of course. Filling a quarter of the wall as per request, Collet's hazy green/gray surface was delicately but unspectacularly banded in the normal pattern of gas giants everywhere. At both its poles was an almost cream-colored haze, while at a dozen spots to either side of its equator I could pick out the spiral patterns of huge hurricane storms, some of which had been raging since the first colonists arrived in the system seventy years ago. Perfectly standard planet . . . until you looked at its rings.

Not the usual gas giant rings, puny circles of dust and ice flakes invisible to all but the most careful observer. These rings literally filled what was left of the wall, stretching outward nearly from the planet's surface in a thousand milky-white bands.

Nowhere in any of the Patri or colony systems did such an anomaly of nature exist, and it had been speculated more than once that if travel to Solitaire weren't so restricted Collet would be a major tourist attraction. Only Saturn, in the old Earth system, could even approach this sight, and those few observers who'd seen both ring systems up close unanimously considered Collet's far more dramatic.

Far more dramatic . . . and incredibly more valuable.

I gazed at the view for a long time, an odd melancholy filling me. It seemed wrong, somehow, for so exquisitely beautiful a creation of God to be ultimately responsible for the Deadman Switch and the human lives that went to feed it. Even from this distance, the computer could probably get a fairly clear look at one of the huge Rockhound 606 mining platforms out there, sweeping leisurely through those rings. Scooping up the rocheoids of ultra-high-grade ore that made Soli-

taire system worth so much trouble . . . and so many
lives . . .

Angrily, I shook my head, forcing the thought away.
Here we were, barely within Solitaire system, and already everything I saw was bringing me back to the
Deadman Switch and the price that had been paid to
get the *Bellwether* here. I was either going to have to
learn better mental discipline, or else brace myself for
an exceedingly depressing two weeks.

*So do not worry about tomorrow; tomorrow will
take care of itself. Each day has enough trouble of its
own . . .*

Shutting off the wall, I dragged myself out of the
contour couch and plodded the two steps back to bed.
Eventually, I fell asleep.

We touched down at Solitaire's spaceport—named,
appropriately, Rainbow's End—at mid-morning the next
day. Mid-morning ship's time, that is; at Rainbow's End
it was already late afternoon. Too late in the day, probably, to get much of anything accomplished; but it might
still be worthwhile to start finding my way around the
local bureaucracy. And so, fifteen minutes after landing, I was in a rented car, driving down a very modern
roadway toward the capital city of Cameo, twenty kilometers away.

The car's computer had been well supplied with cross
references, and after a short discussion we decided the
place I wanted was the Habrin Tsiosky Office of Justice.
I let it do the driving once we reached Cameo's out-
skirts, and within a few minutes it delivered me there.

Within an equal number of minutes, I was again in
the car, on my way back to Rainbow's End.

Kutzko was just inside the *Bellwether*'s gatelock when
I arrived, supervising the placement of a guard booth.
"Mr. Kelsey-Ramos is looking for you," he greeted me
as I stepped aboard. "Hold it a second; I want to give the
weapons sensor a test. Here, catch."

I caught the needler clip he tossed me—puff adders,

of course, Kutzko's usual ammunition of choice—and tried not to wince as I stuffed it into my tunic. I'd seen what these needles could do to a human being, and just holding a clip of them made me slightly queasy. "I told Captain Bartholomy I was going into Cameo," I said as Duge Ifversn stepped over to the booth and flipped a pair of switches.

The archway above me emitted a pig-like squeal. "Looks good," Duge nodded.

Kutzko nodded back. "He must not have checked with the captain, then. You should have taken a phone with you. Anyway, he's in his stateroom with Aikman."

Great. All I needed to make the day complete was to have to face Aikman again. "Joy and rapture," I muttered, returning the clip.

Kutzko peered at me. "You okay?"

"Temporarily, no. But I'm not ready to roll over and give up quite yet." I gestured at the guard booth. "What's all this for? We expecting company?"

"Company, and lots of it," Kutzko nodded. "Mr. Kelsey-Ramos has decided we're going to stay here instead of moving to one of the local hotels."

"Really?" I frowned. "Why?"

He grinned lopsidedly. "You're the expert—you tell me. Real reason, then official reason."

It was an old game for us, but one I didn't really feel like playing at the moment. "Mikha, I don't have time—"

"Come on, Gilead, humor me. Besides, you look like you could use a cheap victory."

I made a face at him; but at this point I was grateful for even bad humor. "Oh, all right."

He put on his best stone face and held it as I, for my part, tried to read past his barriers. It was really pretty easy—despite being in a profession that often attracted the more shady sorts, Kutzko was basically an honest person. "Real reason is that he doesn't trust the hotels," I said slowly. I glanced away at the guard booth arrangement, noting the particular placement and positioning of it— "Not afraid of attack so much as he is of surveillance?"

Kutzko grinned wryly. "Straight set bull's eye. Yeah, we found a couple of tricky little bugs in our suites back on Whitecliff, as well as a *very* cute one built into the records cyl we got from Aikman."

"You think Aikman planted them?"

"Do you?" he countered.

I thought back, remembering the sense of Aikman at that first meeting. "No."

Kutzko nodded agreement. "I didn't think so, either. Aikman's too blazing visible to risk pulling something that underhanded himself. It was probably some faceless assistant hoping to make points. So. How about the official reason?"

I changed gears back to the contest with some effort. "No idea. I suppose Mr. Kelsey-Ramos just claimed none of the hotels here were up to his standards."

Off to the side, Duge Ifversn snickered gently. Kutzko glanced at him, looked back at me. "Two for two," he conceded. "I don't suppose you'd like to take a crack at guessing what we all had for breakfast?"

"You'll excuse me if I find something more useful to do with my time," I said dryly. Still, I *did* feel better. "Thanks, Mikha."

He understood. "No charge. Don't forget Mr. Kelsey-Ramos wants to see you."

"I'm on my way. See you later."

I made my way back through the *Bellwether*'s corridors, simultaneously hoping I wouldn't be so late that Randon would be angry but still be late enough that Aikman would already be gone.

I was halfway lucky.

"About time," Randon growled as I buzzed and was admitted into his stateroom. "Where have you been?"

"Cameo," I told him. I nodded at Aikman with all the courtesy I could muster. He merely stared at me in return, not acknowledging the gesture. "I told Captain Bartholomy where I was going," I added.

A flicker of annoyance touched Randon, but it was more annoyance at himself than at me. If Lord Kelsey-

Ramos had instilled a single quality in his son, it was that of taking internal responsibility for both his actions and his oversights. "I see. Well, no matter." He turned back to his computer—

"What were you doing in Cameo?" Aikman asked shortly, vague suspicion radiating from him.

"Business," I said, deliberately vague.

"More a mercy trip, actually," Randon put in, looking up and favoring Aikman with a thoughtful gaze. "Benedar thinks our outzombi may have been framed for her crimes."

If Randon had hoped for a sharper reaction from Aikman, he was disappointed. Aikman's lip twisted, his sense that of a man whose worst expectations had been realized. "Because she says she was?" he asked pointedly, turning a cynical glare on me. "Or simply because Watchers aren't supposed to do naughty things like murder?"

I started to reply, but Randon beat me to it. "You knew she claimed to be innocent, then?"

"Well, yes," Aikman said, some of his truculance fading before the unexpected iciness of Randon's reaction. "But so what? Convicted felons are always claiming that—what else can they do? If the Outbound judiciary thought she was guilty, I'm willing to take their word for it."

"Yes, well, we may be able to do a bit better than that." Randon shifted his attention to me. "What did you find out?"

I gritted my teeth, still feeling an echo of shame at my failure. "They won't help us."

He frowned. "Why not?"

"Some local law, apparently—"

"Local law, indeed," Aikman snorted. " 'No Solitaran citizen, regardless of crime or levied punishment, will be removed from the jurisdiction of Solitaire system for purposes of navigation, piloting, or piloting assistance on any interstellar craft.' "

In spite of myself, I was impressed. "That's the one, all right," I confirmed.

"I'm sure it was. It happens to be the backbone of the original agreement between the Solitaran colonists and the Patri." His sense was distinctly gloating. "And there are *no* exceptions. None."

"Every law has exceptions," Randon said tartly.

"Not this one. Not even the governor can override it, Patri appointment or no."

"But why?" I asked.

"Why do you think?" he snapped. "Because they don't want their world to become a zombi reservoir, that's why."

It was obvious, of course, in retrospect, and I felt like an idiot for not catching on earlier. If something went wrong with a ship's outzombi, the Solitarans were far and away the most convenient population from which to draw a replacement. Possibly *too* convenient a population . . . and I could well understand the original colonists worrying about that.

"It would never happen," Randon insisted. But beneath his sureness there was a shading of doubt. "The Patri wouldn't let Solitaire become a zombi farm."

"Persuade the Solitarans of that," Aikman countered. "In the past couple of decades there've been at least a dozen threats to the law, any one of which would have set a dangerous precedent."

"I take it they didn't weaken?" Randon asked.

Aikman smiled tightly. "One of the ships was able to beg a replacement zombi from Whitecliff. The rest eventually had to execute one of their own crewers to get out."

My stomach tightened. "And the Solitarans let that happen? How can they justify letting an innocent man die when someone who *is* deserving of death—"

"Innocent?" Aikman sneered. "Since when are any of us oh, so fallen humans really innocent? Sounds a little heretical, if you ask me."

"All right, that's enough," Randon cut him off. He wasn't interested in letting Aikman harass me in his presence; but at the same time I could also sense a subtle decrease of tension within him. Relieved that I wouldn't be rocking any official boats over Calandra now?

If so, he was in for a disappointment. "I haven't given up yet, Mr. Kelsey-Ramos," I spoke up.

He looked warily at me. "Oh? How so?"

"There must be at least ten other ships in Solitaire system at the moment, sir," I pointed out. "If someone aboard one of them should happen to commit a capital crime, perhaps we can persuade the Solitaire judiciary to release him to us."

"In two weeks?" Aikman snarled. "Where the hell is your brain, Benedar?—you really think a court can make a life/death decision like that in just two weeks?"

"It's been done before," Randon reminded him coolly.

Aikman knew better than to really glare at Randon, but the look he threw him was pretty close. "I don't know why I'm even sitting here arguing all this," he gritted out. "The whole thing is nothing but an exercise in futility. Like it or not, Calandra Paquin is guilty of murder; and a hundred judiciaries reviewing the case a hundred times won't change that."

"Then I'm wasting my time," I told him, fighting to hold onto my temper. To have to face such deep hostility and not be able to return it in kind . . . "On the other hand, it's my time to waste, isn't it?"

"And speaking of wasting time," Randon put in, "I have no intention of letting this argument waste any more of *mine*. Benedar, you're authorized to have Captain Bartholomy put a tracer on the local news services, see if anything useful comes up. And don't forget the ring mines—most of the people on the Rockhounds are non-Solitarans, too." He glared briefly at both of us, and I could sense that for now, at least, the subject was closed. "Now. We've been going over the itinerary HTI's got planned for us, Benedar. We'll be meeting with their local managers first thing tomorrow morning, then looking over what they have in the way of groundside facilities."

Which wouldn't be much, of course. All of the real hardware for the extraction and refining of Solitaire's immense mineral wealth was out in Collet's rings, with Solitaire itself hosting little more than basic administration and rest/recreation areas. "Yes, sir. When will we be meeting the governor and local officials?"

He cocked an eyebrow at me, and I knew he could tell that my thoughts were still with Calandra's problem. "Governor Rybakov will be throwing a semiformal dinner for us tomorrow evening at her mansion. Most of the appropriate people will be there. That soon enough for you?"

I flushed. "Yes, sir."

"Good. Then the day after tomorrow we'll be heading out to Collet for a tour of one of the Rockhounds that HTI has contracts with."

The day after tomorrow . . . and it would, I knew, be at least a four-day trip out to Collet. Four days, out of a visit that was supposed to last only two weeks. "And will we be returning to Solitaire after that tour?" I asked carefully.

Randon's eyes bored into mine. "Not unless we have a good reason to do so."

I bit the back of my lip. So that was it. The day after tomorrow . . . and I had less than two days in which to find someone to die in Calandra's place. "I understand, sir."

Randon held my gaze another heartbeat, then turned to Aikman. "So. We've been over the locations, personnel, and local customs. Is there anything else?"

"I have nothing more, Mr. Kelsey-Ramos." Aikman got to his feet. "If you think of anything, I'll be in my stateroom."

"Thank you," Randon nodded. Aikman nodded back, brushed past me and left.

"He's staying aboard ship?" I asked as Randon waved me to a seat. "I'd have thought HTI would have a guest house for visiting employees."

"They've got half a dozen," Randon said dryly. "But Aikman and DeMont were gracious enough to accept my hospitality instead."

I studied him. "You don't want them out of your sight?"

"Let's just say I don't want strangers wandering in and out of the *Bellwether* at their convenience. Particularly bigoted ones." He swiveled his computer around to face me. "You can take all this back to your own stateroom and study it at your leisure, but I want to go over the high points with you first."

I nodded. "I take it you'll be wanting me to come along and watch the proceedings?"

He shrugged. " 'Want' is not exactly the word I would use," he said candidly. "To be perfectly honest, I think that having you around promotes a certain amount of mental laziness. In my opinion, Dad overuses you, and it's cost him some of the edge off his old sharpness."

I already knew all that, but I was rather surprised he was willing to admit to it. "I'm sorry you feel that way. If you'd like, I'll stay in the ship."

He waved the offer away. "Thanks, but Dad would have both of us mined for proteins when he found out." Lowering his eyes, he reached again for the computer, already closing the subject in his own mind. "You may be a crutch, Benedar, but two weeks on a crutch won't hurt me."

"I agree, sir." I braced myself. "Though I believe that in most cases *two* crutches work better than one."

He was sharp, all right. His mind, already on his plans for tomorrow, snapped instantly back on track. "Are you suggesting," he asked quietly, looking up again, "what I think you're suggesting?"

There was, oddly enough, no outrage in his eyes; just a thin layer of ice that was even more intimidating than any anger would have been. But in my own way I was as stubborn as he was, and I refused to back down. "Yes, sir. You have a unique opportunity here, one your father couldn't possibly have anticipated."

"You want me to bring a zombi to a high-level business meeting." The ice in his gaze thickened a bit. "And you want me to believe my father would approve of it?"

"Why not?" I countered. "No one there has to know who or what she is."

"Benedar, she's a *condemned killer*. Remember?"

"Well, *yes*," I admitted. "But as long as we keep her away from tall buildings and bombs . . . "

It had been the right thing to say. Randon's eyes goggled; then, almost grudgingly, he snorted out a chuckle and the ice began to melt. "I trust you realize that if I take a criminal into a meeting with me I'll never live it down."

I shrugged. "A reputation for mild unpredictability can be useful. As your father well knows."

For a long minute he just glared at me in silence. Then he snorted again, gently. "You're not fooling anyone, you know," he said. "I can see through your game. You want me to get as emotionally involved with this little crusade of yours as you are. Making Paquin more useful to me alive than dead would be a good way to start, wouldn't it?"

Sharp, indeed. "I'll admit that's part of it," I agreed without embarrassment. "But the logic still holds. Especially since the HTI people presumably know that I'm coming."

"So they know. What can they do about it?"

"There are several possibilities. Not the least of which would be barring me from the meeting."

"Let them try." But he said it thoughtfully. For a long minute he gazed at me, and I kept my peace and watched the sense of him change. "I'll talk it over with Kutzko later," he said abruptly. "If he thinks it'll be safe enough, I may consider it."

I nodded. "Thank you, sir."

"Uh-huh," he grunted. "Can we get back to the real business at hand now? *Thank* you. All right; let's start with the basic HTI organizational structure . . ."

CHAPTER 6

Randon had a tendency to underestimate just how quickly I could assimilate information, and hitting the "high points," as he'd called it, took about an hour longer than was probably necessary. But at last we were done. Dropping the cyl he'd given me in my own stateroom on the way, I made straight for Calandra's cell to give her the good news.

Or what I had expected would be good news.

"No," she said firmly. "I'm not going."

I stared at her, trying through my stunned astonishment to read her. All I could get was anger and disgust, most of it directed at me. "Calandra, maybe you don't understand what this means—"

"Oh, I understand, all right," she growled. "You thought that I'd leap at the chance to get out of this room, to see the universe in all its glory again."

I gritted my teeth. Once again she was reading me with supremely casual ease. "And why not? Any normal person would."

She glared at me. "Well, then, maybe I'm not normal anymore. Maybe when *you've* been condemned to death you'll have a different outlook on life, too."

51

For a moment we stood facing each other. A thought occurred to me through the haze, and I reached out with every bit of skill I had . . . and this time I found it. Well buried beneath all the anger, I found the fear.

In retrospect, it was obvious. Sometime along the line, during or after the months of her trial and appeals, she'd finally resigned herself to her approaching death . . . and now I was threatening that acceptance. Threatening her once again with uncertainty. "I'm sorry," I said quietly. "I know this isn't going to be easy for you—"

"You *know* that, do you?" she said sarcastically.

"I'm trying to help you!" I snapped abruptly. What with Aikman and now Calandra, I'd finally had enough. "I'm your friend, Calandra. Whether you believe it or not; whether you *like* it or not. You're going with us tomorrow because maybe it'll get Randon Kelsey-Ramos on our side."

"Oh, wonderful," she sneered. "Well, it may come as a shock to you, but I don't happen to *want* your Kelsey-Ramos's help."

"Then you're going to die," I said bluntly.

"There are worse things than death," she shot back. "Such as helping the rich get richer at the expense of everyone else, for instance. If Carillon's money hadn't scraped all the ethics off your precious Watcher label I wouldn't have to tell you that."

A stab of fury slid white-hot through my heart. Fury, strongly edged with guilt. She saw it, and took an involuntary step backward, eyes suddenly wary. "Then don't help," I snarled at her. "You can act like the bottom of a growth tank tomorrow if you want. But you *are* coming along."

She was still standing there, staring at me, as I turned and stomped out.

She was still glowering the next morning when we got into the car with Randon, Dapper Schock, Kutzko, and Daiv Ifversn and headed for Cameo. She was still glowering, and I was still feeling guilty.

Unreasonably guilty, after all, considering that this was nothing less than an attempt to save her life. But the awareness of good motives had always been a feeble kind of comfort with me, and this case was no exception . . . especially since I wasn't fully convinced I was doing the right thing.

So always treat others as you would like them to treat you; that is the Law and the Prophets . . . I was certainly willing to obey . . . but could I really *know* how I would want to be treated under these circumstances? Calandra was right; without being in her position, I could only guess at what she needed from me.

And if I guessed wrong, I would wind up making her last days of life that much harder to bear.

Absorbed in my own thoughts, I withdrew most of my attention from the world around me . . . and was therefore almost startled when I suddenly realized that Calandra was beginning to pay a somewhat grudging attention to our surroundings.

To a normal person, I supposed, it wasn't all that interesting a view. Once out of Rainbow's End itself, the few modestly tall spaceport buildings disappeared, replaced by the squatter structures that nearly always dominated underdeveloped places like this where land was cheap and plentiful. Beyond and between the buildings were scatterings of the giant, multi-trunked native plants that seemed to take the ecological place of trees on this world. Simple, quiet, and at first glance almost prosaic . . . but for Watchers, nothing about God's universe was really prosaic. For me, as for Calandra, the landscape outside was a rich and varied study into the spirit of a world.

A world of people, I quickly realized, who were still not at rest with their planet.

The tension manifested itself in a thousand different ways, through a thousand different details. Here, we passed a home whose owner was fighting to keep aloof from the planet, his property ringed with imported trees and bushes; elsewhere, there were the mute signs of others who'd given up such attempts but still hadn't found any peace. I'd felt all this the night before, and it was no less unsettling in the full light of day . . . especially since I had no idea what it was they were all striving *against*. The Solitaran environment was supposed to be one of the most benign in the colonies.

"Perhaps it's the Cloud," Calandra murmured.

I looked at her, both startled and chagrined that she'd once again read my line of thought so easily. "The Cloud's not supposed to affect people," I reminded her.

"Unless they're already dead?" she retorted grimly.

I swallowed, the sharp-acrid reminder of what she was facing curling my stomach. "Point, I suppose. But a lot of researchers have studied the Cloud, and none of them has ever mentioned any effect on the living."

"How long have any of them been in it?" she countered. "Some of *these* people have probably lived here all their lives. Even then, you can see how subtle it is. Would the average researcher even notice it?"

"Unlikely," I admitted. It would almost certainly take a Watcher to see it . . . and according to Randon, we were the first Watchers to come here.

A slight movement across the car caught the corner of my attention, and I looked over to see Randon eying me in obvious question. "There's a tension overhanging this place, Mr. Kelsey-Ramos," I explained. "A feeling that the people living here aren't really comfortable with their world."

I could tell by the slight cringing in Calandra's sense that she half expected Randon to ridicule either our assessment or us or both. But he just sat there, occasionally turning to gaze thoughtfully out the window, as I tried to put into words what it was she and I had felt.

"So you think it's a side effect of the Cloud?" he asked when I'd finished.

"Or else the paranoia of knowing that their whole existence rests on human sacrifice—" I broke off at the strained patience in Randon's eye. "Or it could be something entirely different," I added. "At the moment all we know is that the tension's there."

He nodded absently, gazing out the window again.

"Any idea," he asked slowly, "how long a person would have to be here for this tension to manifest itself? A year? More? Less?"

"No idea," I shook my head. "You're wondering if that could be part of Aikman's trouble?"

Randon turned to Schock. "How long has Aikman been on Solitaire?"

Schock had his computer out; seated to Randon's other side, Kutzko was fingering the controls of his visorcomp. "Three years," Schock reported. "Station Chief Li, on the other hand, has been here for—bozhe moi!—for eighteen years, ever since HTI got the place going. Assistant Managers Blake and Karash twelve and four, respectively."

Randon nodded. "Yes, I remember those numbers," he said absently. Already, I could see, he was calculating how he might use this insight into Solitaire's planetary ethos to his advantage. The sense of him had altered subtly from the evening before, and I could tell he was rethinking his earlier conclusion that having a Watcher around was merely a crutch. And if he could think that about *one* Watcher . . .

I felt Calandra's presence at my side. *She is far beyond the price of rubies* . . . I could only hope Randon would come to see that, too.

Behind his visorcomp, I could see Kutzko's eyes still moving slightly as he read, and I knew what records he was checking. Tense security guards had a tendency to make their opposite numbers equally nervous. "Well?" I asked him.

"Shouldn't be a problem," he said. He didn't elaborate.

Like most of the rest of Solitaire, Cameo was built relatively flat, with the tallest buildings being only three stories high. The psychology of corporations regarding height and power being what it was, I wasn't surprised that HTI's headquarters was one of the latter, though I wondered on the way in what they could need with even that much room. The autopark guided the car to a VIP spot by one of the Elegy-style columns flanking the main entrance, and as we stepped out a man in a middle-level business capelet emerged from the wrought-styraline doors. A memory clicked as we approached him: HTI's president, O'Rielly, had been wearing an identical capelet clasp when Lord Kelsey-Ramos called to announce Carillon's acquisition of his company. Apparently HTI was one of those corporations which went in for the trappings of team spirit; whether those trappings actually accomplished what they were intended to was something we would soon find out.

"Good day to you, Mr. Kelsey-Ramos; welcome," the man greeted us, nodding with the appropriate deference. His sense belied his words: we were considerably less than welcome here. "I'm Brandeis Pyatt of HTI Transport, Station Chief Chun Li's chief assistant."

"Good day to you as well," Randon nodded back. "I trust Mr. Chun Li is still expecting us."

"Yes, sir, he's waiting inside in the board room." Pyatt's eyes flicked once to me, recognition clearly there, as he turned to lead us inside. "If you'll follow me . . . ?"

We walked in silence down a corridor lined with attractive stonework. A few employees and guards watched with varying degrees of interest—and varying degrees of distrust—as we made our way. Once, I remembered, I'd likened this trip to an ambassadorial visit to a conquered country; now, it was beginning to feel more like an espionage penetration.

Eventually, we reached an inner door. Two guards with duplicates of Pyatt's capelet clasp as collar insignia stood flanking it; at Pyatt's nod, one reached over and pulled the heavy wooden panel open.

It was as if we'd suddenly been transported from Solitaire to a major corporation headquarters on one of the Patri worlds. Nothing in the hallway had prepared me for the vast expanse of space or the lavish display of furnishings, all of them that I could identify having been imported from off-world. A carefully orchestrated sensory bombardment, probably designed to both intimidate the visitor and heighten his subconscious estimation of HTI in the bargain. A thought occurred to me, and a quick check confirmed that the room could indeed be converted with only minimal effort from its current business setup to one more suitable for entertainment.

Seated around the massive formite-topped gemrock table filling out the room's center were two men and a woman I recognized from Schock's data cyl: Station Chief Wilmin Chun Li, First Assistant Manager Tomus Blake, and Second Assistant Manager Angli Karash. Between and around them at the table itself were scattered another half dozen aides and assistants; behind them, against the walls, other aides and guards stood or sat at auxiliary work stations.

"Good day to you," Chun Li nodded gravely, rising to his feet as the others at the table followed suit. "I'm Station Chief Wilmin Chun Li; on behalf of HTI's Solitaire operation, I welcome you."

A proud man, I saw, though not necessarily in the bad sense of that word. Proud of his accomplishments, proud of his organization and of the job he had done here . . . and more than a little nervous. Worried that Carillon would summarily dismiss him? It was a reasonable possibility, and a sadly not unreasonable fear: in corporate acquisitions like this a long and loyal work record often became a liability. Over it all, covering the other emotions like a translucent glaze, was a general sense of tension. The same tension, perhaps, that Calandra and I had sensed in Solitaire as a whole . . .

"Good day to you as well, sir," Randon returned the nod. "I'm honored to be here." He gestured to Schock and me. "May I present my aides: Dapper Schock and Gilead Raca Benedar."

There wasn't a single wisp of surprise from anyone at the table over my name. Not that I really needed further confirmation that they were expecting me.

Chun Li exchanged polite nods with each of us and gestured to his sides. "My assistant managers: Tomus Blake and Angli Karash."

Blake was angry, and he was making little effort to hide it. Tight-lipped, he nodded to Randon with barely adequate courtesy and barely glanced at Schock and me. It wasn't Aikman's version of anti-Watcher prejudice, though: Blake was angry at all of us. Perhaps he felt betrayed at HTI's inability to keep Carillon from taking over; perhaps it was simply that he was now likely to be frozen out of contention for Chun Li's position, a position he very clearly wanted.

Karash, in contrast, was much more phlegmatic than either of the two men; certainly more polite than Blake. Her sense was that of a capable, politically-minded supervisor maintaining a neutral wait-and-see attitude and preparing to roll with whatever rocking occurred. Though with fewer years invested in the Solitaire operation, she of course also had less to lose than they did. All things considered, she was still the most promising potential ally among the three.

The ritual exchange of nods over, Chun Li waved us into our chairs. "Please be seated, Mr. Kelsey-Ramos; gentlemen. I'm sure you have many questions you'd like to ask."

"Yes, indeed," Randon agreed. We sat down, Calandra and the two shields moving to the wall behind us. "First of all, I'd like to bring you greetings from my father, Lord Kelsey-Ramos, and the entire Carillon Group board."

Seated against the wall almost directly behind Chun Li, impossible to miss whenever I looked that direction, was a stunningly beautiful woman.

It was an old ploy, but no less effective for all that, and the woman herself was better at it than many I'd seen. Her almost casual posture subtly emphasized the allure of breasts and legs; while her face, framed delicately by a hairsculpt much too expensive for her indicated corporate position, was coyly provocative. Each time our eyes met—which was practically every time I looked her direction—her lips curled in a barely detectable but nevertheless sultry half smile.

But however many times she'd laid out this snare, it was clear that she'd never tried it on a Watcher. Even as I felt my body stirring with the lust she was trying to distract me with, the rest of her sense came through the allure . . . and of its own accord my desire drained quietly away. She was cold, manipulating, arrogantly amused—so totally opposite, in fact, to the softly sensuous image she was trying to project that her seduction became little more than a gross parody; pitiful and disgusting instead of being alluring. I gazed into her eyes one last time, seeing there that she knew she'd failed—but had no idea why—and turned my eyes deliberately away.

"First of all," Randon continued, "let me assure you that, unlike some corporations, Carillon is not in the habit of automatically replacing the directors and employees of freshly acquired companies . . ."

Perhaps they'd suspected that the long-distance seduction would fail; perhaps they were merely being cautious. Whatever the reason, they'd arranged a second distraction for me . . . a distraction that turned out to be far more effective than the first.

He was one of the HTI guards—or perhaps more precisely, he was dressed in an HTI guard's uniform: a fascinatingly twitch-faced man standing against the wall just inside the range of my peripheral vision. Twitch-faced, and radiating the most unstable emotional state I had ever sensed.

" . . . Our policy is to try wherever possible to maintain continuity and existing relationships, particularly when such relationships are clearly working well . . ."

He wasn't insane, at least not in any way I would have expected to read insanity. His emotions were simply on a permanent scattercoast. One minute he would be tense and nervous, the next fearful, the next inordinately pleased with himself, the next sullen and withdrawn.

" . . . What we *do* demand is ability. There's no place in the Carillon Group for incompetence. Any employee that has been getting a downhill coast while others looked the other way or covered up will be in for an extremely rude shock . . ."

No corporate guard chief could possibly tolerate a man that emotionally unbalanced, which left it a tossup as to whether HTI had raided a treatment hospital or weirded up one of their own guards with some schizm-inducing drug. But at this point the method didn't really matter. Try as I might, I couldn't entirely ignore the man; and the mental effort to do so threatened to become a distraction in itself.

" . . . So. There will be memos and perhaps some reorganizational papers coming down the line over the next few months, I imagine, as soon as we've had time to sift through all the records. But that ought to give you at least a brief overview of our plans. Are there any questions?"

The twitch wasn't just in his face, either. There were echoing spasms in varying degrees from shoulders, knees, and hands.

Including the hand hovering tautly beside the butt of his holstered needler.

I licked the inside of my lip. *No danger*, was my first, back-brain feeling; but under the circumstances that was hardly the sort of conclusion I could afford to trust to a subconscious synthesis of unidentified cues. A schiz-oid man armed with a needler could almost literally mow this entire roomful of people down in the space of a few heartbeats.

On the other hand, none of the other HTI guards were directing any worry at all in his direction. Was that the cue I'd picked up on, that they *hadn't* picked up any danger themselves? Perhaps; but my sense of had felt stronger than that.

"I think I speak for all of us," Chun Li spoke up, "when I say that we'll all do our best to make this transition as smooth as possible, both for Carillon and ourselves . . . "

My phone vibrated its silent call signal. Dropping my gaze with an effort from the twitchy guard, I eased the instrument from its belt case and keyed for nonverbal. Behind me I could hear a faint and unintelligible voice—Kutzko's—while, under the edge of the table, I watched his words flow across the tiny screen:

CALANDRA SAYS TO TELL YOU HIS NEEDLER ISN'T LOADED.
THAT MEAN ANYTHING TO YOU?

An eerie feeling crept across the back of my neck.
She'd done it again. Read my mind with complete ease
. . . and this time without even having to see my face.

She was right, too, of course. Looking back at the
guard—his sense that of almost childlike cunning at the
moment—it was obvious that his needler was riding
much too high in its holster to be carrying even a
partially filled clip. That, plus the way it swung against
his leg when he twitched—the cues had all been there,
and clearly my back-brain had picked up on them in
deciding he wasn't a danger to us. I only wished I could
have identified them faster. At least as fast as Calandra
had.

*Pride goes before destruction, a haughty spirit before
a fall* . . . and, after all, it didn't really matter which of
us picked up on which fact, as long as together we got
all of it. Taking a deep breath, I chased away the tinge
of jealousy from my mind and, my vision clear again,
turned my attention back to Chun Li.

" . . . I presume you'll want to go over our records;
we have them for you right here." Reaching beneath
his capelet, he withdrew a cyl. "This is everything for
the past five years," he added, placing it on the formite
surface in front of him and giving it a gentle push. The
tube rolled across the table, picking up speed as the
formite first concaved, then convexed, coming at last to
a stop in front of Randon. "All previous records will be
on Portslava, where I presume your associates will be
picking them up."

"Thank you," Randon nodded, scooping up the cyl
and pocketing it. "I presume you've also got copies of
those older records on hand?"

A touch of uneasiness flickered through Chun Li's
sense, though he was able to control his face and voice
remarkably well. "Yes, of course," he acknowledged.
"If you'd like copies I can have them sent to your ship
this afternoon."

"Why can't I have them now?"

Blake and Karash were registering heightened tension, too, and it was in fact Blake who answered Randon's question. "The problem is that they're scattered around through the system in rather unreadable code," he said in clipped tones. "It would take at least an hour to chase them all down and put them into coherent form."

"Oh, that won't be a problem," Randon said, voice almost lazy but with a hard edge underneath it. "Schock, here, is quite good at that sort of excavation. If he can borrow a hard terminal for a few minutes he can probably get that out of the way while we finish our talk."

Blake visibly clenched his teeth. "I don't mean to be obstructive, Mr. Kelsey-Ramos, but the data is really *so* scattered through different files and even different listings that it'll take a good deal of time to gather it all."

My eyes turned elsewere, I could still sense Randon smile. "The wonders of modern technology, Mr. Blake. Ever heard of a Templex decoder?"

From the senses of the others, I could tell none of them had . . . and that none of them was looking forward to hearing about it. "I'm afraid not," Chun Li admitted cautiously. "I take it it's something used for this kind of data retrieval?"

"And also for bypassing various blockages," Randon said, choosing his words with care. "Split files, scattered data—that sort of thing."

As well as for getting around intentional barriers. The three across the table picked up on that one at once, and the play of emotions twisting through them became even more interesting. There was just the briefest hesitation, then Karash rose to her feet. "Well, then. If you'll come over here, Mr. Schock . . . ?"

Schock pushed his chair back and got up; Chun Li and Blake followed his motion with their eyes. "Now," Randon said briskly, "while they're doing that, I'd like to hear what sort of projects you've got going at present. Mr. Blake?"

Blake turned his attention back from Schock with an effort. "As you may know, a new Rockhound 606—number four—has recently gone to work in the rings. It's slightly modified to allow it to take in and break up rocheoids of up to a hundred meters across—"

"I was under the impression," Randon broke in calmly, "that it was the pebble-sized rocheoids that contained the purest ores."

An almost-glare leaked out before Blake could stop it. "Yes, sir, that's true," he said with strained politeness. "Though the surfaces of most of the larger rocheoids, down to a few centimeters of depth in some cases, are also rich in heavy metals. However, in this case what turns out to be more important is that the *interiors* of these larger ones contain a more standard distribution of light and heavy elements, and some of those light elements are used in the extraction and refining processes. Getting them directly from the rings will save us having to ship them out from Solitaire."

"I see," Randon said blandly. He'd known all this already, I could tell; as could most of the others. Again simply reminding everyone of his control of the conversation. "So. Rockhound Four is in operation . . . ?"

Blake pursed his lips, smoothed them out. "Yes, sir. Anyway, we're negotiating with them for a share of their light element harvest, as well as for a contract to handle some of their molybdenum and tungsten output. We're also—"

"I was under the impression that you were at your full transport capacity already," Randon interrupted again. "You're authorized for, what, a hundred trips in and out per year?"

The twitch-faced guard made an almost-serious reach for his needler. Even schizoid, I noted, he was careful to stop before he got close enough to the weapon to trigger either of our shields' own combat reflexes. "We're already at our full trip capacity, yes," Blake said stiffly, his tension level rising markedly. "As I was about to say, we also have an order in for a pair of new Fafnir-class freighters. Once those are delivered our total carrying capacity will increase significantly."

"Assuming the Fafnirs are able to keep flying," Randon commented off-handedly. "Those things are right up against the Mjollnir Limit, and I don't know as I'd trust them for more than a couple of trips."

Blake's face darkened; clearly, the Fafnir purchase was his own pet project, and he wasn't the kind to take even implied criticism well. But before he could say anything more, Chun Li jumped in. "We'll make sure they come with an adequate guarantee," he said dryly. "In addition, we have a petition pending before the Patri seeking to raise our trip quota to one hundred twenty per year." A soft beep came from the back wall, where Schock was working under Karash's watchful eye, and the sound seemed to throw Chun Li off stride a little. "We think it may be worth trying to revive the old idea of using terminally ill patients and voluntary suicides to supplement the currently available number of zombis," he went on, a bit distractedly.

"If not, perhaps the crime rate will go up?" Randon said cynically.

Chun Li flushed with anger. "That's not fair, Mr. Kelsey-Ramos."

Randon met his gaze without flinching . . . but he realized he'd indeed gone a step too far with that one. "Perhaps not," he conceded. "My apologies, Mr. Chun Li. Ah—Schock. Finished already?"

The others twisted their heads to look as Schock and Karash returned to the table. "Yes, sir," Schock nodded, holding up three cyls. "I think I've got it all."

I had no doubt of that, myself. Karash's face, as she trailed behind him, was a nice mixture of amazement and tension, with the tension winning.

Randon nodded back. "Well, then, I suppose that will about do it for now," he said, rising to his feet as Schock came around the table. I stood up, too, feeling Kutzko, Calandra, and Ifversn come up behind us, the two shields moving unobtrusively into flanking positions at our sides. "Thank you for your time and hospitality, Mr. Chun Li; Mr. Blake, Ms. Karash. I'm looking forward to our tour of the ring mines later this week; until then, I'll be keeping in touch."

And that was that. In the space of a few minutes we'd

gone in, learned everything of importance—or at least gotten it on cyl—and walked out again . . . leaving tension and perhaps even the first signs of panic in our wake.

Lord Kelsey-Ramos would have been pleased.

CHAPTER 7

It took me over twice as long as the meeting itself had run to describe my observations of it, and when I was finished Randon was impressed.

Though not yet quite willing to admit it out loud. "Interesting," he said thoughtfully, gazing up at Calandra and me as he stretched out a bit more at his stateroom lounge desk. "Very interesting indeed. I'd picked up most of the high points myself, but confirmation is always nice to have. So what exactly do you think they're hiding?"

I glanced at Calandra, got a little confirmation of my own, and shrugged. "No way to tell, sir," I told him. "Also, please bear in mind that they may *not* be hiding anything specific. It could just as easily be a matter of them not wanting to make things easy for you."

He snorted. "Oh, *that* part of the group psyche came through in gigapix. And I still think they're hiding something."

"Probably," I conceded. "I just thought I ought to mention all the possibilities."

"Turning the other cheek again, huh? Well, I suppose we'll just have to wait until Schock finishes his tapment check on the cyls and we can get a look at them." He flared briefly with an almost overwhelming impatience, but he knew perfectly well that Schock couldn't plug the cyls into the ship's computer and download them without checking them first. If HTI had encoded some bookbugs or tapsnakes into any of the information, putting them into the *Bellwether*'s system would be an invitation to disaster. Not only could we wind up losing all the HTI data, but a sophisticated enough tapsnake could conceivably open every other file aboard ship to HTI scrutiny and remote manipulation via the phone system.

There were effective methods to prewash suspected cyls, but they took time. So with an effort Randon forced down his impatience and shifted his attention to Calandra. "So. Having heard Benedar's analysis, do you have anything to add?"

"Not really," she said evenly. "I agree that they're hiding something, probably having to do with either their shipment records or trip quotas or the correlation between the two."

Randon frowned. "Why do you say that?"

"Because it was around those subjects that the tension seemed to peak," she explained. "And they were the only subjects that affected all three of the managers in the same way."

Randon looked at me. "Did you get that, too?"

"I picked up the tension increase," I acknowledged. "I can't confirm that it was all three—Karash was off to the side with Schock at the time—but the other two certainly reacted strongly when you hit those topics. Oh, and that guard—the one put there to distract me?—he also made a particularly bad jolt at the same time."

"That one's coincidence," Calandra shook her head. "The guard wasn't in enough control of himself to turn things on and off that way."

"You sure?" I asked.

"Yes. However, I *was* able to watch Karash, too; as I

said, she reacted the same way Chun Li and Blake did."

Randon grunted. "Um. Interesting."

For a minute the room was silent. I watched Randon closely, trying to detect any subtle changes in his attitude toward Calandra. But if there was anything there, it was buried by the myriad of other things on his mind.

The moment of introspection was ended by the whistle of the phone. Picking up his control stick, Randon waved it toward the instrument. "Yes?"

The picture came on: Brad Seqoya, one of Kutzko's more massively built shields. "Seqoya, sir, at the gatelock. Thought you'd like to know that Mr. Aikman's just returned."

Randon made a face. "Thank you, Seqoya. On his way to see me?"

"Probably, sir. And he didn't look too happy."

Randon's sense took on a slyly amused edge. "All right, I'll be ready for him. Anything else going on down there?"

"Nothing much, sir. We had a Billingsgate rep and his customs escort here half an hour ago to pick up the molecule factory shipment, but nothing since then."

The amused edge disappeared, Randon's sense hardening into distaste. "One of our people went down with them, I hope."

"Yes, sir, as per orders."

Randon nodded, trying to clear his mind and not entirely succeeding. One of the laws governing Deadman Switch usage was that even passenger ships had to carry their share of cargo when entering or leaving Solitaire system, and there had been no exception made for the *Bellwether*. To me it seemed the only decent thing to do: if the toll for our passage was going to be a man's life, the least we could do is make that life count for as much as possible. But Randon didn't see it that way. To him the dead man was a zombi, hardly counting as a human being any more, and it irritated him immensely to have all these strangers traipsing in and out of his ship picking up packages. Aikman, I'd been

told, had tried and failed to find any free space in the
Rainbow's End receiving center where we could unload
the cargo all at once . . . but given the way Aikman felt
about us, I didn't entirely believe that story. "How
much stuff is left down there?" Randon asked the shield.

"Oh, probably something over half, sir," Seqoya told
him.

Randon grimaced, nodded. "You'd better give customs another call and remind them all this stuff has to
be out before we leave for Collet tomorrow. Either
they get the appropriate people here to pick it up, or
else they find some storage space for it. Otherwise we
leave it on the pad when we lift."

Seqoya smiled faintly. "Yes, sir. I'll get right on it."

Randon waved the control stick to break the connection and tossed the instrument on his desk. "You two'd
better get out," he grunted. "Unless you want to face
Aikman in a bad mood."

There was a touch of sly satisfaction beneath Randon's
words. "I'd expected him to be at the meeting today,
sir," I commented carefully. "Was there some trouble?"

"Oh, no—just a long errand I trapped him into." He
shrugged. "After all, I could hardly have him walking in
on the HTI meeting and letting everyone know they
didn't have all the Watchers covered."

That thought hadn't even occurred to me. "I see."

"I wish I could see their faces when they find out
who she is," he said, smiling to himself. "Anyway—" he
picked up his control stick again and keyed it, and the
door behind us opened. "Take her back to her stateroom," he instructed Daiv Ifversn as the latter stepped
into the doorway.

I looked at Calandra as she turned silently to go . . .
and for the first time I could see the stirrings of an
almost grudging hope within her. "I'd like to stay for a
moment, if I may," I said to Randon.

He glanced at me, nodded to Ifversn. "Go ahead," he
told the other.

They left; but before I could figure out how to phrase
the question, Randon saved me the trouble. "All right,

I'll concede the point," he said. "You're a useful person to have at business confrontations; and you and she together are considerably more than twice as useful. Is that what you wanted me to say?"

"More or less, sir," I admitted.

He gave me a tight smile. "I haven't grown up a Kelsey-Ramos without picking up some of my father's tricks. Probably would've made a good Watcher myself if I'd cared to."

And though I have the power of prophecy, to penetrate all mysteries and knowledge . . . "I'm glad we're able to serve you," I said instead. "Will you be wanting both of us along at the governor's dinner reception tonight?"

He threw me a knowing look. "Still trying to make her more valuable to me alive than dead?"

His sense showed none of the rancor the words might have carried. "All people are worth more alive than dead," I returned, keeping my tone light.

He snorted, taking it in the serious but nonthreatening way I'd intended him to. "So you say. You might have trouble proving it. Anyway. You're in charge of getting Paquin ready for the reception tonight—you know what kind of clothes and whatnot women are expected to wear at such things?"

"I can handle it, sir."

"Good. Don't stint, either—there's no point in playing a game like this halfway. Well, go on—get out before Aikman gets here."

"Yes, sir," I nodded. "Thank you."

I passed Aikman on my way down the corridor. From even that brief touch of his sense I was glad I hadn't stayed around.

Kutzko was just where I'd expected to find him: loitering around the exit-corridor storage closets, where he was within easy reach of both the gatelock and the slightly more extensive storage areas where our duty cargo was stored. "All hail the conquering hero," he greeted me. "How'd Mr. Kelsey-Ramos like it?"

"What, our report on the meeting?" I shrugged. "He wasn't as attentive as Lord Kelsey-Ramos would have been, but then he's new to this. He seemed impressed enough."

"I'd say so, yes," was his dry rejoinder. "Considering the order just came through that she'd be coming to the reception tonight." He grinned with a mock-evil-tinged dreaminess. "Can you imagine what the assembled dignitaries would say if they knew they were hosting a zombi?"

I could, and it made me wince. "Mikha, I need a favor."

"Sure. What?"

I hesitated. "I need a complete listing of capital crimes under Solitaire law."

His eyebrows raised a couple of millimeters. "You looking to start a new hobby?"

"It's for a friend," I told him, matching his dry tone. "I also need to know if there are any places in the system—the ring mines for instance—where Patri law might possibly take precedence."

"Solitaire law covers the entire system." He shook his head, eyes boring into mine. "This unnamed friend wouldn't by any chance be our outzombi, would it?"

I hadn't really expected to fool him. "It would, yes," I admitted. "I'm trying to get her a new hearing back on Outbound."

Understanding came into his face. "And having the hearing take place after she's dead kind of defeats the purpose?"

I nodded. "Unfortunately, in order to keep her alive I have to find a replacement for her."

Kutzko's eyes defocused a bit. "So you want a list of capital crimes to see who we could stick with that honor. And you want the ring mines because that's where we'll be leaving the system from?"

"More or less." For the moment, there seemed no reason to mention how limited the pool of potential zombi candidates actually was. "Can you do that?"

"No problem," he assured me. "Now: what's the other favor you want?"

"What makes you think there is one?" I countered.

He smiled slyly. "Oh, come on, Gilead. The blazing Solitaran penal code you could find on your own."

I sighed. "Sometimes I wish you'd been born stupid," I told him. "Okay. At the moment we're scheduled to leave tomorrow, which means the reception tonight will probably be my only chance to talk directly to Governor Rybakov. And I *have* to talk to her—privately or reasonably so."

Again, that knowing look. "And you want me ready to run interference?"

"Basically, yes."

He paused, considering, and I could see that he was weighing the risks of possibly winding up square in the middle of this whole mess. "You really think she's innocent?" he asked at last.

I nodded. "I do. The more I see of her, the less I think she could be a murderer."

He pursed his lips, then shrugged. "Okay, sure, I'll do it. Give me a sign when you're ready and I'll try to make you a bubble to talk in."

I exhaled silently. "Thanks, Mikha. I really appreciate it."

"No problem." He studied my face. "Just one question: is Mr. Kelsey-Ramos one of the people I'm supposed to keep out of this bubble?"

It was a question that had also been nagging at me. At the moment I had at least his tacit approval for what I was doing . . . but making an embarrassing nuisance of myself at a formal reception would evaporate that support in double-quick time. Unfortunately, I had no way of knowing in advance where the crucial dividing line lay. "There shouldn't be a problem as long as I'm discreet," I said as reassuringly as possible. There was no point in him worrying about it, too.

"And if you're not, I pretend I don't know you?"

"Fair enough. Try to be gentle when you throw me out of the building."

He grinned lopsidedly. "I'll bring Brad along and let him do it."

"Oh, thanks a *lot*," I snorted. "I'll either wind up in orbit or in a burn-out trajectory."

His grin faded into seriousness, a seriousness that somehow made me brace myself. "You know, there *is* one other way to get the *Bellwether* a new zombi."

I gazed at him, feeling the cold-steel edge there. "Pick one up ourselves?" I asked carefully.

He nodded in Cameo's direction. "Even Solitaire's got its quota of drifters and generally unwanted people. Some of them might be criminals from the rest of the Patri and colonies who finagled passage here and are hiding out."

"You know I could never be party to something like that," I said, my lips suddenly dry. "It would be murder."

"Which the Deadman Switch isn't?"

I gritted my teeth. "Two wrongs have never yet made a right. Besides, you'd never get Mr. Kelsey-Ramos to go along with something like that."

He cocked an eyebrow. "Maybe. Maybe not. I'll bet there would be a way to rig it to look like someone had stowed away and tried to seize control of the ship." He paused. "You may not know it," he added obliquely, "but Lord Kelsey-Ramos has been trying to find a second Watcher for his staff for a couple of years now."

An odd haze of unreality settled over me, a disbelief that I was even talking about this . . . "No," I said firmly. "Absolutely not. If I can save Calandra legally, I'll do it. Not otherwise."

"Even if the illegal zombi deserved death anyway?" he countered.

All have sinned and lack God's glory . . . "Even then," I told him.

For a moment we looked at each other. Then Kutzko shrugged acceptance. "If that's how you want it," he said. "If you'll pardon my saying so, I think your sense of ethics is on the overdone side."

"Possibly," I said evenly. "But any ethics you can

throw out when they're inconvenient wouldn't be worth much as ethics, would they?"

"I suppose not," he said, and I could sense him backing away from the topic. "I suppose I should start getting my people ready for tonight."

"And I have to get Calandra some formal wear ordered, anyway," I reminded myself aloud.

"There's a catalog listed on the main Rainbow's End phone list," he offered. "I scanned through it some last night, and it seems pretty complete."

"Thanks, I'll take a look."

It was only minutes later, in the privacy of my stateroom, that the enormity of what had just happened hit me with delayed force. Not just that Kutzko, a man I thought a great deal of, had been willing to consider kidnap and murder . . . but that I had actually been on the verge of considering it myself.

And my knees began to shake.

CHAPTER 8

The brighter of the stars in Solitaire's sky were beginning to appear through the dusk overhead as we pulled up to Governor Rybakov's mansion, an imposing edifice that gave out a sense of dignified power that reminded me of the HTI conference room. From the mansions's double-wing design, I guessed it followed the typical Patri pattern for such places, including both office and entertainment facilities as well as living space for the governor. The windows of the ground floor to our left were ablaze with light, and through the half-tinting I could see the shadows of milling people.

"Nice place," Randon grunted as the five of us filed out of the car. "Be interesting to have Schock run the budget sometime and find out just what percentage of Solitaire's income goes to their officials."

"They've got money to spare," I murmured.

He glanced at me. "I suppose they do," he conceded.

Randon and Kutzko in the lead, we climbed the flaystone steps to the main portico. "Mr. Randon Kelsey-Ramos and party," Kutzko told the liveried guards flanking the door. Stepping smoothly in front of Randon, he started to enter—

"Just a moment, sir," one of the guards spoke up. "Is the lady in your party Ms. Calandra Mara Paquin?"

Beside me, Calandra tensed. Randon turned his head leisurely to look at us, turned just as leisurely back again. "Yes, I believe it is," he acknowledged coolly. "Why?"

"I regret to say, sir, that I can't allow her to enter." There was no regret anywhere in the guard's sense that I could detect. "Governor Rybakov's orders."

"On what grounds?" Randon asked.

"On the grounds that she is a convicted felon, sentenced to death, sir," he said stiffly, distaste at both her legal status and her Watcher background coming through his official decorum. "The governor does not wish to have such a potential danger within her house."

There really wasn't any hope of appeal, and Randon knew it as well as the rest of us. But he was too pridefully stubborn to give up quite that easily. "She was assigned to my ship," he told the guard. "Placed therefore under both my care and my legal jurisdiction. I'll take full responsibility for her actions and behavior here."

"I understand, sir. I still can't allow her to enter."

Randon locked eyes with the man for a long moment, then turned slowly back to us and nodded to Duge Ifversn, behind me in rearguard position. "Ifversn, escort her back to the ship," he instructed the other. For a moment his eyes met mine, and I could sense him bracing for an argument. But there was no point to it, and I remained silent. "Turn her over to Seqoya and then come back."

Ifversn nodded. "Ms. Paquin . . . ?"

Calandra turned away, not looking at me, and went with him. I watched them get back into the car, then looked back to find Randon's eyes still on me . . . his eyes, and an almost grudging touch of sympathy. I took a deep breath and nodded to him. Turning, he strode without a word between the guards and into the mansion.

Inside, we found ourselves in a high-arched hallway stretching probably half the length of the building itself.

A greeter waiting just inside welcomed us to the governor's home and directed us to an open pair of double doors down the hall, while a second pair of guards relieved Kutzko of his puff adder needler clips and gave him a single clip of slapshots in return. It was standard security practice—guards usually preferred visiting shields to carry only nonlethal ammunition—and Kutzko surrendered to it with professional good grace.

The buzz of conversation was audible well into the hall . . . and as we reached the double doors it became instantly clear that Governor Rybakov wasn't merely going through the motions on this one. There were at least two hundred people milling around the ballroom-sized space; two hundred rich and influential people, judging by their clothing and deportment and the watchfulness of the unobtrusive shields shadowing many of them. Out of a total planetary population of perhaps four hundred eighty thousand—only half of whom lived in the Cameo/Rainbow's End corridor—getting two hundred of the upper class together in one place was a rather impressive accomplishment.

Randon realized that, too. For a moment he just stood at the doorway, looking around as if committing the room and its occupants to memory. Then, straightening slightly, he led the way into the room.

And all two hundred people turned to look at us.

It was the sort of almost surrealistic scene you sometimes hear about but seldom actually see. The loose knots of people standing nearest to the door spotted us first, their conversations dropping off into silence and then tautly whispered comments as they realized who it was who had just arrived. The sudden quiet made those beyond them turn, many of them repeating the first groups' reactions; until, within the space of a dozen seconds, the wave of notice had rippled across the entire room.

Leaving a blanket of quiet tension behind it.

I'd expected it, of course. After Aikman's obvious anti-Watcher prejudices and HTI's more subtle version of the same antagonism, I hadn't expected open-armed greetings from anyone on Solitaire . . . which was perhaps why it took me several heartbeats more to realize that the cautious attention wasn't directed at me at all.

It was directed at Randon.

There was no doubt, once I finally picked up on the signs. For every subtle movement of a person's face or body there's an equally subtle reaction from those looking at him; and in this case all the reactions I could see were keyed to Randon's movements, not mine.

Vaguely, I wondered why Randon Kelsey-Ramos should make all these people nervous.

The awkward gap lasted no more than a few seconds before an elegantly dressed woman glided toward us from the side. "Mr. Kelsey-Ramos," she nodded, her voice rich with the overtones of a Portslavan native. "I am Governor Lyda Rybakov, the Patri's representative on Solitaire; I bid you welcome."

Randon nodded back. "Thank you, Governor Rybakov. May I present to you my aide, Mr. Gilead Raca Benedar."

Rybakov was definitely an experienced politician. Her nod to me was almost as polite as the one she'd given Randon. At least outwardly. "Welcome," she told me.

"Thank you," I murmured, nodding back.

Her eyes shifted back to Randon. "We're honored to have you here, Mr. Kelsey-Ramos," she continued. "The Carillon Group is well known throughout the Patri and colonies, and we of Solitaire system are looking forward to working with you."

"I'm equally honored to be working with you," Randon said smoothly, throwing a glance around the room to include all the others in that statement. "If you're as diligent at commerce as you are in throwing receptions, Carillon will be hard pressed to keep up with all of you."

A loose, slightly strained chuckle swept the room. Rybakov smiled, the same faint strain evident there, too, and reached out to touch Randon's arm. "Come; let me introduce you to some of the other important people of our world. People much more important than I."

With Kutzko and me trailing a step behind, she led him farther into the room; and as if that was a signal, the buzz of conversation began again. But not quite the same buzz as had been there before. The aura of tension that had taken over at our entrance still lay like bedrock beneath it.

The first group Rybakov led us to consisted of five people—three men and two women—waiting in a loose semicircle and trying hard to look relaxed. "Mr. Randon Kelsey-Ramos, Mr. Gilead Benedar," the governor said, "may I present Danel and Debra Comarow; Dr. Sergei Landau; and Nady and Lize Arritt."

"Pleased to meet you," Randon said as they all exchanged nods. "Let me see: NorTrans of Starlit, I believe?"

A ripple of quiet surprise ran through them . . . as it did through me. I hadn't placed the names, but I'd certainly heard of NorTrans: one of the biggest corporations in the Patri and colonies, almost certainly the biggest with a license to operate in and out of Solitaire.

In other words, we'd found the leaders of the system's business community first crack out of the box. Glancing at Governor Rybakov, I saw it hadn't been mere chance.

"I'm impressed, Mr. Kelsey-Ramos," Landau said, and I could see the comment went for all of them. "I've always thought that I, at least, was too deeply buried in the NorTrans structure for even those *in*side the company to recognize my name."

Randon smiled. "Hardly, sir," he said. "Besides, my father has made something of a hobby of knowing exactly who the major business interests and people are on Solitaire. Some of that was bound to leak down to me."

It was the wrong thing to say. I couldn't tell why, but that much was instantly clear. Almost in unison the tension among the five of them shot up, and the groups nearest us again paused in their own conversations to listen in. "Well, we're certainly honored by your father's interest in us," Comarow said, his voice controlled but with a predator's caution beneath it. "Though speaking for myself, I'm always a bit nervous when someone knows more about me than I do about him."

"Especially as regards his business dealings," his wife Debra put in, her easy laugh breaking some of the hidden tension. I sensed Comarow's approval, realized she'd picked up on whatever he was going for and was carrying on with it. "Danel always gets so paranoid when he has to start doing business with someone new."

"Not paranoid, really, Debra," he chided her gently. All an act; they were clearly two minds headed the same direction. Whatever that direction was. "Just cautious. As I'm sure you understand, Mr. Kelsey-Ramos."

"Perfectly," Randon nodded. "However, I really don't think you have anything to worry about. As I explained to HTI's managers this morning, the Carillon Group tries whenever possible to maintain continuity in the activities of acquired companies."

"So we'd heard," Arritt put in. I sensed Randon's quiet reaction: that the comment implied that Arritt, and possibly all of NorTrans, had a commline into HTI's top management. Not surprising, but worth noting regardless. "And you're right; continuity *is* what's on most of our minds."

"*Most* referring to just NorTrans, or to all of Solitaire?" Randon asked, glancing pointedly at a few of the eavesdroppers around us. A couple of them had the grace to blush.

"Oh, pretty much all of Solitaire," Comarow acknowledged without embarrassment. "You'll find that people who do business here are a fairly close-knit community, Mr. Kelsey-Ramos. We have our methods . . . and we're always a little nervous of newcomers."

"I'm sure you'll find that the Carillon Group business philosophy doesn't change just because we're now on Solitaire," Randon said.

If they found that reassuring, they didn't show it. If anything, in fact, it actually made them a shade more uncomfortable.

"Well, that's nice to know," Comarow said, the easy friendliness of his voice in sharp contrast to the sense beneath it. "I trust you'll find your visit profitable. I understand you'll be leaving for Collet tomorrow?"

"That's right," Randon nodded. "I'm looking forward to actually seeing one of those Rockhound 606's I've read so much about."

Comarow chuckled. "You won't believe it even then. Let me tell you about the first time *I* saw one of the monsters. . . ."

The conversation turned to descriptions of Rockhound mining platforms, drifted to possibly apochryphal stories of life aboard them. It was heading toward social life on Solitaire proper when Governor Rybakov gracefully pulled us away and steered us across the room to another group.

This one composed of the officers of the Elegy-based conglomerate Dragon Hoard Metals . . . and just as interested as NorTrans in making sure Randon knew that Solitaire had its own way of doing business. As, with minor variations in tone, did the third group we talked to. And the fourth. And the fifth.

Eventually, even Randon couldn't pretend to ignore it any more. "From the way everyone's talking," he commented to Rybakov as they collected delicately sculpted appetizers from the serving table, "one might think Carillon just filed its corporation papers last week."

She shrugged, long politician's practice enabling her to cover most of her own flicker of discomfort. She didn't really want to talk about it, and yet on another level knew she had to. "Solitaire is an embarrassment, Mr. Kelsey-Ramos," she said bluntly. "The Patri can't afford to give up the wealth that flows in from the ring mines; but on the other hand, they have to condemn people to death to get it. It's not an especially popular policy." She glanced at me, the first time since our introduction that she'd done so. "We're not just talking fanatical religious minorities like the Watchers or Halloas, either—most people on the Patri and colonies feel at least a little uncomfortable with the whole idea."

"The Halloas?" Randon frowned, also glancing at me. I shrugged fractionally; I'd never heard the reference, either. "What is that, a religious sect?"

Rybakov waved a hand depreciatingly. "I'd hardly call them organized enough to be a sect," she snorted. "They're a group of fanatic-mystics who believe Solitaire is the seat of God's kingdom, or some such nonsense."

Randon glanced at me again. "Why?—because it requires a blood sacrifice to get here?"

Rybakov snorted, and I winced at the contempt underlying her political facade. Clearly, she had even less tolerance than the average citizen when it came to religious matters. Possibly one reason she was a governor. "Not that I've heard, though I wouldn't put it past them," she said. "No, it's supposed to be something about the Cloud being the halo of God. From which it apparently follows immediately that *this* is the heavenly kingdom." She waved a hand around her.

Someone nearby snickered, just audibly; but on Randon's face there was no answering contempt. "Sounds crazy," he agreed evenly. "And you see these Halloas as possibly giving Solitaire even more of a bad image than the Deadman Switch already has?"

Rybakov looked him straight in the eye. "It's possible," she told him. "Most of the corporations holding Solitaire licenses have made an effort to keep the Halloas' existence from leaking out."

"And you think Carillon may not?"

Again, a meaningful glance in my direction. "Your father's . . . peculiarities . . . are well known."

"So are his business skills," Randon returned, his voice a few degrees cooler. "Or are you suggesting he doesn't understand the effect of image on public psychology?"

Surprisingly, she smiled. "Such as the effect a business renegade's image might have on those he's going to be working with, for example?"

Randon frowned, then smiled in return. "Oh, come on, Governor. You aren't going to tell me that all these crafty business professionals are *that* taken in by my father's public posturings, are you?"

She shrugged, eyes still measuring him. "As I said, Mr. Kelsey-Ramos, the business community here is a little touchy. No offense meant."

"None taken." Surreptitiously, Randon's fingers curved in a subtle hand signal. Beside him, Kutzko responded by reaching for his phone, as if a message were coming in. "Actually, Governor—"

"Excuse me, sir," Kutzko interrupted smoothly. "May I speak with you for a moment? Security matter."

"Certainly. If you'll excuse us, Governor . . . ?"

She nodded, and we moved back toward an empty spot on the floor. "Well, Benedar?" Randon murmured, looking at Kutzko as if discussing the imaginary security matter with him.

"The Halloa story is part of the truth, but not all of it," I told him. "In fact, I'd go so far as to suggest the Halloas may be nothing more than a convenient excuse they're using to cover up whatever it is about you that's *really* making them nervous."

He frowned. "What it is about *me*? I assumed *you* were the problem."

"Not this time, sir. You're the one they're all watching like hawkrens."

Randon pursed his lips. "Kutzko?" he invited.

Kutzko shook his head slowly. "I don't think there's any personal danger to you, sir, at least not here and now. But I'd have to agree with Benedar, that you're the one they're interested in."

"And there's something else, sir," I put in. "When Kutzko did his 'security matter' gambit, Governor Rybakov reacted rather strongly."

Kutzko frowned at me. "She did, did she? I didn't notice that."

"She's very good at hiding these things."

Randon eyed me thoughtfully for a moment. "And they all seem to know," he said slowly, "about our meeting at HTI this morning, don't they?"

Kutzko and I exchanged looks. "You think they

might know that Schock got away with more than HTI wanted you to have?" Kutzko ventured.

Randon cocked an eyebrow at me. "Benedar?"

I let my eyes sweep the room, relaxing my mind and letting it dig out every nuance of feeling it could. "I think it might be a good idea, sir," I said, "to make sure the *Bellwether* is ready for trouble."

Randon snorted gently. "Let's not get overly melodramatic," he advised. Still, I could tell that he too was growing uneasy.

As was Kutzko. "Sir, I have to agree with Benedar again," he spoke up. "If it really *is* those cyls that have all these people nervous, they must be blazing valuable. To someone, anyway."

"Probably right," Randon grunted. "All right, go ahead. Keep it quiet, though—if someone tries to get them, I want him to get close enough for us to grab."

Kutzko was already making the connection. "Seqoya? —Kutzko. What's the status on the ship?"

I couldn't hear the answer, but Kutzko's sense indicated everything was normal. "Well, that may be changing in the next few hours," Kutzko told him. "I want the perimeter extended fifty meters, a cat-yellow on the gatelock, and a double cat-yellow on Mr. Schock's stateroom. You'd better warn him that someone may be after those cyls he brought home from HTI today; he ought to know how to protect them." He got confirmation, raised his eyes to Randon. "Anything else, sir?"

And I had a flash of inspiration. "Have Calandra brought to the gatelock," I said.

Both of them looked at me; and after a moment they both understood. "Excellent idea, Benedar," Randon said, a grim smile tugging at the corners of his lips. "Do it, Kutzko."

Kutzko nodded and relayed the instructions. "All set, sir," he said, lowering his hand.

"Good." Randon glanced around. "Let's rejoin the party, then."

A few meters away, Governor Rybakov was talking quietly with a man dressed in the white uniform of a

Pravilo flag officer. Commodore Kelscot Freitag, I remembered from Randon's briefing: in charge of security for Solitaire system.

A man who also clearly enjoyed his vodkyas. Even as Rybakov took his arm and steered him toward us, I could see the slight glaze over his eyes and the twitching of muscles in his cheeks. "Mr. Kelsey-Ramos," Rybakov nodded to Randon. "That security matter all cleared up, I trust?"

"Yes, thank you," Randon assured her.

"Well, if you should have any trouble," Freitag spoke up, "I'm the man to see. Commodore Kelscot Freitag, Mr. Kelsey-Ramos."

"Pleased to meet you." Randon nodded to him, and I revised my opinion of the man a few steps upward. Despite the effects of at least three separate types of vodkyas showing in his face, his speech and eye-focus showed his mind wasn't nearly as touched as I'd first assumed. "Thank you for your offer of assistance, but I suspect any security problems I might have will take place on the ground."

Again, Rybakov's sense flickered with uneasiness. Freitag's, in contrast, remained untouched. "Doesn't matter," he rumbled. "As an offworlder, you come under Pravilo jurisdiction whether groundside or out in the ring mines."

"Though it *is* Solitaran law that applies," I murmured.

Both he and Rybakov frowned at me. "Solitaran law is sanctioned by the Patri and administered by their representative," the governor told me stiffly. "Which makes it as much Patri law as anything else."

"Of course it is," Randon agreed, throwing me an annoyed glance. Out of the corner of my eye I saw Kutzko take a half step backward and pull out his phone, and I hoped fervently he hadn't taken my comment to be his cue. Clearly, Rybakov had some internal conflicts about her position here, and I was going to have to give her more study before I could even attempt to bring Calandra's case to her attention. "What Mr. Benedar was referring to, I think," Randon went on, "was certain minor differences between standard Patri law and certain particular variations that are applied here."

"All colony worlds have their own differences," Rybakov pointed out, still cool. "Local customs, local requirements—all of those enter into it."

Randon nodded. "Which is certainly how the law ought to be—"

"Sir?" Kutzko cut him off; and with that one word I knew something was wrong. "A moment, if I may."

Randon's eyes flicked to him, back to Rybakov and Freitag. "If you'll excuse us . . . ?"

"Certainly," Rybakov said, an almost haunted look flickering across her face as she and the commodore stepped back.

"Trouble at the ship?" Randon murmured to Kutzko as he pulled out his own phone and keyed for the *Bellwether*.

"Actually, sir . . . we're not quite sure," Kutzko admitted.

Randon frowned at him; and then the connection came through. "This is Kelsey-Ramos," he said into the instrument. "What's going on?"

I already had my own phone out. "Well, sir, we're not quite sure," Seqoya's slightly embarrassed voice came. "We have a couple of customs people here who say they're supposed to check on how much cargo we still have and to arrange to have it offloaded."

"Their IDs check out?"

"Oh, yes, sir, all the way . . . but Ms. Paquin says they're frauds."

Randon threw me a quick glance. "Oh?"

"Yes, sir. Unfortunately, she can't tell me who they are or why they're here; just that they're lying about being from customs."

Randon pursed his lips. "They're not armed, are they?"

"No, sir." Seqoya was on more familiar ground here. "We checked them completely. They've got a recorder and package reader; that's all."

"And you *did* run their IDs?"

"Yes, sir. The central Cameo computer says they're legit."

"They could have been suborned," Kutzko murmured.

"Maybe," Randon growled. "Or maybe Paquin is just jumping at shadows." He threw me a glare . . . but it was a worried glare. "All right, Seqoya, tell you what. You have someone call the customs chief on duty at the spaceport and find out what you can about these two. We're on our way; do *not* let them move from the gateway—in either direction—until I get there."

"Understood, sir," Seqoya said.

Randon signed off, threw me another glare, and nodded at Kutzko. "Let's go," he said grimly.

CHAPTER 9

They were still there when we arrived: two men in the official capelets and unofficial hauteur of customs officials, sitting at the gatelock guard station under the watchful eye of the Ifversn brothers. Outwardly, they were mad as hornets at being kept from their duties.

Inwardly, they were badly worried.

It didn't keep them from putting on a good act, though. We'd barely gotten inside the outer lock when the elder of the two was on his feet, glaring at Randon with a fair counterfeit of righteous fury. "Mr. Kelsey-Ramos," he snarled, "I want you to know that if you don't call off your shields *immediately* and let us get about our duties I will be forced to file official and formal charges against you, them, and the master of this ship."

"I'm sure everything will be straightened out in just a few minutes," Randon assured him, giving a good imitation himself of being impressed by the outburst. "Excuse me a moment, and I'll go find out just what the trouble is."

We passed them and headed on into the ship. Calandra and Seqoya were waiting at the door to the first room, the latter looking much more justified than he'd sounded on the phone. "Well?" Randon demanded, throwing a glance at Calandra and then shifting his attention to Seqoya. "What did you find out?"

Seqoya gave him a grim smile. "Something very interesting, sir: our visitors out there don't exist."

Randon frowned. "Explain."

"The customs duty officer at the spaceport doesn't know them," Seqoya said, ticking off massive fingers. "Neither does their central coordination office in Cameo itself. Neither do any of the customs officials, inspectors, or workers that I was able to track down and talk to."

Randon cocked an eyebrow at Kutzko. "Interesting, indeed. How do they explain this?"

"I haven't confronted them with it yet," Seqoya said. "I thought you might want to be here when we did."

Randon nodded. "All right, let's try it." He hesitated, then turned to Calandra. "You have anything to add?"

"You probably won't need to check their equipment," she said quietly. "They didn't seem at all protective of it. But you'll need to search the younger one's capelet—left shoulder, I think."

For a moment Randon looked at her as if she was joking. Then, pursing his lips, he gave her a brief nod. "Call a shield to take her back to her stateroom," he instructed Seqoya, "then meet us back at the gatelock."

Seqoya nodded and stepped to the nearest intercom. Glancing once more at Calandra, Randon led Kutzko and me back to the gatelock. "Sorry to keep you waiting, gentlemen," he said briskly to the two men. "If you'll be so kind as to remove your capelets, I think we can clear this up right now."

There was no doubt about it: Calandra had zeroed in precisely on target. Both men's faces froze for a second, and the younger's left shoulder actually twitched. The elder recovered first. "Why?" he asked.

Randon didn't bother answering. Behind us, Seqoya ambled back into the room; catching his eye, Randon

nodded toward the two men. "Capelets," he instructed.
Seqoya nodded back and kept ambling, an almost lazy
glint in his eye. The others saw it, too, and by the time
he'd reached them both had their capelets off.

"Thank you," Randon said politely as Seqoya collected them. "Now, if you'll just sit back and relax,
we'll take a look and see what we can find—"

We all heard the footstep behind us at the same time;
and for the four shields recognition and reaction were
virtually simultaneous. In a single catlike leap Kutzko
was between the intruder and Randon, his and Seqoya's
needlers out and tracking past my shoulder. The two
Ifversns were just a shaved second slower, their weapons coming to bear warningly on the customs men.
Heart thudding in my throat, I spun around and dropped
to one knee.

For a moment no one moved or spoke. Randon recovered his voice first. "Hello, Mr. Aikman," he said.
"You shouldn't sneak up on people like that. It's bad for
your health."

Slowly, the panic frozen into Aikman's face melted,
and he lowered the foot that had ended up in midair.
"I'm sorry," he managed. "I didn't mean to startle
you."

"You certainly won't do it again, anyway," Randon
said. "May I ask what you *did* mean to do?"

Aikman's eyes flicked past us to the customs men, his
emotional balance already coming back to normal. "I
heard there was some trouble at the gatelock," he said
evenly. "I came to see if there was anything I could do
to help."

Randon gazed at him for a few heartbeats, then nodded. "Certainly. The first thing you can do is tell me if
you recognize those men over there."

Again Aikman looked, and I could sense him brace
himself. "No," he said.

"He's lying," I told Randon quietly.

Aikman spun to face me, a wave of hatred washing
toward me like the burning wind from an explosion.

"And who are you," he snarled, "to pass judgment on another man's mind—?"

"He's a Watcher." Randon's voice was quiet, almost calm . . . but there was a steel underlying it that cut off Aikman's tirade in midsentence. "And if it comes to that," Randon continued, "who are *you* to lie to me?"

Aikman licked his lips briefly, the sense of him abruptly becoming cautious. "I may have seen them before," he admitted grudgingly. "I certainly don't know them personally—"

"Seen them at HTI?" Randon asked.

Aikman's jaw tightened. "Perhaps. I couldn't say for sure."

"I see." Randon nodded. "Well, they've probably changed jobs since you knew them. Happens all the time—people leave low-level corporation jobs for careers with customs."

Aikman ignored the gibe. "What charge are you making against them?"

Randon cocked an eyebrow. "Impersonation of customs officials, for starters. Along with attempted entry into a private spacecraft and probably one or two others as we think of them."

"They have false IDs, then?"

A touch of uncertainty edged into Randon's sense. "Not exactly, but no one knows—"

"Not *exactly*? What does 'not exactly' mean?"

Randon glared at him. "It means that, yes, their IDs check against the customs records, but none of their allegedly fellow workers has ever heard of them."

"That won't hold up for ten minutes before a judiciary." Aikman was on his own territory now, and he knew it. "An ID record is both necessary and sufficient proof of employment in an official capacity." A grim smile quirked at his lip. "Do you know what the penalty is for illegal detention of customs inspectors?"

Across the room, Seqoya cleared his throat. "Is it anything like the penalty for attempted sabotage?"

We all turned to look at him. In one hand was the

younger man's capelet, looking slightly mauled; in the other, a small floppy rectangle that glinted in the light. "What is it?" Randon asked, stepping over for a closer look.

"Not exactly sure, sir, but it looks a lot like the insides of one of our computer data scramblers—see that number on the sicet, there?"

"Probably a scrubber," Kutzko said, giving it a quick glance and then returning his attention to the prisoners. "It's a scrambler gadget for putting into someone else's system."

Randon favored the prisoners with a long, cold gaze, then turned the look back on Aikman. "Any further comments, counselor?"

"Yes," he said calmly. "Do you have any proof that they came here with intent to sabotage?"

"Why else would they be carrying something like this?" Randon snorted.

Aikman's eyes flicked to the prisoners; and the younger picked up on the cue. "We use it to read samples of scrambled data on suspect ships," he said, voice just the right shade of indignation. "Samples that we can then take back and use to decode the scrambler scheme."

Randon glared at them. "Kutzko?"

Kutzko shrugged. "I don't know, sir. You could check with Mr. Schock—he could probably tell you whether this gadget has that kind of capability."

"In other words," Aikman spoke up, "you haven't got proof of any sort that a crime either has been committed or was about to be committed. Correct?"

Randon turned on him. "You can just shut up—"

"No, sir, I will not," Aikman snapped. "My job is the upholding of human rights under Patri law, and I will do that job wherever I find those rights in danger. You will release these men now, or you will hand them over to the Pravilo and formally charge them with a crime. A crime, I remind you, that you'd better be able to prove."

He ran out of wind and stopped, and for a long moment the air was thick with a brittle silence. From

Randon's sense I expected him to explode with fury . . . but his father had trained him better than that, and he waited until his mind was again in control of his emotions. "Benedar?" he invited.

I swallowed. "He's not bluffing, sir. He means it."

Aikman's glance at me glinted with its usual hatred, but he said nothing. "Very well," Randon said icily. "Seqoya: did you run a DNA comparison between those customs IDs and their owners?"

"Yes, sir," Seqoya answered cautiously, clearly wondering if he was about to wind up on the receiving end of Randon's frustration. "They matched perfectly."

"All right, then." Deliberately, Randon turned his gaze from Aikman onto the two prisoners. "They can go. Give them back their capelets."

Seqoya hesitated, then moved to comply. "Not the scrubber, of course," Randon added. "We'll want to let Schock take a look at it."

"That device is customs property," the elder man insisted, his courage clearly having come back with his perception that Randon was giving in. "I must insist on having it back."

Randon gave him a tight smile. "Certainly. Your superior can pick it up in the morning . . . along with Your IDs."

Both men froze in the act of putting on their capelets. "We need our IDs to do our jobs," the elder said through a suddenly tight mouth.

"Then you'd better get your superior over here tonight, hadn't you?" Randon told him coldly. "Seqoya: escort them to the edge of the perimeter. Make sure they leave."

Seqoya nodded. "Yes, sir."

Behind me, Aikman took a deep breath. Randon heard him, too, and turned around. "You have something to say, counselor?"

Aikman did; and he thought seriously about saying it. But he'd lost, and he knew it . . . and like Randon, he recognized the futility of simply lashing out in anger. "No, Mr. Kelsey-Ramos," he sighed at last.

Randon watched him for another moment, just to make sure. Then he turned back, and we all watched Seqoya usher the would-be intruders out of the gatelock. "A-minus for effort," he murmured, more to himself than to any of us. "Come on, Benedar, let's go see what Schock can tell us about that scrubber. Kutzko, keep the shields alert—they may not be ready to give up yet."

Behind me, Aikman turned and stalked back into the ship, his sense a silent blaze of anger. "Yes, sir," Kutzko nodded. "Will you be wanting to head back to the governor's dinner later?"

Randon glanced at his watch, shook his head. "No point to it now." He threw me a sly look. "Besides, someone there may be sweating at our sudden departure. Let's give him time to do it right."

"Cute," Schock muttered, turning the flexible rectangular mesh over in his hand and peering at its other side with his magnifier. "Very cute indeed. Cute *and* nasty." He waved Randon over. "Look here, sir—this sicet here, the one with the number partly scratched off? Odds are it's a preprogrammed bookbug, designed to get into the ship's data records and rescramble selected portions according to a new code."

Randon snorted gently. "Pretty primitive," he growled contemptuously. "Also useless. Even if the main sentinel missed it, there are at least two programs in our library for redecoding data that's gotten fouled up."

"True, but then this wasn't supposed to be anything more than a distraction," Schock shook his head. "Something to keep the sentinel—and us—occupied while *these* other two sicets got to work." He tapped the pair with his probe. "This is the real attack: a highly sophisticated codex mimic, and a miniature phone system switching station. The mimic can—theoretically, anyway —fool a computer into handing control of the phone system over to it, at which point the switching station can set up a link to a phone outside the ship. Without our knowing it, naturally."

Randon swore, the earlier smugness vanished into black anger. The *Bellwether*'s computer could easily defend itself against an autosystem simple enough to fit on a single sicet; defending itself from a human expert with access to a full-range computer was something else entirely. "How hard would it have been for them to hook this into the *Bellwether*'s systems?" he asked.

"Simplicity itself," Schock told him. "There are three induction portals on it, each set to a different voltage and frequency."

"Meaning . . . ?"

"Meaning that all they would have had to do was plant it within electronic spitting distance of any of our electronics," Schock said bluntly. "In a phone, a repeater terminal, even one of the remote locks."

For a long moment Randon was silent, and I could feel the anger growing steadily within him. "Could they possibly have had the thing just sitting around, ready to go?"

"You mean was it put together specifically for us?" Schock shrugged. "Hard to tell. For all I know, everyone on Solitaire could be backstabbing each other with these all the time."

Wordlessly, Randon plucked the thing from Schock's fingers and handed it to me.

One look was all I needed. "It was assembled in a rush," I confirmed. "There are traces of connector fluid on some of the sicets that would normally be cleaned off, and the sealant has ripples in it that imply it was force-dried instead of being allowed to set naturally." I handed it back to Schock.

"Huh," he said in a bemused tone, peering at it again himself. "They're there, all right."

"Which means," Randon said thoughtfully, "that they *did* throw this together solely for our benefit. Hard to do?"

Schock considered. "Not for someone willing to pay the price."

Randon pursed his lips. "There must be something very interesting on those HTI cyls."

"Well, we can find out for sure any time now," Schock offered. "They're clean enough to put into the system and take a look. Incidentally, they'd loaded a passive tapsnake on the cyl they gave us, designed to root around for anything else in our files with an HTI keymark on it. Nothing fancy; it looked almost like they just threw it in out of habit."

"Paranoia," Randon murmured, and I could tell he was remembering the conversation we'd had on the way to the HTI meeting that morning. Remembering the odd tension Calandra and I had sensed overlaying all of Solitaire . . . "Benedar, you said Governor Rybakov reacted when I had Kutzko pull the fake security matter gambit, right? What was she like when we left?"

I thought back. "Much the same," I told him. "Only worse. But also strangely . . . resigned, I think. As if she knew she'd lost a battle or something and was mentally preparing to pull back to a new position."

He stared off into space a minute. "Sort of like the way Aikman acted when I told him I was keeping his friends' IDs?"

"Similar, but more intense." I hesitated, sorely tempted to skip over the next point. But omission of truth was just another form of lying. "For the record, though, I don't believe Aikman was actually in on the scheme, at least not beforehand. He was genuinely surprised to find those men trying to break into the ship."

"Then why did he try to get them off?" Randon demanded.

"Oh, he figured out quickly enough what was going on," I shrugged. "It was obvious that he was trying to get whoever sent them off the hot seat with as little damage as possible."

Randon grunted. "The difference between accessory before the fact and afterwards, in other words."

"More or less."

Randon made a face, then shrugged. "All right, forget Aikman for the moment. Back to Rybakov. What was this battle she'd lost, and where was she trying to pull back to?"

I had to search my memory to find the part of the conversation he was referring to. "My feeling is that she was involved, somehow, with the attempt to get aboard," I said slowly, trying to remember every nuance of the governor's sense. "Perhaps only in knowledge—maybe she was just asked to make sure we didn't leave dinner early."

"Or maybe she was asked to provide someone with a pair of official IDs?" Randon suggested.

I blinked. That thought hadn't even occurred to me. "That's . . . yes, that's possible," I agreed carefully.

"Just a second, here," Schock put in, clearly aghast. "Sir, are you accusing a *planetary governor* of involvement in industrial sabotage?"

"Why not?" Randon countered. "Just because the Patri thought she was qualified to run a minor system doesn't mean she can't be bribed. Or blackmailed or threatened, for that matter."

"But—" Schock struggled for words.

"Especially if she sees us as a threat to the whole of Solitaire, and not just to HTI," I put in.

Randon paused in the act of responding to Schock and stared at me. "*Does* she see us that way?" he asked.

I bit at the inside of my lip. The words had just popped out on their own . . . but now as I reviewed my sense of Rybakov, I could see that my back-brain had again put pieces together ahead of my conscious mind. "Yes," I told Randon.

"How much of a threat?" Schock asked warily.

"It can't be *that* bad," Randon put in before I could answer. "Logic, Schock. Our would-be saboteurs must have reported their failure by now; if Rybakov thought we had to be stopped at all costs, Commodore Freitag's men would already have boarded us under some pretext and carted us and the cyls away." His voice turned thoughtful. "Which means she still hopes we'll be reasonable about whatever we're about to find."

I watched him weigh the alternatives and come to a decision. "Move aside, Schock," he ordered, stepping around the desk. A wary look on his face, Schock slid out of the lounge chair. Randon dropped into it, scooping up the other's control stick and waving it at the phone. "Governor's mansion," he instructed the computer.

"Mr. Kelsey-Ramos—"

"Quiet, Schock. Yes, hello, this is Randon Kelsey-Ramos. I'd like to leave a message for Governor Rybakov—no, don't interrupt her dinner, just give her this message. Tell her that her friends dropped something of hers before they left our ship, and that if she wants the items back she can pick them up here in the morning . . . Yes, personally—I wouldn't think of entrusting them to anyone but her. Thank you."

He waved the stick again and got up off the couch. "And that's that," he said, a note of tension underlying the words. "We'll find out in the morning just how much of a guilty conscience the governor has."

"We won't be here—we're supposed to leave for Collet in the morning," Schock reminded him nervously. Clearly, he considered the whole subject perilously close to social apostasy.

"Then we'll just have to postpone our departure a day or two," Randon told him firmly. "I want to stay here until I know what it is about HTI that has everyone so nervous." He cocked an eyebrow at me. "That's good news for you, of course."

It took me a second to realize what he meant . . . and then it came back in a rush. What with all the intrigue of the evening, I'd totally forgotten the death sentence hanging over Calandra's head. "Yes, sir, it is. If Governor Rybakov does come here tomorrow, I'd like to be present."

Randon's smile was tight, with a trace of bitterness to it. "I wouldn't have it any other way. I'm beginning to see just how potent this Watcher addiction is."

The words were bantering . . . but the hard edge

beneath it was anything but. Like his father, Randon saw himself as a staunchly independent man, master of his life and the people around him. Unlike Lord Kelsey-Ramos, he hadn't yet learned that both independence and mastery had limits. "Good night, sir," I said.

"Okay, Schock, to work," I heard Randon say as the door closed behind me. "Let's get those cyls out and see what in blazing chern-fire is in them."

CHAPTER 10

Kutzko was gone from the gatelock when I returned there. Ifversn, when I asked, directed me to the bridge, a sort of sly amusement about him. Wondering what the joke was, I headed upstairs.

Kutzko was there, all right, sitting beside First Officer Gielincki at the *Bellwether*'s sensor station. "Ah—Gilead," he said, glancing over his shoulder at me before returning his attention to the map spread out in front of him across the control panel.

"Mikha; Officer Gielincki," I said in greeting as I came up behind them. "Am I intruding?"

"Hardly," Gielincki said shortly, not bothering to look around at me. Like most of the *Bellwether*'s crew, she didn't especially like me; unlike many of the others, however, she had both the honesty to recognize her prejudice for what it was and the empathy to feel sorry for me. It gave me an odd and uniquely mixed sense. "—number two just turned again," she said to Kutzko. "North on . . . must be Shupack Avenue."

"Got it," Kutzko said, making a mark on the map. "We're monitoring our two intruders," he added to me, swiveling around in his chair. "Brad slid a couple of trackspurs into their capelets before he gave them back."

I looked at the display, at the flickering spots and glowing grid there. So that was what had Ifversn so amused. "Rather old-fashioned, isn't that? Not to mention obvious?"

Kutzko shrugged. "Sometimes old methods work just because the other side *doesn't* expect them." He waved back at the display. "Besides, what's the point of living in a ship instead of a hotel if you don't make use of what the ship can do?"

I studied his face. He was trying far too hard to control it . . . "Besides which," I suggested, "you found out you couldn't tap into the local police surveillence system without them knowing about it?"

He grimaced. "Something like that," he admitted. "Doesn't really matter—the targets know we're watching. They're just wandering around, killing time probably while they wait for someone who can break them out of our track."

I thought about that. "Then what's the point of doing it?"

"Annoyance value. It bothers them without making any extra work for us."

Gielincki snorted. "Well, it *doesn't*," Kutzko insisted, a little defensiveness creeping into his sense. "You have to be up here on watch anyway."

"Sure. Number one just turned east. Looks like they're starting to drift toward a common rendezvous point."

"Um." Kutzko made another mark. "I wish I'd had enough men to follow them. Might be nice to see who they meet." He turned back to me. "Was there something you wanted, or you just come up here to watch the show?"

"Actually, I was wondering if you'd gotten that information I asked you for this afternoon," I told him.

"Oh—yeah, sure." He glanced at Gielincki and got up from his chair. "Come on back here—Gielincki hates people talking while she works."

That earned him another snort and a semi-mock glare,

both of which he ignored. Together, we walked back to one of the monitor stations flanking the bridge door. "I got your list," he said in a low voice, digging a piece of paper out of an inner pocket, "but I don't think it's going to help you much."

He was right. The list consisted of just four crimes: multiple murder, murder of a police or Pravilo officer in the commission of a Class I crime, death of a kidnap victim, and treason. "This is it?" I asked, checking the paper's other side.

He shrugged. "You're not going to find many other capital crimes anywhere else in the Patri and colonies, either," he reminded me. "And at least one of *these* has only been made a capital crime since Solitaire opened up. Like Governor Rybakov mentioned earlier, people really don't like the death penalty much."

I nodded heavily. "I know. Well . . . thanks anyway."

He studied me. "So what are you going to do?"

"Not much I *can* do. I'll try talking to Governor Rybakov tomorrow morning, see if she can suggest anything."

"Yeah, I heard she was expected. Probably not going to be in the mood for handing out favors, though."

I thought back to the woman's obvious prejudice against religion . . . and about the fact that Randon was prepared to accuse her of complicity in industrial sabotage. "I can only try."

Kutzko grunted. "Well, maybe Mr. Kelsey-Ramos will see his way clear to helping push—"

He broke off, eyes flicking over my shoulder as the bridge door opened behind me. I turned to look—

Just in time to see Aikman come to a sudden halt as he belatedly spotted us. "Ah—good evening," he managed, his sense gone suddenly taut. In his hand was a cyl, a cyl his first reflexive twitching of fingers tried vainly to conceal. "I was looking for the captain; I see he's not here. Excuse the interruption."

He turned to go, stopped abruptly as Kutzko took a long step around me to cut off his exit. "That's okay, Mr. Aikman—we were about finished, anyway," he said easily. "What did you need the captain for? Maybe I can help."

"No, that's all right," Aikman insisted. His eyes flashed at me . . . but on top of the usual hatred there, I found a strong current of nervousness. "I just needed—"

"To call someone?" Kutzko interrupted him genially. "That's right—there's a block on outship calls from your stateroom, isn't there?"

Aikman's forehead darkened in anger. "There are laws against illegal restraint—"

"There are laws against aiding industrial sabotage, too," Kutzko cut him off, his voice hardening. "What's that?"

"What's what?" Aikman asked cautiously, thrown momentarily off-balance by the question.

"That." Kutzko took another half step forward, and his pointing finger abruptly became a darting hand that smoothly plucked the cyl from Aikman's startled fingers.

"*Give* me that!" Aikman snarled, making a snatch for the cyl. For that one brief instant his sense was less that of a human being than it was of an enraged animal, and I felt my muscles tense up as I took an involuntary step backward.

Kutzko's didn't even flinch as his free hand deflected Aikman's grab. "Easy, Mr. Aikman," he warned, voice calm again. "Looks like some kind of tamper-resistant datapack," he commented, peering at the cyl's ends. "Shall we plug it in and see what it is?"

"It's an official legal document," Aikman bit out. "For transmission and filing with the Solitaran judiciary. You break the seal by reading it here and you'll void it."

"Then you'll just have to write it up again, won't you?" Kutzko said coolly. "Unless you'd rather just tell me what it says?"

For a long minute the two men stood motionlessly, facing each other like an echo of the ancient gladiators. The sense of defiance surrounding Aikman bent first. "It's a request for a judicial restraint order," he ground out. "I want the outzombi barred from leaving this ship; and I want *him*—" he nodded his head sideways at me— "also barred, for collusion with a condemned felon."

Kutzko's eyebrows went up in polite surprise. "Collusion?"

"Yes, collusion," Aikman's said sarcastically. "It's a legal term—I doubt that you've had much acquaintance with such things. Except possibly as a defendant somewhere."

Kutzko considered taking offense, decided it wasn't worth it. "I know more about law than you might think," he said. "You want to tell me how collusion applies here?"

"Oh, come on, Shield Chief, let's not let company loyalty blind you to what's going on here," Aikman snarled. "Why do you think Benedar got Kelsey-Ramos to take your outzombi to the HTI meeting this morning?"

"Suppose you tell me," Kutzko invited him.

"Because he's preparing her for an escape, of course. Showing her the lay of the land—helping her to meet the powerful of Solitaire who might be duped into hiring a parasite Watcher, the way Lord Kelsey-Ramos was."

There was a lot in all of that to strain Kutzko's temper, but he held on admirably. "You have any proof of that?" he growled.

"He doesn't need proof," I said quietly. The flicker in Aikman's sense confirmed that I had indeed read his intentions correctly. "If he can even get that restraint order accepted for consideration, it'll be a couple of days before anyone can track through it and find it's nothing but unsupported innuendo."

Kutzko nodded understanding. "Uh-*huh*. By which time we'll be out of here and on our way to the ring mines."

Reaching forward, Aikman plucked the cyl from Kutzko's unresisting hand and stalked across the bridge to Gielincki, who'd been wisely staying out of it. "Officer, I want you to file this document with the Solitaran judiciary in Cameo," he told her, thrusting the cyl in front of her face.

She made no move to take it. "I'm sorry, Mr. Aikman,"

she said, eyes still on her displays. "You'll need to get permission from Mr. Kelsey-Ramos before I can do that. If you'd like, I'll call his stateroom."

"You'll comply, or I'll have you up on charges of illegal restraint," he said coldly. "I don't *need* anyone's permission to file legal papers."

Gielincki never had been the type to take threats well. Slowly, deliberately, she turned to look up at him. "Aboard this ship," she said, her tone even colder than Aikman's, "you need Mr. Kelsey-Ramos's permission to do *anything*. If that offends your democratic sensibilities, you're welcome to go elsewhere."

Aikman glared at her a moment longer. Then, without a word, he spun around and stomped back toward us.

Kutzko still blocked the door, and he made no effort to move. "Of course, if you leave the ship," he said casually, "that cyl has to stay here. We don't have any proof that it's really only a legal document."

Aikman's forehead darkened. "If you're accusing me—"

"Mr. Aikman," I interrupted.

"Shut up, Benedar," he snapped.

"I think perhaps I can help resolve this impasse," I persisted.

That earned me a needle-pointed glance. "How?—by reading my mind? How convenient that you're here. How convenient, too, that there's nobody to corroborate whatever you decide is the truth."

I felt my face flush with anger. "I don't lie about the things I see," I bit out. "I have to answer to God for my actions, you know."

His lip twisted. "Oh, yes, of course. It all comes back to God for you, doesn't it?"

"You have a problem with that?" Kutzko put in.

Aikman looked at him, then turned his attention back to me . . . and abruptly, his sense cooled, his frustrated rage changing to an almost icy bitterness. "Tell me, Benedar, did your Watcher schools bother to teach you any history while you were learning how to invoke God as justification for everything you did? Do you know what finally destroyed the Earth, for instance?"

"It was the increasing economic and political stresses of the last half of the twenty-first century," I told him evenly. "The final disintegration came from a combination of minority demands and unrest, plus a surge of anger over the costs of the StarWay project."

"Yes, that's how I would have expected a *Watcher* school to tell it," he sneered. "This may come as a shock, Watcher, but it wasn't economics or politics that destroyed the Earth. It was religion. Religion that started a thousand fanatic brush wars. Religion that kept terrorism going long after most of the strictly political problems were on their way to being solved. Religion that tore apart every society from East to West and back again."

"That was a long time ago," Kutzko interjected . . . but behind the supportive words I could sense his own hidden doubts. He, too, had grown up being taught that same Patri version of the Final Revolution. "You can't blame—"

"The Watchers?" Aikman cut him off. "Tell that to the people of Bridgeway who lived under the rule of Aaron Balaam darMaupine and his God. *They* know what happens when religion becomes more than just a hobby."

I felt a surge of anger. To equate religion with a *hobby*—

With an effort, I forced the indignation down. *Resentment kills the senseless, and anger brings death to the fool* . . . "As it happens, Mr. Aikman, I *have* heard that theory before," I told him. "It gives the Patri and colonies a good excuse to dislike and even persecute religious practice. Now tell me why it is *you* hate me."

His face went rigid, and for a half dozen heartbeats the bridge was filled with a brittle silence. "You don't need me to answer that," he said at last, very quietly. "You demonstrate it every time I have to be in the same room with you."

"What, because he understands people better than you do?" Kutzko scoffed.

Aikman sent him an ice-edged glare. "Tell me, Shield—you who know so *much* about the law—have you ever read the Patri Bill of Rights and Ethics? *Read* it, I mean, not just heard of it?"

"Yes," Kutzko told him stiffly.

"Do you remember Article Nine? The right against self-incrimination? Good. Then tell me how such a right can exist in the presense of a Watcher."

Kutzko's forehead furrowed slightly. "That right is supposed to be for judiciaries and trial proceedings—"

"No!" Aikman snapped. "It is the most basic of human rights, the right to the privacy of one's own thoughts." He glared at me. "You have no right to do what you do, Watcher. As far as a strict reading of Patri law goes, you don't even have a right to mingle with the rest of society." He held up the cyl, pointing it at me like a needler tube. "And if I can't keep you locked away from normal people forever, I can sure as putrid smert make sure you stay away from the people of Solitaire."

He stepped around Kutzko, headed for the bridge door. "What about Calandra?" I asked. "She has the right to keep her life if she's not guilty."

"The dead have no rights," he shot back. "And zombis are already dead."

I clenched my teeth, feeling a quiet panic bubbling up within me. With Calandra's life hanging by a thread, I couldn't afford to be trapped here in the *Bellwether*, away from the only people who could help. But there was only one way I could think of to stop him . . . and it would only add more fuel to his hatred of Watchers.

So be it. "Mr. Aikman," I called as he opened the bridge door, "if you file that document, I'll have no choice but to tell Mr. Kelsey-Ramos what you did this evening."

Mid-way through the door, he paused. "And what might that be?" he demanded without turning around.

"It was you, not HTI, who called the governor's

mansion and told them that Calandra would be with us."

He still didn't turn; but I didn't need to see his face. The stiffening of back and neck muscles was all the proof I needed that my guess was indeed correct. "You told them Calandra would be along," I continued, "and that she was a Watcher and a condemned felon."

"She *is*," he almost snarled over his shoulder. "She has no legal right to be out of her cell, let alone out of the ship."

"I doubt Mr. Kelsey-Ramos would see it that way," I pointed out. "He might consider it an interference with his mission to collect information here . . . in which case he might well have you removed from the *Bellwether* for the remainder of the trip."

Again, the tightening of muscles told me I'd hit close to the nerve. In the corner of my eye I could see that Kutzko was watching closely . . . and that he hadn't caught either of Aikman's reactions. "And you can't afford that, can you?" I continued. "HTI wants one of their people aboard to keep track of what Mr. Kelsey-Ramos does, and you're it."

"Dr. DeMont will still be here," he countered, striving for off-handedness. "And you can't use the Dead-man Switch without a Patri legal rep aboard."

"Cameo's full of Patri legal reps," I reminded him. "Many of whom don't have any loyalty whatsoever to HTI."

Aikman didn't reply, and after a moment of silence Kutzko stepped over and extended his hand. Without looking at him, Aikman dropped the cyl into the open palm. "It doesn't matter," he said, still with his back to me. "In a week she'll be *dead*. And there's not a putrid thing you or anyone else can do to stop it."

"We'll see," I told him, trying to sound more confident than I felt.

Perhaps he sensed that; or perhaps he knew much better than I what I was up against. "Oh, she'll be dead, all right," he bit out, the confidence in his voice as genuine as the gloating. "And if you don't stay out of my way, I may even arrange to have you as official witness to her execution. Remember that the next time you think about invading my privacy."

He left. "Probably makes friends wherever he goes," Kutzko commented wryly. But I could sense that some of the sarcasm in his voice was merely there for cover. Beneath it—

Beneath it, and in his eyes, was a kind of uneasiness I'd never seen in him before.

"Legal reps are often like that," I shrugged, deciding to ignore the uneasiness I was reading. If what I'd just done really bothered him, he'd bring it up in his own good time. "Just remember that *we* only have to put up with him for a few more days; *he's* stuck with himself permanently."

Kutzko snorted. "He's welcome to it. I wonder if he's like this with everyone."

"I doubt it. Not everyone has a Watcher with them."

Kutzko's uneasiness took on a tinge of guilt. "Yeah. Well . . ."

"What are you going to do with that?" I asked, gesturing to the cyl in his hand.

"Give it to Mr. Kelsey-Ramos, of course. Why?—you wanted to keep it our little secret?"

I shrugged. "I *did* sort of imply that if Aikman surrendered the cyl we'd keep his squalling to the governor to ourselves."

"You shouldn't make promises you can't keep," he growled. "I have to report this, and you know it."

I just looked at him, and after a minute he sighed. "Oh, all right—I'll gloss over that part if I can. Though I'll bet HTI will be madder at Aikman than Mr. Kelsey-Ramos will—getting Paquin thrown out of the reception meant she was here when the saboteurs tried to get in."

I hadn't thought of it that way, but he was right. *God has ensnared the wicked in the work of their own hands* . . . "Good point," I agreed.

Idly, he rolled the cyl across his palm. "I suppose I'd better get this to Mr. Kelsey-Ramos."

I nodded. "When I left him he was in Schock's stateroom getting ready to start sifting through the HTI cyls," I offered.

"Okay." He hesitated. "Gilead . . . does Aikman have a real case?"

"In other words, can I really read minds?"

He grimaced. "Maybe I should ask how *much* of people's minds can you read."

I sighed. "I've been working for Lord Kelsey-Ramos for eight years," I reminded him. "If I could read anything more than emotions and surface impressions, don't you think I could easily have stolen the Carillon Group out from under him by now?"

"Even knowing you'd have to answer to God for doing it?" he asked pointedly.

"Aaron Balaam darMaupine felt God wanted him to establish a theocracy on Bridgeway," I countered evenly. "He would have held onto his power a lot longer if he could have read the minds of those who eventually betrayed him."

"Point," Kutzko agreed, some of the tension in his sense easing. "Old Balaam's Ass *did* crumble pretty quickly once the Patri woke up to what he was doing."

I winced to myself at Kutzko's careless, even automatic epithet. DarMaupine's humility name had been an easy one for the Patri to turn against him: Balaam, the Old Testament prophet who'd had to be told by his own donkey that an angel of death was waiting for him in the road ahead. It was probably the only scriptural passage that even the most rabidly unreligious in the Patri and colonies knew. "Yes, he did," I agreed. "The original Watcher elders didn't unlock any hidden power of the human mind, Mikha. They just learned how to truly *see* the universe around them."

"Yeah. Well . . ." Kutzko grimaced, then shrugged fractionally. "You have to admit it gets blazing spooky sometimes. Anyway . . . I've still got to go find Mr. Kelsey-Ramos. See you later."

"Right."

He left. I waited a minute, then followed, heading back to my own stateroom. He was right, of course:

Watcher abilities could indeed be spooky to those who
didn't understand.

To those of us who *did* understand . . . there were
perhaps dangers the elders had never even considered.
*God does not see as human beings see; they look at
appearances but God looks at the heart . . .*

Had we, in our human pride, tried to usurp that role
for ourselves? Had that been, in fact, the underlying
root of Aaron Balaam darMaupine's treason?—the belief
that with God's power to see even partway into men's
souls he had also inherited God's power to rule?

Had that pride led to the persecution the entire
Watcher sect now suffered under?

I had none of the answers. Not in eleven years of
searching for them.

CHAPTER 11

I'd anticipated it, expected it, convinced Randon it would happen. Even so, I was still surprised when Governor Rybakov arrived at the *Bellwether* the next morning.

"Let me first state for any record you happen to have running," she said after the formalities of greeting were out of the way, "that my presence here is in no way an acknowledgment of any wrongdoing or knowledgeable complicity in wrongdoing."

"Of course," Randon agreed calmly. "Just as by asking you here to retrieve official property I'm in no way accusing you of any such activities."

For a moment they eyed each other in cool silence, while I sat at the third point of the triangle and tried to make myself as inconspicuous as possible. Rybakov broke first. "May I have them?" she asked.

Wordlessly, Randon reached into his desk and pulled out the customs IDs we'd taken from the would-be saboteurs the previous evening. Equally wordlessly, Rybakov took them, gave each a sour glance, and slid them into a pocket beneath her capelet.

"I presume you have an explanation," Randon suggested.

"Certainly I have one. Is there any particular reason you deserve to hear it?"

Randon glanced at me, back to Rybakov. "Would it help if I assured you I don't intend to make any of this public?"

It would indeed help, I could tell. Rybakov's tension level decreased noticeably as she decided he was serious. "It came as most things do in politics," she growled at last. "I owed a favor; it was collected."

"What kind of a favor?"

"None of your business," she said evenly.

Again Randon glanced at me. I shrugged in return—all I could tell was that it was something personal, and that it probably really *was* none of his business. "May I ask, then, who it was who collected on the favor?"

"I'd rather not say."

"It had to be someone from HTI, of course," Randon continued as if she hadn't spoken. "Chun Li?—or was it Blake or Karash? Or one of the middle-level people doing the managers' dirty work for them?"

"I'd rather not say," Rybakov repeated, more emphatically this time.

"Blake," I murmured.

Both sets of eyes turned to me: Randon's with an almost smug satisfaction, Rybakov's with a mixture of anger and resignation. "You sure?" Randon asked.

"It was the name she reacted to," I told him.

"Ah." He shrugged. "Well, it can't always be the unobvious one, can it?"

Rybakov seemed to brace herself. "And now . . . ?"

Randon raised an eyebrow. "And now what? As I said, Governor, I don't intend to either press charges or make this matter public. As far as I'm concerned, it's an internal matter between the Carillon Group and one of its subsidiaries. We'll deal with it from Portslava."

"I see." Again, she seemed to measure his words. "May I ask, then, whether or not you've had a chance to examine the records HTI was so anxious to recover?"

It was as if someone had flipped a switch. Abruptly, the sparring-level tension in the room jumped an order of magnitude. A mutually held secret, I decided, reading the identical emotion in both of them. A secret neither of them really wanted to discuss. "My financial expert and I went over them last evening," Randon told her after a brief pause.

The muscles in Rybakov's face tightened still further. A shared secret, for certain. "And what do you plan to do about it?" she asked quietly.

"That'll be up to my father and the rest of the Carillon board to decide," he said, his voice heavy with condemnation. "And probably the High Judiciary, as well."

Rybakov's face darkened with anger . . . but it was anger tinged with the awareness that she was standing on a warm ice bridge. "Before you pass judgment, Mr. Kelsey-Ramos," she said, "you should do me the courtesy of listening to my side of the story. And perhaps trying to understand the dilemma Solitaire as a whole is in."

He cocked his head slightly to the side. "I'm listening," he invited.

She glanced pointedly in my direction. "Perhaps this is something best kept between the two of us."

Clearly, Rybakov wanted to get rid of me. Just as clearly, Randon wasn't going to have any of that. "I already told you that my financial expert knows," he reminded her.

"Who presumably is better able to see the financial and legal consequences," she retorted. "As well as just the—" She broke off.

"As well as the ethical ones?" Randon finished for her with a snort. He turned to me, and I braced myself for whatever was coming. "We're talking about smuggling, Benedar," he told me. "The illegal transport of metals out of Solitaire system."

The mental bracing did little good. For a half dozen heartbeats I still just stared at him, totally stunned. "But that's impossible," I managed at last. "How do they—?"

And then it hit me, a delayed-action kick, and my

mouth went suddenly dry. "They . . . *kidnap* people for the Deadman Switch?"

"What, is that so hard to believe of our fallen human race?" Rybakov snorted cynically. "I thought you religious types were always weeping and wailing about how wicked we all are."

Randon's eyes flicked back to her. "You were going to tell me your side of it," he reminded her.

She glared at him, softened a bit. "Try to understand, Mr. Kelsey-Ramos, that I'm caught between two diametrically opposed requirements here. I'm sworn to uphold Patri law within Solitaire system, yes; but at the same time I'm under a less formal but no less pressing obligation to keep the supply of metals flowing from the ring mines. There's no easy way to reconcile these two goals."

"When it's a matter of people's lives—" I broke off as, in her eyes, sour contempt mixed with a sense that she'd indeed been right about not wanting to tell me about the smuggling. The righteously self-blind Watcher, unable to see the Broad Scheme Of Things . . .

"In case you haven't noticed," Rybakov told me, "the decision's already been made that Solitaire is worth people's lives."

"Condemned criminals' lives," Randon corrected her. "Not those of innocents."

She glowered at him. "All right, then, fine. You and your Watcher friend want to play God? Tell me how *you'd* go about stopping smugglers from moving in and out of a system this size."

Randon and I eyed each other. "At the risk of stating the obvious," Randon said, "what is Commodore Freitag doing about the problem? Between parties, that is?"

Rybakov snorted gently. "So you noticed the commodore's fondness for vodkyas, did you? That's part of the problem right there."

I remembered back to our brief meeting with Commodore Freitag at the governor's mansion . . . to my sense that the man wasn't nearly as slowed down as he'd appeared. The same tolerance to vodkyas Lord

Kelsey-Ramos had often used to his advantage . . .
"Your father enjoys parties, too," I murmured to Randon.

He eyed me thoughtfully, and I could see he'd picked
up on what I was saying. "The same way?" he asked,
making sure.

"Very similar, at least."

"Um." He looked back at Rybakov. "What size force
does Freitag have to work with when he *isn't* partying?"

"Two Pravilo destroyers and thirteen or fourteen
insystem corvettes," she said. "A shade on the light
side for covering two planets and a gas giant ring system, wouldn't you say?"

"I would indeed," he admitted. "Hasn't he tried to
get a larger force?"

"Roughly twice a month. So far the ships aren't available. Or so the excuse goes."

A sour look flicked across Randon's expression. "As if,
you mean, someone high up in the Patri didn't *want*
him to have any real chance of stopping the smuggler
trade?"

She held his gaze steadily. "You said it. I didn't."

I cleared my throat. "Excuse me, Governor," I spoke
up as they both looked at me, "but you said the force
covers *two* planets?"

"Solitaire and Spall," she said shortly. "Double planet,
remember? Or aren't you religious types able to count
anything that doesn't come in threes, sevens, or twelves?"

"Spall?" Randon frowned. "Since when is Spall
inhabited?"

"Oh, there've always been a handful of scientific parties poking around up there," she shrugged. "The theory being that every planet has *some* value to it, I
guess." Her sense abruptly hardened. "Though at the
moment Spall's primary value seems to be as a dump-
ing ground for Halloas."

Randon threw me a glance. "As a *what*?"

Rybakov waved a hand in a brushing-off gesture.
"Oh, the Halo of God's leaders decided they were
getting too much interference with their God-reception
down here, or some such nonsense, so a couple of

thousand of them pulled up and headed to Spall where they could meditate in peace. We don't especially miss them."

Randon pursed his lips, and behind his usual ambivalence toward religious matters I could sense a clear distaste for Rybakov's blatant prejudice. "I'm sure the feeling is mutual," he told her coolly. "How long have they been up there?"

"A couple-three years, some of them," Rybakov said, her interest in this topic sliding rapidly toward zero. "They seem to be settling in to stay—they've got their primitive settlements scattered all over the planet."

"Perhaps they plan to apply for colony world status," I murmured.

Rybakov snorted, but I could see that the same idea had occurred to her, too. And that she didn't like it at all. "Never in the lifetime of the Patri," she said flatly. "Mr. Kelsey-Ramos, we're getting a little off the main subject here. Even if the Pravilo didn't have to keep an eye on those religious fools on Spall, it would still be hopelessly inadequate to patrol Solitaire and the ring mines, which would *still* leave me in the position of having to enforce an unenforcible law. So before you start laying blame perhaps you'll tell me what you think Carillon can do to change that."

"I don't know what my father will decide," Randon said evenly. "But you can rest assured that he won't settle for a business as usual that allows innocent people to be kidnapped and murdered."

Rybakov's face twisted sardonically. "I can hardly wait to see what the supremely ethical Lord Kelsey-Ramos comes up with." Abruptly, before Randon had figured out whether or not she was being insulting, she got to her feet. "But until that day of miracles, I still have a government to run. Good day to you, Mr. Kelsey-Ramos."

"Good day, Governor." Randon keyed for the door, and as it opened I caught a glimpse of Kutzko waiting to escort her back to the gatelock.

The door closed behind her, and I turned back to

Randon. "I'm sorry if I embarrassed you back there," I apologized. "The idea of smuggling out of Solitaire had never occurred to me before."

"It occurred to someone in HTI," he grunted. "How to get around license limitations, in one easy lesson."

A memory clicked. "A short course other corporations seem to have taken, as well," I said slowly. "Last night—the tension directed toward you at the governor's reception? I would say they all knew you had the raw information that would let you figure out HTI's smuggling connection."

He nodded sourly. "Makes sense. And they're all worried stiff that Carillon will bring the Patri down on them instead of joining in the game."

I shivered. The thought of kidnapping another human being and deliberately killing him . . . "I wonder if there are any smugglers in the system at the moment."

"Probably." Randon's eyes narrowed slightly as he picked up on my tone. "Why?"

"It could be the answer to our problem with Calandra," I told him. "Almost certainly a smuggling ship will be crewed by non-Solitarans, and by definition they'll already have committed murder at least once—"

"*Wait* a minute," Randon cut me off. "Let's not jump overboard on this, shall we?"

I stared at him for a long second. In the space of a single heartbeat his sense had totally changed. "What's the trouble?" I asked carefully. "Carillon *will* be calling a halt to HTI's smuggling arrangements, won't it?"

"That'll be up to my father and the rest of the board," he snapped. "Not to me."

For a minute we just looked at each other. Then, finally, he sighed. "Look, Benedar. I don't have to be religious to agree that what the smugglers are doing is about as odious a business as I've ever heard of. But the minute Carillon or anyone else files that kind of complaint against HTI, their assets and activities will immediately be frozen. *Immediately.*"

And at last I understood. "And since it's HTI, not Carillon, who actually holds the Solitaire license . . . ?"

He grimaced at the accusation in my voice, but nodded. "Carillon will be frozen out of Solitaire," he finished my sentence. "For at least six months. Probably longer."

I bit the back of my lip. "Lord Kelsey-Ramos wouldn't let that stop him."

And knew instantly I'd made a mistake. Randon's forehead furrowed, his facial muscles tightening with a combination of anger and guilt and worry. "But my father isn't here, is he?" he shot back. "*I'm* here, and *I'm* the one who's making the decisions."

The words were limp, and we both knew it. He was out of his depth here, faced with a problem he hadn't been prepared for, and his response was going to be to simply not make any decision at all. He knew it, and I knew it . . . and for that one moment he despised me for knowing it.

I should have backed off right then, dropped the subject until he could discuss it without the weight of his father's own history of decisive action looming over him. But my words were already on their way out, and I couldn't stop them. "Then what about Calandra?"

And in the face of what he clearly regarded as pressure, I could almost see his mind slam shut. "What about her?" he almost snarled. "In a week she'll sit at the Deadman Switch and die, that's what. What do you want me to say?—that I'll risk years of Carillon's future for a condemned criminal?"

"She's innocent!"

"So *you* say. Where's the proof?"

I clenched my teeth. "I've already told you: back on Outbound."

"Fine! So we'll have the records examined. If she's innocent I'll see to it she's posthumously exonerated."

I looked at him, tasting the sour acid of defeat. *Look, I am sending you out like sheep among wolves; so be cunning as snakes and yet innocent as doves . . .* Even Watcher training, I reflected bitterly, was no guarantee against stupid behavior . . . and in talking to Randon as I would have to his father, I had behaved stupidly indeed.

If he couldn't bring himself to make a decision on this, he was nevertheless determined to pretend he was making one. To himself, even more than to me.

It meant that anything I could say now would be useless. But I still had to try. "As I understand it," I said carefully, "you've postponed our departure until tomorrow morning—"

"If you're heading where I think you are, you can blazing well forget it," he cut me off. "We're not going hunting for smugglers."

"No, sir. But if *I* can find one on my own—?"

"Not even if you deliver him to Governor Rybakov gift-wrapped," he growled. "How clear do I have to make it to you?"

I stifled a grimace. "It's clear enough already, sir," I told him stiffly.

"All right. Then get out—and try to remember why you're along on this trip in the first place."

I was back in my own stateroom before the hot flush left my cheeks. *As cunning as snakes . . .* but even as I flopped down on my bed, the beginnings of a new idea began to take shape in the back of my mind. All right; I'd been forbidden to hunt down a smuggler on my own. But if I could give just the right push to just the right person . . .

I thought about it for several minutes, considering possibilities, trying to recall every nuance of sensation I'd gleaned from the governor's reception the previous evening. It was worth a try . . . especially since the option was to give up and let an innocent woman die.

And surely if Randon was presented with a substitute criminal, he wouldn't refuse the chance to let Calandra live. Surely he wouldn't.

CHAPTER 12

I got past two layers of bureaucratic blockages on the strength of the Kelsey-Ramos name; but at the last one my luck ran out. "I'm sorry, Mr. Benedar," the Pravilo lieutenant in the outer office informed me. "Commodore Freitag has an extremely full schedule today. If you'd like to make an appointment, I'll check and see when he can fit you in."

"I'm afraid it can't wait," I shook my head. "I'll be leaving for the ring mines tomorrow morning with Mr. Kelsey-Ramos—"

"Then you're out of luck, aren't you?" he cut me off. "I'm sorry."

"The commodore *will* want to see me," I told him, lowering the temperature of my voice a few degrees.

The lieutenant, unfortunately, was used to such maneuvers. "Then he'll be sorry he missed you, won't he?" he said coolly. "Good day, Mr. Benedar."

I pursed my lips. "Will you at least take a note in to him?" I bargained. "If he doesn't want to see me after he's read it, I'll leave quietly."

He considered telling me that he had the power to make me leave quietly regardless; but by now he was sufficiently intrigued to take a minor risk. "All right," he said, a touch of challenge in his voice.

I scribbled a note on the pad he offered me and then folded it. "For the commodore's eyes only," I said, handing it over.

The lieutenant cocked a sardonic eyebrow at me. "Certainly, sir," he said. Getting up, he tapped a key to datalock his desk and crossed to the commodore's office door behind him.

I held my breath; but I didn't have to wait even as long as I'd expected to. Less than a minute later the other was back. "Mr. Benedar . . . ?" he invited from the open doorway.

This was it. Steeling myself, I walked past him into the office.

Commodore Freitag was seated at an almost neurotically neat desk, situated in what I guessed was probably the geometrical center of the room. "Mr. Benedar," he greeted me, almost lazily, not getting up from his chair. "Thank you, Lieutenant; you may go."

The other nodded silently and closed the door behind him. "I appreciate you seeing me on such short notice, Commodore," I said.

Freitag cocked a sardonic eyebrow. Probably where the lieutenant had picked up the gesture. "On Solitaire, Mr. Benedar, appreciation takes the form of tangible favors."

I gestured at my note, in front of him on the desk. "And my offer doesn't qualify?"

"That depends, doesn't it? 'My name is Gilead Raca Benedar. I know what you're trying to do about the smugglers, and I think I may be able to help.' Not particularly specific."

"It wasn't meant to be," I shrugged. He had, I noted, quoted the note from memory. "It also seems that on Solitaire specifics are handled face to face."

Steepling his fingers, he leaned back in his chair. "Well, we're certainly face to face now," he said. "Why don't you start by telling me exactly what it is I'm supposedly doing about these alleged smugglers?"

"Given your limited resources, you're doing the only thing you can do: going to high-level social events and trying to root out information while you pretend to be enjoying yourself."

He was good. His face didn't show even a trace of his surprise at my statement. Not the surprise, nor the fact that I was right. A non-Watcher would have missed it completely. "You read far too much into a man's weaknesses," he said mildly.

"Do I?" I countered. "You were in far better control of yourself last night than you should have been from your outward appearance. More to the point, you were much too alert for a man who was supposedly only there to indulge in the governor's supply of free vodkyas."

For a long minute he eyed me in silence. "I've never met a Watcher before," he said at last. "Not too many of you venture out of your private settlements these days, do you?"

"It's especially easy for a Watcher to tell when he's not wanted," I told him evenly.

"And being religious types, I suppose, you'd rather roll over and die than fight back at that kind of prejudice?" he snorted.

But I say this to you: offer no resistance to the wicked . . . "Fighting back often does the fighter more damage than his opponent," I said. It was an almost automatic response, echoing back from my childhood days. I'd never yet decided if I truly believed it. "I understood that you were pressed for time, though . . . ?"

He regarded me thoughtfully. "What exactly is it you're offering me?"

"Assistance in what you're already doing: trying to identify which of the corporations working out of Solitaire are dealing with smugglers on the side."

"Why?"

I frowned. "Why what? Why are they using the smugglers?"

"Why are you offering to finger them? What does Carillon hope to get out of it?"

"Carillon isn't involved," I told him. "This is on my own initiative."

"You expect me to believe that?"

I forced my jaw to relax. "It's the truth," I told him.

"Of course. And because you're a Watcher, I'm to believe that you always tell the truth?"

A touch of anger began to stir within me. "Commodore—"

"Or to put it another way, why should I trust you?" he cut me off calmly.

"What does it cost you?" I argued. "All right, suppose for the moment that I *do* have something devious in mind. If you can cut off an arm or two of the smuggling trade, what would it matter if Carillon somehow benefited as well?"

He eyed me for a moment in silence . . . and even as I watched his gaze seemed to harden. "Let me tell you something about this assignment, Benedar," he said at last. "Solitaire is the original no-win post. The Patri are perfectly aware that there's smuggling going on; unfortunately, they're also aware that the people dealing with the smugglers are some of their biggest and most powerful corporations. For that reason and a couple of other equally good ones—" the bitterness in his voice made me wince—"they don't want the boat tipped. Solution?—set up a token Pravilo force under the command of someone who'll spin out his time doing nothing, accept a token promotion at the end of it, and either take a comfortable desk job on Janus or fade gracefully off into retirement." His lip twitched in a slightly bitter smile. "This time around, that person is me."

I studied him. "Sounds like a nicely self-serving plan. What went wrong with it?"

A quiet pain crossed his face. "A few months ago a mining scout ship ran across a body floating out in the rings. An illegal inzombi, dumped by a smuggling ship after getting through the Cloud. Turned out she was the daughter of an old friend."

"I'm sorry," I murmured.

"You belong to Carillon, Benedar. Carillon is a major corporation, based on a Patri world. That makes your offer of help suspect."

I took a deep breath. "Commodore, there's no trickery involved here. The simple fact is that I need a smuggler—need to have him caught, tried, and convicted within the next week."

Freitag's eyebrows rose fractionally. "You Watchers really *do* believe in miracles, don't you? What is this, some sort of private bet?"

I shook my head. "I need to find a substitute . . . outzombi . . . before our ship is ready to leave Solitaire."

The eyebrows rose a bit more. "Something wrong with your current one?"

"Perhaps with her original conviction," I told him. "The details aren't important; what *is* important is that I get hold of a properly convicted criminal before we have to execute her."

Understanding came into his eyes . . . understanding, plus a tinge of anger. "And since the judiciary has told you that you can't have a Solitaran, you decided to come to me?"

"Yes, sir," I said cautiously. The anger was unexpected, and it made me nervous. "But I don't understand why that matters. We would still be helping each other—"

"I don't like being used, Benedar," he cut me off abruptly. "*Or* being toyed with. So I roll over nicely and get you your smuggler and we're all happy, eh?"

"It doesn't have to end there," I said, finally sorting through his emotional labyrinth. "I could still help you track the rest of the smuggler connections—"

"From where?" he shot back. "Portslava? Come on, Benedar, I'm not stupid. You get your outzombi and you'll be off like a shot—leaving me with a job not even half done and with the rest of the smugglers alerted to the fact that I'm not the fool I've worked so hard to convince them I am."

He broke off, suddenly aware that he'd been raging before a total stranger. "But as you said a minute ago, the details aren't important. What's important is that if I don't sweep out the whole smuggler web in one stroke the whole exercise will be for nothing. That, and the fact that you and your allegedly innocent outzombi have no place in that plan. Good day, Mr. Benedar."

I swallowed hard. "Commodore, this is a matter of life and death—"

"Good *day*, Mr. Benedar."

"Commodore—"

Behind me the door opened, and I heard the lieutenant's footsteps coming up behind me. "This way, sir," the other said, almost in my ear. From his voice I could tell he was prepared to use force if necessary.

I gazed into Freitag's face, searching for some indication that there might still be a chance for me to change his mind. But if there was, it was buried too deeply even for me to find it.

Silently, I turned and left.

One by one, in much the same way, all the other possibilities withered and died.

It was near evening by the time I returned to Rainbow's End and the *Bellwether*, footsore and as emotionally weary as I'd been in a long time. Passing through the gatelock, I managed perfunctory greetings to Daiv Ifversn and Seqoya and headed directly for my stateroom.

I made it without running into anyone else. Flopping back onto my bed, I stared up at the ceiling . . . and tried to think.

Commodore Freitag, Governor Rybakov's office, the Police Coordinator's office, even the Solitaran judiciary again—I'd hit them all. Searched the Solitaran bureaucracy from top to bottom looking for someone who could help.

None could. Or none wanted to.

I closed my eyes, squeezing tears out as I did so. Tears of frustration, of helplessness. In less than twelve hours we'd be leaving Solitaire for the ring mines . . . and Calandra would be dead.

Even I couldn't generate any false hope this time. Once we were off Solitaire, away from the center of the system's government and judiciary, all hope would be gone. From Collet to Solitaire was a four-day round trip; with a minimum of at least a few days for a trial—

even assuming the judiciary consented to the use of pravdrugs to speed things along—there was simply no way a smuggler could be convicted and sentenced in the twelve days we had left in the system. Not even if he strolled aboard the *Bellwether* and surrendered to us.

Twelve days left . . . and then an innocent woman would die.

Unless she was not, in fact, innocent.

I shifted uncomfortably on my bed. That was indeed the crux of the whole problem, a question that had haunted me since the moment I met her. The Outbound judiciary had convicted her, after all, based on what they had thought was good and proper evidence of guilt. Whatever that evidence was, it was light-years away, and without it I would never convince anyone on Solitaire of her innocence.

But as for myself . . .

So pride is a necklace to the wicked, violence the garment they wear. From their fat oozes out malice, their hearts drip with cunning. Cynically they advocate evil, loftily they advocate force. Their mouth claims heaven for themselves, and their tongue is never still on earth . . .

Overly poetic, perhaps . . . and yet, there was more than a grain of truth to be found in the words. There was indeed a sort of aura of character that rested within every person I'd ever met; an aura built up over long years of habit in thought and action until it was a clear reflection of the basic personality underlying it. My teachers back at the Cana settlement had likened it to the bedrock beneath an ever-changing surface landscape . . . a bedrock that could not be changed overnight by any act of will.

I'd spoken with Calandra, over several days and in several different situations. I'd read the nuances of her character in her eyes, her face, and her body . . . and for me, there was only one conclusion possible.

Calandra was a human being, not a saint. Her aura showed clearly the same fears and passions and weaknesses that all the rest of us possessed. It did not show the icy callousness of a murderer.

Blessed are the merciful: they shall have mercy shown them . . .

Let the weak and the orphan have justice, be fair to the wretched and the destitute. Rescue the weak and the needy, save them from the clutches of the wicked . . .

I'd tried; I really had. I'd pleaded with Randon, with Commodore Freitag, with every Solitaran official I could find. Every door I'd come up with had been slammed in my face.

Blessed are the merciful: they shall have mercy shown them . . .

"But I've *done* everything I can," I snarled aloud at the thought. The thought, and the guilt playing around the edges of it. "There's nothing else I can *do.*"

But there was. One more thing I could try . . .

And indeed, which of you here, intending to build a tower, would not first sit down and work out the cost to see if he had enough to complete it?

A shiver ran through me. Yes, there was one thing left I could try . . . but it would cost me. It would cost me a great deal.

Be obedient to those who are your masters . . .

How blessed are those to whom God imputes no guilt, whose spirit harbors no deceit . . .

Whoever looks after his master will be honored . . .

Because it wasn't just my job or even my honor that would be at risk here. My entire life would be on the line . . . as would the lives of many others.

I couldn't do it. I didn't *want* to do it.

Blessed are the merciful: they shall have mercy shown them . . .

There was no argument I could make to that. In the end, I gave in.

CHAPTER 13

There are a thousand small sounds and vibrations that exist in a ship the size of the *Bellwether*: the sounds of movement, of machinery and equipment, even the vague background fusion of a dozen mixed conversations. Small sounds, generally: a person newly arrived aboard ship would probably be totally unaware of most of them, and within a short time wouldn t even hear the rest. For me, though, they were always there, hovering at the background of my awareness and frequently intruding on it.

So it was that I was able now to lay back on my bed, eyes closed, and listen as the *Bellwether* shut itself down for the night.

Only partially, of course. One of the senior officers would still be on the bridge, while two or three crewers would similarly be holding station in the engine room and central monitor wraparound. And Kutzko would of course have one of his shields outside Calandra's stateroom. But the rest of the off-duty officers and crewers would be in their rooms, preparing for bed . . . as would Randon and the other passengers.

I waited until the ship had been quiet for fifteen

minutes before leaving my stateroom. No one else was in sight as I made my way forward as quickly and quietly as I could. Second Officer Laskowski would be on duty on the bridge; and if I'd judged things properly . . .

I had. "Mr. Benedar," Captain Bartholomy nodded, his sense showing mild surprise at my presence as I entered the bridge. Laskowski glanced up from his status readouts, returned his attention to his work without saying anything.

"Captain," I nodded in return, fighting to keep my voice normal. "I'm glad I caught you—Mr. Kelsey-Ramos told me you'd probably be here and could give me a hand."

In my ears the lie seemed so patently obvious that for that first horrible second I was certain that there was absolutely no way Bartholomy could fail to detect it. My stomach knotted spasmodically, and I waited an eternity for him to call me on it—

"Yes, I usually do a quick check before I turn in," he grunted. "What can I do for you?"

Through the pounding in my ears I dimly noticed I was holding my breath. "I need to put in a request with the tower," I said through dry lips, beginning to breathe again. "I'm supposed to see if there's something in the way of a small insystem ship I can rent."

Bartholomy's eyebrows rose politely. "Mr. Kelsey-Ramos has decided he doesn't trust the *Bellwether*?"

I matched his smile as best I could. "Hardly, Captain. No, he's decided it might be a good idea for us to take copies of the HTI data out to the ring mines on two separate ships."

He frowned; but in interest, not suspicion. "The stuff's that explosive, eh? I've been hearing rumors about it."

"HTI's already tried to get it back once," I told him, reading both him and the eavesdropping Laskowski as deeply as I could. Not a spark of suspicion in either of them; and it gave me the confidence to throw in a small embellishment. "The problem now is that Dapper Schock says there are ways of at least partially scrambling computer data from outside a ship in deep space."

Bartholomy snorted. "That's a new one on me," he commented. "Did Mr. Kelsey-Ramos say how big a crew he was planning to send on this sidecar?"

"Just me," I said.

The eyebrows went up again, and I immediately wished I'd quoted a larger number. Still no suspicion, but abruptly his sense had switched from interest to uncertainty. "Just you?" he echoed.

"Yes," I nodded, my stomach knotting up again. "Most everybody else is needed here during flight." A flicker of an idea in his eyes—a touch of distaste along with it—distaste that seemed to indicate a personality conflict—"Besides," I added, hoping I had read him correctly, "Mr. Kelsey-Ramos said that if too many people show up missing, Aikman is likely to notice and get suspicious."

I'd indeed read him right. Bartholomy nodded, uncertainties fading as his own thought was quoted back to him. "Yes, I was just thinking that," he grunted. "Well, let's see what we can do."

Stepping back over to his command station, he sat down and keyed the phone. "Spaceport Tower," he instructed it, ". . . Yes, this is Captain Bartholomy aboard the *Bellwether*. I need to locate something along the lines of a shrink-yacht, as soon as possible . . . no, with preprogramming capability . . . yes, I'll hold on." He looked up at me. "She's going to check and see what they've got."

The sense of him was a knowing sort of anticipation . . . "Mr. Kelsey-Ramos said that they *did* regularly rent out ships," I said, daring again.

And again I'd hit the mark. "Yes, that's what she said," he nodded. "It's just a matter of—yes?" he interrupted himself, looking back at the display. ". . . say again?" he said, reaching for his keyboard. "A Cricket V Rockhopper; right. Can you feed me the specs?"

The light reflecting from his face changed subtly, indicating the display had split between the phone and the tower's computer records. One look, and his sense became one of satisfaction. "Sounds good, Tower, we'll take it. When can it be ready?" He looked up at me. "How soon do you want it?"

"As soon as possible," I said. A sense of unreality was creeping over me. This was actually working . . .

"We'd like it stat, Tower," Bartholomy said into the phone. ". . . Yes, an hour will be fine. Provision it for a four-day trip for one, plus a double safety margin. Bill it to our account—no, wait a second." An edge of slyness touched his sense. "Bill it to HTI Transport, care of Mr. Sahm Aikman, aboard this ship . . . Thank you, Tower. *Bellwether* out."

He disconnected and looked up at me, a satisfied smile playing around his face. "You've got your ship, Mr. Benedar—launch cat fifty-seven. Better get out there."

I licked moisture back onto my lips. "Can you really do that? Bill it to Aikman, I mean?"

He shrugged. "Oh, we'll pay the bill when it comes —no one's going to care whose account the money comes out of. But until it's paid anyone checking will find only HTI's name there. Probably won't fool anybody, but it ought to irritate them good."

For a second, superimposed on Bartholomy's satisfaction, I had a sense of how he would feel when he found out I'd lied to him. An almost choking lump of shame and guilt rose into my throat, and I swallowed hard. It didn't seem to help. "Thank you, sir," I said around the lump. "Uh . . . Mr. Kelsey-Ramos wanted it kept as quiet as possible, incidentally."

His eyes twinkled a bit. "Don't worry. I want to be the one who gets to break the news to Aikman when he finally misses you."

I returned his smile as best I could. "Yes, Captain. I'll . . . see you at the rings."

I left. *Blessed are the merciful: they shall have mercy shown them . . . Blessed are the merciful: they shall have mercy shown them . . .* I said it over and over again to myself as I walked back along the *Bellwether*'s deserted corridors . . . trying to erase the mental image of the man whose trust I'd just betrayed.

* * *

In my eight years with Lord Kelsey-Ramos I'd had the opportunity to meet and even study a great many liars, both those who lied only when they considered it necessary and those for whom it had become second nature. From that experience—from watching that downward spiral into habitual deceit—I'd always assumed a second lie would be easier to tell than a first.

It wasn't true.

Bartholomy's face continued to hover before me as I walked down the corridor toward Calandra's stateroom/prison. His face, reacting to my lie . . . reacting to the chewing out he would undoubtedly receive from Randon when my lie was exposed . . . reacting to the possible loss of his job.

The plans of the upright are honest; the intrigues of the wicked are full of deceit . . .

Through his mouth the godless is the ruin of his neighbor . . .

It made me ache inside, and with each step I took I had to fight against the growing desire to call the whole thing off.

Blessed are the merciful, they shall have mercy shown them . . . An innocent life was at stake here . . . and besides, I'd already come too far to stop.

One of Kutzko's shields would be standing guard outside Calandra's stateroom, I knew, but I had no idea which one it would be. One of the Ifversn brothers, I hoped; or even Seqoya, who would probably break me in two if he ever suspected what I was doing. Not Kutzko, though. I didn't want to have to lie to Kutzko.

I reached the intersection of my cross-corridor with Calandra's. Steeling myself, I stepped around the corner—

"Thought those were your footsteps," Kutzko commented genially. "Out a little late, aren't you?"

I forced moisture into my mouth. *Through his mouth the godless is the ruin of his neighbor . . .* "A little. Mr. Kelsey-Ramos's business doesn't always keep neat hours."

I saw his sense shift smoothly from mildly alert boredom to full interest. "What kind of business?"

"My break, maybe," I said, lowering my voice conspiratorially. "Governor Rybakov called Mr. Kelsey-Ramos half an hour ago. She wants me to bring Calandra to Cameo to meet with her right away."

Kutzko's forehead furrowed slightly; and even as the interest sharpened I could sense the first stirrings of suspicion. "What, at this hour?"

"That's what she said," I said, striving hard to control my face and voice. It worked; even through my guilt I could hear how sincere I indeed sounded . . . and the ease of that success chilled me to the bone.

Kutzko pursed his lips. "I don't like it," he said flatly. "Smells like a blazing setup."

I shrugged. "A setup for what? What ulterior purpose could she want us for?"

He glared thoughtfully into space. "No idea. Hang on—"

He keyed his visorcomp, quickscanned whatever record he'd called up. "Aikman seems to have been a good boy today—stayed aboard ship the whole time. I wonder if he could have found a way to get someone else to file that legal thing of his."

I felt sweat breaking out on my forehead. Part of Kutzko's job was to be suspicious, but if he kept at this long enough he was going to wind up ruining everything. "I really don't think this is Aikman's doing," I told him. "Governor Rybakov didn't show any signs of deceit."

"You were there for the conversation?—half an hour ago, you said?"

I could sense the thought underlying the question, that perhaps he ought to discuss this with Randon. The last thing I could afford. "No, I wasn't actually there," I improvised desperately. "I was down in my stateroom when the call came through—like Mr. Kelsey-Ramos, I was getting ready for bed at the time. But he did feed me a copy of the recording afterward."

He frowned, and I could see the idea of consulting

directly with Randon fade with the realization that he would risk waking him up. "I still don't like it," he said at last, "but I guess I'm game. Give me a few minutes and I'll rouse Brad out of bed."

I bit the back of my lip. Right here was where I was going to find out just how good my powers of persuasion were. Just how good a liar I really was. "Sorry—I'm sure he'll be disappointed at not being woken up for this," I spoke up as Kutzko stepped toward one of the wall intercoms. "But the governor said we should come alone."

He paused. "Oh, she did, did she?" he asked quietly. "Interesting."

"Not really as interesting as you might think," I reassured him. "My guess is that certain things she and Mr. Kelsey-Ramos discussed this morning may come out in the discussion, and that she'd rather not have any extra parties along."

"Ms. Paquin isn't an extra party?" he asked pointedly.

"She's involved in other ways," I said, hoping he would let it go at that.

He didn't. "Sorry, Gilead, but this whole thing smells putrid. For one thing, doesn't it seem strange to you that after kicking so much Rybakov should suddenly roll over and start cooperating?"

"It's been her government, not her specifically, that's been opposing us," I reminded him. "More importantly, as of this morning she owes Mr. Kelsey-Ramos a favor. A *big* one."

"And what if she plans to clear the record by doing him a pseudofavor in return?" he retorted. "Such as 'rescuing' a couple of Watchers who just happen to have gotten themselves kidnapped?"

I took a deep breath and braced myself. This one was going to hurt both of us. "All right, then," I said, putting a note of disgust into my voice. "Sure, send Seqoya along. Ruin the arrangement, and maybe a chance for Calandra to see her own record cleared along with it. And, incidentally, maybe send Seqoya to his death; because if someone really wants to kidnap us, they

won't let even him stand in the way . . . and you know
as well as I do that out in the streets a shield can't really
do much more than make a kidnapping or murder more
expensive. They'd kill him for sure, and maybe kill us
in the process."

I'd expected Kutzko to take offense at my little tirade, but I'd expected wrong. For a long moment he
gazed quietly at me, his sense that of indecision mixed
with an odd touch of resignation, almost covering the
hidden pain at the reminder of just how limited even
his considerable shielding skills really were.

And over all of it was a growing sense that he had
little choice but to trust me.

First Captain Bartholomy, and now Kutzko. Trusting
in their betrayer. *Brother will betray brother to death* . . .

"You really believe Rybakov is playing this straight?"
Kutzko asked quietly.

"I wouldn't be going if I didn't," I told him. "It may
be Calandra's only chance." The words, in absolute
terms, were true, and somehow it made them easier to
say. The way he would interpret them, of course, still
made them a lie.

He took a deep breath, exhaled it noisily. "All right,"
he said, suddenly briskly decisive as he stepped to
Calandra's door and rapped twice. "You'd better be
right, though," he added, busying himself with the
lock. "You get yourself killed out there and I'll blazing-
well never speak to you again."

"I'll keep that in mind," I managed.

The door slid open, and Kutzko leaned partway inside. "Ms. Paquin?—good, you're still dressed. Come
on; you and Mr. Benedar are going on a little trip."

"What? Why?" her voice asked softly as she came
around a corner into view. Her eyes flicked over Kutzko,
automatically probing him. She looked past him to me—

Our eyes met . . . and hers were suddenly wide and
alert.

Once again she'd read me with ease . . . and even if
she couldn't know exactly what it was I had planned,
she could clearly tell that something was wrong. With

Kutzko's back still to me, I threw her a warning look, a fractional shaking of my head. Her lips twitched, and she swallowed. "Where are we going?" she asked, the question clearly directed toward Kutzko.

"Governor's mansion," he told her briefly. "Mr. Kelsey-Ramos has gotten you a hearing."

Again her eyes read me . . . read me far too deeply . . . "I don't want to go," she said, stopping abruptly halfway out of her stateroom.

Kutzko threw me a startled glance. "Why not?" he asked.

Her tongue flicked across her upper lip, eyes still on me. "I . . . just don't," she said lamely.

Kutzko snorted. "You don't have a choice," he told her flatly, his sense filling with annoyance. "You're going to Cameo. Period."

She took a deep breath; paused . . . and through the dark screen that seemed to surround her emotions I could sense caution and fear rising within her. She opened her mouth; closed it and gave a short nod instead.

"All *right*," Kutzko said, relieved at not having to continue the argument. "Come on, Gilead; I'll escort you to the gatelock."

And that was it. In a few short minutes—with nothing but my words and my ability to read people, I had persuaded two intelligent and conscientious men to assist me in releasing a condemned prisoner.

We walked down the corridor to the gatelock . . . and in the back of my mind I wondered uneasily if perhaps Aikman's fears about the powers of Watchers hadn't been so exaggerated after all.

CHAPTER 14

We left Kutzko standing at the gatelock; and as the car took us off across the floodlit parking field Calandra turned to me, worry and suspicion hanging around her like a fog. "All right, Benedar, just what in the Patri is going on?" she demanded.

"I'm getting you out of here, that's what," I told her. "There's a ship laid on for us across the field."

Surprise, I was ready for; even confusion, possibly even dazed gratitude. I wasn't prepared for utter fury. "What?" she all but shouted in my ear. "You blazing idiot—have you gone completely out of your mind?"

"Calandra—"

"Do you have any *idea* what kind of trouble you've just gotten yourself in?" she cut me off. "They'll turn you inside out when they catch us."

"That depends on what we find in the meantime, doesn't it?" I said, fighting to regain my balance against the verbal onslaught.

"We'll find your brains scattered across the landscape," she snarled. Abruptly, she leaned forward to the car's microphone. "Car: cancel destination and return us to the *Bellwether*."

138

"Cancel that!" I barked, grabbing her arm and shoving her back into her seat. "Car: cancel destination. New destination: launch catapult fifty-seven, Rainbow's End Spaceport."

I turned to Calandra, a sudden surge of white-hot anger hazing my vision. "We're going into space," I snarled. "We're going because it's the only way to get a replacement zombi for you."

She stared into my face, her own anger draining into fear and dread. "They'll execute you," she said, her voice trembling. "Instead of one zombi, they'll have two. Can't you see that?"

I took a shuddering breath, forcing down my anger. I was battling the whole universe on her account; the last thing I wanted was to fight her, too. "There's a risk, yes," I acknowledged, trying to hide my own fears. In her face I could see that the attempt was only partially successful. "But if we don't try they *definitely* have you. Guaranteed."

She licked her lips. "Gilead . . . I'm not worth it. I'm really not. Please—turn back and forget all this. Please."

I sighed. "I'm sorry, Calandra. You're asking me to sit by and let an innocent person be killed. I just can't do that."

A stab of pain flicked across her face. "What if I told you I *wasn't* innocent?" she challenged. "That I really *did* kill all those people?"

She was good, all right. I could almost believe the sincerity behind the words was real . . . but equally strong, and equally believable, was the fear she felt for me. "And I suppose then that you'd like me to believe that you, a cold-blooded murderess, would actually care what happened to me, a near-total stranger?" I asked pointedly.

She closed her eyes, blinking back tears. "Gilead . . . I don't want to go to my death knowing I caused yours. Please, *please*, take me back."

Hesitantly, I reached over and took her hand. It resisted for a moment, then reluctantly accepted the touch. "I can't let you die without a fight," I told her gently. "Not while there's a chance to clear you. Certainly not when there are people far more deserving of death within our reach."

She opened her eyes again. "What do you mean?"

I looked upward, at the stars dimly visible above the spaceport floodlights. "There's a thriving smuggler trade operating out there," I said, hearing more bitterness in my voice than I'd expected. "They kidnap people to run their Deadman Switches in and out of the Cloud . . . and the Patri look the other way while they do it."

Calandra shivered, my own disgust and horror mirrored in her sense. "And you think the two of us can stop it?"

"I'm not *that* much of an idiot," I snorted. "No, I've met the only man who has a real chance of doing that. The problem is that he wants to kill it with a single blow, and he's not ready yet to do that."

"So then . . . ?"

"I think he was basically sympathetic to our plight," I said. "But he was also afraid that if he came down on a single smuggler now the rest would suddenly realize he's not the ziphead everyone thinks he is and instantly bury themselves out of his reach."

She considered that. "So you think," she said slowly, "that if *we* can pinpoint a group of smugglers, he can go ahead and pick them up without risking that?"

I grimaced. With Randon backing my demand for such official action, I had no doubt Commodore Freitag would have been willing to do exactly that. Now, though . . . "I hope he'll be that reasonable," I said.

"You don't know for sure, though," she said quietly. "Do you?"

"It's a calculated risk," I conceded.

She took a deep breath. "Gilead . . . look, I deeply appreciate what you're trying to do for me. But the risk's not worth it. Please take me back."

"We've already been through this," I said gruffly. "Whether you remember or not, part of a Watcher's job is to stand up for the helpless."

"To the point of ruining your career?"

"To the point of giving up my life, if necessary."

She swallowed. "There's still no need for me to be along," she said, making what I could sense was her last effort. "You can take me back to the *Bellwether* and then go out alone and find your smuggler."

"And what happens if I can't do it in time?" I asked her. "You'll be executed on schedule."

"But you'll be in less trouble than you are now," she countered. "I'm willing to take the chance."

"I'm not," I told her flatly. "Besides, I'm going to need your help. Spall is a big planet for one person to search."

Possibly for the first time that evening, I'd taken her by surprise. "*Spall*?" she echoed, blinking in confusion.

"Spall," I nodded. "Though no one seems willing to talk about it, I get the distinct impression that at least some of the smugglers are thought to have their permanent bases there."

"But—" she floundered.

"It makes sense, when you think about it," I continued. "The only two places in the system where they can have both a reasonable amount of room and a shirtsleeve environment are Solitaire and Spall, and Solitaire's got too much traffic coverage for them to sneak in and out easily."

"And Spall's got the exact opposite situation," she pointed out. "No one lives there at *all*—which means a smuggling settlement would stand out like a floodlight on even the simplest spectrum scan."

"Except that it turns out Spall isn't as uninhabited as we'd all thought," I said, shaking my head. "They've got scientific groups poking around all over the planet . . . and also a group of permanent settlers called the Halloas."

Something either in the name or in the way I said it . . . "A . . . religious group?" she asked cautiously.

I looked at her. Behind her eyes, I could almost see the memories of her childhood with the Watcher's Bethel settlement passing through her mind. Bittersweet memories . . . "Yes," I confirmed. "Apparently treated with the same contempt every other religious group gets. Possibly one of the reasons they left Solitaire."

She winced. More bittersweet memories. "Are you planning to make contact with them?" she asked.

I heard the reluctance in her words. "We have to," I told her firmly. "We'll need supplies, transportation, the likeliest places for smugglers to have dug in—things only the Halloas will be able to provide."

"And what makes you think they'll cooperate?"

I shrugged. "Faith. And the hope that they'll recognize the rightness of what I'm doing."

To that she made no answer. Sitting next to her in the relative gloom, I watched the spaceport pass by outside the car. And tried to plan out just what I'd say to the ground crew when we reached our ship.

"Okay, now, here's the main control bank." The crew boss pointed the panel out to me, his words slightly distorted by the pepperstick hanging out one corner of his mouth. "Lot of stuff here you can ignore—these Crickets were built for rock hunting, but all the fancy grappling equipment's been taken off."

Though it could undoubtedly be put back on if necessary. Like everything else I'd run across on Solitaire, even these minor shuttle ships had apparently been chosen with an eye on their possible use in the ring mines. Just one more reminder of how thoroughly the mines—and the wealth from them—permeated every aspect of Solitaran life. "And my course settings?"

"Idiot-simple," the boss assured me. "That box there is a set of course cyls. Just plug in the one you want— right there—and hit the button here." He tapped it. "Not till you clear atmosphere, of course—up till then the cat'll have override jurisdiction and all you'll get is a loud beep and a nasty 'nostic on the status display." He grinned.

Beside me, Calandra stirred. "Not too many options, are there?" she murmured, indicating the small number of course cyls in the box.

"Not a lot of places to go in the system," the boss

shrugged. "You got four Rockhounds, you got six ring research platforms, you got Solitaire. What else is there?"

"How about Spall?" I asked.

He snorted. "What, you mean Halloa Heaven? Who'd want to go there?"

"We do," I told him, putting some firmness into my voice. I was, after all, supposed to be the one in charge here. "I have to drop my friend here off before continuing on to Collet."

He frowned slightly, his sense suddenly becoming uncertain. "I thought this was supposed to be a one-man trip," he said. "I mean, that's what we've got her serviced and stocked for—"

"Minor change in plans," I cut him off. "And I seem to recall the *Bellwether*'s captain specifying double safety margins for the supplies."

A surge of professional pride overpowered the uncertainties. "Oh, sure, there won't be any problem like that—I mean, Spall's just five or six hours away."

"Good," I nodded. "Then if you can dig us up a course cyl for Spall, we'll be ready to go."

"Yeah, well—yeah, sure. Let's see . . ." He scratched his chin thoughtfully. "I guess the tower banks'll have a complete set on file. It'll take a few minutes, but I could send someone over and have them make you some copies. Or if you can tell me where exactly you'll want to land, I could have a copy of that particular one fed to you while we get you loaded into the cat."

"Don't we have to go to wherever Spall's launch catapult is?" I frowned. "Or do they have more than one?"

"They don't have any at all," he shook his head. "People who go there pretty much land anywhere they want. All you have to do when you want to leave is gimp your way up a couple thousand meters and then kick in the fusion to get you to ram speed. Uses more fuel than with a cat, 'course, but not as much as you'd think."

The thought of using a fusion drive that close to a

planetary surface . . . "What does it do to the land-scape?" I asked.

"Not much good," he conceded. "Doesn't matter much, though—practically the whole planet is desert, anyway. So; you want one cyl or the whole batch?"

I glanced at Calandra, thinking fast. It would be handy to have a complete set—aside from having a wider range of choices, it would help spread the search around when my web of lies eventually fell apart. On the other hand, a list of reference points or even place names wouldn't do us much good by themselves. "Would the nearest convenient place to the main Halloa settle-ment be okay with you?" I asked her.

Once again, she deciphered my train of thought with ease. "A list of all the settlements would be better," she said. "You *do* have maps of Spall programmed in, don't you?" she added to the boss.

"Oh, sure. For all the good they are—cartographers haven't exactly fallen over themselves getting the place fine-gridded out. Tell you what; I'll have the tower feed you course cyls for the six biggest Halloa places, okay?"

I raised my eyebrows questioningly. "Yes, that should be satisfactory," Calandra nodded.

"Okay," the boss said, relief in his sense as he brushed past us to the control panel. From a box next to one of the contour seats he scooped a handful of blank cyls and laid them out neatly in a row on a grip next to the computer feed. "You put them in here," he said over his shoulder, demonstrating with the first. "When it beeps, you replace it with the next one—"

"I *am* familiar with the procedure," I told him mildly. "Thank you."

"Yeah." He straightened, took one last look around the cabin at the displays and indicators. "Well, every-thing seems ready. Just sit down and make yourselves comfortable, and I'll get the crew started on loading you into the cat. And I'll get the tower going on those cyls, too."

"Thank you," I said again. He shifted the pepperstick

to the other side of his mouth, gave us each a brief nod, and left.

"Now what?" Calandra asked nervously as the door was sealed behind us with a hollow *thud*. Her aura of calm, adopted for the boss's benefit, was gone without a trace.

"We sit down and make ourselves comfortable," I told her, trying to keep my voice light. "And we try to think optimistic thoughts."

She snorted. Turning her back on me, she chose one of the twin control seats and began strapping in. I followed suit with the other seat, noting that my suggestion about optimistic thoughts didn't seem to be working for her.

Not really surprising. They weren't working for me, either.

CHAPTER 15

Six hours later, we began our final approach to Spall.

It had been a quiet trip. Both of us had tried to get some sleep, with varying degrees of success; neither of us had felt much like talking. Calandra, I could tell, was still unhappy with both me and the situation, her worrying underpinned by a low-level anger that wasn't showing much sign of subsiding.

I could hardly blame her. Once away from Solitaire, with my adrenaline-fueled tension fading as it became clear we had indeed gotten away, I had started having second thoughts myself. Two people, setting off to search an entire planet—it was so utterly ridiculous I couldn't believe I had actually considered it a rational scheme. And yet, that was all we had left. Two people against a world, with nothing but faith to go on . . . and *my* faith very possibly having to do for both of us.

He brought out his people like sheep, guiding them like a flock in the desert . . . I could only hope that there was more than poetic imagery behind the words.

"Doesn't look very inviting," Calandra murmured from beside me.

I looked at the display she was indicating. "The crew boss said it was mostly desert," I reminded her.

"I've seen other deserts," she said shortly. "They didn't look like this."

I pursed my lips, studying the landscape slowly scrolling down the screen. She was right; there was far more variation in color and visual texture than in the handful of deserts I'd seen from space. "Well . . . desert in this case may just mean that most of the soil isn't easily arable," I suggested.

"Maybe."

I shifted my eyes to her. "Worried that the Halloas may be just barely scraping a living for themselves, and therefore not inclined toward helping strangers?" I asked.

The muscles of her face tightened slightly. She could read others without compunction, but she didn't much care to have the roles reversed. I felt a flash of annoyance at her double standard; a heartbeat later it belatedly occurred to me that I felt exactly the same way. "The thought *had* crossed my mind, yes," she growled. "That, along with the normal pattern of outcast societies." She glanced at me. "Or did the Cana settlement conveniently leave that one out of *your* curriculum, too?"

"I'm not sure I know what you mean," I said, getting the distinct feeling I wasn't going to like this one.

"Really," she said, her voice heavy with contempt. "Well, it seems that religious groups that go off and establish their own societies to escape persecution almost always wind up being just as bad to their own minorities."

"The Watchers didn't—" I began; then broke off.

A bitter smile touched her lips. "That's right," she agreed, following my unspoken thought. "Aaron Balaam darMaupine's Bridgeway was heading exactly that direction when he was finally stopped."

I clenched my teeth. "You don't *know* that it would have become that," I pointed out. But it was a weak argument, and I knew it—besides which, what was I doing playing advocate for darMaupine in the first place?

"I don't recall learning that in Cana, no," I added, getting back to the issue at hand. "But I wouldn't think the Halloas have been here long enough to have forgotten their own problems with intolerance."

She shrugged uneasily. "I guess we'll find out soon enough," she said, nodding toward the display. "We're coming down."

The whole thing went reasonably smoothly, I suppose, especially considering that the Cricket's autopilot probably cost less than a hundredth of the one aboard the *Bellwether* and was operating without benefit of a spaceport tower system besides. A few jerks and stomach-wrenching jolts—a couple of sudden swerves for no reason I could discern—one final *thud* and a last-second drive shriek that left my ears ringing, and we were down.

The drive shut itself off, and in the silence Calandra and I looked at each other. "I don't care if they execute me tomorrow," she announced evenly. "I'm *not* riding one of these things again."

I took a deep breath. "That's not especially funny."

"It wasn't meant to be." Moving stiffly, she began to unstrap. "Any signs of life out there?"

I found the control for the outside cameras, got them sweeping. "Um . . . small dust cloud forming over one of the hills. Probably a vehicle approaching."

She craned her neck to look; and right on cue, a pair of cars topped the hill and headed toward us. "Reception committee from the Halloas?" she ventured.

"Probably. I don't see anything official-looking about the cars." I hit my own strap releases. "Come on—let's get the ship ready for the next leg and then go out and meet them."

They were waiting patiently outside their cars as we emerged from the Cricket: two men and a woman. At first glance all three struck me as impressive . . . and it was several seconds before I realized how remarkable that subconscious conclusion actually was. Standing next to old mul/terrain vehicles, dressed in neat but drab clothing, there was no immediately obvious reason why I should find them anything but perfectly ordinary.

And yet I did . . . and a couple of seconds later I realized why. There was something in their faces, in the senses of each of the three, that seemed to radiate peace. Not the artificial and short-lived counterfeit of peace available from bottles and pills, nor even the genuine kind of peace that most people experience only rarely and for similarly brief periods. This was a far deeper and more permanent sort of peace; a peace, moreover, with an unshakable dignity of soul attached to it.

It was the sort of peace I'd seen occasionally among the Watcher elders of my youth . . . and nowhere else that I'd ever traveled.

"Good day to you," the man in the center said with a smile as Calandra and I approached them. "Welcome to Spall."

"Thank you," I nodded to him. About fifty years old, I estimated—perhaps twice the age of each of his companions—with a neatly trimmed fringebeard and the sort of wrinkling about his eyes that comes of long outdoor work and frequent smiling. The eyes themselves . . . measuring me with a keenness almost Watcher-like in its intensity. "You must be from the Halloas," I told him. "An elder, I presume?"

A slight ripple of distaste touched his companions, but the spokesman didn't flinch. "I'm a shepherd of the Halo of God, yes," he said, correcting my terminology. "The term 'Halloa' is considered derogatory, by the way."

"I'm sorry," I apologized. "We'd never heard you referred to as anything else."

His eyebrow twitched. "Ah. I take it, then, that you haven't come here to join us?"

I shook my head. "No, I'm afraid not. We have some rather pressing business on Spall . . . which we were hoping you might be able to help us with."

His sense shaded toward wariness. "What sort of business?" he asked cautiously.

"Life and death business," I said bluntly, watching him closely. "If we're unsuccessful, someone will die."

His eyes continued to measure me. "People die all the time," he said, a hint of challenge in his voice. "And death is, after all, only the passage from this life back to God."

"Perhaps," I acknowledged. "But injustice should not be the ticket to that passage."

His eyes flicked to Calandra, returned to me. "I'm Shepherd Denvre Adams," he said; and with his name came a sense of at least provisional acceptance of us. "Two of my associates from the Shekinah Fellowship: Mari Ray and Danel Pommert." He gestured to his companions.

"I'm Gilead Raca Benedar," I told him, watching carefully for reaction. "This is my friend, Calandra Mara Paquin."

There was some reaction, certainly, among the three. But not at the level I would have expected from people on the alert for a pair of fugitive Watchers. Carefully, I let out the breath I'd been holding; apparently the alarm hadn't yet made it this far.

"So. Watchers." Adams nodded as if finding a piece to a puzzle. "I should have guessed right away. The aura of alertness surrounding you is very distinctive."

"We find it so ourselves," I agreed, wondering how much of that had been made up on the spot to impress his companions. "Most people manage to miss it, though. Is there some place where we can talk in private?"

"The Shekinah settlement is only about fifteen minutes away. We can talk there." His eyes flicked over my shoulder at the ship. "I take it you could use a ride?"

"Yes, thank you," I said. "If you'll give us a minute, though, we need to get our supplies off. And to set our ship to take off."

Beside me, I could sense Calandra's displeasure at my telling him that. I didn't much like it myself, but I couldn't see any way around it. The faster we got the ship headed for the outer system, the less inevitable it would be that the search would zero directly in on us here; and trying to concoct a lie about how the ship had accidentally launched itself could easily lose us any Halo of God support we could hope to get.

Adams's eyebrows raised slightly. "Without you aboard?" he asked.

"Yes, sir."

I stopped, waiting for the questions. Adams's eyes flicked to Calandra, to the ship, back to me. "Very well," he said at last. "We'll wait and drive you to Shekinah." His sense suddenly went very solemn indeed. "And there, Mr. Benedar, we *will* talk."

If Shepherd Adams was our first surprise, the Shekinah Fellowship settlement was our second.

With only a sparse scattering of native plant life across the hills between our landing area and the settlement, I had formed a mental picture of a cluster of rude huts clumped together, its inhabitants struggling to eke a living from rocky fields. Nothing could have been further from the actual truth. Even as I unconsciously braced myself for the drab ugliness ahead, we came over the final hill into a shallow valley . . . and a virtual explosion of greenery.

Not just small fields, but also well-tended private gardens and even a grassy parkland where a handful of adults could be seen relaxing and conversing as a group of children played a short distance away. The houses, prebuilt sectionals, were nevertheless clean and attractive, their positioning well thought out. "I'm impressed," I told Adams as we drove down toward it.

"Thank you," he said. "Some visitors have thought it a bit extravagant for people who are supposed to be seeking God and not their own material comfort. But it's been my experience that attractive surroundings usually improve one's meditative abilities instead of detracting from them."

I frowned, and took another look at the group of adults in the park. Sure enough, they weren't talking together, as I'd first assumed. We were close enough now that I could see their closed eyes, the odd combination of concentration and relaxation on their faces. "Scenery is all good and well," I commented, gesturing toward them, "but wouldn't they do better to choose a quieter place?"

"Probably," Adams agreed easily. "And we certainly don't start beginners that way, out in the middle of the park. But the more advanced among us can listen to God anywhere at all." He waved at the surrounding hills. "You see, Mr. Benedar, we believe Spall to be the actual center of God's kingdom, with the Cloud a manifestation of His halo. Here we can touch Him more easily than anywhere else in the universe; but our goal is not simply to become modern-day monks."

Beside me, Calandra stirred. "You mean the way the Watchers have?"

Adams shrugged, his sense becoming a bit uncomfortable. "It's not my place to judge anyone else," he said evasively. "The Watchers were dealt a terrible blow by the actions of Aaron Balaam darMaupine, and if you must withdraw into yourselves for a time, I can understand that. But if we're truly to be the light of humanity, none of us can hide like that indefinitely." He gestured again to the surrounding landscape. "Our goal is to become so attuned to God's presence here that we'll be able to go anywhere in the Patri and colonies and still feel His touch. No matter the distance, no matter the distractions."

I nodded. "Hence the meditation in the park, amidst the universe's best shot yet at perpetual motion machines?"

Adams smiled, a crinkling of his face. "Aggravating though they may be at times, children are still one of our most prized treasures. The Watchers proved that the art of observation is best begun in childhood; we hope that will prove true for the art of meditation, as well."

Adams's house was situated near the center of the settlement: an unpretentious structure, indistinguishable at least externally from the others surrounding it. I wasn't especially surprised; the sense of the man was clearly not that of someone in the job for the wealth or the prestige.

He parked the car under a two-sided overhang, and we went inside . . . and got down to serious business.

Carefully, Adams poured himself a cup of tea, his third since we'd begun our story. He offered us refills, was turned down, and set the pot back to the side. "I'm sure you realize," he said, gazing into the swirling liquid in his cup, "the awkward position you put me in."

"Yes, sir," I acknowledged, "and we're sincerely sorry about that. But we really had no one else to turn to."

He raised his eyes to me. "Your very presence here threatens our existence," he said bluntly. "Harboring fugitives is a serious offense—serious enough that the Solitaran authorities could easily use it as an excuse to disband our fellowships and ban us from Spall entirely."

The sense of him was not nearly as strong as the words . . . "Except that they won't," Calandra spoke up before I could. "You're a religious group, which makes you an embarrassment to them, and the last thing they want is to have you around where visitors to Solitaire might stumble over you. Where could they possibly send you where you'd be less visible than you are now?"

She had, I noted, echoed precisely Adams's own private thoughts. "Perhaps," he admitted grudgingly. "And if it was just you involved I would probably agree. But now you seek to prove that there are smugglers hiding among us; and *that* the authorities won't be so willing to ignore."

Again, I could sense a private argument about that going on in his thoughts. I probed, trying to pick out a part of that I could use . . .

And again, Calandra beat me to it. "And yet, if you prove yourselves cooperative in rooting out these smugglers, won't that clearly weigh in your favor?" she pointed out.

"Besides," I added, "we certainly don't expect to find smugglers hiding out in your actual settlements, masquerading as Hallo—as members of your fellowships. The fact that you may be sharing a planet with them can hardly be considered collusion."

"True," he sighed.

For a long minute he continued to gaze into his cup . . . and abruptly I realized his sense had changed—changed so subtly I hadn't noticed it happen. Somehow, even as he sat before us, it was as if he no longer was aware of our presence. As if his attention had wandered—

Or wasn't there at all.

I looked at Calandra, tilted my head fractionally toward Adams. She nodded, her own sense growing oddly troubled as she studied him.

I know a man who fourteen years ago was caught up right into the third heaven . . .

It was a scripture that had always intrigued me as a child . . . but now, faced with something that might very well be similar, I found myself sharing some of Calandra's uneasiness. It seemed impossible . . . but could Adams and his group truly have discovered holy ground here?

"Sorry," Adams said suddenly. I jumped; again I'd missed whatever transition there might have been. "I was trying to see if God would provide me an answer."

I could still sense a great deal of indecision in him. "And . . . ?" I prompted.

He shrugged. "Nothing that I can take as guidance. Touching the cloak of His mind is one thing; truly understanding what He is saying is something considerably harder." He took a deep breath, and I felt some residual tension slowly leave him. Apparently this form of meditation wasn't exactly easy on its practitioners. "He seems, as usual, to be leaving this decision up to me," Adams continued. "So tell me: just exactly what is it you want from us?"

I took a deep breath of my own. "On the way here we spent some time studying the ship's maps of Spall, and we've picked out one area that we'd like to concentrate on."

"How big an area?"

"A few hundred square kilometers." I read the look on his face and shrugged. "I know: a drop in an ocean. But we're only two people, and we haven't got much time."

"Yes, I understand. It's just that—never mind. Please go on."

"The target area is about two hundred sixty kilometers southeast of here, about eighty kilometers from your Myrrh settlement—that *is* one of yours, isn't it?"

He nodded. "So what you need is transportation to Myrrh; and while there you'll need a vehicle, power for it, and lodging."

"Yes, sir," I said. "I realize that's a lot to ask."

He waved a hand. "Physical goods aren't that much of a problem. Would you want a guide, or assistance in the search?"

"No," Calandra spoke up firmly before I could answer. "We'd rather do it ourselves."

I frowned at her. "Calandra—"

She turned intense eyes on me. "We're getting these people involved too much as it is, Gilead. We do it alone, or not at all."

It wasn't a point I could really argue with. "All right," I agreed, turning back to Adams. "I guess the physical goods will be all we need, then."

He nodded slowly. "Those I think we can provide. There's still one more thing you'll need, though: time. How much?"

How much time to search a world? "We'll take as much as you feel comfortable giving us," I said honestly. "If you were able to plead ignorance as to who we were—" I shrugged helplessly. "But of course it's too late for that now."

"Not unless they ban the use of pravdrugs tomorrow," he agreed soberly. "Still, as long as you don't tell anyone else, I'm the only one they can charge with knowing collusion." His eyes hardened. "And it *will* remain that way. Understand?"

I swallowed, a rush of guilt and shame flooding in on

me at the reminder of what I'd done to Kutzko and Captain Bartholomy. They, too, would escape any direct charges of collusion . . . but it would likely be small consolation to either of them. "I understand very well," I told Adams evenly. "There's too much already in the balance for us to want to add to it."

The hardness faded slowly from his sense. "I'm glad we agree." A faint smile twitched at his lips. "Though before you get the wrong impression about us, let me say that I'm glad you were honest with me. No matter what it costs, truth is always preferable to lies." He took a deep breath, let it out in a long sigh. "I can give you three days. No more."

I caught Calandra's eye. She shrugged, a touch of helplessness in her sense. Three days was horribly short . . . but then, anything less than a decade would be too short for the task we'd set ourselves. "Whatever you think is right," I told Adams.

"I'm sorry I can't give you more," he said, genuine regret in his voice. "But in actual fact, I suspect you'll have even less time than that. Your absence will surely have been discovered by now, and sending your ship out into space isn't likely to fool anyone for very long. The Pravilo will probably be here by nightfall."

Unfortunately, he was probably right. "All the more reason for us to get moving at once," I said.

"Agreed. What I think I'll do is simply give you one of our cars and let you drive yourselves to Myrrh—that'll save me having to ask one of my people to make the ten-hour round trip, and also keep you from tying up one of Myrrh's vehicles with your search."

"Fine," I said. "Semi-auto drive, I presume?"

"Yes, but you won't have any trouble getting to Myrrh," he assured us. "We've done the trip enough times that we've got the best route programmed in." He got to his feet. "If you'll excuse me, then, I'll go get things started. I'm afraid there won't be time enough for me to offer you a proper meal, but my kitchen is back that way—please help yourselves to whatever you'd like to take for the trip."

"Thank you," I nodded, also standing up. "We appreciate all your help."

For a moment we locked eyes. "I only hope," he said quietly, "that it'll be enough."

He left, and I looked down at Calandra. "Do you think we can trust him?" I asked her.

She shrugged slightly. "We don't really have much choice any more, do we?"

I grimaced. "Not really."

With a sigh, she stood up. "Anyway, the Halloas are probably the least of our worries at the moment. Come on—you heard the man. Let's go pack up a lunch."

CHAPTER 16

We set out from Shekinah half an hour later in a mul/terrain that Adams assured us was the best in his small fleet. The vehicle's exterior was in such bad shape that it made me wince, but the motors ran well enough and the sucon rings seemed to hold their charge without any obvious leakage, so on balance I really had no grounds for complaint. Perhaps, I reflected, eight years among Carillon's wealth had spoiled me more than I'd realized.

We headed off, following a barely distinguishable path that looked more appropriate for livestock than for vehicles. Calandra, I could tell, wasn't in the mood for conversation, and I had no particular reason to try and draw her out. So I got as comfortable as I could in a perpetually bouncing seat, prepared myself mentally for a long five-hour trip, and settled back to watch the landscape.

It was, I found, a surprisingly interesting landscape to watch. Even the sections of untouched native area we'd seen around Shekinah had hardly been the lifeless desert I'd been expecting, and now I was finding that even that had been relatively sparse.

Not that any of it was truly spectacular, at least not by normal human aesthetic standards. Most of the plants were a drab bluish or gray-purple in color—clearly based on something other than chlorophyll—and most of them were built low to the ground, with only a few types even as large as a mid-sized bush. But they were numerous enough, and with considerable variety. Idly, I wondered how many of those who so confidently described Spall as a desert had ever actually seen the place.

"I wonder why the plants are so thin around Shekinah," Calandra spoke up into my thoughts.

I shrugged. "I'd guess Adams's people are doing something to the soil to help their own crops grow—fertilization, or something. Maybe whatever it is interferes with the local flora."

"Maybe," she said slowly. "On the other hand . . . maybe it's a result of running fusion drives that close to the surface."

I sensed a cautious glint of optimism within her, and saw where she was headed. If the fusion drive was indeed responsible for the thin flora, we might have found a visual sign of human habitation. "What could the mechanism be?" I wondered out loud. "The heat wave from the landing?"

"Or else perhaps some chemical peculiar to a fusion exhaust," she suggested. "I wish we had some detailed information on the biochemistry here."

"And had a biochemist along to explain what the information meant?" I added dryly.

Almost unwillingly, she smiled. "That's a point, I suppose," she admitted. "Well . . . maybe someone at Myrrh will know something."

I nodded. The Halloas at Myrrh had, after all, been farming this soil for a couple of years now. Hopefully, somewhere along the line they'd taken the time to learn a little about their new home.

It was almost sunset when the car finally drove us into the center of a small cluster of homes and came to a stop.

The Myrrh settlement was in many ways a fainter echo of the Shekinah one. Considerably smaller, with a slight feeling of roughness around the edges, it was obviously still in the early stages of its life and development; but obvious too was the fact that it was indeed a true offshoot of the Halo of God. The young man who came out to greet us—a bit shabbier, in a frontier sort of way, than those at Shekinah—had the same underlying sense of peace about him that I'd seen in Adams and his followers.

"Greetings," he nodded as Calandra and I got stiffly out of the car. He did a double take as he realized he didn't recognize us; and then his smile came back. "Sorry—we don't get many strangers here. What can I do for you?"

"We're here to see Shepherd Joyita Zagorin," I told him, stretching aching muscles. "We've got a message for her from Shepherd Adams."

"Ah—I should have guessed," the boy nodded, his smile becoming more of a grin. "I've driven the Shekinah/ Myrrh road myself—great fun, isn't it?"

"Marvelous," I grunted. "You should go into partnership with a kidney regrowth company—you'd both clean up."

"Probably. If you'll follow me, please . . . ?"

"Where is everyone?" Calandra asked as we crossed the open square-like area toward a large meeting-house sort of building.

"We're having a common dinner tonight," he explained over his shoulder, "and many are working on that. The rest are either finishing up the day's chores or are out meditating."

He waved off between two of the buildings, and I saw a group of perhaps half a dozen people sitting a short distance off from the settlement, clearly deep in meditation. "You people certainly take this meditation seriously, don't you?"

He didn't take offense, not even privately. "There wouldn't be much point in doing it half-heartedly, would there?" he countered.

I couldn't argue with that.

The meeting house was full of busy people and delectable aromas that made my stomach growl. Our guide led us past the large, C-shaped tables to a small room in the back, where a young woman was diligently working with an old computer. She looked up as the youth tapped on the open door. "Yes, Thomaz?"

"Visitors from Shekinah," he told her, indicating us.

"Ah," she said, rising gracefully to her feet. "Welcome to Myrrh Fellowship. I'm Shepherd Joyita Zagorin; what can I do for you?"

I shouldn't have been surprised—even in those few seconds Shepherd Zagorin's twin auras of inner peace and leadership had been clearly evident, had I gotten past my expectations enough to notice. But I hadn't, and with my embarrassment at missing the signs came an even more embarrassing tongue-tangling. "I—uh—my name is Gilead Raca Benedar," I managed. "This is Calandra Mara Paquin. I—we—have a message for you from Shepherd Adams."

"Who failed to mention my gender?" she asked dryly.

"Who failed to mention your age," I corrected, spurred by an urge to explain myself. "In my—admittedly—limited experience, a congregation's elders have seldom been as young as you are. Particularly in a frontier community like Myrrh."

She nodded, and to my relief I could see she wasn't offended. "In the Halo of God, positions are based on faith and gifts, not seniority or status," she told me. Her eyes flicked to Calandra, back to me. "From which I take it neither of you is even a prospective Seeker?"

I caught the sense of the word: the proper name for what we'd been calling Halloas. "No, we're not," I confirmed, digging out the envelope Adams had given us. "Perhaps this will explain."

She opened the note and read it . . . and, watching her face, it was clear to me that the situation wasn't being explained nearly to her satisfaction. A sense of uneasiness began to color her basic calmness, and she took the time to read the note a second time. "I hadn't

caught the significance of your middle names," she said
at last, looking up again and giving us each a brief but
probing look. "I've never met any Watchers before."

"We haven't met many Seekers, either, if it comes to
that," I shrugged.

She tapped the paper with her fingernail. "Shepherd
Adams would like me to extend Myrrh Fellowship's full
hospitality to you—which, of course, we're more than
willing to do." She hesitated, searching for a delicate
way to ask the indelicate . . .

"We can't tell you any more than Shepherd Adams
already has," Calandra spoke up. "For your own protection as well as ours."

Zagorin's lips compressed momentarily. Shepherd Adams, I gathered, was generally very open with his people, and I suspected it was this unusual secrecy as
much as anything else that was disturbing her. "If it
helps," I added, "we ought to be out from underfoot in
two or three days and that'll be the end of it."

She cocked an eyebrow at me. Seeker Shepherd or
no, I could see that there was still a strong latent layer
of skepticism built into her view of the universe. But at
least she was too polite to call me on it aloud. "Well,
until then, Myrrh Fellowship and I are at your complete disposal," she said instead. "Shepherd Adams men-
tions lodging and power for your car; can I assume the
first is the priority at the moment?"

"Definitely," I nodded. "I don't even want to *see* that
car for the next few hours."

That got a smile from her. "Yes, I've done the Shekinah
route myself on occasion. Well, then. Dinner will be in
about half an hour; while we're waiting, why don't I get
your lodging arrangements settled?"

I glanced at Calandra, read agreement. "Sounds good,"
I told Zagorin.

"All right," she said, coming out from behind the
desk. "Let's go see what we can turn up."

The dinner was well attended, with about a hundred
twenty people gathered around the tables, twenty per-

cent or so of them children. Shepherd Zagorin had us
seated next to her, an arrangement which enabled her
to answer or deflect any awkward questions about what
we were doing in Myrrh. The fact that she did so at
least twice during the meal showed that, in spite of her
own private reservations about us, she was nevertheless
willing to trust Adams on this one.

The food itself was a little startling at first. So far I
hadn't really had an opportunity to sample genuine
Solitaran-style cooking, of which I assumed this was a
variant, and it was far tangier than I had guessed from
its aromas. But it was good enough, once my palate had
gotten over its initial shock.

And as I ate, I took the time to study the Seekers.

The children were the easiest, of course. Full of
energy and mischief-tinged high spirits, with few social
barriers yet in place, they were like children everywhere else throughout the Patri and colonies. It brought
back to mind Shepherd Adams's offhanded comment
about beginning their meditation training early, and I
felt a twinge of concern. Our own Watcher elders had
struggled long and hard with the problem of how to instill
observational discipline without overloading or even
breaking their children's natural spirits, and I could
only hope Shepherd Adams and his people were tread-
ing as lightly.

Especially given the obvious effectiveness of their
training on their adult members.

It was vaguely astonishing. Granted, only a handful
of those close enough for me to read showed anything
even approaching the degree of inner peace that I'd
seen in Adams and Zagorin—the majority, in fact, still
showed strong traces of the same tension and low-level
despair that we'd sensed down on Solitaire. But even in
those the tension was clearly on its way out . . . and for
perhaps the first time in eleven years I found myself
actually beginning to relax.

Eleven years away from the Watchers of Cana
settlement—eight of those years immersed in the greed-
saturated atmosphere of Lord Kelsey-Ramos's circle of

associates—had almost erased the memories of what a simple, loving community felt like. Here there was no competition for riches or power; no arguments that couldn't be swiftly worked out between the parties involved; no greed or grasping for things that ultimately didn't matter. All that mattered to them was each other and God.

It was like the warm touch of the sun on chilled skin; and I was eagerly soaking it in when Calandra stirred next to me . . . and as I turned my attention to her the whole comfortable sensation vanished like a soap bubble.

"You all right?" I murmured, keeping my eyes on those across the table from us. "What's the matter?"

Her tension was a subtle thing, well under her control. But it was no less real for all that. "It's this place," she whispered tautly. "These people. Don't you feel it?"

I frowned, stretching out again. Nothing. "No."

She glanced me an odd look. "The sameness," she murmured, shivering. "The placidity—don't you understand?"

I shook my head. "All I feel here is peace and contentment."

Her tongue flicked across her lips. "It reminds me of Bridgeway."

A cold chill ran up my back. Bridgeway . . . and Aaron Balaam darMaupine. No. No, it couldn't be. "Are you saying—?"

To Calandra's left, I sensed Zagorin preparing to speak to her. "Later," Calandra hissed, and turned her attention in that direction.

I took a deep breath. It couldn't be, I told myself. Calandra was simply misreading the peace here as something overly malleable; the strong leadership as something sinister. Surely Adams had nothing of darMaupine's insane ambitions in him.

Surely not . . . and yet, darMaupine had managed to hide his intentions from the Watchers of his era. Many of whom had been far more discerning than I.

After a moment I returned to my meal, and as I ate I

continued to chat and smile with those around me. But the friendliness was guarded . . . and the food had lost much of its earlier flavor.

Dinner was followed by a worship service and then by a short fellowship hour; and so by the time Shepherd Zagorin led us from the meeting house it was full night outside.

"Beautiful view," I commented to Zagorin, nodding at the star-filled canopy overhead as we crossed the square. "It's been a long time since I've seen a night sky like this."

Zagorin nodded. "I know what you mean—I lived in Cameo before I joined the Halo of God. I've sometimes thought that even without the rest of it, the stars alone would make life here worthwhile."

Something caught my attention, off to our right . . . "Something's out there," Calandra said sharply, peering into the darkness. "An animal?"

Zagorin followed her gaze. "No, there aren't any animals that size on Spall," she assured us. "Probably one of our people meditating."

"What, at this hour?" I frowned.

"God takes calls around the clock," Zagorin reminded us dryly.

I swallowed, my mouth oddly dry. "Tell me, Shepherd Zagorin . . . what's it like?"

Even in the darkness I could sense Calandra's disapproval of the question. Zagorin, on the other hand, gave the distinct impression she'd expected me to eventually ask. "You mean, what's it like to be in direct contact with God?" she asked.

I nodded. "Do you actually hear Him speak? Or is it more like just a sense of His presence?"

She hesitated. "It's really sort of midway between the two," she said slowly. Prepared for the question or not, it was clearly not an easy thing to put into words. "It's a . . . well, a *presence* is probably the best way to describe it. A presence above and beyond that of humankind, circling us and filling us."

"And speaking to you?" I asked.

I felt her wry smile. "I'm sure He's speaking," she said. "Whether or not we know yet how to listen properly is another question."

Almost exactly the same words Adams had used at his failure to get guidance as to what to do about us. "But there *are* words to it?" I asked. "Or is it more like emotions or abstract thoughts?"

"For some of us, it's all three," she shrugged. "There's no obvious pattern—God seems to have chosen to speak to each of us differently. We don't know why."

Who has ever known the mind of God? Who has ever been his adviser? "Does it come clearer with experience?" I asked her.

"Usually, but there are those among us who were gifted at hearing Him from the first." She hesitated, just a bit. "As well as some for whom no amount of practice seems to help."

I heard something in her voice . . . "Such as the man who's out there now?" I suggested, waving toward the movement we'd seen.

I could sense Zagorin's surprise, and the wry acceptance that followed it. "You Watchers do live up to your reputation, don't you?" she said. "I wonder how you'd be at hearing God."

There was no insult or challenge in the comment that I could detect, merely genuine interest. "We're not likely to be here long enough to learn your methods," I reminded her.

"It isn't all that hard," she told me, beginning to warm to the idea. "I could probably teach you the rudiments in a couple of hours."

"We won't have time," Calandra put in. Her voice said to drop the subject.

Zagorin caught the tone, too, and reluctantly gave up. "Well, if you change your mind—either of you— just let me know. So. Shepherd Adams's letter implied you'd be heading out from here in the morning. Will you be coming back at nightfall?"

I shook my head. "Probably not. We have a lot of

territory to cover, and we've only got three days to do it in."

She very much wanted to ask me what exactly we were looking for, but politeness won out. "All right. I'll have the computer figure out the likely power you'll need for three days and have the sucon rings loaded into your car. We also have a couple of fold-down shelters on hand—if you've got room for them, they'll certainly be more comfortable than sleeping in the car."

I tried to remember whether or not a spaceship's standard survival pack included that kind of shelter. "If you can spare them, we'd certainly appreciate it," I agreed. "But if you're using them—"

"It's no problem," she assured me.

I thought back to Calandra's fears that the Seeker communities would be hostile to outsiders. I would have to remind her of that sometime. "In that case we accept," I told Zagorin with a nod. "Thank you very much. Tell me, what do you know about the territory east-southeast of here?"

"Not very much, I'm afraid. It gets hillier out there— that'll be obvious a kilometer or so after you leave Myrrh—with some genuine mountains and buttes cropping up here and there. You'll find thicker vegetation about where the hills start up, too, though it shouldn't be too thick for you to drive through."

I sensed Calandra's sudden interest. "Thicker vegetation of the same type as around here?"

"Mainly," Zagorin said. "There's also more variance in species, especially the larger types like thunderheads."

"More plentiful ground water?" I hazarded.

She shrugged. "I really have no idea. It could just as well be something in the soil or in the plants themselves, for all I know."

Calandra's guarded interest was beginning to fade, and I had to privately agree that we'd reached a dead end on this one. Still, the assumption that a smuggler's fusion drive would do *something* detrimental to nearby plants seemed reasonable enough; and even if we didn't know exactly what type of damage we were looking for, the more plants that were around getting scorched the easier it ought to be for us to spot that scorching. "What about animal life, then?" I asked Zagorin. "Any predators big enough for us to worry about?"

"In the middle of God's kingdom?" she asked, gently reproving. "No."

Beside me, I sensed Calandra's grimace. "Of course," I murmured. "Well, then . . ." I paused, groping for something else to say.

"Here we are," Zagorin spoke up smoothly into the gap. "I see the Mustains aren't home yet—will you be all right inside alone, Calandra?"

"No problem," Calandra assured her. "They prepared my room and showed me where everything was before dinner."

"Good. I trust the Changs did likewise for you, Gilead? Good. Well, then, if you'll both excuse me, I'll need to get back to my office and get that power-use calculation done. Sleep well, and please let me know before you leave in the morning."

We assured her we would, on both counts. Exchanging good-nights with her, we watched as her dimly lit silhouette headed back toward the lights of the meeting house.

"Predators in God's kingdom, indeed," Calandra murmured from beside me as Zagorin's footsteps faded away. "How silly of you to even ask."

"Let's be a little less sarcastic, shall we?" I growled, annoyed by the condescending tone in her voice. "Try to remember they're doing us a favor."

"Yes, well, you'll forgive me if I get uneasy relying on people whose brains don't fit right, won't you?" she shot back.

"Since when—?"

"Come *on*, Gilead. They come all the way out here just so they can worship Solitaire's Cloud? What would *you* call them?"

I sighed. "So you think that's what their meditations are picking up, too?"

"What else could it be? The option is that they're all

suffering from hallucinations or genuine mass insanity. Unless you want to suggest that this really *is* the heavenly kingdom?"

The twelve gates were twelve pearls, each gate being made of a single pearl, and the main street of the city was pure gold, transparent as glass . . . "If it is, the accepted description is way off," I conceded. "You know, it just occurred to me . . . on the way into Solitaire system Mr. Kelsey-Ramos asked me to try and see if I could sense whether or not the Cloud was alive."

"And was it?"

Even now, the memory of what I'd been asked to do made me shudder. "I couldn't bring myself to try," I had to admit. "My point was whether the question itself might imply the Solitaran officials are starting to notice the Seekers' success with their meditation."

"You mean we're back to the old knot about just what the Cloud really is?" Calandra asked thoughtfully, interested in spite of herself.

"And maybe whether or not we can locate its source," I pointed out slowly. "Because if there *is* a source and we can find it . . . it can presumably be shut off."

Calandra chewed at her lip. "So you're suggesting that maybe the Patri aren't just tolerating the Halloas, after all? Or letting them spread out over Spall just to get rid of them?"

"Triangulation, maybe," I said doubtfully. "I don't know, though. How do you gauge the strength of a meditation contact?"

She shrugged. "Don't ask me. This is *your* crazy idea, not mine."

I glared through the darkness at her. "Oh, right. *Your* crazy idea was that Adams is organizing the Seekers to follow in Aaron Balaam darMaupine's footprints."

She actually winced, her irritation coloring into embarrassment. "I only said the sense here was similar," she muttered. "There's too much placidity here. Too much comfort. Too little curiosity—don't you think they ought to care at least a *little* about the ecology of the planet they're living on? To me that says they're letting their leaders do their thinking for them."

"Sorry, but those all sound contradictory to me," I told her, feeling a twinge of remorse. I knew darMaupine and Bridgeway were a sore spot with her; I shouldn't have hit her there. "And I don't see any signs of that kind of twisted ambition in Adams, either."

She shook her head. "It doesn't matter. Whatever Adams has planned for the future, I'm not going to be around to see it."

I reached out and put my arm around her shoulders. "Yes, you will," I said with as much assurance as I had. Plus as much more as I could fake. "Don't forget we've now got *two* potential targets to go for: a smuggler base, and the origin of the Cloud."

She snorted. "Oh, great. And if we're *really* lucky maybe we'll find the origin with a smuggler base built on top of it. And an iridium mine next door."

The sarcasm displaced some of the depression, as I'd hoped it would. "That's the spirit," I told her lightly, trying to push it a bit more. "Hey—if we find a rich enough mine, we'll just go ahead and buy out Lord Kelsey-Ramos's interest in Carillon. Then Randon can scream at us all he likes."

Again she snorted. "You'd better get to bed—you're starting to hallucinate."

I nodded. "Sure. You, too; we'll want to get an early start in the morning." Besides which—I didn't add—a good night's sleep would do a lot to quiet at least the worst of her fears.

"Yeah." She hesitated. "Gilead . . . I still think you're a suicidal fool to be doing this. But . . . thanks."

I found her hand, squeezed it reassuringly. *For he hides me away under his roof on the day of evil, he folds me in the recesses of his tent, sets me high on a rock. Now my head is held high above the enemies who surround me . . .* "It'll all work out," I told her.

"Sure," she sighed, not even trying to pretend she believed me. "Good night."

"Good night."

I waited until she was inside, then trudged along the edge of the square to the house where I'd been given a room. Trying to bolster Calandra's spirits like that, I hadn't realized just how tired I really was. But it was all catching up with me now: the nighttime flight from Solitaire, the debilitating ride across Spall, the continual strain of having to lie with a straight face. Not to mention simply having to contemplate the enormous task looming before us.

The lights were out as I approached the Changs' house, for which I was grateful. Pleasant though I'd found the family earlier, the last thing I wanted at the moment was to have to face them. However paranoid Calandra might feel about the Halo of God, my own respect for both the Seekers and their goals was only increasing . . . and along with it was similarly growing a quiet dread that our presence here was somehow going to be used to destroy them.

On the threshold of the house, I shook my head sharply. Fatigue depression, I told myself—it was nothing more than that. As long as Myrrh Fellowship was unaware of who and what we were, they couldn't be held responsible for aiding us. Not legally, not rationally.

And yet . . .

I looked upward. Hanging overhead, like some kind of bluish fruit, was the partially lit disk of Solitaire, with three abnormally bright stars off one edge. Three of Commodore Freitag's ships, coming for us . . . and it occurred to me that the law was usually designed to serve the purposes of those in power. And that for those same people, rationality was more an occasional option than it was a requirement.

CHAPTER 17

We left just after sunrise the next morning—a totally ungodly hour, to my way of thinking. Even so, quite a few of the Seekers were up before us, though that was hardly remarkable once I reminded myself that Myrrh was economically an agricultural community. Still, to my city-oriented biological clock, the thought of doing this day in and out made my eyes ache.

My skills at manual driving were probably ten years out of date, but given there was no road to stay on and no other traffic to avoid, I didn't expect to have any real problems. Calandra, clearly more wide awake than I was, suggested she take the first turn at the wheel, an offer I had to regretfully decline. The way my eyelids were sagging I wasn't at all sure how good an observer I would be, and it would be better for us to hit a few extra bumps than to miss some possibly vital clue off on the horizon somewhere.

Fortunately, Zagorin had anticipated the problem. Two mugs and a thermac full of a hot, tart-sweet-tart drink had been placed into the car along with the promised supply of sucon rings, and even as we drove out of the settlement I found I was gradually sipping my eyes fully open.

The fields surrounding Myrrh were more extensive than I'd realized from our approach the evening before. Our southeast heading took us through several hectares of cultivated land, a good scattering of Seekers and small-scale farm equipment already hard at work among the rows of greenery. "What do you know about farming?" I asked Calandra.

"Nothing more than I picked up as a child." She craned her neck to both sides. "I'd say they've got enough cropland here to support their community, though, if that's what you're getting at."

"It was," I acknowledged, too groggy to be irritated by her customary ease at reading my thoughts. "Can you identify any of those plants?"

She shrugged. "That's corn over there, and I think those short broadleaved things are trelapse. The rest—" She shook her head.

"Not important," I said. A movement off to the left caught my eye: a Seeker, head down, walking slowly through the native flora bordering the fields. "I wonder what he's looking for," I commented.

"Valeer, probably," Calandra said, leaning forward to look past me. "The Mustains told me about it last night before I went to bed. It's a native plant they extract a spice from."

"Ah." I thought back to the exotic flavors of the food at dinner last night. No wonder I hadn't been able to identify the ingredients. "Interesting. They planning it for export?"

"I'm sure the leaders have toyed with the idea—the Mustains certainly have. At the moment, though, they seem to be keeping it to themselves."

Something in her voice . . . "Trying to find out if they're being fed a placidity drug, were you?" I asked.

I sensed a grudging embarrassment from her. "The thought *had* occurred to me," she admitted.

"We both ate it last night," I reminded her. "Even

with just a single dose either of us would have noticed if it produced that kind of effect."

"If they're using one native plant, they could be using others," she countered. But her voice lacked any real conviction. And rightly so—with a multitude of vodkyas in vogue around the Patri and colonies these days, both of us were well acquainted with the outward signs of such use, and none of the Seekers in Myrrh had exhibited any of them. That Calandra would even consider such an unlikely possibility meant she was determined to find a darker explanation for the Halo of God than a loving community spirit.

She wanted to believe the worst of them . . . and down deep I knew that nothing I could say would change that desire. Even Watchers could blind themselves to reality if they wanted to badly enough.

Perhaps that was how Aaron Balaam darMaupine had managed to get as far as he had.

A stray fact ticked at my consciousness: the Seeker out there had been wearing gloves. "Are the valeer plants sharp-edged?" I asked Calandra, as much to change the subject as anything else.

She glanced out at the Seeker again, and I could tell she was also relieved that another argument about Adams's group had been deflected. "It could be just the plants themselves. The Mustains told me that Spall's soil is highly acidic."

I grimaced. Great. And us about to go out poking around in it without any protective clothing. "How acidic is acidic?"

"Oh, it's not dangerous or anything like that," she assured me. "Just gives you a rash if you dig around in it too much."

Yes—the Seeker had been wearing the same general style of daywear clothing we'd seen at the settlement dinner the previous night, which hadn't struck me then as particularly thick or chemical-resistant. "I suppose that means they have to lay down some kind of alkaline solution before planting their own crops," I commented.

"Probably," Calandra nodded. "Whatever the method,

it seems pretty effective—I haven't seen any signs at all
of native plants where the soil's been treated. I wonder," she added thoughtfully, "if that means it's the
chemicals in the fusion drive exhaust, after all."

My stomach tightened as academic curiosity faded and
the huge task facing us flooded back on me. "Could be.
Speaking of which, I suppose we'd better get down to
business."

"Right." Calling up a map of the area on the car's
display, she tapped for a contour overlay. "I presume
you'd planned to do as much searching as possible from
high ground?"

I nodded. "Unless, of course, we spot some place
straight out that looks like it would be a good hiding
place for an illegal shuttle or starship."

She peered at the display, then slowly scanned the
landscape around us. "Not really. Anyway, we're still
too close to Myrrh."

"Agreed." I tapped a spot on the display, ahead and
to our left. "That's probably that hill over there," I said,
pointing to a small rise in the distance. "Ten to fifteen
minutes away, I'd guess. Shall we start there?"

She shrugged, and I could sense her brace herself.
"Might as well."

With only the unfamiliar plant life around to judge
by, the distance proved deceptive, but we still made it
to the hill in under half an hour. The only slope gentle
enough for the car to manage was unfortunately also too
rocky for me to want to risk the tires on, and so we
wound up spending another ten minutes struggling to
the top on foot.

Shepherd Zagorin had been right: both the landscape
and the flora facing us were remarkably different from
that which we'd seen on the drive between Shekinah
and Myrrh. Added to the basic blue and gray-purple
we'd already seen were touches of red, dark yellow,
and even a delicate lavender. Most of the color seemed
to belong to flower-like structures, but some was simply
the plants themselves.

There was animal life out there, too, the first we'd

yet seen on Spall. Dozens of tiny spots flitted low over the ground or circled the flowers in the semi-random pattern of insects everywhere, and I discovered that if I watched the nearest foliage carefully I could see the subtle leaf movements that implied small ground animals underneath.

And in the midst of the thickest and richest patches of plant life stood the thunderheads Zagorin had mentioned.

Even never having seen one before, I had no doubt as to their identity. Growing up to probably a meter in height, standing singly or grouped together in twos or threes, their oddly asymmetric, flat-topped breaking-wave shapes towered over the shorter plants surrounding them. Their shape, coupled with their dirty-white color, made the name "thunderhead" practically inevitable.

"They seem to prefer the lusher areas," Calandra commented into my thoughts.

I dug out the noculars from our ship's survival pack and studied a quick sampling of the thunderheads within view. She was right—each one was indeed surrounded by several meters of colorful plants, making a sharp contrast with the thunderheads' own whiteness. "Lusher areas, or the presence of some particular insect," I offered, lowering the noculars. "I can see small clouds of something surrounding each one."

"Probably coincidental," she shook her head. "More likely the insects are going for the more attractive plants around them."

"Though who knows what's attractive to an insect?" I shrugged. "You suppose they're some variety of fungus?"

"They sure don't have whatever the local equivalent of chlorophyll is," she said. "I don't know, though—those don't exactly look like ideal places for dead vegetation to have collected."

"Maybe a parasitic fungus, then," I said, reaching back as best I could into the classroom biology I hadn't used in years. "It would make sense—any parasite that size would have to have a lot of host material around to live off of."

Calandra nodded thoughtfully. "Sounds reasonable. If so . . . it may mean they're a sort of reverse indicator for fusion-damaged plants."

I considered. "Maybe," I agreed. "Assuming the pattern here also holds further out, anyway. We'll have to keep an eye on that."

"Right. Well . . ." Straightening her back, she took a deep breath and fell silent. Taking the cue, I raised the noculars again and began my own search.

Nothing. No indication of the sort of inhibited plant growth we'd seen at the landing area near Shekinah Fellowship. Also no scorch marks, no landing skid tracks, and no odd reflections that could be from plastic or metal.

I didn't have to look to sense Calandra's disappointment. "Like you said," I reminded her gently, "we're still pretty close to Myrrh."

Her eyes, when I turned to look, were haunted. Haunted with the threat of failure . . . or with the threat of the death that would follow that failure. "Come on," I said softly. "We can do it."

She closed her eyes briefly, and when she opened them the haunted look was gone. "Sure," she said. Almost as if she believed it.

Biting the back of my lip, I slipped the noculars back in their case. Taking her hand, I led her carefully down the hill and back to the car.

I don't know how many hills we drove or climbed up that day. There were at least ten—that many I remember clearly—but much of the ordeal remained afterward little more than a fatigued blur in my memory. The pattern of that first attempt remained with us the rest of the day: choose a local high point, drive there across bumpy ground, climb or drive up—driving being the rare exception—and gaze out at the landscape until our eyes ached. Climb or drive back down, head for the next spot, and repeat.

It was incredibly draining. Physically, it was clear that neither of us was in shape for this kind of activity, and by the time the first fluffy clouds began to form about noon my eyes, head, and legs all ached with fatigue. Calandra, with the normal woman's higher stamina in such things, fared a shade better, but not enough to really matter. By midafternoon she was stumbling as much as I was, and leaning on me for balance as much as I leaned on her.

But as bad as it was physically, it was even worse emotionally.

I'm not sure really what I was expecting when we started out that morning. That God had guided me in a lucky guess, I suppose, and that within a couple of hours we would spot the telltale signs of fusion-drive damage and could scamper back to Shekinah and call Commodore Freitag down on them. But it wasn't happening. To gaze at an unfamiliar landscape and try to pick something "abnormal" from it took incredible amounts of both painstaking attention and equally painstaking imagination. The existence of the thunderheads helped, but not as much as we'd hoped it would. The dirty-white plants grew in small clumps, never with more than three or four together, and never in the kind of widespread daisy field that would eliminate large sections of territory from our consideration.

And as the work continued—as the hours dragged by without even a hint of what we thought we were looking for—the optimism slowly faded . . . to be replaced by depression and finally despair.

We both felt it—both tried to hide it from the other for pride's sake, if for no other reason. But as the sun dipped toward the horizon, and Calandra started us toward yet another distant hill, she finally gave up the pretense.

"It's not working, Gilead," she sighed, abruptly letting her foot off the accelerator. The loud background swishing of the plants against the car faded to a half-imagined ringing in my ears as we rolled to a stop. "We're not going to find anything this way, and we both know it. Let's give it up and go back."

I ground my knuckles into my eyes, trying to rub the

soreness out of them. Watching the landscape from a
bouncing car, we'd discovered, was even harder on the
eyes than repeatedly sweeping the horizon from the
tops of hills. "We can't do that, Calandra," I told her,
hearing her same tiredness in my own voice. "Besides,
we've just barely reached our main target section. All
this up to now has been practice; tomorrow is what
really counts."

She turned to face me. "Do you really believe we're
going to find anything?" she asked bluntly.

"There's always hope—"

"That's not what I asked."

I clenched my teeth. "You've given up on faith completely, haven't you?"

"What I believe or don't believe isn't the issue," she
said stiffly. "And if it comes to that, don't forget that
you've left the Watchers, too."

My stomach tightened. "It's not the same."

"Oh? Tell me how—and don't forget to include how
much Carillon's paying to rent your soul."

I took a deep breath, trying to will my anger and
depression away, and broke my eyes away from her
glare. A short ways ahead, a little off to our right, was a
rocky pair of close-set bluffs rising out of the vegetation
surrounding them. "I don't think either of us is in the
mood for a rational discussion at the moment," I said.
"Tell you what; let's drive over to those bluffs over
there and make camp for the night."

She hesitated a long minute, then shrugged. "I suppose we might as well," she agreed with a tired sigh.
"It's probably too late to get back to Myrrh before dark,
anyway."

We headed out . . . and as we approached the bluffs
I discovered that my original guess had been wrong.
There were, in fact, *four* bluffs in the group, not two,
sitting closely together in a rough square. Probably
with a fair amount of reasonably sheltered space in the
middle of the formation, judging from what little of
their shapes I could see. It would indeed be a good
place to spend the night.

Perhaps an equally good place for a smuggler to spend the night. Possibly even a good place in which to hide a small shuttle . . .

I felt the hairs on the back of my neck stiffen. If there *were* smugglers in there, watching our approach . . .

Beside me, Calandra stirred. "There's a thunderhead on the top of the bluff," she said.

I felt heat rise to my face as I squinted against the bright sky behind the bluff. She was right, as usual; in fact, I could see one of the large plants on each of the two bluffs whose tops were visible from here. "Oh, well," I said. "It was just a thought."

"Yeah. How close do you want me to get?"

"Might as go all the way in, if you can," I told her, pointing to the nearest of the gaps. "If last night was any indication, it's likely to get pretty chilly tonight, and those bluffs may at least break the wind for us."

"Or funnel it right down our throats," she muttered.

"So we'll find someplace out of the line of fire," I growled. "Let's just go, okay?"

She flashed me a glare and drove on in silence.

The place was clearly not being used by smugglers . . . but the closer we got, the more I realized it could easily *have* been. All four of the bluffs were tall and—from this side, at least—unusually straight-walled, which meant the gaps between them remained narrow all the way up. A cozy hideaway, indeed, with virtually no visibility except from directly overhead. The ground leading to our target gap began a gradual rise about a hundred meters out from the bluffs, and from glimpses I caught through the opening I got the impression that the ground fell away again toward the center of the enclosed area.

"What do you think?" Calandra called over the swishing of plants around and beneath us.

I studied the gap and the terrain in front of it. "Looks like we can get in all right," I told her. "Let's try it. We can always stop if we hit a patch of sharp rocks or something."

She nodded. We passed the outer edges of the bluffs,

the sunlight from behind us cutting off abruptly as we passed into shadow. The walls of the bluffs curved toward us, and I could see now that the narrowest part of the opening would indeed be large enough to admit us. Calandra saw that, too, and kept going. A couple more meters of slope up; and then we were through the gap, angling down now toward the slightly depressed center—

And Calandra slammed on the brakes. "God in heaven," she breathed, almost mechanically.

Directly ahead, filling the enclosed area from the base of one bluff to the next, was a literal sea of thunderheads. The plants which always before we'd found in the centers of lush vegetation . . . and never in groups larger than four.

I took a deep breath. "Offhand," I heard myself say, "I'd guess we've found a very healthy place to camp."

The words seemed to break the spell. "Right," Calandra said dryly. "At least if you're a thunderhead." She stared at them for another minute before shaking her head. "Well, come on, then," she growled, getting stiffly out of the car. "Let's get those shelters put together before the sun goes down."

CHAPTER 18

Calandra had been correct about the gaps funneling the wind. They did, and with a vengeance, converting the gentle breeze outside into a steady whistle that here in the shadow of the bluffs was already beginning to be chilly. Fortunately, I'd also been correct in the assumption that we'd be able to find someplace sufficiently sheltered from the blast. The northernmost bluff had two gentle ridges extending from its top all the way down into the mass of thunderheads, and between those ridges was a hollow with plenty of room for both of the shelters Shepherd Zagorin had lent us. The shelters themselves proved to be both simple and idiot-proof, and in perhaps twenty minutes we had a fairly cozy camp put together.

For a long time afterwards we just lay there on the ground, too exhausted even to talk. I watched the clouds passing overhead, framed by the towering buttes, and wondered if my legs would ever feel like walking again.

"Gilead . . . ?"

"Hmm?" I said. There was no reply, and with an effort I turned my head to look at her. Flat on her back, her head propped almost vertical against a rolled-up sleeping bag behind her neck, she was staring down at the mass of thunderheads. Staring at them with a troubled expression on her face. "Something wrong?" I asked.

"I don't know," she said slowly. "What are they all doing here?"

"What, the thunderheads?" Feeling vaguely resentful at having to make the effort, I propped myself up on my elbows.

She had a point—even tired and irritated I had to admit that. Every other thunderhead we'd seen today, without exception, had been growing smack in the middle of heavy concentrations of plant and insect life, neither of which was present here in even moderate amounts. Not to mention the sheer unexpected number of the things growing together in the first place. "Could be there's enough shelter from the proper seasonal winds in here that spores don't get very far," I offered.

Calandra shook her head. "That might explain why there are so many here. It doesn't explain why they're alive."

I chewed carefully at a sun-chapped lip. "Maybe they can feed more than one way," I suggested. "Parasitic when they're out among other plants, something else when they aren't."

"Maybe."

For another moment we lay there in silence. Then, moving stiffly, Calandra rolled over and got to her feet, her sense that of someone bracing for unwanted but necessary activity. "What are you doing?" I asked, not at all sure I wanted to hear the answer.

She nodded up at the bluff towering over us. "There's a thunderhead up there, remember? I'm going to go take a closer look at it."

I looked up, a sinking feeling starting in my stomach and seeping down into my legs. It wasn't enough that we'd climbed forty million hills today already; Calandra wanted to do it some more. "Why?" I growled. "Or at least, why now?"

"You don't have to come," she said shortly. Glancing

at the two ridges stretching to either side of us, she chose the leftmost and started up.

I watched her climb for perhaps a minute. *Let every valley be filled in, every mountain and hill be levelled* . . . As far as I was concerned, the fulfillment of that one couldn't come too soon. Swallowing a word I'd once been severely punished for saying, I got to my feet and followed.

It was, fortunately, not as bad as it had looked from flat on my back. Fairly gentle in slope to begin with, the ridge was also heavily studded with large and solidly inlaid rocks, giving it the appearance in places of a highly irregular staircase. Even so, it was a good fifteen minutes before we finally puffed up onto the flat top.

For a few minutes I just stood there in the brisk wind, well back from any of the edges, my eyes reflexively sweeping the horizon as my legs trembled slightly with fatigue. As usual, nothing that seemed out of the ordinary was visible out there.

"There's a thunderhead on each of the other bluffs, too," Calandra said in an odd voice.

I turned to look. She was right—precisely right, in fact. One thunderhead, exactly, perched atop each of the four bluffs.

From the top of the tall cedar tree, from the highest branch I shall take a shoot and plant it myself on a high and lofty mountain . . . A shiver ran up my back, totally unrelated to the wind. "All right, I give up," I said, trying to keep my voice light. "How *did* they get up here?"

Calandra licked her lips. "You feel it too, don't you?" she asked quietly.

I waved my hands helplessly. "I don't know *what* I feel," I had to admit. "Something here isn't right . . . but I have no idea what it is."

Calandra took a deep breath. "Me neither. And I don't like not knowing." She gestured to the lone thunderhead on our bluff, quivering in the breeze a half meter from the bluff's outer edge. "Let's have a look."

Standing at my cubicle window in the Carillon Building, a hundred twenty stories above ground, I'd never had even a twinge of acrophobia. Walking in a steady wind toward the edge of an open-air bluff a tenth that height was something else entirely, and I had to force myself to go the last couple of meters. "Looks reasonably normal to me," I said, dropping to my knees beside the thunderhead.

"Pretty hard rock it's dug into," Calandra pointed out, scratching at the cracked rock at its base with a fingernail. "The spore or whatever must have found a crack or hollow to germinate in."

I thought about that. "Maybe. On the other hand . . . there are an awful lot of cracks up here."

She hissed softly between her teeth. "Or in other words, why is there just one." Slowly, she shook her head. "I don't know."

I looked at the thunderhead again. A fungoid plant, stuck all alone in the middle of a rocky clifftop without other plants or decaying material anywhere around. A deep root system, perhaps, tapping into some source of nutrients within the rock itself? "Maybe it just so happens that thunderheads *like* fusion drive emissions," I suggested, only half humorously.

She shivered. "I don't like that idea at all," she said quietly.

I thought about it. If we were, in fact, sitting on top of a smuggler hideout . . . "Neither do I," I admitted.

Almost hesitantly, she reached out and touched the thunderhead's outer skin, resting her fingers there for a moment. Then, with a sigh, she lowered her hand and climbed back to her feet. "There's nothing here. Come on—let's go back."

We headed back across the bluff to where the two ridges began their sloping way down. "You want to try the other one this time, or stick with the one we already know?" I asked.

"Let's stay with the known," Calandra said. "I'm too tired to have to figure out new footing."

"Yeah," I nodded. Something on the second ridge

caught my eye—"Hold it a second," I said, catching hold of her arm.

"What?" she asked, her voice suddenly taut.

I pointed down the ridge. "Discolored spots in the rock, about twenty centimeters across each—there and there; see? In fact," I amended, an odd tightness settling into my stomach, "they go all the way down."

She stared down the ridge in silence for a long minute. Then, still without speaking, she started down toward them.

The second ridge was, fortunately, as easy to climb as the first had been. The nearest of the discolorations was perhaps ten meters down, and we reached it without difficulty. Squatting awkwardly on the slope, Calandra below the spot and I above it, we gave it a careful look.

It was clear right from the start that the discoloration hadn't been my imagination; equally clear was the fact that it wasn't just a chance placement of different colored rock. The patch was obviously a changed section of the stone immediately around it . . .

I reached out to touch it. Smooth, or at least smoother than the rest of the surrounding rock. Wind or water treating could account for that, possibly, except that there was no reason I could see why one section would be so affected and a nearby one not. Off-colored rock; with a shiny, almost glassy hint to it . . .

I looked up and met Calandra's eye . . . and I could tell she'd reached the same conclusion I had. "It's been heat-treated," I said quietly.

Calandra licked her lips. "There's nothing here that could do that," she almost whispered. "Nothing at all."

The mountains melt like wax before the God of all the earth . . .

I swallowed hard, fighting back the dark, half-remembered fears of childhood. Spall was not—*could not be*—the seat of God's kingdom. Period. There was a reasonable explanation for what had happened here—a reasonable, scientific, non-miraculous explanation for what had happened here.

All I had to do was find it.

My probing fingertips caught something else. "Hair-line cracks," I grunted to Calandra.

She nodded. "There's a whole network of them," she said absently. "More visible from my angle, I guess. They seem to radiate from the glazed part outward into the surrounding rock."

I leaned forward to see. "Cracks from the heating?" I hazarded.

She shrugged, oddly hunch-shouldered. For all her current rejection of her faith, she'd had the same up-bringing I had . . . upbringing that would have in-cluded the same scriptures about God's fire and lightning that were currently bouncing around my own mind. "Maybe," she said. "They look a lot like the cracks around the thunderhead up there, though."

I looked back down again, chagrined that I hadn't made that connection myself. "Maybe that's the an-swer, then," I suggested slowly. "Maybe these are spots where there were once thunderheads."

She snorted. "Oh, certainly. What, no one ever taught them not to play with fire when they were seedlings?"

Under other circumstances I might have tossed out a pointed reference to God's lightning. But with a sense of creepiness growing steadily around me, I couldn't even resent her sarcasm. "It's not *that* crazy an idea," I told her. "I've heard of plants whose seeds germinate best after a forest fire has passed through the area. Why not one which spontaneously burns down at the end of its life to give that kind of seed a good head start?"

"Have you ever *heard* of a plant like that?" she countered.

"No. But neither of us is exactly steeped in botanical knowledge."

Her eyes seemed to defocus for a moment . . . as if trying to see something that still wasn't quite there. "True," she said at last. "I just hope it's really that simple."

There were housekeeping chores to be done when we reached bottom; chores that enabled me to temporarily ignore the odd feeling hovering at the edge of my mind. By the time we'd set up our firepatch flatlantern and gotten it started, the sun was down; by the time we'd sorted out and eaten our pac-heated meals, it was full night.

And as we sat quietly on opposite sides of the firepatch, lost in our own private worlds, the mystery inevitably returned to my thoughts.

"Any progress?" Calandra asked, her face eerie looking in the glow of the firepatch.

I shrugged. Irritating though Calandra could be, a portion of my mind noted dimly, it was sometimes nice to be with someone who didn't have to communicate entirely through words. "Maybe," I told her. "I presume we can eliminate right away the possibility of volcanic activity on those slopes?"

"I know even less about geology than I do about botany," she said dryly. "But I find it hard to believe this is volcanic rock."

I nodded. "Okay, then. Suppose, for sake of argument, that the thunderheads have a high metallic content."

"All right," she said after a slight pause. "I guess I can suppose that. So . . . ?"

"So high metal content would imply good electrical conductivity," I said. "Which would make them likely targets during thunderstorms."

"So all the ones that happened to grow on the slope got blasted off, while the ones right on top didn't?"

"The ones on top might be younger," I reminded her. "We don't have any idea how old the heat-treated parts are, or how long a thunderhead's lifespan is."

She waved upward, the motion casting a ragged shadow on the ridge behind her. "It still doesn't make sense," she sighed. "None of it does. Why would one group of thunderheads prefer—no; *insist* on—living among a tangle of other plants out in full sunlight, while another group works very hard to drill its members into solid rock on cliff faces? While a *third* packs together in shadow like lonely walruses," she added, gesturing at the sea of thunderheads faintly visible in the reflected light.

I shrugged helplessly. "Maybe they're three different species," I said. "Maybe they behave differently at different parts of their life cycle. Maybe they're just highly adaptable and can live and grow no matter what happens around them. Some things are like that; others aren't."

I hadn't intended the comment to sound accusing . . . but it did anyway, and both of us heard it. "Sometimes that kind of struggle isn't worth it," she said quietly, her eyes steady on me.

For a moment we gazed at each other, and I felt the rush of suppressed emotion flowing like white-water through her. "What happened?" I asked softly.

Her eyes were still on me, but her attention had turned inward. To thoughts, and memories, and feelings . . . and, perhaps, to the need to talk about it all. "Aaron Balaam darMaupine happened," she said at last. "Do you remember what it was like to be sixteen?"

I thought back. Awkwardness, both physical and social. Confusion, and the questioning of things long taken for granted. A profound need to be accepted, to be like all the others. An equally profound terror that I wasn't, and would never be. "I remember enough of it," I said.

"I was sixteen when darMaupine's Kingdom of God was toppled," she said, her voice echoing old pain. "When the Patri and colonies began to truly hate the Watchers." She took a deep breath, let it out slowly. "You were, what, ten when that happened?"

"Eleven."

"Eleven. Which meant you were still pretty much locked safely away in the Watcher womb." She shook her head. "I wasn't. I'd already spent a lot of time out in the non-Watcher world—darMaupine practically ordered us to do that. 'Do you not realize that the holy people of God are to be the judges of the world?'—that was one of his favorite quotes. I'd spent time out of the settlement. Made a lot of . . . friends."

She dropped her gaze to the firepatch, a hand coming up to daub briefly at her eyes. "I was sixteen, Gilead. I . . . couldn't take the hatred and . . . rejection I felt everywhere. And I couldn't believe a loving God would have permitted someone as gifted as darMaupine to be so badly corrupted."

I licked my lips. "We're creatures of free will," I said quietly. "By definition, that means God allows us to choose whether to use our talents for or against Him."

"I know all the arguments," Calandra said, shaking her head. "But arguments didn't help. I was hurting . . . and all the Watchers who were left were too busy fighting off their own destruction to care about something as unimportant as a teenager's crisis of faith. I left just as soon as I could."

"And have been running ever since?"

A bitter smile touched her lips. "But the running's going to stop now, isn't it? Can't run any more after you've been at the Deadman Switch."

"Calandra—"

"You suppose it's my punishment for quitting?" she asked, her voice trembling slightly. "You suppose God considers it heresy that I ran out when my questions outnumbered my answers?"

"If God were that impatient He would have rolled up the universe by now and put it away in a closet," I sighed. "We just have to trust that He's got things under some kind of control. Whether we understand what He's doing or not."

She raised her eyes back to mine again. "So why did *you* run away?"

I hesitated. I had promised myself never to tell this to anyone else . . . "I left because there wasn't any way to make money in Cana," I told her. "And I wanted to make money."

She stared at me for a long minute. "I don't believe you."

"Everyone in Cana believes it," I said, feeling a flicker of pain. Pain I thought I'd laid to rest long ago.

"Then they haven't seen you lately. Have they?"

I shrugged fractionally. "It's been about nine years."

Her gaze hardened. "Don't lie to me, Gilead. DarMaupine and his people lied to me; I won't be lied to again."

I took a deep breath. "I earn about a hundred fifty thousand a year working for Lord Kelsey-Ramos."

She snorted. "I've lived on as little as six."

"I live on five."

Silence. Then, slowly, she nodded. "Who knows?"

"Cana's chief elder. No one else."

"Why not?"

"What purpose would it serve? To save my reputation among them?"

"Your reputation's very important to you."

I bit at the back of my lip. She was right, of course. "So is their dignity as human beings," I said quietly. "Your Bethel settlement got crushed in the aftermath of darMaupine, Calandra—for Cana, it's a matter of being slowly strangled to death. Without my contribution, I really don't think they could survive as a community any more." I caught her eye. "You really want them to know that?"

Her lip twisted. But it was a soft sort of twist, with more sympathy to it than contempt. "And you risk throwing that away to help me?"

It was something I'd thought about a great deal lately. Usually late at night, alone in the dark. "I have a weakness for lost causes, I suppose," I said, forcing a smile.

She dropped her eyes, turned her head to gaze out at the thunderheads. "Can't get much more lost than I am . . ."

She trailed off, and abruptly her sense sharpened. "What?" I whispered.

For a half dozen heartbeats she didn't answer . . . but slowly her sense changed to disbelief. Disbelief, and quiet horror. "Do you feel it?" she whispered.

I followed her gaze, stretching out with all my skill. The thunderheads were a ghostly sea of faint white patches, some of them seeming to quiver in the breeze. The air about me was rich in subtle sounds . . . subtle aromas . . . subtle sensations . . .

And at last I saw what Calandra had seen.

I looked back at her. Our eyes met; and together we uncrossed our legs and stood up, picking up our survival pack flashlights as we did so. She moved around the firepatch, stepped close to me, her muscles trembling with emotion. For another moment we stood like that, holding each other tightly, our shadows stretching across the milky white sea. Then, setting my teeth, I raised my light, set it for tight beam, and flicked it on.

A narrow cone of light lanced out . . . and even as I squinted against it, I felt the responding ripple, and knew that what we'd both sensed had indeed been the truth.

The thunderheads were alive. Alive, and aware . . . and watching us.

CHAPTER 19

For a long moment we just stood there. "This is crazy," I said at last. "I mean, *really* crazy. They're *plants*, for heaven's sake."

Close beside me, Calandra shivered. "Are they?"

"Of *cour*—" The reflexive retort died halfway out. "What else *could* they be?"

"There are things called sessile animals that spend all or part of their lives attached to trees," she said mechanically, her eyes darting about the dirty-white shapes laid out before us. "I just don't . . . how could the original survey teams have *missed* something like this?"

I moved my flashlight, watched the incredibly subtle ripple of reaction move with it. "Because they weren't Watchers," I said grimly.

She took a deep breath. "Let's take a closer look."

Together, we walked across the uneven ground. Calandra knelt down beside the first thunderhead we reached, touched it lightly. "Turn the light on it."

I did as instructed. "Well?"

She pursed her lips. "There's a . . . it's a little like a vibration, but not exactly. I felt it in the thunderhead on top of the bluff, too, when we were up there."

I twisted my head, looking up at the dark shape silhouetted against the stars. "You think they could be mobile at some stage of their lives?"

"Either that, or else they're awfully good at throwing seeds . . ."

She trailed off, and we looked at each other. "The discolored spots," I said, an odd sense of unreality seeping into me. "The one on top is the last of a whole line of the things."

Calandra nodded, her eyes haunted. "They could only get their seeds a short ways uphill. So they just kept at it until they got one onto the top."

"But why—" I stopped, turning again to look at the sea of thunderheads crowded between the buttes. No; not a *sea* of thunderheads . . . "It's a city," I breathed. "A *city*." Which meant the ones atop the buttes—

" 'I shall stand at my post,' " Calandra quoted softly. " 'I shall station myself on my watch-tower, watching to see what God will say to me.' "

I looked again at the sky, my mouth dry. "They're sentries," I whispered. "Guarding the approaches."

Calandra followed my gaze. "But guarding *how*? And against whom?"

I shook my head. "I don't know." But even as I said it I thought about the heat-treated spots on the ridge up the bluff . . . "What do you say," I said carefully, "we kind of ease back, break camp, and get out of here."

She hunched her shoulders fractionally. "It won't help. They know we're here."

She was right—I could sense the unblinking attention focused on us. "Maybe they don't realize we know what they are," I told Calandra. Something in the back of my mind was screaming *danger!*— "Come *on*," I snapped, taking her hand and pulling her all but bodily away from the thunderheads—

It came as a half seen, half felt sense of a dark mass falling from the sky; and even as we both ducked reflexively there was the sharp *crack* of suddenly released pressure, and we were abruptly in the middle of a cloud of thick white smoke. A sweet-bitter smell flooded my nostrils, and I clamped a hand over my face to try and keep it out. But too late. Already I could feel my arms and legs going numb. I tried to take a step, stumbled instead to my knees, dragging Calandra down with me as my hand refused to release its grip on hers. Together we sprawled onto the ground, and a moment later I found myself on my back. Overhead, the fog parted slightly, enough to give me a glimpse of the pattern of lights hovering overhead.

The last thing I saw were those lights, beginning their descent . . .

CHAPTER 20

From somewhere beside me came the quiet sound of someone shifting position in a chair.

Eyes still closed, I let myself come fully awake, stretching still-groggy senses as best I could. From the sound and its echo I could tell that I was in a small, metal-walled room, and that my unknown companion and I were the only ones here. Outside the room . . . probably a corridor, with others there. Which meant I was in some kind of small building or ship, possibly the one I'd glimpsed attacking us in the buttes. Commodore Freitag's Pravilo force, arriving sooner than I'd expected them to? Or had we indeed found the smuggler we'd been seeking?

And then I paused to evaluate my own condition . . . and realized with a shock that I'd been asleep for at least two days.

There was no doubt about that. The acid feeling in my stomach, plus the emptiness there, was certain proof that I'd skipped more than a couple of meals, while the general lack of hunger and the tenderness in my right upper arm indicated intravenous feeding had taken place.

And from the odd taste in my mouth I could guess that during those lost days I'd undergone pravdrug interrogation.

My unknown companion shifted again . . . and there was no point in putting off the confrontation any longer. Mentally bracing myself, I opened my eyes.

Seated across the small room, watching me closely, was Kutzko.

Relief flooded across my tension . . . and then I looked deeply into Kutzko's face, and the relief was replaced by shame.

Stone-faced, he tapped the phone on the molded table beside him. "Kutzko, sir," he spoke into it. "He's awake."

He got an acknowledgment and turned the instrument off, and for a long moment we eyed each other. "Would—?" I broke off, worked moisture into a desert-dry mouth. "Would it help," I tried again, "if I said I was sorry?"

He regarded me coolly. "I once killed a man in front of you," he said. "You remember?"

How could I forget? He'd been a corporate saboteur, surprised in the act by Lord Kelsey-Ramos, and he'd been practically on top of me when Kutzko had blown three needler cartridges into him. "I remember," I said with a shiver.

"I said I was sorry. Did it help *you*?"

I sighed. "Not really."

His face didn't change, but his sense seemed to soften a bit. "You could have let me in on it," he said. "Could have let me help."

I shook my head. "I couldn't let you put your neck on the block like that for me," I told him.

"Why not?" he countered.

"Because—" I broke off at a sound from the door beside him. The panel whispered open . . . and Randon Kelsey-Ramos strode in.

For a half dozen heartbeats he just gazed at me. "I trust," he said at last, his voice cold, "that you're pleased with yourself."

I swallowed. "Not really, sir," I said.

"No?" he asked, eyebrows raised sardonically. "You mean that spiking through half a dozen major laws—not to mention making your friends look like a lot of smert-heads—you mean that's not really what you were trying to accomplish?"

I gritted my teeth. I'd heard Lord Kelsey-Ramos shrivel people this way before, and Randon definitely had the proper tone of voice. And yet, somewhere under the anger I could sense something that didn't quite fit. "You know why I did it, sir," I said quietly. "And I make no excuses. I knew the consequences, and I'm ready to accept them."

"Ready to accept the consequences, are you?" he shot back. "Ready to accept charges of fraud, grand theft, kidnapping, aiding and abetting a prisoner escape, and a half dozen smaller charges? Ready to accept a sentence of psychological blockage or even total reconstruction? Let me tell you straight out, Benedar, that the *only* reason you're not in a jail cell back on Solitaire is that I laid myself and Carillon down on the line for you."

"I appreciate your support, sir," I said between suddenly stiff lips. *Back on Solitaire*—did that mean we *weren't*, in fact, on the planet? That we were already in deep space, tunneling through the Cloud with Calandra at the Deadman Switch?

My heart froze; but an instant later my fear evaporated. I knew, after all, the sounds of a ship on Mjollnir drive, and I knew the subtle ways Mjollnir-space pseudogravity differed from the real thing. We were still planetside; and if we weren't on Solitaire—

"Well, I'm glad you appreciate *something* about this mess," Randon growled sarcastically.

"But it wasn't just for me that you're fighting Governor Rybakov," I said, trying to interpret the sense I was reading from him. "In fact . . . you're not really having to fight them at all. Are you?"

"I fought them when you were first recaptured," he ground out. "And I may have to do it again. At the moment . . . it turns out that you may be more asset than liability. It all depends."

"On what, sir?"

He grimaced. "On whether or not you and Paquin were hallucinating out there." He took a step toward the door. "Come on."

I glanced at Kutzko, read nothing useful there. "Where are we going?" I asked Randon, swinging my legs carefully over the edge of the bed and sitting up. A rush of dizziness came, faded.

"To see your pet thunderheads, of course," he said. "And you'd better hope the study team out there has come to the same conclusion about them that you have. Otherwise—" he looked me straight in the eye— "I *will* have to fight for you. And decide how much fighting you're worth."

Turning, he headed out into the hall. Swallowing hard, I followed.

The three of us emerged from the Pravilo ship, and I found that we were in the center of a hastily thrown-together encampment about two hundred meters from the four buttes where Calandra and I had been recaptured. A row of mul/terrain cars like the one we'd borrowed from Shepherd Adams was to our left, and fleetingly I wondered what sort of trouble he was in over this. "Where's Calandra?" I asked Randon.

"Still locked up," he said shortly, turning us toward the vehicles. A Pravilo sergeant was waiting at the wheel of the nearest car, clearly expecting us. Randon got in beside him; Kutzko ushered me into the back seat and then joined me.

A couple of minutes later, we were at the buttes.

The encampment at the ship should have prepared me, but I still found myself gaping at the sight that greeted us as we bounced through one of the gaps and came to a halt. The hollow where Calandra and I had set up our camp was crammed full of shiny equipment racks, a half-dozen young techs working busily among them. From the central monitor-type station three flat cables snaked to the edge of the thunderhead city, connecting there to what was probably several square meters of sensor bands and patches liberally plastered across the three nearest thunderheads. Besides the techs at the monitors, there were probably another ten people crouching by the thunderheads or milling about generally, with another five or six Pravilos lounging at various points around the perimeter. One of them—like the driver, clearly alerted in advance—was waiting for us. "Mr. Kelsey-Ramos: gentlemen," he nodded. "This way, please."

We followed him to the group around the thunderheads, and as we approached an older man straightened up. He glanced at Randon and Kutzko, then focused on me, his sense a combination of interest and distaste. "Mr. Benedar," he nodded, his voice and manner reasonably civil. "I'm Dr. Peres Chi, in charge of this so-called thunderhead project of yours."

"You don't believe they're intelligent," I said. It wasn't a question.

His lips compressed momentarily. "Humanity has been waiting to run into another intelligent species for better than four hundred years now," he told me stiffly. "We've put a great deal of thought into the question of identifying and communicating with one, should we ever be lucky enough to run across it. I'll tell you flat out that *these*—" he waved a hand back toward the thunderheads— "don't match up with any of the established guidelines." He took a deep breath. "Having said that . . . I'll admit that we really don't yet know *what* to make of them."

I shifted my eyes over his shoulder. In full daylight, the sense of intelligence and attention was even more apparent than it had been in the dead of night. But it was oddly shifted. Those thunderheads furthest away seemed the most alert, while those closest to us—including the monitored ones—seemed virtually lifeless. "What exactly have you been doing with and to them?" I asked Chi.

He glanced back himself. "Just what you can see.

Metabolic monitoring, full electromagnetic scans for any sort of brain waves, real-time layerscans for organs or organ-like structures. All perfectly non-destructive."

"I'm surprised you had all that equipment lying around Solitaire," Randon put in. His interest was genuine, I sensed; apparently, he was seeing the setup for the first time, as well.

"It's not much more than basic biological study gear," Chi told him. "That plus some variations borrowed from one of the hospitals. Also standard." He fixed me with a cool stare. "We're learning a lot more about thunderheads than anyone up to now has ever wanted to . . . but I can tell you right now that whatever you thought you saw in them, it wasn't sentience."

"If those are the only ones you studied," I said, "I'm not surprised you're having trouble. Those particular ones don't seem very alert at the moment."

The Pravilo officer beside me snorted. "I've heard this one before. You tell people you can put a rock to sleep with hypnosis, and when they ask you to demonstrate you tell them all the rocks in sight are already asleep."

Chi threw him a glance, cocked an eyebrow at me. "Crudely put, perhaps, but you have to admit—"

"There!" I snapped. All three of the thunderheads had abruptly come to life.

Chi spun around. "Where?"

"The thunderheads! Don't you . . . ?"

I hissed through my teeth. The brief flash of intelligence I'd sensed there had gone as quickly as it had come. "It was there. It *was.*"

Chi turned back, eyes flashing with irritation. "Look, Benedar—"

"Why don't we check your monitors?" Randon suggested. "If something really happened, it should have shown up there."

Chi looked at him, took a deep breath. "If you insist. I can tell you right now, though, that it'll turn out to be a false alarm. We've seen them before."

He stalked over to the hollow and the central monitor station. "Give me a composite for the last two minutes," he instructed the young woman sitting there. "All three subjects."

She nodded and tapped keys, and three traces appeared on the display. "There you go," Chi said, waving at them. "Spurious data."

"Wait a minute," I objected. "Who says it's spurious?"

He gave me a patient look. "Just look at the traces. All three virtually identical, *and* all three beginning and ending at the same time. Doesn't that suggest that whatever caused it was some external effect—a mild ground tremor, perhaps—and totally unrelated to the thunderheads?"

I bit at the back of my lip. But I'd sensed their intelligence—could *still* sense it, at least in the further ones—

"Or else," Randon said thoughtfully, "it means they're deliberately turning it on and off in synch."

Chi snorted. "You're arguing your premise."

"Or looking for internal consistency," Randon corrected mildly. "Indulge me a moment, Doctor, and assume they're capable of something that sophisticated. Why would they want to do that?"

"To shake us off their trail," Kutzko spoke up unexpectedly, a hard edge beneath the words. I turned to look at him, found him gazing out at the thunderheads . . . and a chill ran up my back. Kutzko's stance, his eyes, the way his hand hovered near his needler—I'd seen it before. He was sensing the presence of danger . . . "They're trying to make us think that the readings are wrong."

"Ridiculous," Chi snorted. "You're not just postulating intelligence, now, but intelligence equal to humanity's own. Not to mention a sophisticated social structure."

I thought back to the sense Calandra and I had had, that this collection of thunderheads was a city. "You implied you've had other readings like this?" I asked.

"A few," Chi acknowledged grudgingly.

"Exactly the same?"

"I doubt it—we really haven't done the complete

analysis on the data yet." He sighed. "But if it'll make you happy—Karyn, call up all such events, will you? Give a time line, too."

The tech did as instructed. Four records appeared on split sections of the display . . . and Chi hissed between his teeth. "Bozhe moi," he muttered.

"What?" Randon asked sharply.

Chi pointed. "This one was the fourth we've recorded . . . and the time lapse between it and the third is the same as between the third and second . . . *and* between the second and first."

Randon and I exchanged glances. "So they can go dormant," Randon said slowly, "but not indefinitely. Something like a water mammal having to come up at fixed intervals for air."

Chi rubbed his cheek. "Maybe," he conceded reluctantly. "Maybe. It still doesn't prove it's not a natural non-intelligent phenomenon. A normal biologic cycle, perhaps."

"The others aren't following any such cycle," I told him. "It's only the ones you're studying. The rest are watching us."

"So you say," Chi countered. "Can you prove it?"

Randon snorted. "Oh, come on, Doctor. He pointed out to you the exact moment when those three reacted. What more proof do you want that he's seeing something real?"

Chi glared at him. "I'm a scientist, Mr. Kelsey-Ramos," he said evenly. "I deal in facts—provable, scientific facts. Watchers like Benedar deal in feelings and interpretations and beliefs. Faith, not science. I understand the political reasons you want to make him a hero in this, but I have no intention of letting those reasons get in the way of my work."

For a long minute Randon just looked at him, and I watched as Chi went from righteous indignation to discomfort to the distinctly nervous feeling that perhaps he shouldn't have spoken quite so sharply to the heir of the Carillon Group. Randon let him squirm another moment, then turned to gaze again out over the thunderheads. "Tell me, Doctor," he said calmly, "why would something as plant-like as a thunderhead develop intelligence in the first place?"

Chi blinked at the unexpected question. "I don't understand what you're asking."

"They're not mobile, are they? I've seen the original survey team reports—their roots go pretty deep into the ground. Surely they aren't able to pull them up and move elsewhere."

"No, of course not. That's why the whole idea of them being intelligent—"

"Is ridiculous," Randon finished for him. "Yes, we know. And yet, they're aware enough to know that you're studying them. True?"

He hesitated. "We don't yet have any hard evidence of that."

"So check me on it," I suggested, beginning to feel annoyed with the man. "Have Calandra brought here—I presume she's being held somewhere nearby? We'll watch one of your test thunderheads and see if we can both spot the exact moment when it returns again."

Chi made a sour face. "The collusion between two Watchers would hardly—"

"Wait a minute," Kutzko interrupted him, turning to me with a frown. "What do you mean, when it returns again? Returns from where?"

"It was just a figure of speech—" Chi began.

"Quiet," Randon said. "Well, Benedar?"

I opened my mouth . . . closed it again. It *had* been just a figure of speech . . . hadn't it? No; it hadn't. "I don't understand it fully myself," I said at last. "But the thunderheads don't feel dormant so much as they feel . . . empty."

The word seemed to hang in the air, held there by the thick silence that had settled into the hollow. Even without looking I could tell that the techs around us had all ceased their work and were listening.

Chi could tell it, too, and it perhaps kept him from being as sarcastic aloud as he would otherwise have been. "Well," he said at last. "That's a rather interesting interpretation. To say the least."

Randon ignored him. "Are you suggesting that it's not the thunderheads themselves that are sentient? That they're just playing host to some kind of non-physical consciousness?"

"It doesn't have to be that sharp edged, sir," one of the techs spoke up, a bit hesitantly. His eyes flicked to me, as if seeking moral support. "It could be that the thunderheads are indeed sentient, but that they've learned how to . . . well, to allow their spirits to disassociate from their bodies."

Chi glared at his subordinate. "If you don't mind, Allix," he growled, "I'd like to try and handle this without resorting to mysticism. Religious upbringing," he added with thinly veiled contempt to Randon.

The natural person has no room for the gifts of God's Spirit; to him they are folly; he cannot recognize them, because their value can be assessed only in the Spirit . . . "Dr. Chi—"

Randon silenced me with a wave of his hand. "So why is it so ridiculous?" he asked Chi coolly.

The other blinked in surprise. "*Why?* Mr. Kelsey-Ramos—well, all right; for starters, it makes no sense from an evolutionary standpoint—"

"Why not? Especially given that they can't move physically, why shouldn't they have found a way of getting around on a different plane?"

"You're talking mysticism—"

"I'm talking different levels of reality," Randon snapped. "Mjollnir space used to be considered mysticism, too, you know. Superluminal travel, electric currents creating artificial gravity—the whole thing's patently unreal by all the rules that were known half a millennium ago."

"Spare me the history lesson, if you please," Chi said stiffly. "The problem is that there's no way an evolutionary process could have come up with this sort of thing."

"Then forget evolution," I said, suddenly tired of

swimming upstream against this man. "Surely somewere in the Patri and colonies there are more sensitive instruments available—"

"Or in other words," Chi cut me off, "you want the Patri to make a nova-class fuss over this, simply on the strength of a Watcher's word. Let me explain something, Benedar: I have a reputation and a career, and chasing ghosts is *not* how I got them. If we find some evidence—*hard* evidence, I mean—in the next couple of days, then we'll see."

"And if you don't?" Randon asked.

"Then we pack up and go back to Solitaire." Chi's lip twitched knowingly. "And you'll have to make some other kind of deal to get your Watcher back."

Beside me, Kutzko stirred. "Hard evidence, huh?" he asked.

We all looked at him . . . and again I shivered. He was preparing for action . . . "Mikha—"

He turned hard eyes on me, and I shut up. "Your permission, Mr. Kelsey-Ramos?" he asked.

Randon frowned, but nodded. "Go ahead."

Kutzko nodded back and turned to the Pravilo officer still standing nearby. "Sir, I'll need my needler. Please signal your men not to react."

The other eyed him thoughtfully, gave a brisk nod. "Guards!—clear weapon!" he shouted.

"Thank you." Carefully, Kutzko eased his needler from its holster, keeping it pointed at the ground. "Dr. Chi, would you say that the smarter something is, the faster it ought to learn?"

Chi licked his lips nervously. He had no idea where Kutzko was headed with this, but already he didn't like it. "I suppose it would be a fairly accurate generalization."

"Fine." Kutzko looked at me. "Which ones are the most awake, Gilead?"

I swallowed. "Pretty much all of them, except the ones being monitored."

"That one, for instance?" he asked, raising his needler to point it at a nearby thunderhead.

I studied it a moment. "Yes," I acknowledged.

"No change right now?"

"No."

"Fine." He lowered the weapon again and took a quiet preparing breath. "Keep watching it. See if it learns that a needler is something to be afraid of."

He took a few steps toward the thunderhead. Beside me, Chi and Randon were both watching him unblinkingly; from the tight silence in the hollow, I could tell everyone else was doing the same. Lifting his needler, Kutzko aimed at the far bluff and fired twice.

The shots shattered the silence, their ringing echos almost covering the faint insect-whine of the needles ricocheting harmlessly off the distant rock. The silence returned . . . and Kutzko lowered his aim deliberately to the thunderhead he'd indicated—

An icy hand grabbed my heart. "Stop!" I shouted. "Don't shoot!"

The gun didn't move. "I'm not going to," he frowned. "Did it leave?"

I took a deep breath. "Yes, it did," I told him. "Please—lower the gun."

He held the pose another moment, then returned the needler to its holster and started back toward us. "What's wrong?" Randon murmured at my ear.

I shook my head, my brain scrambling to sort out the sensations that had jolted me into shouting my warning. "I don't know, exactly. I felt a sudden surge of emotion from the entire city, directed at Kutzko. And there was a . . . it was like a flicker of light, only too short to really see."

"A flicker of light you couldn't really see, huh?" Chi said dryly. "Well, *that* makes sense."

My stomach knotted with frustration. Peripherally, I noted that the threatened thunderhead had now returned to full consciousness. "The flash was there," I insisted.

Kutzko reached us and stopped. "Well, Doctor?" he asked coolly. "That convince you?"

Chi grimaced. "Not especially. I'm sorry, but again

all we've got here is one man's impressions, without a shred of hard evidence anywhere—"

And a hunch clicked. "Mikha, give me your needler," I cut Chi off.

Kutzko's forehead furrowed slightly. "Sir?" he asked the Pravilo officer.

The other nodded. "Go ahead."

Drawing the gun from its holster, Kutzko offered me the grip. I took it and, gingerly, looked down the muzzle.

A centimeter down the barrel, a spiderweb had appeared, blocking the opening. A spiderweb composed of a dozen ultrathin filaments of metal . . .

Wordlessly, I handed the weapon to Randon. He looked . . . raised his eyes back to mine. "It's blocked," he said, his voice hollow as he offered it to Chi. "Like it'd been . . . spot welded or something."

I nodded, feeling cold all over. "They thought Mikha was going to start shooting at them. This was their way of stopping him."

Chi looked up from the gun, a haunted look in his eyes. "But it *wouldn't* really have blocked the shot. Would it?"

Kutzko took the needler back, and his face hardened as he gazed in at the metal spiderweb. "Probably not," he said. "Does it blazing-well matter?"

Chi took a ragged breath, his gaze drifting almost unwillingly to the thunderheads. To the thunderheads; who in the space of a few seconds had observed, evaluated, and taken precise action . . . "No," he told Kutzko with a shiver. "I don't suppose it matters at all."

CHAPTER 21

I was returned to Solitaire and placed under what seemed to be a form of house arrest aboard the *Bellwether* . . . and for the next six weeks nothing happened.

Or at least, nothing that I expected to happen did so. No one came to charge me with any crimes, or to take me before the judiciary or even to a more official prison; the *Bellwether* made no attempt to leave the planet, let alone the system; and from what I could gather from my limited information sources, there was no reaction at all from the general Solitaran populace over the news that an alien intelligence had just been discovered on their sister world.

All of which implied that, even as courier ships were undoubtedly burning their way through Mjollnir space to bring the news to the Patri hierarchy, somewhere the decision had been made to keep the discovery secret. A bad idea, I thought, for several different reasons. But no one was asking my opinion.

I didn't see Calandra at all during that time. From the face and body language of the guards who brought me my meals I gathered that she too was back aboard, though no one would verbally confirm that. They also wouldn't tell me what, if anything, was happening with her case, and I spent many of the long hours replaying all that had happened and brooding about whether my fumbling attempts had made things any better for her. There was no way to know, and I could only console myself with the knowledge that I certainly hadn't made them any worse.

And finally, six weeks to the day after my imprisonment began, they came to get me.

We landed near the Butte City encampment where I'd first awakened from my pravdrug interrogation, an encampment that had changed drastically in the time I'd been locked up on Solitaire. The ship that had been at its center was still there, but the handful of soft-wall structures had been replaced by ten gleaming prebuilt sectional buildings, including what looked like a clean-room lab and two military-style barracks. The whole area had been cordoned off by a sensor fence, a fence that also enclosed our landing area and stretched out to define a wide corridor to the buttes. From my angle I couldn't tell if the buttes themselves had been fenced off, but I rather thought they had.

I was taken into the lab, and to a large office/workroom already starting to show signs of cluttering . . . and there I met the new head of the thunderhead project.

That he was the head was instantly clear. His manner, his bearing, the subtle exchange of body language between him and my guards—all of it pointed to absolute authority, and to a man accustomed to wearing it. From the way he looked at me—the thoughtful, probing way he sized me up as I walked with my Pravilo escort from the doorway to his desk—it was similarly clear that he was a man of science and not simply some Patri official or bureaucrat.

Just as it was clear that he didn't especially like me.

"Gilead Benedar, sir," the head of my escort identified me. "Brought here as per your instructions."

The scientist's eyes flicked to him. "Thank you, Captain. You and the others may go."

The other nodded and signaled to his men, and the scientist and I were left alone.

For a long moment he continued to study me, giving me a vague feeling of being under a microscope. "So *you're* a Watcher," he said at last. "Not exactly what I was expecting."

I looked at his face, read the lie there. "That surprises me, sir," I told him evenly. Another flicker—"Especially since you've read all the information the Patri has on Watchers in general and on me in particular."

His reaction was mild surprise, open and obvious enough to practically light up the room. More confirmation, if I'd needed it, that he'd spent his life in science, insulated from the darker political and business worlds where a man usually learned to shield his thoughts and emotions more carefully.

But the surprise disappeared quickly, replaced by a strong and probably habitual skepticism. "Easy guess," he grunted. "Of course I would have learned all I could before deciding to send for you."

Another lie . . . "Perhaps," I nodded. "Except that it wasn't really your idea to send for me. You don't like me, you didn't want me here, and you'd very much like an excuse to toss me back off Spall and be done with it."

His face turned to stone, whatever traces of patronizing amusement he'd been feeling vanishing like smoke. "I see," he said through stiff lips. "Oh—please continue, since you know so much. If I don't want you, why are you here?"

"Because you need my help," I told him. "Because something about the thunderheads has you stymied, and you've been reduced to grasping at straws."

He gazed steadily at me. "Do you know who I am?"

I shook my head. "My experience lately has mostly been in business and—"

"I'm Dr. Vlad Eisenstadt."

I swallowed. It was a name even people preoccupied

with business had heard of. A true Renaissance man of science, he was said to be equally proficient in biology, chemistry, cybernetics, and neuropsychology. In retrospect, I suppose, it was obvious that the Patri would have picked someone like him for this job. "I see, sir," I said, not knowing what else to say.

"I'm a scientist, Benedar," he continued. "I deal with the objective world, and I distrust anything that is by nature subjective. Near the top of that list are mind-reading stunts and religions of all sorts."

"You sound like Dr. Chi," I murmured.

His sense took on a distinctly sour tinge. "Perhaps. It was he who recommended we call you in."

I blinked. "That's . . . very interesting, sir."

Something like a breath of relief touched his sense. Relief, and—paradoxically—a touch of disappointment, as well. "So you *can't* really read minds," he said, almost as if to himself.

"No, sir," I shook my head. "I would think the Patri files on the Watchers would have made that clear."

His lips tightened, and I could see he was trying to decide whether to terminate the interview right here and now. "If it helps, Dr. Eisenstadt," I offered, "I *was* able to sense what seemed to be emotional changes in the thunderheads the last time."

He nodded, not particularly impressed. "That much our sensors can do," he told me. "What we need—" He hesitated. "What we want is some way to determine when one of them is dead."

I blinked. "Excuse me?"

"What's the matter?—isn't the question clear enough?" he growled. "I want to know if there's a way to distinguish between a thunderhead that's dead and one that's just out . . . visiting."

I looked at him, listening to the way that last word echoed through my mind. "This bothers you, doesn't it?" I asked him quietly. "The idea that there could be something in us that exists independently of the physical body—"

"If you want to talk religion, Benedar," he cut me off

harshly, "you can do it alone in a Solitaran prison cell. All I want from you is one answer, yes or no: can you find me a dead thunderhead?" He glared at me. "And if the answer is no, then we'll just have to go out and choose one at random to dissect."

I stared at him, throat tightening as understanding belatedly poured in on me. *Man of God, he said, may my life and the lives of these fifty servants of yours count for something in your eyes* . . . "What if you guess wrong?" I asked, striving for calmness. "What if you kill one of them?"

"What if we do?" he countered.

I took a deep breath, searching for some sort of non-religious answer to give him . . . and in that pausing, the emotion cleared somewhat from my vision, and I saw that the answer I sought was already there, buried in Eisenstadt's own expression. "If you do," I told him evenly, "what happened to Mikha Kutzko's needler could happen again. To your people."

His mouth twisted derisively; but it was a habitual derision, devoid of any strength. The attempt to block the muzzle of Kutzko's needler was abundant proof that the thunderheads had both the intelligence and the means to defend themselves, and Eisenstadt knew it. "There are ways to safeguard against that," he said anyway, clearly determined not to admit even rational fears in front of me. "But if it turns out that these things are more intelligent than, say, dogs or horses, it might strain future relations if we began by killing one."

His sense held very little doubt that such an intelligence level did in fact exist, but I passed over the chance to call him on yet another half-truth. "I understand," I told him, "and I'll do what I can. But I'll need Calandra's help."

Again, his mouth twisted. "Yes, I rather expected you'd ask for her—your crusade to save her from the Deadman Switch borders on the obsessive. Give me one good reason why I should let her get any more involved with this matter than she already is."

"Because two of us together will have a better chance

of finding what you want than either of us singly," I told him simply. "And because it's in your best interests and those of the Patri to make the chances of failure as small as possible."

He snorted. "By that logic, I should invite a whole colony of Watchers here."

I shrugged. "I agree."

He glared at me, a token attempt at intimidation as he pretended to be weighing my words. In actual fact, I could tell he'd already decided that Calandra's presence was something he could tolerate. Especially given the potentially disastrous consequences if he didn't. "All right," he growled at last, shoving his chair back and standing up. "Let's go collect your friend and get out to the test area. Just remember that she'll be right up there with you when we start cutting . . . and if you choose wrong, you two will be among the first the thunderheads will fry."

And if that happened, the *Bellwether* would have to choose from one of its own to man the Deadman Switch on its journey out . . . "Yes, sir," I said, my lips dry. "I understand."

We didn't go ourselves to wherever Calandra's cell was—Eisenstadt changed his mind at the last minute and sent a pair of Pravilos for her instead while he and I proceeded along the fenced-off corridor to the Butte City. We were there, and I was studying and marveling at the elaborate sensor gear that had been attached to several of the thunderheads, when she was finally brought in.

I didn't know where she'd been kept all this time, or under what conditions; but it was abundantly clear that she hadn't been treated as politely as I had. Her face was pale and noticeably thinner, her movements as she got out of the car vaguely hesitant. I took a step toward her, paused as I saw the warning in her guards' eyes, and waited instead for them to come to us.

"You all right?" I asked her quietly, reaching forward

as she approached to take her hand. The skin was cool, but was warming up even as I held it.

"As well as can be expected," she said, her sense a mixture of irritation and tiredness and resignation. And in her eyes—

Abruptly, it clicked. "Pravdrugs?" I asked, turning my head to stare at Eisenstadt. "For the whole six weeks?"

A muscle in his cheek twitched. "Off and on during them, yes," he said coolly. "We needed to know as much as we could about the thunderheads; and as you yourself implied, she was a somewhat better observer than you were."

"And, of course, no one with the Carillon Group's influence was watching to make sure no one abused her like that?" I bit out.

His forehead darkened with anger. "If I were you, Benedar, I wouldn't push my luck too far. You're out on a pretty warm ice bridge yourself, and the minute you stop being useful there's likely to be a very fast thaw."

I glared back at him; but before I could say anything Calandra squeezed my hand warningly. "It's okay," she said. "He's right. And besides . . ." Her eyes drifted out over the sea of thunderheads, and I felt her hand stiffen. "Whatever's going on here, it's something we need to know about."

I looked at her, back at Eisenstadt, and swallowed my anger. "Where do you want us to start?"

A flicker of relief touched Eisenstadt's face. "Let's try over here," he said, the same relief evident in his voice. Clearly, Calandra and I weren't nearly as expendable as he wanted us to believe. I filed the fact away for possible future reference and we followed him to the edge of the thunderhead city.

"We've found several places along their skin where we can pick up neuroelectric signals," he said, squatting down beside one of the thunderheads and gingerly indicating places along its side and atop the curving crest. I noticed that he was careful not to actually touch the creature, wondered if perhaps the scientists had

had a second demonstration of the thunderheads' defensive capabilities. "We can detect well enough when the thing is . . . vacant . . . but so far every one we've found has come back within the decay limit."

"The what?" I asked.

"Decay limit." Eisenstadt's general discomfort deepened a bit. "While the bodies are empty there's a subtle form of tissue decay going on. Nothing particularly serious, but our projections indicate that if the thing stays away longer than about two hours, irreversible damage will begin to set in."

Calandra shivered. "As if they really were dead."

The word hung in the air for a moment. Temporarily dead thunderheads; permanently dead zombis. Nowhere in Solitaire system, it seemed, could you get away from death.

"Whatever," Eisenstadt said at last. "We suspect that that limitation implies that this wasn't a talent that evolved along with their physical development."

I cleared the image of death from my mind. "So. You set up your sensors on one of the thunderheads, who promptly runs out when he sees you coming, and then you have to wait another two hours before you can tell whether it's dead or just off somewhere hiding."

Eisenstadt nodded sourly. "That's basically it—and we'd just as soon not have to go through the whole exercise with all two hundred forty-one of the smertputrid things. And *then* maybe have to go outside to hunt one down anyway."

I looked at Calandra. "What do you think?"

A slight frown creased her forehead. "It would be a little like trying to single out a particular conversation in a crowded room," she said. "And from a fair distance, too. It's going to be tricky."

"Why from a distance?" Eisenstadt demanded. "Why can't you just go up to one of them—?"

He broke off, looking annoyed with himself as the answer came. "Oh. Right. They spook too easily."

Slowly, Calandra let her gaze sweep the thunderheads. "There," she said, pointing. "Fourth back from the edge. Is that one . . . ?"

She trailed off. I stared at the thunderhead she'd indicated, searching with all my powers of observation for signs of sentience . . . "I don't know," I murmured finally. "It's hard to tell."

Out of the corner of my eye, I saw Calandra lick her lips. "Well . . . there's one way to find out. Maybe."

She started forward, walking carefully out toward the thunderhead. I watched closely . . . and saw the subtle change. "It's gone," I called to her.

"Yes," she agreed, coming to a halt. For a moment she stood there watching it; then, almost reluctantly, she turned and came back to where Eisenstadt and I stood. "I don't think this is going to work, Dr. Eisenstadt," she sighed. "The signs are too subtle—" she waved a hand helplessly— "and there's just too much interference from the others around here."

He gave her a look that was equal parts contempt and disgust. "What about you, Benedar?" he said, turning the look on me. "You giving up, too?"

The threat beneath the words was abundantly clear: if we couldn't or wouldn't help his investigation, we would be summarily returned to our cells. From which I would go to stand trial before the Solitaran judiciary; from which Calandra would be taken to her long-over-due execution aboard the *Bellwether*. "What about the thunderheads outside the Butte City?" I asked, searching desperately for a straw to grasp at. "Surely some of them must have died, too."

"Some of them have," Eisenstadt growled. "Unfortunately, the two or three we've located have been dead long enough for the local scavengers to have made a mess of them. More to the point, they never show up in groups of larger than four out there, and I have no interest in trekking all over Spall sifting through groups that small for a fresh corpse. This—right here—is our best chance; and it's your *only* chance to put all those high-minded religious principles of yours to work. If you can't, then we go out and pull up one of the things at random."

I took a deep breath. "Sir . . ."

And at my side Calandra suddenly seemed to tense up. "What?" I interrupted myself, turning to her.

She was gazing unseeingly out over the thunderheads. "Perhaps, sir," she said quietly, her voice taut with a strange reluctance, "we could try asking the thunderheads themselves."

Eisenstadt snorted. "Oh, certainly," he said, dripping sarcasm. "What do you suggest we use: sign language or dot code?"

Calandra hesitated. "It . . . may be easier than that," she said hesitantly. She looked at me, eyes pleading—

And suddenly I understood. "Yes," I agreed, my stomach tightening. A long, long shot indeed; and I could just hear what Eisenstadt would say when I suggested it. The thought made me wince . . . but if there was even a chance it would work . . . "Yes," I said again, putting as much confidence into the word as I could and bracing myself for what was to come. "It's certainly worth a try. Dr. Eisenstadt . . . we're going to need an aircar."

CHAPTER 22

Shepherd Denvre Adams listened in silence until Eisenstadt had finished. He looked at me, at Calandra, at the sea of thunderheads beside us. "What you're suggesting," he said quietly, "is blasphemy."

Eisenstadt's lip twisted. "Look, I understand how you feel about this—"

"I doubt that, sir," Adams cut him off. "I doubt it very much. At any rate, I won't do it."

Eisenstadt threw a razor-edged glare at me, and I cringed at the raw frustrated anger boiling out at me. Just convincing him to give this a try had taken every bit of my persuasive powers, and he'd made it abundantly clear at the outset that it was going to be on my head if it didn't work out. Now, it didn't look like we were going to get even that far. "I wonder, sir," I said to Eisenstadt, "if Calandra and I could talk with Shepherd Adams privately."

"Why?" he demanded.

Calandra got the answer out first. "Because we *do* understand how he feels," she said.

Eisenstadt turned his glare onto her. Unexpectedly, though, the reflexive refusal he'd been preparing to

219

give seemed to get lost somewhere en route. "You've
got five minutes," he said instead. Turning his back, he
stomped away to the central monitoring station.

"You can't convince me," Adams warned me . . . but
there was more than a hint of uncertainty beneath his
quiet defiance.

"What are you afraid of?" I asked him.

"I already told you. Blasphemy. To even suggest that
God is nothing more than a group of sentient plants—"

"No one's suggesting that," I insisted. "All we're
saying is that the thunderheads may be what you hear
when you're meditating."

"Is that all?" he asked with probably as much sarcasm
as the man was capable of. "You just want to prove that
God isn't speaking to us?"

"But if He's not—"

"If He's not, there are still benefits to be had from
the act of meditation," he said stubbornly. "As well as
from our fellowship here."

I eyed him, mentally preparing myself. For years I'd
watched Lord Kelsey-Ramos appeal to logic and self-
interest to persuade people to his point of view; now, it
was my turn to try. Fleetingly, I wished he was here
to do it for me. "I realize that, sir—don't forget that I
had the chance to observe some of those benefits first
hand. But that's not what's at issue here. The question
is whether Halo of God doctrine does, in fact, conflict
with the real universe . . . and if it does, you know as
well as I do that you can't hold it back."

"Not forever, no," he said evenly. "But perhaps for
awhile."

Calandra snorted. "And what would that gain you?
Unless you plan to get out from under your creation
before the whole thing collapses."

The corners of Adams's mouth tightened in anger. "I
did not 'create' the Halo of God," he bit out. "Not for
my own gain, not for anything else. It happened far
more spontaneously than that, among a great many
people."

"Then why be afraid of the truth?" I asked.

He looked back at me, and his gaze hardened. "You think it's for myself that I'm worried? I'd have thought a Watcher would understand me better."

I waited, and after a moment he sighed. "All right. Assume for a moment that your theory is right, that Dr. Eisenstadt's people have proved God isn't actually speaking to us here. How long do you think it will be until someone makes the obvious generalization?—that *all* manifestations of God must be similarly in error?"

It wasn't, unfortunately, a scenerio that could be totally dismissed. "Those who've experienced God's presence in their own lives will know better."

"And what of those who are young in their faith?" he countered. "I've seen what the subtle pressures of this society can do to them."

But as soon as the sun came up they were scorched and, not having any roots, they withered away . . .
"You can't protect them forever," I said.

"I know that." He hesitated. "But perhaps I *can* protect them until their roots are a little stronger."

"Protect them," Calandra asked quietly, "with a lie?"

A muscle in Adams's cheek twitched. "I'm sure they'd understand. Afterwards."

"Do you really believe that?" Calandra demanded, a hard edge to her voice. On her face I could see her struggle with all the memories she would have preferred to have left buried. "Well, I don't. Because I lived on Bridgeway under Aaron Balaam darMaupine. Do you know what happened to his followers after his theocracy was overthrown?"

Adams winced in sympathetic pain. "They were scattered. Those who weren't tried as accomplices and imprisoned."

"That's right," she nodded. "And there's a curious thing about that. Those accomplices—the ones who were closest to him, the ones who knew what he was doing—many of them have kept their faith. Such as it was." The hardness in her gaze faded into a sort of bitter sadness. "Most of the others, the ones he lied to . . . we didn't."

For a long minute the quiet background conversation of the techs at their stations and the hiss of wind whistling between the bluffs were the only sounds in the hollow. Adams gazed out at the thunderheads, his sense a no-win struggle between the logic of the situation and his desire to protect his people. "When we first met," I reminded him gently, "you told us you appreciated our honesty. If you really meant that, you have to offer that same honesty to your followers. And to yourself."

He closed his eyes, and I could see moisture at the edges of the eyelids . . . and I knew that he was seeing the beginning of the end. "It would probably be best," he said at last, the words coming out with difficulty, "if there were at least two of us present. To try and confirm between us . . . what it is we hear."

Eisenstadt was far from happy at the prospect of letting still another outsider in under his tight-locked security umbrella, and he again came very near to vetoing the whole experiment right then and there. But as a scientist he could hardly argue against the reasonableness of having more than one interpreter present, and in the end he gave in. Adams suggested Shepherd Joyita Zagorin be the other Seeker, and a Pravilo aircar was sent to bring her from the Myrrh settlement.

And an hour later, all was ready.

They sat side by side at the edge of the thunderhead city, looking up through the tangle of sensor leads attached to them as Eisenstadt ran through his instructions one final time. ". . . And remember, nothing fancy this time around," he told them, trying mightily not to let his complete skepticism over this whole thing show through. "Concentrate on expressing our goodwill to them, and see if you get any kind of similar feeling in return."

"Don't you want them to ask about recently dead thunderheads?" I murmured to him.

A flash of annoyance. "Let's take this one step at a time, Benedar, all right?" he muttered back. "*If* the sensors show evidence that this trance state of theirs has anything unusual to it, *then* maybe we'll try to go for some specifics."

And if not, I heard the rest of his thought, there was no point wasting any more time than necessary listening to gibberish from religious fanatics. Fleetingly, I considered making some kind of comment; but there really wasn't anything to say. The only thing that would make a dent in his skepticism would be clear and positive results.

I could only pray there would be some.

Adams nodded. "We understand," he told Eisenstadt. He took a deep breath. "Silence would be helpful to our concentration."

Eisenstadt took the hint and shut up, and I watched as Adams and Zagorin closed their eyes and slipped into their meditative trance.

The last time this had happened in my presence I'd missed seeing the actual transition. This time, paying close attention, I still almost missed it. One moment Adams was sitting quietly, his breathing slowing as all emotion seemed to drain from his sense; the next, it was all somehow different.

"It's started," I murmured to Eisenstadt. At his other side, Calandra added her agreement.

Eisenstadt nodded. "Kiell?" he called softly over his shoulder.

One of the techs stirred in his seat. "Well . . . *something's* happening," he said, his tone vaguely troubled. "The readings started looking like normal rest mode, but now . . ."

"But now what?" Eisenstadt prompted, his sense wavering between irritation and genuine interest.

The tech never got the chance to answer. Abruptly, Adams and Zagorin straightened simultaneously where they sat, and both sets of eyes came fully open. Open . . . but with a disturbing glaze to them. "Greetings to you," the two Seekers said in unison, both voices the same husky whisper. "We are the—" something I couldn't catch. "We welcome you to our . . . world."

CHAPTER 23

For a long moment we all just stood there. Eisenstadt was the first to move; and, predictably, it was to me he turned, an uncertain thunder in his expression. "If this is some sort of game, Benedar . . ."

The reflexive accusation died midway, and he swallowed hard. Even to him, it had to be clear that this was no trick. The odd blankness in the two Seekers' eyes, the subtle contorting of their faces, the abnormal timbres in their voices—none of it could have been faked. "It's no game, sir," I murmured. "They're in contact—somehow—with the thunderheads."

Eisenstadt exhaled between his teeth in a snake-like hiss. Adams and Zagorin were still sitting as they had after delivering their message, faces and bodies frozen as stiffly as normal human muscles could handle. Waiting for Eisenstadt's response . . . "Aren't you going to say something?" I prompted him quietly.

Eisenstadt's jaw tightened. "I . . . greet you as well," he managed. A touch of annoyance crossed his face as some of the initial shock faded and he abruptly realized that he was now speaking for posterity. And not doing a particularly memorable job of it. "I am Dr. Vlad

Eisenstadt, representing the Four Worlds of the Patri and their colonies," he continued, somewhat more firmly this time. "Who, may I ask, have I the honor of addressing?"

A moment of silence. Then Adams and Zagorin spoke, again in that oddly hoarse whisper, and again in unison. "My identity can . . . not be put into this . . . kind of speech. We are . . ." The voices faded.

Eisenstadt leaned forward slightly, cocking one ear forward. "I'm sorry; what was that?"

"They can't answer," Calandra spoke up, a slight wavering to her voice. Her face—what I could see of it—looked both awestruck and more than a little shaken. "Their faces—watch their faces and the way their throats contract. Whatever the word is, they simply can't pronounce it."

Eisenstadt pursed his lips, considering. "With your permission, then," he said, "we'll continue to call you by our name for you: thunderheads. Unless that word should be used to distinguish between you and your physical hosts. They *are* just hosts for you, aren't they?"

A pause; and when Adams and Zagorin spoke again, I could hear a slight hesitation in their voices. "Not hosts. Bodies . . . homes . . . fortresses. Safety. Life."

"Ah," Eisenstadt nodded, a bit cautiously. "Yes—bodies." He considered. "You mention safety. What kind of safety do these bodies provide you?"

Silence. To me it was obvious that Eisenstadt was fishing for details about the thunderheads' defenses. Perhaps it was obvious to the thunderheads, too. "I don't think they're going to answer," I murmured after a minute.

"Afraid to?" he asked. "Or just a lack of vocabulary?"

I considered. "Afraid or distrusting, I'd say. The sense here is different than it was when they were trying to find a way to describe their body-homes, so I don't think it's a vocabulary problem."

He grunted and turned to Calandra. "You agree?"

"That the senses were different in the two instances, yes," she nodded. "Whether the emotion behind it should be interpreted as fear or something else, I don't know."

"I thought you Watchers were supposed to be able to read anybody you wanted to," he grumbled.

"Anybody human," she corrected him softly. "At the moment . . . they aren't."

The muscles in Eisenstadt's cheeks tightened . . . and abruptly his sense, too, changed. "Yes, well, maybe you religious types believe in demonic possession," he said, almost briskly. "But I don't. You—Smyt—swivel Adams around a little so that he and Zagorin can't see each other."

I frowned as Smyt and one of the other techs moved to obey. "Sir, there's no way they can be cueing each other. The synchronization is just too close."

"We'll see about that, won't we?" Eisenstadt said coolly. For just a minute, I realized, he'd been caught up in the same sense of awe and wonder as Calandra and I over what was happening; but that minute was over, and now the scientist in him had reemerged, hard-headed and skeptical. "What kind of readings are we getting?" he added over his shoulder to the techs at the monitors.

"Weird ones," one of them reported. "Heart rate, blood pressure, and cell metabolism index are way down. Neuron and brainwave patterns—" he hesitated. "Frankly, Doctor, I don't know how to read this. There are strong elements of mental hyperactivity—localized at highly unusual sites—but there are also elements of deep sleep. *Really* deep sleep—just barely this side of comatose. By all rights, they should both be flat on their backs, snoring away."

Eisenstadt chewed at his lip. "Does any of it correspond to other known forms of meditation?"

"Not that I can tell. Of course, the records we've got here weren't designed to be an exhaustive listing."

"Sir," another tech put in, "it looks like their metabolic rates are still going down. Gradually, but noticeably."

"Potentially life-threatening?" Eisenstadt asked.

"I . . . don't know. Possibly."

Eisenstadt nodded, a slightly sour expression on his face. "You—thunderheads—are you still there?"

Adams's and Zagorin's faces contorted slightly in unison. "Where is *there?*"

"I meant are you still . . . in contact with us." Eisenstadt took a careful breath, his emotional resistance to accepting all this at face value fighting visibly against the recognition that we could be running up against a time limit. "We'd like to learn more about you—sharing knowledge of us in return, of course. Part of the study we would like to do—"

"We have no desire to . . . learn more about you."

Eisenstadt floundered a second, his line of thought bent by the interruption. "Yes. Well. Part of the study we would like to do would involve a dead thunderhead and a procedure called dissection. Would it be possible for us to have—?"

"There is no death."

Eisenstadt took a careful breath. "Ah . . . yes. Perhaps I didn't make myself clear. What we'd like—"

"Body-homes may die. We do not."

"Yes—that's what I meant," Eisenstadt tried again. "It's one of your body-homes that we'd like to study. If you could indicate an unused one for us and give us permission—"

"You may have a drone to . . . study."

Eisenstadt paused in mid-sentence. "A drone? What's that?"

"Body-home grown from ster . . . ilized seed for use of . . . any who needs it."

For a moment Eisenstadt seemed taken aback. "What do you mean, any who needs it? Don't all of you have your own body-homes?"

Again, the answer was silence. "They told us their body-homes can die," Calandra reminded Eisenstadt softly. "Perhaps growing spare bodies is their version of immortality."

Eisenstadt threw her a sharp look. "Let's try and keep metaphysics out of this," he growled at her . . . but behind the words I could hear his acute uneasiness with the idea. "All right, thunderhead, we accept. Can you point one of these drones out to us?"

A slight pause. Then, in unison as always, Zagorin and Adams each raised an arm and pointed. "There," they whispered. "Two thousand four hundred . . . eighty-seven heights."

"Which heights?" Eisenstadt asked. "Ours, yours? These mountains'?"

"Doctor!" one of the monitors called before the Seekers could answer. "Getting cardiac runaway in Adams!"

"Adams! Break contact!"

It took me half a second to realize that the shout had come from me. The twisted expression on Adams's face—the sudden tension throughout his body—it almost literally screamed to me of lethal stress. I took a step toward him—

And was brought up sharply by Eisenstadt's hand on my arm. "Doctor—!"

"Let's wait and see what the thunderheads do," he told me, his voice rigid. "Whether or not they release him on their own."

I twisted my head to stare at him, not believing it. "And if they don't?" I snapped.

His eyes stayed on Adams. "We need to know what kind of value the thunderheads place on human life. This is as good a time as any to find out."

Because Adams was a Halloa. A religious fanatic . . . and therefore expendable. I clenched my teeth hard enough to hurt and turned back to the Seekers. Adams's stress was still growing—becoming critical— "Thunderhead!" I shouted. "You're killing him! Let him go!"

For a long second nothing happened. Then, abruptly, the alien sense was gone from both Adams and Zagorin. Zagorin slumped, breathing hard through slack lips—

As Adams collapsed, unconscious, to the ground.

The physician on Eisenstadt's team was young, brisk, and—unlike many I'd known—perfectly willing to admit to a certain degree of professional ignorance. "If you want the bottom line," he said, shaking his head, "it's that I can't tell you what exactly happened to him."

Eisenstadt glowered. "And that's the best you can do?"

"Oh, no," the physician said, undaunted by his superior's displeasure. "I said I didn't know what happened; that's *not* to say I can't treat the results." He leaned over his desk to call up a display. "Here, for instance, he shows signs of having had a mild stroke—we're already cleaning up the damage there." Another display. "Cardiac trauma. We'll probably wind up having to rebuild parts of his heart, but for the moment he's perfectly stable. Ditto for the other bits of scattered damage he sustained."

Eisenstadt nodded. "What about the woman?"

The physician shrugged. "Mild stress-related traumas in heart and central nervous system. No permanent damage, though."

"Why not?" I asked. "Because she's younger than he is?"

"That's a large part of it," the physician nodded. "Mr. Adams also had a definite predisposition to cardiac problems going into . . . whatever it was he went into."

"Which the stress then triggered," Eisenstadt nodded, ignoring the physician's thinly veiled curiosity. "Could you say, then, that any normally healthy person, having undergone the same stress, would come out of it all right?"

The physician cocked an eyebrow. "I'd hardly say *that*, Doctor—certainly not with just two casepoints to extrapolate from. It could just as easily be that Ms. Zagorin has stronger than average resistance to whatever it was happened to the two of them."

Eisenstadt considered that a moment. "All right, then," he said slowly. "Having seen what this stress does . . . would it be possible to somehow pretreat someone so as to minimize the resulting damage?"

The other shrugged. "If the results of the stress remain consistent, certainly. Again, having seen only two casepoints I can't guarantee that the next person won't develop something entirely different."

Eisenstadt's lip twisted. "I suppose it's a chance we'll just have to take. When can we see Ms. Zagorin?"

The physician called up another display. "Give her another few minutes, anyway," he said. "No permanent damage doesn't mean that the thing wasn't traumatic for her. Besides which, the longer you give us to wash the preventatives and diagnostics out of her system, the more coherent she'll be."

Eisenstadt nodded. "Thank you," he said.

We left the office. Calandra, along with her usual pair of Pravilos, was waiting out in the hall; without even looking at her, Eisenstadt took her arm and led the two of us down to an empty conference room. "Wait outside," he told the Pravilos briefly. Ushering us in, he closed the door.

For a long minute he just looked at us, a whole range of conflicting emotions following each other across his face. "Well?" he growled at last, somewhat reluctantly. "Let's have your opinions."

Not our report, I noted, but our opinions. Boldfacing the subjectivity of our talents. Still, he *had* asked, and even grudging interest was a step up. "Both Shepherd Adams and Shepherd Zagorin were in contact with one or more of the thunderheads," I told him. "There simply isn't room for fraud or error in what happened out there."

He snorted. "Much as I might wish it were otherwise, I have to agree. Assuming, of course, that the search teams find a dead thunderhead in the direction they gave us. So. The thunderheads are alive and sentient and they really *can* travel out of their bodies. What can you tell me about them?"

I gestured Calandra to go first. "They're clearly intelligent, first of all," she said slowly, forehead furrowed in thought and memory. "I'd guess they've been studying *us* for quite some time. At least as long as the Halo of God has been here; possibly since the first colonists arrived at Solitaire."

"What makes you say that?" Eisenstadt frowned.

"Their ability to use human speech apparatus to communicate, for starters," Calandra said. "Besides that—" She hesitated, looking at me.

And a piece fell into place. "The general paranoia on Solitaire," I said. "It's a subconscious resistance to the thunderheads' presence, isn't it?"

Her eyes were oddly haunted. "I think so, yes."

I could see Eisenstadt debating whether or not to pursue this line further, deciding to shelve it for the moment. "All right; so you think the thunderheads are intelligent and that they've been studying us. What else?"

Calandra took a deep breath. "Obviously . . . they're also the ones who've been guiding our ships to Solitaire for the past seventy years."

The muscles in Eisenstadt's jaw tightened . . . but the thought was clearly not a new one to him. "They're certainly the most likely candidates," he admitted. "You have anything on that besides guesswork?"

"The way their arms moved," I said slowly, replaying the contact in my mind's eye. "The muscle sequences they went through when they pointed the way to the dead thunderhead." I focused on Eisenstadt, found him looking intently back at me. "It was virtually identical to the hand movements I saw in the *Bellwether*'s . . . on our trip into Solitaire system."

His eyes bored into mine. "You certain?"

"As certain as I can be," I said.

"So why, then," he asked softly, "has it taken them this long to communicate with us?"

I shook my head. "I don't know."

He pursed his lips, and for a moment the room was silent. "What about Zagorin?" he asked at last. "Could she have picked up anything herself during the contact, or was she acting purely as a medium?"

"No idea, sir." I looked at Calandra. "You?"

She shook her head. "You'll just have to ask her yourself."

He nodded, an odd reluctance evident in his sense. "Yes, I'd planned on doing that. I just thought—well, never mind." He seemed to brace himself. "I suppose that . . . now that we know how to get through to the thunderheads, your part in this is pretty much over."

He stopped . . . and I saw what it was he couldn't allow himself to say. "With your permission, Dr. Eisenstadt," I said into the silence, "Calandra and I would both very much like to continue on with this. Having gone this far, we'd like to see it through." I looked at Calandra, saw she understood what I was doing, and why. "Curiosity aside, we might still wind up being of some use to you."

Relief virtually flooded into Eisenstadt's sense, all the confirmation I needed that my reading of him had been correct. To verbally acknowledge our worth and ask us to stay on had been a sacrifice of humility he hadn't been willing or able to make. But now that pride had been satisfied—now that he could see himself as doing *us* a favor, instead of the other way around—he could get what he'd wanted all along. "You might be of some value, at that," he agreed. "I'll pull some strings with the governor, see what she can do. In the meantime—" he glanced at his watch— "let's go talk to Zagorin. See what she remembers about her contact. If anything."

I nodded, and together we left . . . and it wasn't until we were out of the room that the significance of what I'd just done suddenly struck me. Barely two months ago I'd felt real agony over the ethics of using my Watcher insight to manipulate people to my wishes; now, I'd done precisely the same thing to Eisenstadt without the slightest qualms or hesitation.

For the best of motives, of course: those of protecting Calandra's life. *No one can have greater love than to lay down his life for his friends* . . . I let that scripture run over and over through my mind as we walked down the hallway with the two Pravilos. And tried to ignore another saying, nearly as old, nagging at the back of my mind. A saying that spoke of the road to hell . . . and how that road was paved.

CHAPTER 24

After what the physician had said about the effects of the drugs Zagorin had been given, I wondered privately whether trying to talk to her now would wind up being a waste of time. Those fears, at least, proved groundless. Zagorin was awake, alert, and coherent, and though she was clearly tired she was willing to help.

Except that in her case, good intentions merely paved the road to nowhere.

"I'm sorry, Dr. Eisenstadt," she said tiredly, for probably the fifth time. "Believe me, I would be happy to tell you everything, if only to get this over with. I just don't have the words—I don't *have* them, period. The contact was like—" She waved a hand vaguely, let it drop back to the bed beside her. "The feelings, the sensations . . ." Her face contorted with the effort, but again she was forced to give up.

Eisenstadt stared at her a moment longer, his sense going through contortions of its own as he struggled to hang onto his patience. "Opinion?" he growled, turning to me.

"She's not just being uncooperative," I assured him. "She really *can't* find the right words."

"Perhaps a dose of pravdrug would help her vocabulary," he suggested, throwing her a darkly sour look.

"I doubt it," Calandra spoke up, her first words since we'd entered the room. "The problem isn't vocabulary. There's some sort of blockage in her ability to speak."

Eisenstadt frowned at her. "You mean a mild aphasia? Nothing like that showed up on her brain scans."

Calandra shrugged fractionally. "It may not be totally physical in origin. Perhaps it was a side effect of the way the thunderheads used her speech center to talk to us."

"Perhaps." Eisenstadt stroked his chin thoughtfully, his sense suddenly suspicious. "Or maybe it was done deliberately."

I looked at Zagorin, saw her own sudden tension there. "Why would they do something like that?" I asked Eisenstadt. "If they didn't want to talk to us—"

"Oh, they wanted to talk, all right," he grunted. "But if you were paying attention, you may have noticed that they didn't exactly give us a gigapix of useful information. Certainly nothing we didn't already know or couldn't easily find out. Maybe there was something they didn't want us to know, but that they couldn't hide from their co-opted mouthpieces."

I felt the first stirrings of annoyance. There he was, jumping to worse-case conclusions again. "I don't suppose it occurred to you that they might just be nervous," I pointed out with perhaps more heat than was really called for.

"Oh, it occurred to me, all right," he countered. "Did it ever occur to *you* that they could just as easily be hiding some massive plot against humanity?"

"What?—here in the middle of nowhere?" I snorted.

He eyed me coldly. "You and Ms. Paquin have already stated you believe the thunderheads are creating tension in the people of Solitaire. Our communication with them so far has been entirely on *their* terms and under *their* control; now, you tell me that—intentionally or otherwise—they're hanging onto that control even after the communication is ended."

Coincidence, I thought. Coincidence, or else simply the normal misunderstandings and gropings that should be expected in a first contact between two such different species. "If you assume the worst of people," I murmured, "you'll often get it."

"Maybe," he conceded stiffly. "And I'm sure you religious types would rather err on the generous side than take the risk of bruising someone's pride. But we can't afford that kind of naivete here." His glare flicked to Calandra, came back to me. "Part of my job—and yours—is to make sure the thunderheads aren't a threat, to humanity in general and the Solitaire colony in particular. You can cooperate with me in that or you can get out. Understood?"

"Yes," I said between clenched teeth. Deep down, I had to admit it wasn't an unreasonable attitude for him and the Patri to take. In some ways, that made it worse.

"All right, then," he said. "So. Somehow, Ms. Zagorin can't talk about her little visit with the thunderheads. We know there's no physical brain damage, or at least none of the kind usually associated with aphasia. That leaves us either something very subtle or else something psychological. Opinion: would hypnosis help? Either standard or drug-induced?"

I looked at Calandra. She chewed her lip briefly, then stepped up to the bed. "I'd like to try something less drastic first, if I may. Shepherd Zagorin, I'd like you to try to relax and think back through the contact, remembering it as fully as you can. Words, impressions, emotions—whatever comes to mind. Don't try to talk about them; just remember."

I turned to explain to Eisenstadt, saw that he'd already caught on to what she had in mind. "Go ahead," he nodded to Zagorin.

She clenched her teeth momentarily. "All right." Closing her eyes, she settled herself back against the pillow.

Calandra reached over to take her left hand as I

moved to the other side of the bed and took her right.
Zagorin's skin was warm, the muscles slightly tense,
and I could feel the faint throbbing of her pulse. "All
right, now, Joyita," Calandra said, her voice calm and
soothing. "You're sitting down by the thunderheads and
going into your meditative trance."

A sense of the normal. "Everything's going as usual,"
Calandra continued. "And now—suddenly—it's different."

Surprise—a touch of fear—recognition of a heretofore
only vaguely sensed personality. "Yes," Calandra confirmed my own reading. "For the first time you're
really in communication with the presence you've felt
during previous meditations."

"It's strong," Zagorin whispered, eyes still closed.
"So very strong."

"Overpoweringly strong?" Eisenstadt asked.

A pause. "N-no," Zagorin said hesitantly. "But . . ."
She trailed off.

"She broke contact easily enough when Adams was in
trouble," I reminded Eisenstadt. "Remember that they
were in a very passive state at the time of the contact—
your tech described it as almost a coma."

He considered. "You're saying it was more a matter
of their weakness than it was of any inherent thunderhead strength?"

"I don't think they can take over unreceptive minds,
if that's what you're worried about," Calandra said.

"I'd agree," I nodded.

Eisenstadt's lip twisted in a grimace. That was indeed
what he was worried about, and he wasn't entirely
convinced otherwise. "We'll get back to that later," he
said. "Go on."

Calandra turned back to Zagorin. "You've made contact, now, Joyita. The thunderheads are talking to Dr.
Eisenstadt through you and Shepherd Adams. Can you
hear the conversation? Either end, or both?"

An oddly reticent eagerness flicked across Zagorin's
sense. Eagerness, combined with . . . it felt almost like
urgency. "They very much want to communicate with
us," I murmured to Eisenstadt.

"Uh-huh," he grunted. "So again: what's taken them so long?"

"Quiet," Calandra ordered us. "Joyita, is there anything else? Something they want to tell you?—or that they're trying to hide from you? Something besides what's being asked?"

"I . . . don't know." Zagorin's face contorted with concentration. "There's something there. Something important. But I can't . . . I can't remember it, exactly."

"Something having to do with the dead thunderhead we're looking for?" Eisenstadt asked.

Confusion, frustration. "I , , , don't know."

Eisenstadt muttered a curse under his breath. "This isn't getting us anywhere."

"Maybe," I said. "Maybe not." I caught Calandra's eye. "You ever play Process of Elimination at Bethel?"

She frowned at me, then her expression cleared. "Yes, I see. Can't hurt to try."

"What can't hurt?" Eisenstadt growled.

"It's called Process of Elimination," I told him. "It was originally a Watcher children's game, but I know the method's been used in serious therapy, too. What we're going to do is to name several topics and see if any of them sparks a response."

"When you use a pravdrug you usually reach only the conscious mind," Calandra added, anticipating his next question. "This approach can sometimes get a little deeper—and if the blockage is in the conscious speech center, we may be able to get around it."

"So we should be able to just wire her up to sensors and try it that way, right?" Eisenstadt asked.

"Yes, except that the sensors would only record the fact of a reaction," I reminded him. "Calandra and I may be able to read the emotion behind it."

He grimaced, then nodded. "All right. Give it a try."

I turned back to Zagorin, realizing with a pang of guilt that while she'd been lying there listening we'd been discussing her like a lab specimen. But if she was irritated by it, I couldn't find the emotion. "You ready?" I asked.

She nodded. "Go ahead."

"Thunderheads."

Nothing. "Defenses. Fortresses. Body-homes."

Still nothing. "Solitaire," Calandra put in. "Spall. The Halo of God. Humans. Fear, or distrust."

"Anything?" Eisenstadt murmured.

"Quiet," I said sharply. There had been just the briefest of flickers . . . "Fear, Joyita? Fear of us? Fear of death?"

Another flicker. "Death," Calandra said, almost pouncing on the word. "Death?—the Deadman Switch?"

I glanced at Calandra . . . and in her sense I found confirmation of my own impression. "The Cloud?" I asked Zagorin quietly.

And there it was. Subtle, but unmistakable. "The Cloud," Calandra said, and shivered.

I turned to Eisenstadt. "It has to do with the Cloud," I told him.

He chewed at his lip, his eyes on Zagorin's taut face. Uncharacteristically, he didn't seem inclined to doubt our conclusion . . . at least as far as it went. "I need more details," he said. "Is it just that they're the ones guiding us through it?"

I watched Zagorin, replaying her earlier responses in my mind. Replayed especially her reaction to the word *fear*. "I don't know," I had to admit. "But whatever it is, it's important. And it's something that includes fear."

Eisenstadt took a deep breath. "Ms. Zagorin . . . do your records back at the—whatever the place is called; at your Myrrh settlement—do the records there include a list of your best meditators?"

Zagorin gazed up at him, and I could see her bracing herself. "I can't ask my people to do this," she said.

"I'm afraid I have to insist," he told her firmly. "We need to talk to the thunderheads again, and neither you nor your friend Adams is up to it—"

"And why isn't Shepherd Adams up to it?" she cut him off. "Because he nearly died, that's why. How do you expect me to ask one of my people to take that kind of risk?"

"It's not that much of a risk," Eisenstadt insisted, trying hard to be soothing. "We know what the contact does—"

"And you know that I'm the only one who's been through it safely."

Eisenstadt sighed. "Ms. Zagorin, I thank you for your offer—at least, I assume I hear an offer in there. But to be perfectly honest, we can't afford to let you be our only contact with the thunderheads. In the first place, even with proper medical preparation I doubt you'll be able to make contact more than once a day at the most, and I don't want to be stuck with that kind of limitation. In the second place—" He hesitated. "I don't want all our communications to go through a single person."

Zagorin's forehead creased slightly with puzzlement. "Why not?" she asked.

"Dr. Eisenstadt?" I put in quietly, before he could answer. "May I talk to you a moment? In private?"

He hesitated, eyes measuring me. Then, with a quick nod, he led the way out into the hall. "Well?" he asked, closing the door behind him.

"You're worried about the possibility that repeated contacts may subtly alter her," I said. "Bringing her emotionally onto the thunderheads' side, or even making her an agent of their will. Correct?"

He smiled grimly. "Maybe you're not as naive as I thought," he conceded. "Yes, that's exactly what I'm worried about."

I nodded. "In that case, sir, I think you ought to let Shepherd Zagorin be our only contact, at least for now."

"Oh, really? And what happened to all that stuff about how the thunderhead presence was affecting people over on Solitaire?"

I thought back to our dinner in Myrrh settlement, the odd passivity Calandra had thought she'd sensed among the people there. "It affects people here on Spall, too," I told Eisenstadt. "Only not in the same way. Maybe because the Seekers' meditation leaves them more in a position of cooperation than of competition with the thunderheads—"

I'd been thinking out loud, and I could see that along the way I'd completely lost Eisenstadt. "Calandra and I found a sort of relaxed passiveness here when—"

"I get the main picture," he interrupted my attempt to explain. "Assuming that you're not talking nonsense—and that may be an invalid assumption—all I'm really hearing is that the closer the contact, the more dangerous."

"Maybe, maybe not," I shook my head. "We don't know for certain—which is why it would be safest to keep these direct contacts limited to as few people as possible. Besides which . . . Calandra and I spent some time with both Shepherd Adams and Shepherd Zagorin when we first came to Spall. We don't know any of the other Seekers nearly as well."

Eisenstadt frowned at me for a long moment . . . and then he understood. "You really think you could spot any alterations the thunderheads might make in them?"

"I don't know," I said honestly. "But we'd have a better chance with them than with anyone else, at least until we've gotten to know them better."

Eisenstadt pursed his lips, considering. "Your boss—Kelsey-Ramos—told me that you have something of a gift for persuasion. Specifically, that you'd probably try to make you and your friend too valuable for me to easily get rid of."

"Mr. Kelsey-Ramos exaggerates," I said between dry lips.

"Perhaps." Eisenstadt grimaced. "Unfortunately, even knowing the hook's there, I seem to be stuck with the bait." He took a deep breath. "All right, you've convinced me. For now, anyway, we'll stick with Zagorin. I suppose it would make sense to wait a day or two before talking to them again, anyway—give us a chance to study the dead thunderhead we're allegedly getting." He glanced at his watch. "Which reminds me, I ought to go check on their progress."

"Would you like Calandra or me to come with you?"

"When we actually find the thing, probably. Until then—" he jerked a thumb at the door behind him—

"your job is to spend your time getting to know Zagorin as well as you can. Just in case."

I sighed quietly. "Yes, sir."

He eyed me. "Something else?"

"I . . . don't know." I shook my head slowly, trying to identify the uncomfortable darkness hovering like a nighttime predator at the edge of my mind. "I guess I just don't like having to guess what it is about the Cloud that the thunderheads don't want us to know about."

He snorted. "I don't much like it myself. Do try to remember that it was *you* who just talked me out of sending for more Halloas and dragging the secret out of the thunderheads right here and now."

"I know, sir. But . . ."

"And anyway," he added, "whatever it is, they've kept it to themselves for at least seventy years. A few days, one way or another, isn't likely to make any difference."

He was right, of course, I told myself as he strode briskly away to check on his search team. After seventy years, a couple of days could hardly be important.

I hoped.

CHAPTER 25

It was, in fact, considerably more than a couple of days before Eisenstadt was ready to talk to the thunderheads again. Though Shepherd Zagorin seemed ready and willing to make another attempt by the next morning, the physician charged with preparing her was reluctant to administer his proposed pre-treatment mixture without doing a few more tests on both it and her; and before he had time to complete them, Eisenstadt's search team finally located the dead thunderhead.

Most everyone, I gathered—from Eisenstadt on down—had privately concluded that the directions we'd been given had somehow been misread, and it was only through mule-headed persistence on the search leader's part that the dead thunderhead was located at all. The "height" the thunderheads had used in giving distance, it turned out, was neither their own physical height nor ours, but a length that was finally identified as the height of the common building in Shepherd Zagorin's Myrrh settlement. For me, it seemed just one more indication that the thunderheads had been observing the Halo of God settlers since their arrival; Eisenstadt, conversely, wondered aloud whether it was a deliberate

242

delaying tactic. But it wasn't long before the sheer scientific excitement drove such political/military considerations into the background of his mind and allowed the pure scientist to shine through again.

To shine through with a vengeance. For all but his inner circle he virtually ceased to exist, disappearing into the project as if inhaled by it. Every waking hour was spent either in the clean room with the examination team or else in his office studying the data that was being extracted by the double cylful. His rare sleeping hours were probably spent dreaming about it.

I'd spent eight years with Lord Kelsey-Ramos, who hadn't pushed Carillon to the top by being lazy; but even by those standards Eisenstadt's capacity and energy were astounding. Armed with a full clearance to the information—a courtesy that I suspected for a long time had been an accidental oversight on his part—I did my best to keep up with as much of the flood of information as I could. But even just following the nontechnical summaries was almost more than I could handle.

Thunderheads, it turned out, were in many ways an almost even mixture of plant and animal characteristics. Our dead drone, once extracted, left behind it an extensive network of hairlike roots extending up to twenty meters into the ground, a nutrient-gathering system which at least partially explained how they were able to survive on top of barren bluffs as well as amid lush vegetation. The root system contained an unusual twist, though: a close examination showed that each of the fibers went through a living/dead/decomposing cycle that actually encouraged nearby plant growth by flooding the soil with vital trace elements.

The discovery, exciting though it was to the scientists, was greeted with a certain chagrin by those who had had to dig the drone up and would presumably be called on to do so again. Along with the problem of having to slog through matted plants to get to the thunderhead, they had quickly found that those same plants sheltered the nests of a fairly nasty species of stinging insect, insects who had had to be gassed before the drone could be approached. For a day or two afterward there were rumors that the workers had asked either that the next specimen be taken from Butte City, where no such plants or insects existed, or else that Eisenstadt assign the next sampling run to a fully armored Pravilo team.

The rumors faded with time. I doubt Eisenstadt ever even noticed them.

There were a great many other plantlike characteristics, too, cellular structure among them. But at the same time there were enough animal-like qualities to keep the thunderheads from simply being labeled as sessile, sentient plants. They had almost the entire set of normal animal senses, for one thing, including sight, hearing, a limited sense of touch, and a combined chemical analysis system nestled beneath the wave-like overhang that combined smell and taste. Their sight, in particular, was surprisingly well developed, especially given that it relied on fairly simple cellular lenses scattered in a semirandom pattern across the whole of the body. It took a great deal of computer modeling time to finally show that the hard-wired neural pathways connecting the lenses to each other and the brain actually acted as as sort of organic computer, combining and cleaning up the blurry images into something as clear as human eyesight.

The drone had a true circulatory system too, not just primitive ducts for transporting sap and water, though the system operated via a combination of vascular pressure, capillary action, and gravity instead of a heart. There were also several distinct organs scattered throughout the body, though there was a great deal of heated debate as to the functions each might serve. The brain and central nervous system were fairly decentralized, though the neural density increased markedly near the various sensory organs and each of the cellular eyes.

There was more to be learned—a great deal more— and Eisenstadt's "couple of days" stretched ever longer as they took their prize apart bit by bit, arguing and discussing each new discovery. Off to the side, largely ignored, Calandra and Shepherd Zagorin and I waited . . . and speculated quietly among ourselves whether giving Eisenstadt the drone might have been part of a thunderhead plan to distract him from whatever it was about the Cloud that they seemed determined to hide.

We waited three weeks . . . until, finally, Eisenstadt decided he was ready.

Calandra and I were taken to the Butte City at mid-morning the next day, to find the preliminary preparations nearly complete. Shepherd Zagorin, sitting alone this time at the edge of the thunderhead mass, was being fitted with sensors and monitor leads as Eisenstadt stood fidgeting over her. Further back, in the ridge hollow, the techs were checking out their equipment and taking readings with a sense of quiet chaos that reminded me of an orchestra warming up before a concert.

Physically, it was like a replay of the last contact. Emotionally, it was drastically different. Three weeks ago the men and women here had been contemptuously amused by the suggestion that a simple religious practice could accomplish something their science had so far failed to do. We'd offered them a miracle, and it had been granted . . . and as I looked around the Butte City now I found only sober anticipation and even traces of respect.

Beside me, Calandra snorted gently. "Look at them," she murmured, nodding fractionally at the busy techs.

"What about them?" I murmured back.

"The way they look at Joyita—you see it? They've adopted her as an honorary member."

I frowned, studying their faces more closely. Calandra was right; I could indeed sense an odd camaraderie when they looked in her direction. "I don't understand."

"The last time they did this she and Adams were just religious fanatics," Calandra said, a trace of bitterness in her voice. "Not worth more than basic legal tolerance. But their method worked, and every scientist and tech *knows* that only science works. So the method must be science, and she must be a scientist."

I felt an echo of her bitterness in my own stomach. *For the wisdom of its wise men is doomed, the understanding of any who understand will vanish* . . . "It's always easier to come up with a rationalization than to change your basic assumptions," I reminded her. "At least it gains her some acceptance—maybe even gains some acceptance for the Halo of God in general."

Eisenstadt spotted us, beckoned us over. "We're about ready here," he told us as we approached, his voice and expression rich with slightly nervous anticipation. He raised his eyebrows questioningly—

"We're ready, too," I assured him. Calandra and I had kept up our end of the bargain with Eisenstadt, spending a good seventy or eighty hours with Zagorin over the past three weeks. If the thunderheads were planning any intellectual or emotional manipulation, I had little doubt that we'd be able to catch it.

Eisenstadt nodded, the tension in his sense easing just a bit, and turned back to Zagorin. "Whenever you feel ready, Ms. Zagorin."

She nodded and closed her eyes. Eisenstadt stepped back to stand between Calandra and me, and together we waited.

My subjective feeling was that the contact was made faster this time than the last, but as nearly as I could tell everything else was the same. Zagorin straightened abruptly from her meditative slouch, glazed eyes opening to stare at us. "Greetings to you," she whispered, the husky sound again containing overtones that never existed in her normal voice. "We are the thunderheads. We have waited long for . . . your return."

Eisenstadt cleared his throat, and I could tell he was mildly impressed by the thunderheads' easy acceptance of our name for them. "I greet you as well," he said. "Yes, I'm afraid it *has* been a while. We had a great deal of work to do, and it seemed best for us to finish it before talking to you again. For one thing, this sort of communication is rather hard on the humans you speak through."

A slight pause. I glanced back at the techs monitoring Zagorin's biological functions, read no alarm or danger in their faces. Apparently the medical pre-treatment was successfully warding off the more extreme side effects of the contact. "We mean no harm," Zagorin whispered. "It is not possible . . . for us to change this."

"Yes, we understand," Eisenstadt assured the speaker. "It may be possible for us to do something from this end—we're still experimenting with it." He paused, and I felt him brace himself. "We appreciate your generosity in letting us examine one of your dead. We've learned a great deal from our work; however, there are still some questions we've been unable to answer. Several weeks ago, for instance, you used a heat weapon—we think probably it was a chemically-pumped laser—against a human that you thought was about to attack you. We're very interested in the commercial and industrial possibilities of such a device, but we've been unable to identify either the mechanism or the biochemistry from the drone we studied. If you could enlighten us—even give us a clue as to where the source is located—we would be most grateful."

Zagorin gazed at him with those flat eyes, but remained silent. "Even a second demonstration would help," Eisenstadt tried again, uncertainty and uneasiness creeping into his sense. "Under controlled conditions, of course, with recording instruments in place—"

"The Cloud," Zagorin cut him off. "You seek the origi . . . nation of the Cloud, do . . . you not?"

Eisenstadt threw a slightly startled glance at me. "Well . . . yes, of course we do. We've, uh, been speculating that it was your people who've been guiding our ships through the Cloud all these years—"

"We will take you to the . . . origination of . . . the Cloud."

Eisenstadt stared at Zagorin, and it took him two

tries to get any words out. "You mean . . . the mechanism that generates the Cloud? Where is it, on Spall?"

"In space," Zagorin whispered. "Deep in space."

Eisenstadt nodded slowly, his sense that of a man who has seen the answer to a long-time puzzle. "I understand. We'll need some time to get a ship ready. Can we communicate like this with you off of Spall?"

"There is no need. When you are ready, speak . . . to the pilot. To—" Zagorin hesitated, and I could sense the thunderhead searching his host for the right word. "To the zombi."

"All right," Eisenstadt said, forehead furrowed slightly. "We'll get started on the preparations. In the meantime—"

"Farewell until then," Zagorin said.

"Wait!" Eisenstadt barked; but it was too late. Zagorin slumped over, her face and eyes returning to normal.

Eisenstadt took a step toward her, fury in his eyes. "Who told you to break contact?" he snarled.

Zagorin blinked up at him; but Calandra spoke up before she could reply. "It wasn't her doing, Doctor," she told him. "The thunderhead left her of his own volition."

Eisenstadt glared at her, and I could see him fighting to choke down his anger. "I wasn't through asking questions yet," he bit out, to no one in particular. "Couldn't he see that?"

"Perhaps he could," I said. "Perhaps *he* was through giving answers."

Eisenstadt paused in mid-sentence, swinging around to focus on me . . . and as I watched, the scientist within him gave way once again to the official representative of the Patri, with all the political and military considerations that role included. It was something of a shock; I hadn't really appreciated how different the man had been without those encumbrances.

"I see," Eisenstadt said at last. His voice, too, had subtly changed. "Sounds like they don't really want to discuss their organic laser, doesn't it?"

"Or else," I offered, "they consider whatever it is about the Cloud to be far more urgent."

Eisenstadt looked sharply at me, and I could tell he was remembering back to that Process of Elimination game with Zagorin three weeks earlier. "You could be right," he admitted grudgingly, and I could see him thinking about how much trouble it would be to organize a trip out into space to actually take a look. There was a long moment of indecision; and then his face cleared. "Lieutenant?" he called, turning to look for the Pravilo officer in charge.

The other stepped forward from the monitor area. "Yes, sir?"

"I want you to contact Commodore Freitag for me. Find out how soon we can have one of his destroyers ready for a short trip."

The lieutenant nodded and turned back to one of the consoles. Eisenstadt looked over at Zagorin, currently the focus of attention of a half dozen medical people. "How do you feel, Ms. Zagorin?" he asked.

"Fine," she said, sounding a little out of breath. "Much better than the last time."

Eisenstadt nodded, caught one of the physicians' eyes. "I want you to do an extrapolation of her physical condition," he told the other. "I'm interested particularly on how long she could have stayed under without harm."

The other nodded and returned to his examination. "You're planning to take her along with you?" I asked quietly.

Eisenstadt nodded. "It might be useful to find out just how far away from Spall we can get before we can't raise them anymore."

"But if the thunderheads are guiding us through the Cloud—"

"We have no evidence of that," Eisenstadt reminded me. "Not even an unsupported statement by the thunderheads. All of that is pure speculation on our part, and pure speculation always makes me nervous."

I looked at him, read the sense of uneasiness there . . . "Because if it's not the thunderheads guiding us through the Cloud, it's someone else?"

He threw me a patient look. "Come on, Benedar—surely it's obvious there are at least two intelligences working at cross-purposes here. Or do you want to try and tell me that the thunderheads built the Cloud as a defense or something and then couldn't remember how to turn it off?"

I thought about that. "It doesn't have to be that monochrome, though, does it?" I suggested hesitantly. "Couldn't it just as well be that they don't mind us mining the rings but want to limit how many of us live next door to them on Solitaire?"

"Or even be the reverse," Calandra added. "That they don't mind us living on Solitaire but want to limit our plundering of the ring minerals."

"For all the good the rings do *them*," Eisenstadt growled. "They're hardly in a position to do any mining themselves. Unfortunately, neither of those theories will hold air. If that's all they wanted, all they needed to do was to make a treaty with us covering population size and mining rights and then shut off the Cloud."

"What if we reneged?" I asked.

"They turn the Cloud back on, of course—trapping, incidentally, everyone who was in the system at the time. With that kind of threat hanging over us, they'd hardly have to worry about treaty violations."

"Before the Halo of God came along, maybe there wasn't any way for them to talk to us," I reminded him.

"The way's there now," he countered. "And they haven't mentioned anything along those lines. No, either the thunderheads are the ones guiding our ships and *aren't* responsible for the Cloud, or else they're running the Cloud and someone else is bringing our ships in. It doesn't make sense any other way."

I bit at the back of my lip. He was right—the logic of it was indeed hard to argue against. And yet . . .

"You don't seem convinced, Benedar."

I focused on him. His expression was gruff, tolerant, as befit a scientist who didn't officially give much credit to my Watcher skills . . . but beneath that official veneer I could sense a genuine interest. "There's something else about the thunderheads," I said, trying without success to pin down the elusive feeling nagging at my back-brain. "Something that bothers me."

"You think they're lying to us about something?"

I looked at Calandra, saw her equally helpless shrug. She didn't have it, either; but like me, she recognized there was something here we weren't getting. "No, I don't think they're *lying*. Not . . . exactly."

It was a sloppy enough statement, and I fully expected to get a scornful glare for it. But Eisenstadt merely rubbed his cheek, his sense thoughtful. "Could it be that this invitation out to the Cloud is some kind of a trap?" he suggested.

"I can't see what they could hope to gain," I shook my head. "They must know that information about them has long since left the system. It's far too late to try and keep their existence secret, even if that was what they wanted."

Calandra stirred. "I don't think it's a trap," she said slowly. "But Gilead's right—they *are* hiding something. I get a sense of manipulation, as if they're deliberately feeding us just enough information to keep us moving in the direction they want."

"You think they're going to take us to the Cloud generator and then ask us to shut it off?" Eisenstadt asked bluntly.

She looked at him steadily. "I'd be very careful about doing anything like that," she told him. "If you're right about them not being responsible for the Cloud, then it could only have been put there by someone else for the purpose of isolating them."

Eisenstadt nodded grimly. "That thought has already occurred to me," he acknowledged. "Which is why I want to take a Pravilo warship instead of just requisitioning some freighter. The generator may be defended."

Across the way, the Pravilo lieutenant straightened from his board. "Dr. Eisenstadt?" he called. "All set. Commodore Freitag has ordered the *Kharg* to return from ring patrol duty; ETA approximately six days." He hesitated. "However . . . the commodore asks me to remind you that none of the Pravilo ships in Solitaire system is equipped with a Deadman Switch."

For a second Eisenstadt just stared at him. Then he swore under his breath. "Chern-fire!—I forgot all about that."

I glanced at Calandra, read my own puzzlement there. "I don't understand," I said to Eisenstadt. "It can't be *that* hard to install a Deadman Switch."

"The hardware's not the problem," he growled. "It's the fact that the Pravilo doesn't have a general license for Solitaire transport. Trips in and out of the system are authorized on an individual basis by the Patri. And for that authorization you have to go all the way to Portslava."

"It's not quite that bad, sir," the lieutenant spoke up. "The judiciaries on Miland or Whitecliff can also grant authorization."

"All that means is that you apply to them and *they* send the request on to Portslava," Eisenstadt shook his head. "Could take weeks—not to mention the paperwork involved in getting the actual zombi."

I looked at Calandra, feeling my stomach muscles tightening. Except that there was a zombi already on hand, if Eisenstadt ever happened to remember that . . . "Surely there are emergency procedures available," I said.

"I doubt this could be made to qualify," Eisenstadt snorted.

"Well . . ." I hesitated. "The last I knew, Governor Rybakov owed Mr. Kelsey-Ramos a rather large personal favor. You might talk to him, see if he can wheedle a zombi for you from among Solitaire's own death-sentence criminals."

He looked at me; and from the way his eyes carefully avoided Calandra I could tell that he, too, had suddenly remembered her status. I held my breath . . . but practically before the idea was fully formed it was smothered by a strong sense of rejection. Like Randon, it seemed, he had quickly learned what an asset Watchers were, and he had no intention of throwing that asset away. "I was under the impression Solitaire law forbade that," he said. "Worth a try, though. Anyway—" He glanced at Zagorin. "I'd like you two to accompany Ms. Zagorin back to her quarters when they're through with her."

His voice and sense were heavy with significance. "Yes, sir," I said, trying to convey my understanding of his order without being too obvious about it. If the thunderheads had done anything to her, a couple of hours with her should bring it to light.

"Good," Eisenstadt nodded. "I'll let you know what happens with the governor." Nodding to Calandra and Zagorin, he turned and set off toward the gap in the buttes where the cars were parked.

I watched him go; felt Calandra's presence as she stepped to my side. "He wants the Cloud turned off," she murmured.

I nodded. "I know."

She shivered suddenly. "I hope we're not all going at this too quickly. That we aren't about to undo something that . . . shouldn't be undone."

I chewed at the back of my lip. "I don't think he'll do anything rash. Besides . . . there's still something about this that doesn't work. Why would *anyone* go to all the trouble of creating a ten-light-year barrier when all it does is lock in creatures who are rooted to the ground?"

Calandra shook her head. "I don't know. But I still don't like it."

I put my arm around her, felt the tension in her muscles. "I know," I said quietly. "Neither do I."

CHAPTER 26

It was late evening, and I was in my quarters—somehow, I thought of them as quarters now, instead of as a prison cell—when a pair of Pravilos came to take me to Eisenstadt's office. One look at his face was all I needed. "What's wrong?" I asked, stomach tightening.

In answer he waved me to a seat and swiveled his phone display around so that I could see it. Randon's face was on the screen . . . and he, too, looked worried. "Why don't you repeat what you just told me, Mr. Kelsey-Ramos," Eisenstadt invited sourly as I sat down.

"Benedar," Randon nodded to me from the display, his eyes briefly searching my face. "How are they treating you?"

"I'm fine, sir," I said. "What's the problem?"

His mouth twisted briefly. "I've just been in contact with Governor Rybakov," he said.

It was obvious what was coming next. "I take it she won't suspend the no-zombi law for us."

"It's worse than that," he said grimly, holding up a cyl. "I have here a copy of a petition that was filed with the governor's office two days ago. It reminds Rybakov that the duly mandated sentence of death passed against

Calandra Paquin has been unlawfully suspended . . . and it requests that said sentence be carried out without further delay."

I stared at him. "Aikman?" I asked between stiff lips.

"Who else?" Randon growled. "What's worse, Rybakov really has no choice but to give the request proper consideration . . . and she tells me privately that he *does* have a case."

"How?" I demanded. "Calandra's been co-opted by a representative of the Patri for official purposes."

Eisenstadt cleared his throat. "Unfortunately, Benedar, my authority doesn't actually extend that far. It was only through Mr. Kelsey-Ramos's generosity that she's here on Spall at all, and he could legally call her back to the *Bellwether* at any time."

I stared at the display, the thudding of my heart like the distant sound of crumbling hope. My belief in Calandra's innocence—my efforts to buy her enough time for a new hearing—all of it threatened by a legal trick. *But he said, Alas for you lawyers as well, because you load on people burdens that are unendurable, burdens that you yourselves do not touch with your fingertips . . .* Clenching my teeth, I forced my mind to unfreeze. "All right," I said slowly. "But since Calandra was assigned to the *Bellwether*, shouldn't that mean that her sentence can only be carried out aboard the *Bellwether*?"

"And since the *Bellwether*'s been temporarily grounded for security reasons," Randon finished for me, in a voice that told me they'd already thought of this, "the sentence ought to be temporarily grounded, too. It's a nice idea; the problem is that her actual assignment is to HTI Transport, not to the *Bellwether*. It happens that there are two other HTI freighters inbound in Solitaire system at the moment, either of which could be used to carry out her sentence."

"Except that they both have zombis of their own—" I stopped short as a horrible thought struck me.

"Of course they do," Randon said, frowning at my tone. "But since their zombis' sentences are presumably dated after Paquin's, it wouldn't be unreasonable to switch zombis between one of them and the *Bellwether*."

Aikman's face flashed through my mind: his face, his hate-filled and vengeful soul, his devious mind . . . and I suddenly knew what it was he was trying to do. "They won't be giving you anything in exchange," I said, my stomach knotting even tighter. "If the governor accepts that petition, they'll take Calandra and leave you stranded here."

"What are you talking about?" Eisenstadt demanded. "They have a zombi of their own—"

"Who will already be dead or dying when the *Bellwether* gets him."

They both stared at me . . . and slowly, the understanding came. "You mean . . . they'd deliberately *kill* one of their zombis?" Eisenstadt asked, a look of horrified astonishment on his face.

"He may even be already dead." I looked at Randon, all my instincts screaming with the need for immediate action. "Have any of the HTI board been in contact with those freighters?"

"I can probably find out." Randon's own disbelief had vanished, replaced by an angry determination. "Cute— very cute. A blazing lot of trouble and risk to go to, but I wouldn't put it past that gang of vultures."

"Especially with Aikman goading them on," I said, my voice trembling. "Sir, we may not have much time left—"

"Easy, Benedar, easy," he soothed. "They'd be stupid to jump their cue and kill any of the zombis until they had an official ruling in hand—otherwise *they* might wind up stuck here instead of us."

I hadn't thought of that. It helped, but not very much. "I don't think we should count on them to be that logical," I told him. "The sooner you can get word of this to the governor, the better."

"Agreed," Eisenstadt seconded, his voice grim. "And while we're at it, let's try a little legal offensive of our own. What we need to do is file a counterpetition, requesting that Rybakov grant an indefinite suspension of Paquin's sentence until the Patri can confirm her service with my team here."

"And maybe ask that Commodore Freitag assign some Pravilos to take over zombi guard duty aboard the HTI freighters," Randon agreed. "Certainly worth a shot. Unfortunately—" he looked back at me. "All that really does is block off Aikman's easiest route. His petition is still the major problem; and coming as it does practically on top of your own request for a zombi, Dr. Eisenstadt, it leaves Rybakov the obvious move of combining the two by transferring Paquin's sentence to whatever this jaunt is you want to make. Aikman couldn't have planned things better if he'd had a straight pipeline out to you."

I sent Eisenstadt a sharp look; but he shook his head. "No, it's just coincidence. Remember we didn't decide ourselves until today that we'd even be needing a zombi."

Though there had been strong hints earlier on . . . but it was too late to worry about possible leaks now. "And there's no provision at all for using a Solitaran criminal?" I asked.

"None," Eisenstadt answered heavily. "Wouldn't really matter if there was. Breaking that strong a legal tradition would mean her own political suicide—Solitaire would demand her removal, and the Patri would pretty much have to bow to their wishes."

But as one man they howled, Away with him! Give us Barabbas! "I understand," I murmured, trying not to be bitter.

Randon cleared his throat. "Benedar . . . the original reason you took Paquin to Spall in the first place. Did you have any luck at all with that?"

Our search for a smuggler base. So much had happened since then I'd nearly forgotten. "No, sir," I had to admit. "If we'd had more time—" I shrugged helplessly.

"What about the Pravilo?" Randon persisted. "I'd think *someone* there would be interested in helping out."

I shook my head, Commodore Freitag's face at our

last meeting floating up from my memory. His face, and his sense of unbreakable determination on the issue. "I talked to Commodore Freitag before we left Solitaire," I said. "He was uninterested in anything but a total solution to the problem."

"Uninterested?"

"Violently so." I hissed frustration between my teeth. "And I have to say that I agree with his reasons."

Randon grimaced, but I could see he was willing to trust my judgment. "I see. Well, you can tell me all about it some day when we have more time and a secure line. For the moment—" his eyes searched out Eisenstadt— "do you have any more ideas, Doctor?"

Eisenstadt shook his head. "Nothing except what we've already come up with. I'll get my counter-petition worked up and send word to Freitag about putting Pravilos on those HTI zombis. Aside from that, I can't think of anything."

Randon nodded. "I'll turn up what heat I can here and see what I can find out about unofficial HTI involvement. If I can catch an important hand in the cashbox, maybe I can force them to back down."

"Worth a try," Eisenstadt agreed. "Well . . . I appreciate your help on this, Mr. Kelsey-Ramos. Good luck, and keep me informed."

"Right. Good-bye, Doctor."

"Good-bye."

Eisenstadt waved his control stick and the display blanked, and for a moment we sat in silence. Then he stirred in his seat. "I just thought you'd want to know," he said, almost gruffly.

The gruffness was a shield; but it couldn't hide his genuine concern. "Thank you," I said, getting to my feet. "I'd better let you get on with your work."

He hesitated. "Paquin is out at the Butte City," he told me. "If you want to go and talk to her, I'll have one of the Pravilos escort you there."

In other words, would I like to accept the burden of telling her the bad news. It was the last thing in the universe I wanted to do . . . but I knew it would be better coming from a friend. "Yes, sir," I sighed. "I'll do it."

There were a set of lights strung along the fences that enclosed the two-hundred-meter-long corridor between the encampment and the Butte City, but with no one officially on duty there tonight the lights had been muted to firefly level. My Pravilo escort had planned to drive me across, but the night was cool and quiet, ideal for a short walk. Besides which, I needed the time to think.

It was the first time I'd been really outside after dark—away from the encampment's lights, anyway—since Calandra and I had first camped at the buttes, and as we walked I found myself gazing up at the starry sky, a sharp bitterness swirling within me. Practically singlehanded, she and I had opened up mankind's first contact with an alien race—found them, identified them, even discovered how to talk to them . . . and none of it seemed to make any difference whatsoever to the coldly impersonal web of laws which Aikman was manipulating in his obsession to destroy us.

Us; because once Calandra was dead, I would be his next target. Aboard the *Bellwether* I'd forced him to back down, and for a man like Aikman such a goring of his pride was as deadly an insult as I could have given him. Stranding Randon and the *Bellwether* in Solitaire system without an outzombi would be a nice start to his revenge; in the time that would buy him, I had no doubt he would find the right thread to pull to wrap the web around me, as well.

And there was nothing I could do to stop him.

Like the corridor, the Butte City was only dimly lit, but there was enough starlight filtering between the cliffs for me to pick out the three forms standing near one of the gaps. Calandra and her two Pravilo escorts. My own escort trailing along behind me, I headed over.

She saw us coming, of course, and identified me well before there was enough light for her to properly see my face. "Hello, Gilead," she called softly. "Come to look at the stars?"

"Not really," I said.

Her silhouette stiffened slightly as she heard the tightness in my voice. "What's the matter?"

I hesitated, suddenly very conscious of the strangers listening in. "Could Ms. Paquin and I have a minute alone?" I asked my escort.

"I guess that'd be okay," he said genially. Pulling out his phone, he keyed in a code, and the lights that had been strung around the Butte City brightened to the level of a fashionably dim room. "Take all the time you want," he added. Signing Calandra's escort to follow, he stepped back around the thunderheads.

"What's the matter?" Calandra repeated when they were out of earshot.

I related my conversation with Eisenstadt and Randon. The words felt like molten lead in my mouth. "I see," she said when I'd finished. Her eyes were focused somewhere past my face; her sense was dread combined with a strange calm. "Well . . . we knew it was just a matter of time."

I clenched my teeth hard enough to hurt. "I haven't given up," I told her. "Neither have the others."

She shook her head. "You might as well. It's over."

"Calandra—"

She silenced me with a look. "I never asked for this," she reminded me quietly. "Never asked you to get involved with this crusade—begged you, in fact, not to. Please, Gilead—just let it go."

They have filled this place with the blood of the innocent . . . "And let them trade an innocent life for money?" I demanded.

She sighed, and her eyes closed briefly. "The powerful have always built their wealth on the lives of other people," she said tiredly. "You of all people should know that—the Carillon Group has certainly done its share. Solitaire just happens to be a more blatant example than most."

"There ought to be room for both wealth *and* ethics in a civilized society," I ground out.

She shrugged. "The last person to try running a government that way was Aaron Balaam darMaupine. Want to trade?"

I glared at her. "I can't let this happen."

"You can't stop it." She took a deep breath. "But if it helps any . . . you've already done more for me than I could ever have hoped."

She turned slightly, her eyes turning upward to the stars. "You remember the parable of the talents?"

To one he gave five talents, to another two, to a third one, each in proportion to his ability . . . "How could I forget it?"

She nodded. "Me, too. The teachers at Bethel really drummed that one into us. You ever wonder—late at night—whether you were living up to their expectations?"

I swallowed. "No more than a hundred times a year."

"Same with me," she said. "I'd pretty much given up even trying; but it was always there anyway, somewhere way in the back of my mind. I guess I soothed it by assuming that when I was older I'd find something great to accomplish. Now, of course . . . I won't be getting much older."

I bit at the back of my lip, and wished I knew how to comfort her. "I'm sorry," was all I could think of to say.

She looked at me. "Don't be. Don't you see?—this crazy quixotic quest of yours has given me more of a memorial than I ever dreamed of having. You and I, Gilead, have literally changed mankind's history."

I looked at the sea of thunderheads, vague ghost-white shapes in the dim light. "I suppose so. Though whether we were here or not, it was only a matter of time before someone made contact with them."

She snorted. "Someone like who?—the Halloas? Come on; they were perfectly content to sit here thinking they were walking around on heaven talking directly to God. They'd never have made the connection by themselves."

From heaven God looks down, he sees all the chil-

dren of Adam, from the place where he sits he watches all who dwell on the earth; he alone molds their hearts, he understands all they do . . . "Imagine the impression on mankind's history if that *had* been true," I murmured.

"The thunderheads hardly conform to the popular concept of angels," Calandra said, a touch of humor glinting through the solemnity.

I smiled in return; and right then it hit me, like a brilliant flash of lightning. *From heaven God looks down* . . . "God in heaven, Calandra," I breathed. "That's it. *That's it!*"

She stared at me. "What—?"

"Come on!" Grabbing her hand, I almost literally pulled her toward the Pravilos still waiting nearby. "I need a phone—quickly," I called to them.

We met them halfway, and a phone was handed to me. "How do I get Dr. Eisenstadt?" I asked, fumbling with the instrument with trembling hands. It was so blatantly *obvious*—

One of the Pravilos keyed in the code, and a minute later Eisenstadt's face appeared on the tiny display. "Hello?"

"This is Benedar," I identified myself. "Where is Commodore Freitag?"

He blinked, clearly taken aback by the unexpected question. "On Solitaire, I presume."

"Call him," I said. "Get him here." I glanced at the Pravilos, looking as puzzled as Eisenstadt did. "And after he's on his way, better keep this whole place incommunicado. We still haven't proved Aikman didn't have an information source here, and this can*not* be allowed to get out."

"*What* can't be allowed to get out?" he growled, starting to grow irritated. "Calm down and—"

"We need a non-Solitaran criminal," I cut him off. "Right? And the best candidate for one is a smuggler. Right?"

"Y-y-yes," he said slowly. "Except that you said Freitag wasn't interested in a solution to the—"

"In a *partial* solution," I corrected him. Couldn't he *see* it—? "He wants to take all the smugglers in a single sweep, before any can slip through the net."

"And you know where they all are?"

"No!" I all but shouted at him. "*But the thunderheads do!*"

Beside me, Calandra whispered something startled and yet oddly reverent sounding . . . and Eisenstadt, for the first time since I'd met him, was speechless.

CHAPTER 27

It wasn't quite that easy, of course. The thunderheads had no way of distinguishing legitimate ships and settlements from smuggler ships and bases, for one thing, and it was quite a job explaining to them how to use human maps and skytracks. But with patience and computer wizardry on Freitag's part and stamina on Zagorin's, the job was eventually done.

A week later, Freitag had his clean sweep.

I learned later that no fewer than five smuggler ships were caught in the Pravilo's grand net, as well as four rather cushy bases buried in the wilds of Spall. Unraveling all the entanglements—some of which were rumored to stretch as far afield as Janus and Elegy—and bringing all those involved before the appropriate judiciaries would take months or even years. But for the leaders of one crew, caught red-handed with a kidnap victim still aboard, the Solitaran judiciary authorized the use of pravdrugs. From those five men, two were chosen whose clear and willing guilt was matched only by their complete ignorance of the group's business contacts.

Guilty, but at the same time useless to the Pravilo investigation . . . or in other words, perfect candidates for filling Eisenstadt's request for a zombi.

I expected the judiciary to take at least a week to make it official. It took, in fact, barely five days.

I'd expected the second time would be easier. Or perhaps merely hoped it would.

It wasn't, of course.

The Pravilo doctor stepped back from the *Kharg*'s helm chair, returning the hypo to its place in his small case. My stomach a hard knot, I forced myself to watch as the dead hands lifted delicately and reached for the helm board. I shuddered—those hands could have been Calandra's. They settled there; and abruptly the stars vanished from the bridge displays.

"Deadman Switch in control, Commodore," the man at the ditto helm announced. "Taking us out on bearing twenty-two mark four zero, fifty-six mark three three."

Freitag nodded. "Navigation?"

The navigator's hands were already playing over his board. "There's nothing in particular listed for that direction, sir," he reported. "No large planetoids or cometary bodies. Though that may not mean much— except for Solitaire system itself, data for this part of space is pretty sketchy."

"Which should encourage all of you to keep sharp," Freitag reminded the bridge in general. "Wherever the Cloud generator is stashed, it's likely to be either well hidden or well defended. Or both." He swiveled another quarter turn. "Dr. Eisenstadt?"

Standing beside the ditto nav chair, Eisenstadt leaned over to peer into Shepherd Zagorin's glazed eyes. "Thunderhead? You still with us?"

"I am," Zagorin whispered.

"Are we on the right path?"

"Yes," she assured him.

I watched her closely, trying with all my skill to read past the words to what might lie beneath them. As usual, the attempt failed. There were subtle differences in the sense between one encounter and another, I could tell now, differences that might be related to thunderhead emotional coloring the same way it was to that of human beings. But it could equally well be a result of Zagorin becoming acclimated to the contact, or to different thunderheads handling their end of the communication each time, or to any of a dozen other factors.

Beside me, Calandra shivered. "You were right, Gilead," she murmured. Her eyes, I saw, were on the body at the Deadman Switch. "It *is* the same. The same motions, the same sense, the same . . . everything."

She trailed off. I turned to Eisenstadt, to find him looking in turn at Calandra. His eyes flicked to mine, then shifted to the helm and Commodore Freitag sitting stiffly in his command chair. His sense . . . "Something wrong?" I asked quietly.

Eisenstadt hesitated, shook his head. "Just . . . thinking. Wondering about . . . well, the logic involved here."

The logic of the Cloud. With all his attention focused on getting a zombi for this trip, Eisenstadt had apparently lost sight of all the questions and contradictions that had sparked this trip out in the first place. "I presume you and Commodore Freitag intend to move carefully," I said.

"Give us a little credit for brains," he grunted. "I just wish the thunderheads would loosen up and tell us exactly what they expect us to do for them out here."

His eyes dropped to Zagorin's impassive face, but if the thunderhead listening through her ears recognized the cue he ignored it. Zagorin remained silent, and after a minute Eisenstadt grunted again and gave up. "Anyway," he said to me, "we should know within ten hours. Wherever it is they're taking us, it has to be inside the Cloud itself."

I nodded down at Zagorin. "Are you going to have her maintain contact the whole way?"

Eisenstadt pursed his lips, shook his head. "No, I suppose not. They're not," he added dryly, "exactly being fountains of information, after all. Ms. Zagorin?

—you can go ahead and break contact. Thunderhead, we'll be talking to you later. If there's anything we need to know, you'd better tell us now."

Zagorin straightened slightly. "Farewell," she said . . . and with a loud sigh slumped in her seat.

Eisenstadt looked at me, a sour expression on his face. "Or in other words," he growled, "they're still playing it coy."

"Don't worry about it," Freitag advised him coolly. "Whoever or whatever is out there running the Cloud generator, we'll be ready for them."

Woe to those going down to Egypt for help, who put their trust in horses, who rely on the quantity of chariots, and on great strength of cavalrymen . . .

Quietly, I slipped out of the bridge, leaving Freitag and the others to their watch. And their confidence.

It didn't take the ten hours Eisenstadt had been prepared for. It was, in fact, just under an hour later when the *Kharg*'s pseudogravity abruptly vanished.

We had arrived.

There were no warning sirens, no terse announcements of red alert or whatever as I left the command ready room and floated hurriedly across the small lounge to the bridge proper. Not that that was really surprising; Freitag would hardly have left matters to a last-second scramble for battle stations, any more than he had permitted me to stray farther from the bridge than the nearby ready room. Still, somehow, the silence was more unnerving than the sounds of even a pitched battle would have been. As if the bridge crew—perhaps even the entire ship—had been suddenly killed or disabled . . . Heart thudding in my ears, senses fully alert, I slid open the bridge door and pulled myself in.

And, naturally, instantly felt like a fool. Everyone was still alive and well, working quietly at their posts. The overall sense of the room was concentration, underpinned with tension and controlled nervousness, but there was nothing that seemed to indicate imminent danger.

I took a deep breath, privately embarrassed by my sudden wild imagination . . . and preoccupied with that, it took me another second to realize that that very lack of danger sense was in itself a signal that something here wasn't right.

Calandra was sitting quietly to one side, strapped into a ditto station chair where she could observe without being in the way. Giving the wall a push, I floated over to her. "What's wrong?" I murmured.

She shrugged fractionally, her sense uneasy. "There doesn't seem to be anything out there," she said.

I frowned, giving all the displays within eyeshot a quick scan. They meant little to my untrained eye. "Error?" I asked.

She flicked a glance at Eisenstadt and Zagorin, the latter working on getting into a meditative state—

I was looking at Zagorin, not any of the displays; but even so my peripheral vision was dazzled by the brilliant flicker of light that flashed across the room. "What—?"

I was drowned out by the warble of warning sirens. "Radiation attack," one of the crewers snapped. "Bow-starboard hull registering particle fluxes of—it's off the scale, sir." His voice sounded awed and more than a little shaken. "Heavy magnetic flux residue—focused particle beam weapon, almost certainly."

"Backtrack it, Kernyov," Freitag ordered another man. "Pinpoint the source. Costelic, how much got through?"

The first crewer opened his mouth to speak . . . paused. "Uh . . . virtually none, sir," he said slowly, frowning at his displays in disbelief. "The inner hull sensors are recording just barely above background."

"The hull *is* designed to block radiation, isn't it?" Eisenstadt asked.

"Not from particle weapons that go off the scale," Freitag said tartly. "You got a spectrum profile yet, Costelic?"

"It's coming in now, sir." Costelic paused, his puzzlement growing even deeper. "It . . . doesn't appear to have been a beam, sir. The distribution suggests an extremely hot thermal spectrum, almost like residue from a point source."

"Some kind of nova or star-collapse remnant, maybe?" Eisenstadt suggested doubtfully. "A wall of radiation sweeping past might give readings like that."

Freitag shook his head, studying Costelic's readings. "Too sharply defined for that. Kernyov!—where's that backtrack report?"

I looked at Kernyov in time to see him wave his hands helplessly. "It doesn't backtrack, sir," he said, voice rich with frustration. "I can pull a vector from the particle velocities—it's vague, but it's there—but there just isn't anything in that direction."

"What do you mean, isn't anything?" Freitag demanded. "That radiation came from *somewhere*."

"I know, sir, but there's nothing larger than a few microns in the indicated direction."

Freitag rubbed his fingertips together thoughtfully. "We're well within Solitaire system's cometary halo. Anything nearby large enough for a ship to be hiding behind?"

"I've already checked, sir," was the prompt answer. "There are eight good-sized comets visible on scope, but none of them is even remotely near the radiation vector. Also checked for neutrino emissions that might indicate fission or fusion going on, again, negative."

Freitag snorted and turned to Eisenstadt and Zagorin. "I want some answers, Doctor. When'll she be ready?"

"Thunderhead?" Eisenstadt asked, peering at Zagorin's impassive face. There was no repsonse. "Thunderhead?" he repeated, throwing a questioning glance at Calandra and me.

"Doctor—" Freitag began.

"It's not Zagorin, Commodore," Calandra spoke up. "She's in the proper meditative state."

Freitag's eyes flicked to her, as if he was going to argue with her diagnosis. "Then why isn't it working?" he demanded instead.

I could see her brace herself. "I'd guess, sir, that the trouble is on the thunderhead side."

Freitag transferred his glare to Zagorin. "Is it, now. Sort of as if they led us out here and then deliberately pulled back?" He shifted the glare once more, this time to Eisenstadt. "I don't suppose, Doctor, that you'd care to speculate on why these friends of humanity would do something like that?"

It was the first time I'd heard the thunderheads referred to in that way; and from the way Eisenstadt winced, I gathered the phrase had been his own coinage. For the first time I realized just how hard he'd pushed to get this trip approved, and how much of his reputation and prestige he'd put on the line for it.

And now, with it threatening to crumble right in front of him, I saw his mind frost over in the face of Freitag's question. He glanced at me, an unspoken plea behind his eyes— "Perhaps," I spoke up, "they're simply unable to make contact."

"They can run a zombi over nine light-years farther from Spall than this," Freitag countered.

"But we've never had a ship come in from this direction," I pointed out, feeling sweat breaking out on my forehead. Now it was *me* on the hot spot, and I wasn't at all sure where I was even headed with this. "None of the colonies is anywhere near this path."

"And?" he challenged.

"Well . . ." I floundered a bit. "Perhaps the radiation here is a clue. Coming from seemingly nowhere, and all—"

"I hope you're not going to suggest the radiation is scaring them off."

I clenched my teeth. "I don't think the radiation per se is bothering them, no. But perhaps there's something else associated with the Cloud generator that *is*."

Freitag cocked an eyebrow. "Oh? What Cloud generator is *that*?" he asked, hand waving across the empty displays.

"There's nothing that says the Cloud generator has to be in normal space, is there?" I asked doggedly. Spur-of-the-moment idea or not, I had no intention of letting myself be bullied into just abandoning it. "The Cloud itself certainly doesn't seem to be. And if the Cloud was created to keep the thunderheads inside Solitaire system, maybe the generator itself was designed to keep them *out*."

Freitag's mouth opened . . . closed again. "Uh-*huh*," he said at last, thoughtfully. "Interesting, indeed. It's supposed to be impossible for something to be at rest in Mjollnir space, but let that pass for the moment. Costelic, have we got a solid fix on our position here?"

The navigator was opening his mouth to reply when, without warning, the *Kharg* lurched and gravity abruptly returned.

"*Hold* it—!" Freitag snapped, his flash of anger turning to equally sharp embarrassment as he suddenly remembered he was yelling an order to a dead man. "Kernyov!—get his hands away from that thing."

"No!" Eisenstadt barked as Kernyov reached for the Deadman Switch board. "We could lose our path!"

Freitag threw him a stabbing glare. "We may already have lost it—"

And, mid-sentence, the circuit breakers cracked and gravity again vanished. Freitag swore under his breath, and for a long second seemed to be trying to regain his mental balance; then the gears meshed and he was back in control again. "All right, let's sort this out. Costelic, where are we now?"

The navigator peered at his displays. "Not too far from where we started, Commodore. Looks like we basically did a short loop, back around to a point about five million kilometers closer in to Solitaire. I can give you an exact location in a minute."

Freitag eyed me. "You want to try and explain *this* one, Benedar?" he suggested. "You've got a choice: two separate Mjollnir-space generators or one *extremely* large one. Take your pick."

I took a deep breath, trying desperately to come up with an answer that wouldn't sound overly stupid—and as abruptly as the last time, the displays again flashed with light.

Eisenstadt yelped something, the words drowned out

by the warbling of the radiation alarm. "What in chern-fire—?"

"Shut up," Freitag snapped. "Costelic?"

"Same as before, Commodore," the other reported. "Hot radiation, but without any of the penetrating power of a beam weapon."

For a moment longer the activity continued on the bridge, with crewers reporting generally the same findings as before. But I was watching Freitag . . . and because I was, I saw the moment when his irritated puzzlement turned suddenly to something cold. "Commodore?" I asked tentatively.

He ignored me. "Costelic . . . did we get anything on the aft-starboard instruments?"

"The flash came from the bow-starboard side again—"

"I know where it came from," Freitag said tightly. "I'm asking about *aft*-starboard. Specifically, ninety degrees from the flash."

"Ah—yes, sir." Costelic's fingers skittered across the keys. "There's not really much of anything there, sir. Solitaire system is that direction, of course; a couple of comets in the distance . . . just a moment."

"What is it?" Eisenstadt asked.

"We'll know in a minute," Freitag told him.

I watched as Costelic's sense took on a tinge of awe . . . and when he lifted his gaze from his displays his eyes were haunted. "Aft-starboard instruments show a tube-shaped region of high particle density, Commodore," he said, the words coming out with some difficulty. "Expanding rapidly into an even larger tube of . . . extremely hard vacuum. A large fraction of the high density material reads as superexcited helium."

The muscles in Freitag's back visibly tightened. "And the optical scanners?"

Costelic braced himself. "It's there, all right, sir. Computer's doing a cleanup and compensation now—be just a few more seconds."

"It *who*?" Eisenstadt asked. "What did you pick up, one of the thunderheads?"

"Hardly, Doctor," Freitag said darkly. "That splash

of light and particle radiation . . . was the backwash of a spacecraft."

Eisenstadt blinked. "A space—?"

And all at once his sense turned to quiet horror. "You mean . . . traveling space-*normal*?"

Freitag nodded grimly. "And over nine light-years in from the edge of the Cloud, too. Even at—looks like they're doing something over ten percent lightspeed— even at that rate they must have been doing this for one smert of a long time. Costelic?—where's that adjusted data?"

"Coming through now, Commodore . . . oh, *bozhe moi.*"

The last word was an abrupt whisper. For a long moment Freitag gazed at his displays . . . and I watched his sense go from disbelief to something akin to horror.

Slowly, he looked up, turning to face Eisenstadt. "My error, Doctor," he said, his voice icy calm. "It's not, in fact, *one* spacecraft heading inwards toward Solitaire. It's something close to two hundred of them."

Eisenstadt stared at him. "A war party?"

"I don't see what else it could be," Freitag nodded.

I suddenly noticed my hands were clenched tightly at my sides. "Couldn't they simply be colony ships?" I asked, moved by something I only vaguely understood to give the strangers the benefit of the doubt.

Freitag looked at me. "Does it matter?" he asked bluntly. "Whether they want territory or a fight, the end result is still the same.

"Solitaire is under attack."

CHAPTER 28

" . . . The ships, fortunately, are only about half the size we'd originally estimated," Freitag said, splitting his display to show both an actual photo as well as a computer-scrubbed rendition. "Nearly forty percent of the size and mass is taken up by this umbrella-like thing, apparently a scoop-and-shield arrangement that magnetically grabs interstellar hydrogen and funnels it into the drive—those four nozzles on the underside—while simultaneously protecting the passengers from any atoms and micrometeors that the fields missed. The main body of the ship is back *here*—" he indicated it— "hanging about a kilometer beneath the drive section."

"Held there by what?" Governor Rybakov asked coolly. All things considered, I thought, she was taking this with considerable composure.

"A cable, we assume," Freitag told her. "Unfortunately, the *Kharg*'s cameras weren't good enough to resolve it. That gives us a lower limit for its strength, though, and it's considerable."

"How considerable?" Rybakov demanded. "Beyond Patri capabilities?"

Eisenstadt shook his head. "I've done some checking

and we *could* duplicate it. Tricky and expensive, but possible."

The tension in the governor's sense eased a bit. "At least they've got similar technology," she murmured. "I suppose we should be grateful for small favors."

Freitag and Eisenstadt exchanged glances. "Perhaps, Governor," Freitag said cautiously. "But don't forget that these ships have been running, probably constantly, for something like eighty-five *years*—and without putting in at a port for maintanence, I might add. That implies a tremendous technological consistency; and for them to be willing to ride the things in the first place implies an equally impressive confidence in that technology."

"Although we don't really *know* the ships are manned, do we?" Rybakov countered. "They could just as easily be robots. And as far as your assumed consistency is concerned, remember that we also don't know how many ships they had when they first started out. These one hundred ninety-two could conceivably be just the tail end of a fleet that originally numbered in the thousands."

"Unlikely," Freitag grunted. "Easy enough to check, though—all we have to do is search their backtrack for derelicts or debris."

"Provided the thunderheads will cooperate in such a search," Rybakov said, turning her gaze on me for the first time. "Which is why I wanted Benedar to be in on this conference today."

I gazed back at her . . . and it was only then, faced with the contrast in attitudes, that I suddenly realized just how much Eisenstadt's original antagonism toward me had diminished over the past few weeks. "I'll help in any way I can," I said evenly.

She almost grimaced, her sense a mixture of distaste and determination reminiscent of when she'd come to Randon to retrieve her illegally issued customs IDs. "I understand you've been keeping an eye on these Halloas Dr. Eisenstadt is using to talk to the thunderheads," she said.

"Yes," I nodded. "Though at the moment there's only one Seeker there to keep an eye on."

"And . . . ?"

I shrugged. "So far things seem to be going all right. Shepherd Zagorin is exhibiting some subtle changes, but they seem to be mainly adjustments to the thunderhead presence. There's no indication that they're subverting her or anything like that."

Rybakov glanced at Eisenstadt; peripherally, I saw his nod of agreement. "For the moment we'll assume you're right," she went on. "So. If they're so cooperative and friendly, explain why they didn't tell us about the Invaders sooner."

I winced. "We don't actually know they're deliberate invaders—"

"You can practice turning the other cheek on your own time," Rybakov cut me off. "Just answer the question, and save the moralizing for your religious friends."

"I *was* answering it, Governor," I told her, fighting back my own irritation. "I was trying to suggest that the thunderheads may not have said anything about them because they themselves may not see it as an invasion."

She snorted. "Ridiculous. What do they think they're coming for, a picnic?"

Eisenstadt cleared his throat. "It's possible they've examined both the ships and their passengers and concluded they won't be wanting Spall," he said. "We think it likely they did the same with *us* before they first started guiding us through the Cloud."

"The fact remains that, unlike the Invaders, they let *us* in," Rybakov countered. "Or are you going to suggest the Invaders were offered the same Deadman Switch approach and were turned down?"

"The Invaders may not have Mjollnir drive," Eisenstadt pointed out. Just as I was doing with the aliens, he was clearly trying to give the thunderheads every possible benefit of the doubt. "We won't know until we can take better pictures and see if the ships are equipped with the necessary hull lacings."

Rybakov grimaced. "All right, then, let's try it from another direction. According to the report you filed when you first asked for a Solitaran zombi, the thunderheads were offering to show you the Cloud generator. They lied about that; what's to say they aren't lying about other things, too?"

"Yes, well, we wondered about that too," Eisenstadt said, embarrassment seeping through his professionalism. "If you go back and check the tapes, you find that the thunderheads promised to take us to the origination—their word—of the Cloud. 'Origination,' my dictionary tells me, is something that gives origin to, or something that initiates. I assumed at the time that they meant the generator of the Cloud; what I gather they actually meant was the *reason* for the Cloud's existence."

"In other words, as a protection from invasion," Rybakov snorted. "As I said."

Eisenstadt glanced at Freitag. "Again, not necessarily, Governor," Freitag said. "It's possible that they're maintaining the Cloud in order to protect *us*."

Rybakov opened her mouth, a retort ready . . . closed it again as her sense turned suddenly thoughtful. "Uh-*huh*," she said at last. "Well, that's hardly a flattering thought—rather reduces our role here to something like pets or valuable wildlife."

"Or an equally valuable scientific study," Eisenstadt offered. "That might explain, too, why they hid their sentience from us for so long."

"Perhaps. Hardly an improvement over being pets, to my mind." She frowned into space for a moment. "Didn't they say at your first contact that they didn't have any interest in studying us?"

"What they actually said was that they had no desire to learn any *more* about us," Eisenstadt corrected her. "If they already had seventy years of such studies behind them, they would hardly need any more."

Rybakov snorted gently. "Again, a strictly truthful statement that nevertheless manages to mislead. I don't like the pattern I see forming here."

There was considerable irony in such a complaint coming from a professional politician, but Eisenstadt had the sense to pass up the obvious barbs. "At least they seem reluctant to tell out-and-out lies," he shrugged.

"Don't forget, too, that they've already demonstrated respect for human life. When that shield—what was his name, Gilead?"

"Mikha Kutzko," I supplied. A pang of guilt poked in under my concentration; I'd hardly thought at all over the past few weeks about what might be happening with him and the others on the *Bellwether*.

Eisenstadt nodded. "When Kutzko did his little experiment to see how fast the thunderheads could learn, they could presumably have tried to kill him instead of going after his needler."

"Protecting their scientific experiment," Rybakov said sourly. "—yes, I know, Doctor, it's better than being considered enemies," she added as Eisenstadt started to speak. "Anyway, the issue of thunderhead perceptions is low on the priority list at the moment. What's important is how we're going to deal with the Invaders. Any ideas, Commodore?"

Freitag waved a hand uncomfortably. "I've done a couple of preliminary scenerios, but none of them is especially promising."

"What's the problem, the speed they're making?"

"Basically. You have to remember that they're doing twelve percent lightspeed; that's thirty-six thousand kilometers a *second*. None of our weapons has the slightest chance of even tracking something that fast, let alone connecting with it."

"What about shooting at them from the front?" Rybakov asked. "We *know* what their course is, after all."

"Wait a moment," I objected. "Isn't this a little early to be thinking about shooting at them? We haven't even *tried* to talk to them yet."

All three looked at me; Rybakov with impatience, Freitag with an almost guilty impatience, Eisenstadt with genuine regret. "The problem, Gilead," the latter said, "is that their speed also pretty well precludes any kind of communication. We'd have to use high-density pulses, fired from close range the instant they passed, and signals like that are notoriously sensitive to the sort of electromagnetic fluxes they've got operating."

"But surely they know how to compensate for that," I argued. "I mean, they must have some way of watching ahead of them, at the very least."

"I'm sure they do," Freitag said, his discomfort putting gruffness in his voice. "But they'll be watching out for cometary masses, not pulsed radio signals. And besides . . ." He seemed to brace himself. "It might not be a good idea to tip them off that we're even aware of them. It would lose us any advantage of surprise we might still have."

I looked at him, feeling the blood draining from my face. *Look at them, lurking to ambush me, violent men are attacking me, for no fault, no sin of mine . . .* "You can't do that," I said quietly. "It would be nothing less than mass murder."

"It's called survival," Rybakov said sharply.

"Since when?" I demanded. "This isn't some sudden, split-second assault we have to react to—they're not even going to *be* here for, what, ten years?"

"More than that," Freitag grunted. "Somewhere along the line they'll have to flip their ships over and start decelerating; depending on what kind of thrust their engines can handle, it could be anything from twelve to twenty years before they arrive."

"Which means that everyone involved will have plenty of time to weigh the alternatives," Eisenstadt told me soothingly. "I presume, Governor, that 'everyone,' in this case, will be people other than us?"

Rybakov nodded. "The Patri will almost certainly want to set up a commission to examine the situation and make recommendations." She turned to me. "*Your* job, Benedar, will be to continue assisting in the thunderhead study. That is, if Dr. Eisenstadt still needs you."

"I do," Eisenstadt said. Almost too quickly. "Both he and Ms. Paquin are proving indispensable."

Rybakov shrugged, striving for off-handedness but not entirely succeeding. "Fine. Let me know when either of them becomes superfluous. Well. Thank you, Doctor; Commodore. I congratulate you both on your work in this, and I'm sure the Patri will find a way to put their appreciation into more concrete form. Good day to you all; Dr. Eisenstadt, keep me informed on your work."

Freitag parted company with us outside the governor's mansion, heading for his office at the main Solitaran Pravilo HQ, as Eisenstadt and I headed back to Rainbow's End and the shuttle awaiting us there. I waited until we were aboard, out of earshot of drivers and crewers, before asking Eisenstadt the obvious question. "What did the governor mean, that you should let her know when either Calandra or I became superfluous?"

"Oh, there've been some further legal rumblings about you two," he shrugged, trying hard to sound unconcerned. "Same sort of thing as before."

"You mean that Calandra's execution should be carried out?"

"Mainly," he said. "There's also some noise that you ought to be charged for your role in her escape. Completely ridiculous, especially given the importance of what it was you two stumbled onto poking around Spall."

I thought about that a moment. One of the immediate implications— "Then the Patri are still planning to keep all of this a secret as long as possible?"

He nodded, throwing me a lopsided smile. "Uh-huh— and that's very much to your advantage right now. As long as they're reluctant to bring any more people than absolutely necessary into this, you two are by definition the only Watchers available. As long as I need you, Rybakov's not about to take you away."

"Yes, sir," I murmured. To our advantage, certainly . . . and even more to the Patri's. No public knowledge meant no public opinion . . . and no public opinion meant they could plot the aliens' destruction with complete impunity. *Though a thousand fall at your side, ten thousand at your right hand, you yourself will remain unscathed . . .* "Yes, sir," I said again. "I understand."

CHAPTER 29

For the next three weeks nothing much happened. Eisenstadt talked with the thunderheads once every couple of days, Calandra and I watching each contact and trying to learn how to read and interpret the aliens' sense as they spoke through Shepherd Zagorin. Eisenstadt didn't learn all that much from the conversations, and now that I was looking for it I realized that Governor Rybakov's comment had indeed been correct: the thunderheads really *did* like making strictly truthful statements that were nevertheless misleading. At one point Eisenstadt got mad enough to consider calling them on it, but eventually decided not to. It could, after all, be merely an odd quirk of their psychology, in which case objecting would accomplish little and probably be insulting in the bargain.

Of the approaching fleet they would say nothing at all, no matter how many creative ways Eisenstadt found to rephrase the questions we wanted answers to. Eventually, he gave up asking, but only after he managed to obtain assurances that they would cooperate in guiding the observation ships the new Patri commission would undoubtedly be sending out.

The commission itself arrived, bringing with them a pair of Pravilo ships, a selection of highly sophisticated sensor and photographic gear, and—I heard—upwards of a dozen zombis. The thought of the latter made me wince, and I wondered how I was going to handle living in the same camp with a full-fledged death-cell prison. But my worry turned out to be for nothing; instead of joining us, the commission opted to set up their head-quarters a few hundred kilometers away in one of the now-abandoned smuggler bases. Settling in for a long, leisurely study, apparently, and unwilling to spend it in what was still something of a makeshift camp.

It made me wonder what kind of people had been chosen for the commission; but after a little reflection I decided it might actually be a hopeful sign. Business and political leaders who liked their comfort might be less inclined to shoot first and sift the rubble later than would a group drawn strictly from the Pravilo's military strategists. Indeed, after a meeting at their encampment, Eisenstadt told me that despite Freitag's expectations to the contrary, the question of whether the Patri should try to open up communication with the fleet was indeed on the commission's agenda. It was, I had to admit, as much as I could have hoped for.

And so the commission sent out their ships, and I returned to my duties and let thoughts of the alien fleet sink into the distant background of my mind . . . and so was totally unprepared when, two weeks later, it all crumbled at my feet.

Eisenstadt and Zagorin had had one of their—as usual—largely futile conversations with the thunder-heads that morning; now, in late afternoon, the Butte City was deserted except for a pair of Pravilo guards keeping a fairly casual eye on the fenced corridor lead-ing from the encampment. It was a good time to just sit and observe the thunderheads with a minimum of dis-tractions, something I'd been doing a fair amount of lately. Ultimately, my goal was to learn to read them the way I did human beings; but like everything else connected with the thunderheads, this project seemed to be at a standstill. There were a great many subtle signals I could draw from the whitish shapes—movements, color changes, even the hint of soft, high-pitched sounds—but putting them together into anything more meaningful than simple awareness/unawareness was still far beyond my capabilities. It was frustrating in the extreme, but as long as they seemed determined to evade vital questions I had to keep trying.

Especially if—I was honest enough to admit—it could make Calandra and me that much more valuable to Eisenstadt.

The shadows from the dipping sun were crawling up the sides of the buttes, and I was just wondering if I should give up for the evening when the breeze brought me the faint sound of approaching tires.

I frowned, wondering who else would be coming out here at this hour. The Pravilo guards were standing together, looking down along the corridor . . . and abruptly, both stiffened with sudden alertness.

My heart seemed to skip a beat. Danger?—no. Sudden alertness, but neither man had made any move toward needler or phone. Sudden alertness . . . as in formal, parade-ground ceremonial. Some important official, then, on an unscheduled tour? It seemed likely; and if so, he and his shields might not be pleased to find me hanging around. I gritted my teeth, wondering if I would have time to make a discreet withdrawal before the approaching car blocked my exit; and then it was too late. The front of the car nosed into view and came to a stop, and two men climbed out . . . and I caught my breath. Even at that distance, with their faces too silhouetted against the sky to make out, their stances and movements were far too familiar to be mistaken.

The taller of the two was Mikha Kutzko . . . and the shorter was Lord Kelsey-Ramos.

I stared at them, feeling my mouth drop open as my brain fluttered like a stunned bird. Lord Kelsey-Ramos, *here*? I'd been told that travel to and from even Soli-

taire had been heavily restricted lately, let alone travel
to this part of Spall. And for him to be allowed into the
Butte City itself . . .

They were talking to the Pravilo guards now, and one
of them pointed through the gathering shadows to me.
Lord Kelsey-Ramos nodded his thanks and together he
and Kutzko started across. Abruptly, my brain cleared
enough for me to remember my manners, and I scrambled to my feet. "Lord Kelsey-Ramos," I nodded, fighting hard to keep the surprise out of my voice. A lot got
through anyway.

"Good to see you too, Gilead," Lord Kelsey-Ramos
said dryly. His voice was good humored, even friendly
. . . but behind the facade was something grim. Something very grim indeed. "Wondering how I managed to
run the Patri blockade of Solitaire system?"

I glanced at Kutzko, got cool formality in return.
Apparently he still hadn't entirely forgiven me. "I imagine, sir," I said to Lord Kelsey-Ramos, "that you called
in some of your high-level favors—no," I interrupted
myself, the obvious answer filtering in through my still-
sluggish brain. "You're on the commission studying the
incoming fleet, aren't you?"

He smiled, a smile that didn't even dent the grimness in his eyes. "I've really missed having you around,
Gilead—you so seldom waste my time with the need
for long explanations. Yes, I have indeed been honored
with one of the seats on the panel."

"I congratulate the Patri on their fine choice, sir."

"Thank you," he nodded. "Though in all fairness I
should remind you that I had a good head start on
getting my name in front of the proper people—with
the *Bellwether* stuck here and every query I sent
coming back with vague and clearly censored answers, I
knew that *some*thing unexpected was happening." He
half turned to look at the sea of thunderheads. "But I
never guessed it was anything like *this* . . ."

"What's wrong, sir?" I asked.

He turned back to face me. "The commission has
finished the first phase of its study, Gilead," he told

me, a quiet ache in his voice. "The decision's been made to destroy the Invaders."

I stared at him. "*What?*" I whispered.

He shook his head wearily. "I'm sorry. I tried to find an alternative—I tried blazing hard. But there just wasn't anything that would work. Not in the time available."

"What 'time available?' " I demanded. "They won't be here for *years*—surely we can find a way to communicate with—"

"We don't have years. We have four to six months."

My argument froze in its tracks. "*Months?*"

He nodded. "Admiral Yoshida's experts have gone over the Invaders' engine efficiencies at least five times, from five different directions. They estimate that in four to six months the Invaders will be shutting down their drives, turning their ships around, and reconfiguring for a long deceleration phase."

"But if they'll be slowing down—?"

"Oh, they still won't actually get to Solitaire for seventeen years," he shrugged. "But once they're in deceleration mode . . . well, there's no need for their drives to be angled at all away from their line of motion."

And suddenly I understood. "In other words," I said slowly, "their exhausts will be aiming forward, where they'll vaporize anything we throw at them. So if we don't destroy them now, we won't have another chance until they get here. Is that it?"

A muscle in his cheek twitched, a deep and genuine pain twisting through his sense. "It's a *war fleet*, Gilead—the more Yoshida's experts study it, the more they're convinced of that. If we let them get to Solitaire, the colony is lost—pure and simple."

"We have seventeen years to prepare—"

"It wouldn't matter if we had a *hundred* years—there's no way we can fight that many ships in face-to-face battle."

I locked eyes with him. "There are less than half a million people on Solitaire. They could surely be relocated somewhere else."

He didn't flinch from my gaze. "Just clear out of the system, then? Is that what you suggesting?"

"Why not?"

"Two reasons." He held up two fingers. "One: it would mean abandoning the ring mines."

A cold knot formed in my stomach. Yes, of course—it had to have been something like that. "So for a few million tons of metal we deliberately murder thousands of—"

"And two," Lord Kelsey-Ramos cut me off firmly, "it would mean abandoning the thunderheads, leaving them to face the Invaders alone. *Now* tell me where the ethical path lies."

My righteous anger faded, replaced by uncertainty. *If you have resident aliens in your country, you will not molest them. You will treat resident aliens as though they were native-born and love them as yourself—for you yourselves were once aliens in Egypt* . . . "I don't know," I had to say. "All I know is that mass murder isn't it."

Lord Kelsey-Ramos sighed. "Deep down, I'd have to agree . . . but intellectually, I just don't see any alternatives. It would probably take all the time we have until turnover just to figure out the raw mechanics of sending messages to the Invaders, let alone finding a common language to talk to each other in."

"Wait a minute," I said as a sudden thought occurred to me. "What about the thunderheads? Maybe *they* know how to talk to them."

"Maybe," Lord Kelsey-Ramos agreed. "And if you can get them to give you either a method or a language, I'm sure the commission will be interested. But we've asked them about it ourselves at least a half dozen times, and they've so far completely ignored the request."

I grimaced. "They know something about it—I'm sure they do."

"I agree," Lord Kelsey-Ramos nodded grimly. "But if they won't say anything, there isn't much we can do about it."

"But then how can we assume they're the threatened

party?" I argued. "All right—suppose the ships *are*, in fact, a war party. Who's to say it isn't the thunderheads who brought it on themselves?"

Lord Kelsey-Ramos eyed me. "And if they did, what do you propose we do about it? Take sides with the Invaders against the thunderheads?"

Frustration welled up within me, settled into a bitter pool in the pit of my stomach. *Blessed are the peacemakers* . . . "I don't know."

For a long minute we stood there in silence. Then Lord Kelsey-Ramos stirred, looking up at the buttes towering above us. "Interesting place, this," he said, almost conversationally. "Unique, too—we've been over the satellite photos of Spall with a fine mesh and there's nothing even remotely like this city anywhere on the planet."

"The thunderheads have many human-comparable senses," I told him mechanically, my thoughts still on the terrible vision of mass murder hovering before my mind's eye. "They told us they like having this kind of close-packed community when it's possible."

"Uh-huh," he nodded. "And what is it, do you suppose, that makes it possible here?"

The vision of carnage vanished, and I looked at Lord Kelsey-Ramos sharply. There was something new in his sense; something part of, yet distinct from, the overall grimness there. "What is it?" I asked quietly.

"Suspicion," he said. "Nothing more—for the moment, anyway. My question wasn't rhetorical, incidentally."

I looked around the Butte City. "I really don't know, sir," I admitted. "It's somewhat sheltered from violent weather, but that's about all I can think of."

Lord Kelsey-Ramos nodded, turning to eye the slope that Calandra and I had climbed the first night we'd camped here—years ago, it seemed. "The transcript of your pravdrug interrogation mentioned that you'd found a line of heat-treated places going up one of those slopes," he said, pointing. "Show them to me, will you?"

"Certainly. This way . . ."

I led him and Kutzko over to the base of the proper slope and pointed out the lowest of the spots. "We thought perhaps they marked where thunderheads had once been," I explained. "They apparently needed several stages to get one of their seeds all the way to the top of the butte."

"A watchman," Lord Kelsey-Ramos nodded. "Yes, I remember that speculation from the transcript. Has it occurred to you since then to wonder why a physical watchman should be of any use to beings who can leave their bodies and travel about at will?"

I frowned. It *hadn't* occurred to me, as a matter of fact. "To watch for the approach of threatening weather?" I suggested hesitantly.

"I think that unlikely," Lord Kelsey-Ramos shook his head. "Most creatures tend to do things along the line of least energy expenditure, and I can't see them going to that much trouble for something they don't have any control over."

"Do we *know* they don't have any control over their weather?" I countered. "I would think that the heat from a massed set of organic lasers might make it possible for them to—I don't know; perhaps at least alter storm tracks somewhat."

Lord Kelsey-Ramos looked hard at me, and abruptly his sense sharpened. "What?" I asked, my heart jumping in sympathetic reaction.

"Maybe nothing," he said slowly. "Maybe everything. Coordinated use of their organic lasers . . . interesting." He thought for a moment longer, then shook his head fractionally, putting whatever it was into mental storage for later. "Anyway. For now, back to the original topic: the thunderheads' watchmen. According to Dr. Eisenstadt's reports, the way the thunderheads located the smuggler ships and bases was by finding isolated groups of humans for you. Correct?"

I nodded. "I remember them specifically mentioning that inanimate objects such as ships weren't detectable to them in that state."

"Right. Word for word, in fact, with the report."

"Dr. Eisenstadt seemed to think it was reasonable enough," I told him, wondering where he was headed with this. "If they could see everything around them while out of their bodies, there wouldn't be much need for the bodies themselves to have developed duplicate senses."

"Agreed," Lord Kelsey-Ramos said. "Eisenstadt speculated that it was some kind of 'life-force' that they pick up—our souls, if you wish," he added, obviously expecting me to make the identification if he didn't. "It occurred to me that perhaps we were once again being too generous with something the thunderheads were saying. As you pointed out, they themselves told you they couldn't see inanimate objects; but it was *our* assumption that it was *only* inanimate objects they couldn't see."

And finally, I got it. "You think there are animal predators around that they also can't detect?"

"It would seem reasonable," Lord Kelsey-Ramos shrugged. "Given the thunderheads' organic lasers, a predator would almost have to be able to sneak up on them."

I frowned at him, reading his sense. "This isn't just speculation, is it?" I asked carefully. "You've done some checking on this already."

Lord Kelsey-Ramos gazed upward at the buttes again. "There's a small weasel-like animal that seems to have a taste for thunderhead flesh," he said. "Often hunts in packs of up to thirty family members. I wonder how clearly a group like that could be seen from up there."

"Thunderhead eyesight is pretty good," I told him, a shiver running up my back. In retrospect it was obvious that the balance of nature on Spall would include predators for the thunderheads to cope with . . . but the fact that the thunderheads had again deliberately obscured important information set my teeth on edge. "So when the watchmen on each of the buttes see a pack approaching . . . the others get ready to fight?"

"Kutzko?" Lord Kelsey-Ramos invited. "This is your specialty. What do you think?"

Kutzko looked slowly around the area, eyes measuring. I read his sense, realized the idea was new to him, as well. Lord Kelsey-Ramos had apparently been playing this one very quietly indeed. An indication that he was very worried . . . "It's a good setup," Kutzko said at last. "Only four approaches, none of them very wide, and with a layered defense in place at each."

"Layered defense?" Lord Kelsey-Ramos frowned.

"Yes, sir." Kutzko pointed. "See, near each gap, how there's a group of five to seven thunderheads positioned slightly upslope? In standard military placement, those would be forward sentries, responsible for stopping any lone weasel or small group who'd managed to slip in past the topside sentry." He waved toward the larger mass of thunderheads. "Then, for larger groups—which the topside sentry would presumably have warned them about—there's a good potential for concentrated firepower from the main community. See how the shorter ones tend to be at the edge, the taller ones at the middle? Again, reminiscent of a standard kneeling/standing arrangement."

I licked my lips. "Many of the shorter ones are drones," I told him. "Extra bodies, not originally sentient."

Kutzko nodded. "So much the better. They can still probably be used to fight from, and are expendable if the weasels get in that close."

"In other words," Lord Kelsey-Ramos said, something dark in his voice, "the thunderheads understand warfare."

Kutzko shrugged. "Not necessarily. Evolution often hammers this sort of strategic ability into a species."

"Except that these are intelligent creatures," Lord Kelsey-Ramos growled. "*And* this city isn't part of their standard living pattern."

"Yes, what about that?" I asked him. "Out in the wild, they don't have anything like this arrangement to protect them."

"They also don't cluster together in large groups that could as easily attract predators," Lord Kelsey-Ramos pointed out. "Perhaps the thick vegetation that they encourage to grow around them is supposed to discourage attacks."

"I wouldn't think so," Kutzko disagreed. "Especially since having all that stuff in the way would also interfere with their lasers."

"Mmm." Lord Kelsey-Ramos thought for a moment; and again, I could see his sense harden as some new and clearly unpleasant thought occurred to him. "What are you doing tomorrow morning, Gilead?" he asked abruptly.

"As far as I know, nothing special," I told him cautiously. "I don't think Dr. Eisenstadt has a contact session planned."

"Good. I'll pick you up at nine—be ready." He motioned to Kutzko, turned to go . . . hesitated. "Oh, by the way," he added, sounding almost embarrassed, "I've sent a request to Outbound for the transcripts of your friend Paquin's trial."

"Oh . . . thank you, sir," I said, surprised and oddly ashamed. With all the focus on the thunderheads and alien fleet, I'd almost forgotten what the original point of all this had been.

"No problem," Lord Kelsey-Ramos grunted. "Just keep in mind that I can't make any promises. Well, I'll see you in the morning. Good-night, and sleep well."

Sleep well. With a hundred ninety-two alien spacecraft streaking toward destruction . . . "Yes, sir," I sighed. "Good-night."

CHAPTER 30

They arrived precisely at nine the next morning, flying in from commission headquarters in a sleek Pravilo aircar. We left half an hour later by mul/terrain vehicle, the intervening time taken up largely by a quiet yet sharp argument between Lord Kelsey-Ramos and Dr. Eisenstadt. I wasn't close enough to hear any of the words, but from the body language I could see I gathered that Eisenstadt, his curiosity piqued, was asking to come along on this expedition and that Lord Kelsey-Ramos was refusing him. From Eisenstadt's expression it was obvious he thought Lord Kelsey-Ramos was simply trying to cut anyone else out of whatever credit might come out of it, and he was understandably irritated by the thought of an amateur poking around scientific matters and possibly fouling them up in the process.

I could almost have wished it was indeed something that petty. To me, knowing him as I did, it was uncomfortably clear that Lord Kelsey-Ramos was limiting the group to himself, Kutzko, and me because he was expecting trouble and wanted to limit the number of potential casualties.

A noble attitude . . . but as we drove off into the wilderness, I couldn't help but reflect how much easier it was to applaud such consideration when it was someone else's neck on the line.

We drove for about an hour before Lord Kelsey-Ramos finally found what he was looking for.

"There," he pointed, offering me his noculars for a closer look. "Up there on the hillside—that single thunderhead in the middle of that weed patch?"

I nodded. The "weed patch," as he called it, was familiar enough—the sort of thick growth that Eisenstadt's studies had found was encouraged by the thunderheads' periodic root disintegrations. A few small insects were visible circling the vegetation, but other than that I could find no sign of other animal life. Shifting my angle, I gave the entire area a quick sweep. There were other thunderheads scattered around on nearby hills, but as near as I could tell none of them were in direct line of sight with the one Lord Kelsey-Ramos had picked out. "It's as isolated as we're likely to find," I agreed. "Do we get to know yet why that's important?"

He swung the car door open, and I could sense him bracing himself. "Take the noculars and head up," he said over his shoulder, an odd tightness in his voice. "Not too close—maybe by that rock outcrop over there." He pointed. "Some place where you can see everything. And keep your phone on—I don't want us to have to shout back and forth. Kutzko, where did you stow the box?"

"Left side storage," Kutzko told him. "I'll get it."

"No, I'll do it. You take the recorder and get up there with Gilead—find some place more or less opposite from him."

I looked at Kutzko, read the same uneasiness and uncertainty there that I was feeling. "Lord Kelsey-Ramos—"

"Get moving," he cut me off, moving around the back of the car to the storage compartment Kutzko had indicated and popping it open.

I didn't move. "Lord Kelsey-Ramos, there's only a

limited amount of help we can give you if we don't know what it is you're trying to do."

He paused, indecision in his sense. Glancing past him, I saw a long box in the open storage compartment, a box made of metal and a heavy, opaque mesh. Lying beside the box was a set of heavy gloves; from the box itself came a faint scratching sound . . .

I looked back up at Lord Kelsey-Ramos, found his eyes on me. "It's one of the weasels you talked about yesterday, isn't it?" I asked carefully.

"The proper scientific name is *laska myesist*-something-or-other," he said with forced casualness. "And there are actually four of them in there."

"You want to see how the thunderheads fight," Kutzko said quietly, hand drifting automatically closer to his needler.

"I want to see how the thunderheads defend themselves in the wild," Lord Kelsey-Ramos corrected. "There's a difference."

Kutzko looked up the hill at our target thunderhead and slid the recorder strap off his shoulder. "Here, sir," he said, offering it to Lord Kelsey-Ramos. "If you and Gilead will get in position, I'll bring the cage."

Lord Kelsey-Ramos shook his head. "Sorry, Kutzko, but this one is mine."

"I insist sir," Kutzko said, an edge to his voice.

"As do I," Lord Kelsey-Ramos told him icily. "This is my idea, and it could be dangerous. I'll do it."

Kutzko's sense hardened a bit more. "My *job*, sir, is to protect you," he said. "I intend to carry out that job . . . and if I have to lock you in the car, you won't be able to watch what happens very well."

Lord Kelsey-Ramos locked eyes with him. "I'm giving you an order, Kutzko. You will blazing-well obey it."

"Gilead?" Kutzko invited.

I took a deep breath. The last time the thunderheads had even suspected they were about to be attacked they'd brought enough heat energy to bear to melt and fuse metal. What this one might do in the face of what was, in effect, a genuine attack . . . "I'm willing to handle the recorder," I sighed, "if you need to lock him in the car."

Lord Kelsey-Ramos turned his glare on me; but behind the anger I could detect a growing resignation . . . and more than a little grudging appreciation. "When we get back I'm going to have to teach you two the distinction between loyalty and disobedience," he growled at last, reluctantly taking the recorder that Kutzko still held out. "Take them no closer than ten meters to the thunderhead, Kutzko, and watch out for teeth and claws when you open the box. And then get back down the hill."

"Yes, sir," Kutzko nodded, reaching for the gloves.

"And be careful," he added. "Come on, Gilead, let's get up there."

We climbed together for the first thirty meters or so, then split apart, me heading for the outcropping he'd pointed out earlier as he made for a slight dimple in the ground that would shield him at least somewhat from anything the thunderhead chose to shoot his direction. I watched the thunderhead the whole time; but though I could tell he was aware of us, there was no hostility that I could detect. I could only pray that that wouldn't change.

Kutzko waited until we were in position before starting up himself. I kept my eyes on the thunderhead, wondering if I could shout a warning fast enough if I detected hostility . . . wondered if I would even know in time what thunderhead hostility looked like. Heart thudding in my ears, I almost missed hearing Lord Kelsey-Ramos's quiet words from my phone: "Okay, Gilead, he's released the laskas. He's falling back—no sign of any attack on him . . . the laskas are moving forward . . . okay, here they come. Keep watching the thunderhead."

I bit tightly down on the back of my lip. In my peripheral vision, now, I could see the four laskas stalking their way forward through the light undergrowth.

And the thunderhead had noticed; I could sense the heightened awareness, though how much of that was now focused on the animals and how much still on us I couldn't tell. I risked a glance at the laskas, saw no sign that they were in any kind of distress.

So the thunderhead hadn't yet fired. Was he waiting for the predators to get closer? I thought back to the Butte City, trying to recall every nuance of the sense I'd felt when the thunderheads there had lashed out at Kutzko's needler. "No lasers yet," Lord Kelsey-Ramos murmured into my thoughts. "Maybe he knows we're recording and is hoping he won't have to demonstrate his weaponry for us."

A thought that hadn't occurred to me . . . but if that was what the thunderhead was banking on, I could already see that it was a futile hope. The laskas had the sight or scent of him now, and were moving steadily forward.

Steadily, but still slowly . . . and suddenly I realized that that really didn't make sense. "Something's not right here," I murmured toward my phone. "The laskas ought to be rushing the thunderhead by now—there's not nearly enough cover here for them to sneak up through."

"You're sure the thunderhead has spotted them?" Lord Kelsey-Ramos asked.

"I'm almost certain he has," I told him. "But all I get from him is a sense of—oh, watchful waiting, I'd have to say."

Lord Kelsey-Ramos grunted. "All right. Keep watching."

The laskas continued their cautious pace, moving forward until they'd nosed their way right to the edge of the vegetation that surrounded the thunderhead. There they paused, heads ducking and weaving as if checking visually or aurally for danger. I waited for them to charge . . . and with the same patience they'd already demonstrated, they eased their way forward through a gap between two bush-like plants—

And without warning the bushes suddenly exploded with a buzzing cloud of insects.

Reflexively, I ducked lower behind my outcropping, suddenly remembering the complaints of the men who'd gone out to dig up that first thunderhead drone. "Watch out—they sting," I snapped into my phone.

"Understood," Lord Kelsey-Ramos said, glacially calm . . . but there was an odd mixture of distaste and quiet horror in his voice. "I see now what the organic lasers are for—they don't shoot at predators directly, but use them to stir up their insect neighbors. Stay down and keep watching."

I gritted my teeth and complied. For a dozen heartbeats nothing seemed to happen; and then, with a flurry of leaves and branches audible even over the loud drone of the insects, the four laskas shot out of the bushes, heading downslope at a dead run. For a second it looked like the insects were going to pursue; but they were apparently content with merely driving the intruders away. For a minute longer they swarmed around the thunderhead before gradually disappearing again into the thick vegetation surrounding him.

Slowly, Lord Kelsey-Ramos straightened back to his feet. "All right," he said, his voice tight. "Gilead?—what's the thunderhead doing?"

"He's watching us," I told him, forcing my own voice to stay calm. It wasn't over yet, I reminded myself, a hollow sensation in the pit of my stomach. We still had to make it back to the car . . . and on the way we would have to pass within view of the rest of the thunderheads on the surrounding hills. "I can't tell—wait a minute," I interrupted myself. A subtle change in the thunderhead's sense— "He's gone," I reported. "He's left his body."

"Uh-*huh*," Lord Kelsey-Ramos grunted. "Not unexpected, if I understand what's going on. I think it's time for a dignified yet brisk retreat."

"Stay there, sir," Kutzko put in, his voice the tone of command I'd heard him use so often before. "I'll come up and get you in the car."

Lord Kelsey-Ramos hesitated, then nodded. "All right.

I don't think we're in any real danger . . . but then again, we don't know how desperate they are to keep this a secret, either."

"To keep *what* a secret?" I demanded. It was abundantly clear that Lord Kelsey-Ramos had seen something significant in the scene we'd just witnessed; equally clear was that whatever it was, I'd missed it completely. A dash of humility to add to the tension and danger already knotting up my insides. "I don't understand."

Lord Kelsey-Ramos sighed, the sound just audible over the phone. "No, I don't suppose you do," he said, a strange sadness beneath his own tension. "The problem with you religious types is that your view of reality has some built-in limitations. There are things in this universe that only someone with a deceitful, manipulative mind can properly comprehend."

I was still searching for a reply to that when Kutzko brought the car to a bouncing halt, stopping between his employer and the still-vacant thunderhead. Lord Kelsey-Ramos ran for the vehicle; clenching my teeth, I got my feet under me and did the same.

No attack had come by the time Kutzko started us down the hill again. I tried to watch the scattering of other thunderheads over my shoulder as we came within sight of them, but we were too far away and jolting too wildly for me to read anything of consequence. All I could get was the sense that they, too, were watching. "What now?" I asked.

Lord Kelsey-Ramos took a deep breath, the tension flowing out of him to leave a tired anger in its place. "We head back," he said wearily. "Head back, and tell Admiral Yoshida and the rest of the commission just how the thunderheads have been using us all these years."

I felt my stomach muscles tighten. "I still don't understand."

He turned grim eyes on me. "Don't you see? *That*—" he jerked his head sharply back at the hillside behind us—"was a demonstration of the thunderheads' natural defense mechanism. A mechanism they simply adapted for their system as a whole."

And, finally—finally—it was clear. "The Cloud," I breathed. "It's nothing but a gigantic version of that plant barrier."

Lord Kelsey-Ramos nodded bitterly. "And we're the stinging insects that live there. The insects they've lured in to defend them."

CHAPTER 31

Temperatures the previous night had dipped toward freezing, a sure sign that winter would be arriving in this part of Spall. Even now, four hours after sunrise, the air was still respectably chilly—a fact that clearly weighed upon the minds of the engineers working hard to prepare the new housing area that was being added onto the compound. I watched them as I walked, finding it a little hard to remember the encampment as it had been at the beginning. From a single Pravilo ship and a handful of soft-wall structures, its occupants grudgingly investigating the babblings of a pair of pravdrugged Watchers, it had now become a veritable city of offices, labs, and prebuilt individual houses.

And somewhere in all that influx of money and personnel, I could sense that something had gotten lost. The pure, almost childlike excitement of scientific discovery was all but gone now; in its place was the equally strong but far darker motivation of being part of an important, life/death problem.

Dr. Eisenstadt, though he wouldn't admit it aloud, could feel that loss. Many of the others didn't. For some, bigger and more important and better funded was always the definition of progress.

The house I was looking for was just inside the original security fence, about as far from the main work areas as it was possible to get at the moment. Like all the other houses in the cramped and inadequate space, there wasn't a great deal of land surrounding it; but as I neared the front door I could tell from the faint whiffs of familiar vegetation that there was enough room between house and fence for at least a small garden. The muted sound of metal implements on dirt accompanied the smells, and I changed direction to circle around that way.

Shepherd Adams was on his knees in the middle of a small section of turned dirt, poking with a fork trowel around the roots of three knee-high plants. He looked up as I came around the corner of the house, and for that first unguarded instant his sense was full of unfriendliness, vague bitterness, even betrayal. "Mr. Benedar," he nodded, his voice tightly neutral.

"Shepherd Adams," I nodded back, fighting to hold my ground against the strong feelings radiating from him. "I'm sorry to intrude on your privacy—"

"I have little else these days *except* privacy," he countered.

There was just a hint of irony in his voice; a chink in the armor he was trying to throw up around himself . . . "Gives you an idea of what it would be like to be a monk," I offered. Another flicker in his sense— "As you once considered becoming."

He snorted gently, another chunk of the armor coming down. Adams simply wasn't constituted to hold onto grudges. "I'd forgotten how little one's thoughts are one's own in the presence of a Watcher," he sighed. "It's a hard reminder of how open we always are to God."

I looked at him, read the quiet pain there. "I'm sorry," I said softly. "Sorry for . . . everything."

He favored me with a bittersweet smile, a portion of the anger within him turning back against himself. "You mean for your part in exposing the Halo of God as a lie?"

I flinched at the bluntness. "A mistake, Shepherd Adams. Not a lie."

He grimaced. "Was it? I've spent the last month wondering about that. After all, we both know the Halo of God wouldn't have grown as large or as quickly without the mystical allure we presented—the chance to actually stand here on the very physical manifestation of God's kingdom." He dropped his eyes away from mine. "Who's to say I didn't deliberately blind myself to the inconsistencies in that claim?"

I shook my head. "For whatever it's worth, I looked very hard for signs of perverted ambition when we first met—and Calandra looked even harder. Neither of us found any."

His lip twitched. "Calandra never really trusted us, did she?"

I thought about Calandra's admitted loss of faith. "She has a hard time trusting anyone these days," I told him.

He nodded. "I suppose it comes of being a Watcher living after the darMaupine's fiasco." Lowering his eyes, he tapped one of the plants with his fork trowel. "Know anything about valeer plants, Gilead?" he asked.

The name was vaguely familiar. "They provide one of the spices you use in cooking, don't they?"

He nodded. "I found these growing inside the fence after Dr. Eisenstadt's people decided they didn't need me and buried me out of the way back here. Tricky sort of plant to harvest, actually—something we discovered the first time we tried it." He gestured at five fat leaf-like structures at the top of one of the plants. "These are the spice pods," he identified them. "What happens is that, as winter approaches, the plant's entire supply of nutrients—its life-force, if you will—is drawn into the seeds in these pods. By the time the process is complete, the plant has become a dead stalk, and at that point the next wind just blows it apart, scattering the seeds all over the landscape. The trick for the gardener is to wait long enough to get the maximum yield, yet not so long that the wind destroys the harvest."

I looked at the plant, seeing the analogy he was making. "Perhaps it's now time for the Halo of God to scatter," I suggested.

"Oh, they'll scatter, all right," he sighed. "But not as viable seeds. They're too young, most of them, to withstand something this hard."

"You think it'll be harder on them than Aaron Balaam darMaupine was on us?" I countered, suddenly angry at his defeatist attitude. "The Watchers have been considered little better than dormant traitors by much of the Patri and colonies for the past two decades. Yet we survive."

He smiled bitterly. "You were old and established, and faced suspicion and hatred. We are young, and face ridicule. Which do you think the human spirit can more easily withstand?"

I knew the answer to that one. All too well. "Don't underestimate them," I said instead. "They may be stronger than you think."

His gaze drifted to the security fence. "I should be out there with them," he murmured. "Preparing them for this."

I took a deep breath. "You may be of more value here."

He shrugged. "I'm of no use at all. Shepherd Zagorin seems to be—" He broke off, eyes shifting back to me as his brain belatedly noticed the tone of my comment. "Has something happened to her?"

"No, she's fine," I assured him. "She's still handling all the contact work, but she seems to be acclimating to it well."

He snorted. "There's no need for her to be doing all of it alone," he growled. "They fixed my heart and brain weeks ago—I'm perfectly capable of taking some of that load off her."

"I know, sir. That's why I'm going to ask you to contact the thunderheads for me."

His sense was startled, then cautious. "Why me?"

"Because I can't use Shepherd Zagorin." I braced myself; this was likely to be painful. "What do you know about what's happening?"

His forehead furrowed slightly. "The thunderheads are intelligent, with what seems to be a complete society, though we don't yet understand how it works. There's also a fleet of sublight spaceships a little under a light-year from Solitaire and due to reach us in about seventeen years."

"Did you know the Patri is planning to destroy that fleet?"

The skin around his eyes tightened, his sense turning to horror. "God save us all," he murmured. "But . . . why?"

"Because we're afraid of them," I said simply.

He licked his lips, and I could see him struggling with the enormity of it. "How do they intend to . . . do it?"

I grimaced. "A hundred ninety-two of Collet's biggest rocheoids are going to be fitted with Mjollnir lacings and tethered to tugboats equipped with Deadman Switches," I told him, my stomach tightening as it always did at the thought of it. "Zombis will be put aboard, and the thunderheads will guide them to points directly in front of each of the ships. Too close, of course, for the aliens to veer or take any kind of countermeasure."

For a long moment Adams was silent. I watched, also in silence, as he slowly forced his horror back. "How will they know how close they'll have to get?" he asked.

I nodded. "The same thought occurred to me. Apparently the thunderheads know more about this than they'll say."

"They know who the Invaders are, then." It wasn't a question.

"I'm certain of it," I agreed. "But they won't tell us anything."

He thought about that. "What is it you want to ask them?"

"I want to know how to communicate with the aliens,"

I said. "If we can talk to them, maybe we can figure out what's going on here, as well as what side of this confrontation we should be on."

He gazed steadily at me. "And what makes you think there *is* a side we should be on?"

I blinked, the question catching me off-guard. "We have to take a stand on this *some*where."

"Do we?" he demanded. "'Blessed are the peacemakers'—or had you forgotten that?"

I clenched my teeth against a rush of anger . . . anger tinged uncomfortably with guilt. "Are you suggesting I've forgotten the goals of my faith?"

"Have you?" he asked bluntly.

The emphatic denial I'd planned died in my throat. "If eight years in Lord Kelsey-Ramos's business world didn't break me," I ground out, "a couple of months here certainly didn't."

A faint, sad smile touched his lips. "The business world of Lord Kelsey-Ramos is one of the acquisition of money and the stabbing of competitors in the back," he said quietly. "Here, you've been offered a chance to use your talents to explore a part of God's universe. Which world do you think it would be easier for you to fit comfortably into?"

"Neither," I retorted, feeling uncomfortably on the defensive. To even suggest I could be so easily seduced by the secular world was utterly absurd, even insulting. "And anyway, that's beside the point. The point is that unless we can find an alternative, the Pravilo is going to snuff out a great many intelligent lives."

He nodded, but I could see that the issue of my path was merely being shelved, not abandoned. "So why won't they let you talk to the thunderheads?"

With some effort, I forced myself back to business. "They probably would, actually, if that's all I was going to do," I told him. "But I'm going to have to do more than just talk. I'm going to have to reveal to the thunderheads that we know a secret about them."

Adams's frowned. "What kind of secret?"

"One that shows they aren't the poor, picked-on victims they've been pretending to be. That they deliberately drew us to Solitaire system in hopes of embroiling us in this dispute with the aliens."

"Interesting," Adams murmured. He pondered for a moment. "You don't think revealing that will make trouble?"

I shook my head. "The thunderheads almost certainly know by now that we know it. And in the two weeks since Lord Kelsey-Ramos figured it out they haven't shown any signs of being particularly worried." Which, if that was true, meant that its use as a lever might well be vanishingly small. But there was nothing left for me but the grasping of such straws.

For another moment Adams gazed at me, his sense a kaleidoscope of indecision and thought and the weighing of possibilities. Then, abruptly, it cleared; and he nodded briskly. "All right. Are you ready?"

The quickness of the decision surprised me. "Well, yes, but *you* aren't. We'll need to get some of the drugs they've been using to prepare Shepherd Zagorin."

"And you have access to these drugs?" he asked pointedly.

"I can get them," I insisted. "We can't risk the kind of trouble you had the first time."

"Why not?" he countered. "I lasted several minutes then, and with my rebuilt heart and cerebral circulatory system I shouldn't be in even that much danger this time."

I felt my stomach muscles tightening up. I couldn't ask him to do this—not now, not unprepared. But he was right. The first batch of rocheoids were already being prepared, and the schedule called for the rest to be finished within another month. The longer we delayed, the less likely anything we learned would be able to stop the holocaust. "All right," I sighed at last. "There shouldn't be anyone at the Butte City at the moment."

"I'm glad to hear it," he said dryly. Laying his fork trowel aside, he shifted to cross-legged position and closed his eyes.

I felt a rush of heat to my face, feeling like an idiot. Of course there was no need for us to physically go to where the thunderheads' bodies were. Sitting down in front of Adams, I took a careful breath and tried to clear my mind of extraneous thoughts. Adams slipped into his meditative trance . . . reached what seemed to me to be the proper point . . . "Thunderheads?" I invited.

The response was immediate. "I am here," Adams whispered hoarsely. "What do you wish?"

I braced myself. This was it. "I wish information," I said. "I'd like you to teach me how to communicate with the aliens who are approaching this world."

Eisenstadt had made the identical request before; and, as with that time, there was a long moment of silence. I kept my eyes on Adams, watching for any signs of physical distress. "There is no way to talk . . . to them," the thunderhead answered at last.

Predictably, the same answer as last time. "Then perhaps we humans will choose to leave this place," I told him. "Perhaps those in authority over us will decide they don't like being lied to and manipulated by others."

I'd half expected the thunderhead to feign innocence; but perhaps I'd underestimated the creatures' sophistication. "Your race has gained much from . this place," he said through Adams. "You seek certain miner . . . als for your machines. They are worth lives to you. You will stay and fight for . . . what you want."

"I'd advise you not to underestimate the strength of human pride," I warned him. "You see, we now know all about your natural defense strategy, with the stinging insects and all. We know that you're playing the exact same game with us, right down to luring us here by creating the mineral wealth of Collet's rings for us."

"We do not create," he said calmly.

"Semantics," I snorted. "Perhaps you'd prefer the word *enhanced*. Regardless, we know all about it. Must have been quite a project: an entire planetful of thunderheads focusing their organic lasers on the rings for years at a time, slowly boiling off the lighter elements and leaving the heavier metals behind."

"Such an accusation . . . is utterly fantas . . . tic."

I shook my head. "I agree it's wilder than most of the theories that have tried to account for the heat-treating of the rocks out there, but once Lord Kelsey-Ramos made the connection it was a trivial matter to show that the heating was done by the same set of wavelengths as the melted spots on that ramp in the Butte City."

There was another long silence, and I had the distinct impression that the thunderheads were a little taken aback. For all their remarkable natural abilities, their lack of any kind of technology severely limited their knowledge of the physical sciences. To their minds, the analysis I'd just described—a very straightforward one, I'd been told—probably sounded identical to magic. "Well?" I prompted after a moment.

A sense of firmness touched Adams's face. "You will stay and fight for . . . the minerals in the . . . rings," the thunderhead repeated.

I bit at my lip. This was getting me nowhere. "Will you at least tell me *why* they're coming?" I asked him.

"They are invaders."

The stock answer. "Yes, so you've told us," I said, feeling my frustration level beginning to rise. "But *why* are they coming? What quarrel do they have with you that they're willing to spend a hundred years coming through your Cloud to get to you?"

"They are invaders."

I focused sharply on Adams. Something in his voice on that last sentence . . . ? "Thunderhead, we haven't got much time left," I said, watching Adams closely. The contact was beginning to get to him. "We can't simply kill the aliens in cold blood—we just *can't*. Don't you understand how unethical such a thing would be for our species?"

Adams's glazed eyes turned up to me . . . and suddenly I felt a chill run up my back. There was a hard edge to his sense, something I'd never before seen in a thunderhead contact. "You are defenders," he whispered; and even with a whisper's usual lack of tonal cues I could hear the contempt there. "You will destroy them be . . . cause that is your nature. That is why you are here."

I gritted my teeth hard, anger and frustration combining into a violent urge to somehow lash out at the thunderhead. But I couldn't. A nerve was twitching in Adams's neck, and I could see the palpitation of the carotid artery, and there was nothing I could do except swallow my fury and break off the contact. "We are human beings," I gritted out. "We go where we wish, do what we wish. As you *will* find out. Adams!—break contact."

For a second I had the horrible feeling that the thunderhead was going to refuse to allow it, that he was going to let Adams die as a demonstration of thunderhead power. But a second later the stiffness went out of Adams's back, and he was free.

I watched him closely, finger resting lightly on the Emergency button on my phone. But the worrying turned out to be unnecessary; compared with the last time, this recovery was practically instantaneous. Within a minute his breathing and eyes had returned to normal and he was able to sit up straight again. "So," he said at last. "It didn't work."

Defeat had a bitter taste. "No," I shook my head wearily. "I'd hoped there might be something else there . . . but there isn't. We really *are* nothing but overgrown insects to them. They're playing with us—*have* been playing with us, for seventy years now. And if the Pravilo gets their way on this one . . ."

Adams turned his head to gaze through the security fence. "Perhaps they aren't simply being blind or greedy," he suggested quietly. "Perhaps they don't see any safe alternative to cooperation at this point." He hesitated. "The thunderheads' lasers—did they *really* burn the light elements out of the rings?"

I saw what he was getting at. "Yes, but Lord Kelsey-Ramos told me that it took them literally years to do it. At least ten, probably closer to twenty. The individual lasers aren't all that powerful, really—they seem to have come about mainly as a means for stirring up their insect protectors when a predator approached. It wouldn't be all that effective a weapon against us."

"They fused the end of a needler with it," he pointed out.

"Melted a few drops across the opening," I corrected him. "And it probably took the entire Butte City population to do it. Agreed, a direct confrontation would carry a certain risk. But I can't see the Patri knuckling under solely because of that."

Adams snorted gently. "Then you're right: it has to be either blindness or greed."

I nodded. "My guess is greed."

For a minute we sat there silently. I found my eyes turning upward, toward the glistening white clouds drifting serenely across the blue sky . . . and in my mind's eye the clouds became Mjollnir-equipped rocheoids. Massive chunks of death, moving into their appointed places in front of the approaching ships.

Ships that would probably never even know what had happened to them.

"You can't give up," Adams said.

I turned back to find his eyes on me. "I don't *want* to give up," I retorted. "But I've tried everything I can think of, and I'm out of ideas. Even if the thunderheads were willing to tell us how to talk to the aliens, there's no guarantee we could get a dialogue going fast enough to figure out what the conflict is between the two races."

"Still, if the aliens could tell us their side of things, you can bet the thunderheads would open up and give us *their* version," Adams pointed out.

"For whatever good that would do," I shrugged. "Whatever the morality of the situation turns out to be, the fact remains that siding with the thunderheads keeps us the ring mines. I don't think the thunderheads would let the Patri forget that."

"As if the Patri would need reminding."

"Right." Carefully, I got to my feet, the muscles in

my legs protesting as I did so. "Thank you for your time, Shepherd Adams, and for your willingness to risk your life in this."

He waved a hand, figuratively brushing the gratitude away. "What will you do now?"

"I don't know." I looked toward the Butte City. "Go talk to Dr. Eisenstadt or Lord Kelsey-Ramos, I suppose. Keep nagging people until they get tired enough of me to do something."

He smiled. " 'For a long time he refused,' " he quoted, " 'but at last he said to himself, Even though I have neither fear of God nor respect for any human person, I must give this widow her just rights since she keeps pestering me, or she will come and slap me in the face.' Is that it?"

"More or less," I said. "Except that unlike the judge in the parable, they don't really have to put up with me any longer than—"

I broke off as my phone twittered. I frowned as I pulled it out, wondering who could possibly be calling me. "This is Benedar," I identified myself.

"Gilead, this is Eisenstadt." The scientist's voice was tight. "Where are you?"

"Out near the fence, talking with Shepherd Adams," I said, stomach muscles tightening. "What's wrong?"

His sigh was just barely audible. "You'd better get back to the ship right away. There are some Pravilos here . . . with a warrent for your arrest."

CHAPTER 32

The prison cell was simple, small, and unadorned—a sort of sardonic parody, I thought more than once, of my cubicle in the Carillon Building back on Portslava. Without the magnificent view, of course. Or even a reasonably good intercom system.

"As near as I can tell, it's sort of a forced misunderstanding," Lord Kelsey-Ramos said, his image on the display fuzzing just enough to make it exasperating to try and read. "What's happened is that someone labyrinthed a writ through the central judiciary on Portslava, ordering the Pravilo to detain you here on charges stemming from your running off with Calandra Paquin. Total nonsense, of course, given what's happened since then, but until we can backtrack it there's not a lot I can do about it."

I nodded heavily. "I don't have to guess who's behind it, do I?"

He grimaced. "Not really. I've talked to Randon and we both agree it was almost certainly this smert-headed Aikman you kept locking horns with. Something of a farewell present to you, I expect."

I frowned. "Farewell present? He's gone?"

"Left about a week ago. Took a new position on Janus, the HTI people tell me."

"How very convenient for him," I murmured.

"How, indeed," Lord Kelsey-Ramos said grimly. "Don't worry, though—we'll track him down."

I sighed, a bitter taste in my mouth. "Don't bother, sir. He's not worth it."

Lord Kelsey-Ramos glared at me. "You'll forgive me, I trust, if turning the other cheek isn't part of *my* philosophy."

"It's not that, sir," I told him. "It's just that he really *isn't* worth the effort. You can get me out of here just as fast through normal channels as you could by chasing him down, and even hauling him back here wouldn't do anything but give him the chance to gloat in my face."

"Give *you* the chance to gloat, don't you mean?"

I shook my head. "No, sir. You see, he's already lost his original battle—I've kept Calandra away from the Deadman Switch. He can't make me watch her die, the way he wanted to . . . so instead he's arranged for me to be locked away and helpless while the alien fleet dies in her place."

Lord Kelsey-Ramos made a sour face. "I understand. Yes, it could easily take the three weeks we've got left to sort all of this through to Portslava and back." He studied my face. "Unless, that is, I make an all-out fight of it."

I shrugged. "What would be the point? I've already done everything I can think of to get the Patri to change their minds about talking to the aliens first. Whether I sit here or in the Butte City encampment makes no real difference."

Lord Kelsey-Ramos sighed. "I'm sorry, Gilead. If there was any way I could help, I would."

"I know, sir," I assured him. "You've done all *you* could, too."

"Yes." He paused, his sense turning inward. "It's interesting, you know," he said in a meditative voice. "Ever since I took over Carillon I've pretty much had things my own way—been the man making the decisions, both the good ones and the bad ones. This commission takes me back to earlier days."

"Days you'd rather forget?" I suggested.

His gaze came back to me. "I like having power, Gilead—I admit that. No one gets to my position who doesn't. What I hate about this commission is being saddled with a share of the responsibility for actions which I haven't really had any power to influence."

Something in his voice . . . "Are you saying," I asked carefully, "that the Pravilo had already made up their minds to destroy the aliens, no matter *what* the commission recommended?"

"Oh, come on—you don't think Aaron Balaam darMaupine originated the echo council, do you?" he growled. "Sorry to be crude, but there it is. Of course the Pravilo had already decided the Invaders were a threat; the commission's only real choice was to either rubberstamp that opinion for them or else prove conclusively that the Invaders weren't dangerous to us. I imagine you know all about proving a negative."

As in proving the Watchers weren't a threat to the rest of humanity . . . "I know it very well, sir," I said quietly.

He grimaced, and I could see he'd followed my line of thought. "Yes, well . . . sorry I jumped down your throat like that. As I said, I'm willing enough to accept the responsibility that goes with power, but I hate like blazing chern-fire to have the responsibility all by itself."

I managed a smile. "That's what makes you different, sir," I told him. "Most people prefer to have the power without any of the responsibility."

He snorted. "Yes, we at Carillon certainly are a noble bunch," he said dryly.

I thought about the Solitaran executives' fears that Carillon would put a stop to their profitable smuggler trade. "Yes, sir. In many ways, you are."

He eyed me sharply, and even with the fuzzy picture I could sense his embarrassment. Nobility was not exactly the sort of image he'd tried to project to his competitors. "Thank you for the vote of confidence," he rumbled. "Anyway, I've got to get back up to Spall, consult with my fellow commissioners. I'll be back to talk to you in a week or so—sooner if I make any headway against the judiciary."

"Thank you, sir. I appreciate all you're doing."

"No problem. Take care."

He stood up and turned away, and I caught just a glimpse of the visiting-room wall behind him before the guard blanked the screen. For a moment I stayed where I was, staring at the blank display for lack of anything better to do. But the seething frustration within me was too great to let me sit still for very long. Getting to my feet, I went the four steps over to the cell's outer wall.

Outside the tiny window was fifty meters of open ground, ending at a two-story wing I'd been told was part of the Pravilo headquarters here. The windows facing me were black squares—polarized ninety degrees to mine, presumably, to give the officers working there privacy from prying eyes. Blank people behind blank windows, I thought with a touch of bitterness. Faceless people wielding power without having to take the responsibility for the use of that power. Doing their daily work without knowing—probably without even caring—what the ultimate results of that work would be. It was why bureaucracies grew and flourished. Why people like Aaron Balaam darMaupine had been able to seize power . . .

And without warning, my mind suddenly and inexplicably froze. Aaron Balaam darMaupine. Aaron *Balaam* darMaupine . . .

Balaam . . .

I have no explanation for the idea that burst, virtually full-grown, into my mind. Perhaps my back-brain had already come up with it, and had merely used the name as a trigger; perhaps it was a genuine case of divine inspiration. Either way, it was as if a star had exploded in my mind, showering light where before there had been only darkness. And in that light, I saw the answer.

Or at least, a possible answer.

For a handful of heartbeats I stood there at the

window, my full attention inward as I sifted frantically through the idea, searching for errors or flaws. But if they were there, I couldn't find them. It could be done—it could definitely be done.

And then my eyes focused again, and I remembered where I was; and spinning around, I dove for the intercom.

It seemed like an eternity before the monitor answered my signal. "Has Lord Kelsey-Ramos left yet?" I snapped at him.

He frowned at my tone, but apparently decided prisoners who rated a visit from someone like Lord Kelsey-Ramos should be treated with at least marginal politeness. "Hang on, I'll check," he growled.

"I have to talk to him right away," I insisted as his eyes shifted to a different display.

"Yeah, well, we'll see if he wants to talk to *you*," he grunted. "Lemme see . . . Rayst?—yeah; give a shout to that guy who just passed, will you? Tell him Benedar's calling for him."

I licked my lips, trying to organize my thoughts, the taste of black irony in my mouth. Aikman's final, pitiful gesture of hatred . . . and it was beginning to look like it might do far more damage than either he or I had believed.

A minute later the monitor's face vanished from the screen, and I was again looking at Lord Kelsey-Ramos. "Yes, Gilead, what is it?"

"I have to get out of here," I told him, voice trembling slightly with emotion despite my efforts to control it. "Right away. It's urgent."

He frowned. "I just finished telling you it'll take some time," he reminded me.

I bit the back of my lip, suddenly mindful of how easy it would be for one of the guards to eavesdrop on the line . . . and that my idea could very likely be construed as treason. "I know, sir," I said, wracking my brain desperately to find some kind of private cue to feed him. Something the guards wouldn't be able to interpret . . . and for the second time in as many minutes, inspiration struck. "It's just that this room is so *small*—so small and so plain. I thought I could handle things being this dull, but I can't."

His eyebrows lifted in surprise; and abruptly there were tension lines in his face. "I see," he said carefully. His eyes flicked to the side, where a guard was presumably standing. "Yes, I understand how that would be hard for you to take—you're used to so much more luxury back at Carillon. More privacy, too, naturally."

"Exactly, sir," I nodded, feeling a small surge of hope. He was with me, now, correctly hearing both what I was saying and what I wasn't saying. In eight years with Carillon I'd learned a great deal about the man; now, for the first time, I realized how much he'd learned about me in the process. "Besides, I hate the thought of wasting time here," I added. "There's always so much work to be done."

His eyes were locked with mine. "I know the feeling," he said. "I'll talk to Commodore Freitag and Admiral Yoshida right away, see if you might at least be . . . reassigned, perhaps, to somewhere closer to home?"

Closer to home. Here, on Solitaire, that could only mean the *Bellwether*. "I'd very much appreciate that, sir," I said, speaking the words clearly. "You might speak to Governor Rybakov, too—I believe she still owes us a favor."

"I'll do that," he agreed. "Let me get started, and I'll see what I can do." He paused, and his gaze seemed to intensify. "Are you certain this will do it?" he asked, his voice deliberately casual.

I swallowed. Was I sure this would solve the problem of the alien ships. "I'm not certain, no," I had to admit. "But I believe it's worth a try."

He nodded. "All right. Sit tight, and I'll get back to you."

"Thank you, sir," I said.

His lip twitched in a tight smile. "I'll do what I can," he said . . . and in his tone I heard a promise that went beyond the immediate situation. That if my idea had any chance at all of success, he would stand behind me all the way.

"Thank you, sir," I said again, and watched his image blank from the screen. Taking a ragged breath, I once more went over to the window, trying to still the tension roiling within me. The aliens' lives were still hanging by a thread, but at least now I had a plan. A plan and, more importantly, an ally.

I could only hope he would be as enthusiastic when he found out what the idea was . . . and what carrying it out was going to cost.

CHAPTER 33

Three weeks. Twenty-one days.

The number hovered before me like a personal specter, its presence a black poison in the background of every waking thought. An emotional expression of the solid walls and locked door of my tiny cell; a maddening reminder of my utter helplessness.

And every morning, the number taunted me by growing one smaller.

There were a great many scriptures that dealt with patience; a similarly impressive number dealing with faith and hope. I quoted every single one of those verses to myself during those long hours, grabbing through the hurricane of growing anger and frustration for something solid to grasp onto.

It didn't seem to help. I tried to tell myself that it *was* doing some good, that without their comfort I would have sunk into a mind-crippling despair. But lurking at the edge of my mind was another, more sobering possibility: that it didn't help because Shepherd Adams had been right, that I had indeed become too entangled with the rewards of the secular world to find strength in the spiritual realm. It was a frightening and debilitating thought, a dark nightmare shadow which seemed to begin and end each day.

And finally—when it seemed as if I couldn't take the fear and forced solitude a single day longer—finally, on the afternoon of the fourth day, my cell was opened and I was escorted under guard to the Rainbow's End starport. The starport, and the waiting *Bellwether*.

"It took every string I could find to pull," Lord Kelsey-Ramos commented, offering me a steaming mug as I sat down across from his desk. "Including that favor the governor owed us," he added, "though I can't say she was all that happy at having to pay it off."

"I appreciate it, sir," I said, carefully taking the mug with fingers that still trembled with vague reaction. The heat was soothing to my hands, the smell flooding my mind with memories of home and safety. It was exactly the medicine I needed, and even as I sipped at the drink I could feel the fears and doubts of the cell beginning to recede.

"I was glad to do it," Lord Kelsey-Ramos said, frowning slightly as he gazed into my face. "I'm just sorry it took so long—on Portslava I'd have had you out in half an hour."

"Four days was soon enough, sir," I assured him, trying to sound as if I meant it.

He wasn't fooled. "It looks to *me* like we just barely made it," he said pointedly.

I sighed, giving up the pretense. "It was harder than I'd expected," I admitted. "A lot harder. Just the thought of those ships heading toward their deaths—and me locked away where I couldn't do anything about it . . ." I shuddered, and took another sip of my drink.

"Um," he grunted. "Interesting. You know, I've always thought that too much of that empathy you religious types pride yourselves on might be a handicap at times." He pursed his lips. "On the other hand . . . I wonder if maybe not all of it was really you."

I frowned at the suspicion in his sense. "Are you suggesting," I asked slowly, "that the Pravilo might have *drugged* me?"

The flicker of surprise showed that hadn't been what he'd been suggesting at all. "I suppose that's not impossible," he nevertheless conceded. "I doubt that Admiral Yoshida would go that far to keep you out of his face for these last couple of weeks, but some eager subordinate might have thought it would make a nice early birthday present for him. I was thinking more of the thunderheads, actually."

A cold knot formed in my stomach as, abruptly, something like a hazy curtain seemed to vanish from in front of my memory. The overall sense of tension and struggle Calandra and I had noticed on Solitaire—of course; that was precisely what I'd just spent four days struggling against. Or rather, a highly magnified form of that sense. Magnified from scientific tool or side effect into a weapon . . . "Yes," I said, voice wavering slightly—with disgust, dread, or anger, I couldn't tell which. "Yes, it was them. It had to be. They were *attacking* me. *Deliberately* attacking me."

"Don't let it throw you," Lord Kelsey-Ramos growled, his voice rich with suppressed anger of his own. "After spending seventy years patiently leading us to this point by our collective nose, they're hardly going to look kindly on someone who's trying his best to upset their plans."

"Then they're going to have some readjusting to do," I gritted. The pressure was still there, I could see now, resting up against my consciousness like a dull toothache. But now that I knew its origin and purpose its power over me was gone.

Lord Kelsey-Ramos cocked an eyebrow. "Well, we'll see about that, won't we?" he said. "So, let's hear this plan of yours."

I took a deep breath, my anger at the thunderheads fading into the distance . . . leaving a tinge of uncertainty in its place. Perversely, what had seemed like a gold-plated idea while I was alone in my cell was tarnishing almost visibly under Lord Kelsey-Ramos's unblinking gaze. "To begin with," I said, deciding to go with the least arguable part first, "I'll need to talk to the thunderheads again. The only way this is going to work is with their cooperation."

Lord Kelsey-Ramos blinked, his anticipation turning slightly sour. "These are the same thunderheads who've just spent four days trying to drive you into a nervous breakdown?" he asked pointedly.

"Yes, sir," I nodded, "because I'm going to show them why their plan isn't going to work. And why cooperating with me is literally their only chance."

For a long moment he gazed into my eyes, and I could see him measuring his knowledge and trust of me against the obstacles that stood arrayed against us. I held my breath; and the trust won. "All right," he said at last. "I presume you'll need a Halloa for that. I'll have Captain Bartholomy get the earliest possible lift clearance from the tower and we'll head out to Spall."

"Am I allowed to leave Solitaire?" I asked, a bit startled.

"As long as you're with me, you are," he said. "You've been released into my custody, the only stipulation being that you stay within Solitaire system."

A significant fraction of the weight resting on my back seemed to lift. I'd been very much afraid that I would once again have to steal a ship—somehow—and escape Solitaire on my own. Now—

Now, unless I could shake him later, I would have Lord Kelsey-Ramos along with me the whole way. Sharing fully in the dangers, and in the legal consequences if it didn't work . . . or perhaps even if it did. "Well, then, let's get going, sir," I said.

He nodded and waved his control stick at the intercom; and as he did so, I felt all the eased weight settle back in again. Along with perhaps a bit more.

CHAPTER 34

We reached Spall six hours later—the middle of the night there—and put down at a freshly-built landing area about fifty kilometers from the Butte City. An aircar and Pravilo escort were waiting as Lord Kelsey-Ramos, Kutzko, and I disembarked; twenty minutes later, we were at the encampment.

To my surprise, Dr. Eisenstadt was waiting for us, obviously alerted in advance that we were on our way. "Lord Kelsey-Ramos," he nodded, getting up from his desk as we entered. "Good to see you again. Gilead; glad you're out of prison."

"Thank you, sir," I nodded back, hiding my irritation with Lord Kelsey-Ramos for dragging Eisenstadt into this. We hardly needed his help or his permission to go talk with Shepherd Adams; all his presence here was going to accomplish would be to get his name on the Pravilo's list when this was over and they went looking for my accomplices. "With your permission, Dr. Eisenstadt, I'd like to go and talk to Shepherd Adams—"

"Yes, Lord Kelsey-Ramos told me what you'd need," he nodded briskly, slipping past me toward the door. "If you'll all come with me, Adams is just down the hall."

He led us out again into the hall, and I again had to fight to hide my irritation. We weren't in such a hurry that we couldn't have simply gone out to Adams's house and talked to him there—all we needed now was to bump into someone working late who might ask awkward questions.

Eisenstadt had at least had the sense to put Adams nearby, in one of the abandoned dorm-type rooms that the housing boom outside had made superfluous. He was dozing on a cot, and as we filed quietly in and Eisenstadt turned the lights up to a dim glow he awoke. "Hello?" he called tentatively, rolling over and propping himself up on one elbow.

"It's Eisenstadt," Eisenstadt identified himself as Adams blinked his eyes back to focus. "I've brought you some visitors."

Adams nodded greetings to Lord Kelsey-Ramos and me in turn, his sense more one of worried tension than real surprise. "Has something gone wrong?" he asked, his eyes coming to rest on me.

"Possibly just the opposite," Lord Kelsey-Ramos grunted. "Something may actually be going right. Gilead? —this is your show now."

"Yes, sir. I need to talk to the thunderheads," I told Adams. "There may be an alternative to destroying the alien ships, but I'll need thunderhead cooperation to do it."

Adams frowned slightly at that, but nodded his willingness to assist. "All right," he said, rearranging his legs into cross-legged position. "Give me a minute."

He closed his eyes again, and I could see him reaching for the proper meditative state. "I gave him the prep drugs earlier this evening, incidentally," Eisenstadt murmured in my ear. "First time he's used them, but if they work the way they do on Shepherd Zagorin he should be fine. What is it you've come up with, Gilead?"

I kept my eyes on Adams, searching for an answer that wouldn't be a true lie. "I think I've found a way to communicate with the aliens," I said. "Maybe. Thunderhead?—are you there?"

Adams's glazed eyes opened. Focused on me . . . and hardened. "You are Gilead Rac . . . ca Benedar," he whispered harshly. "Our enemy."

A shiver went up my back, and in my mind's eye I saw the muzzle of Kutzko's flash-welded needler . . . "I'm not your enemy," I told him as firmly as I could through a suddenly dry mouth. "I seek only life and safety for all—including both you *and* your enemies."

Abruptly, Adams gasped, his back stiffening. I jumped forward, searching his sense for clues as to what was happening—

And, moving with shaky clumsiness, he unfolded his legs and lunged at me.

I was caught utterly by surprise, my momentum still carrying me toward him as his legs straightened out to drive his body awkwardly forward; and even as I tried to throw my own arms up into some kind of defensive position, I knew I wouldn't make it in time. His hands, curved into wiry claws, reached upward toward my face—

And dropped suddenly down again as the butt of Kutzko's hurled needler caught him squarely beneath the rib cage.

The thunderhead screamed; a thin, eerily wavering sound of frustration or pain or fury. Curling against the pain of the blow, he scrabbled around for the needler; but he wasn't even close before Kutzko was there, brushing smoothly past me to capture both of Adams's wrists in his hands as he kicked the needler out of reach. The thunderhead screamed again, this time unmistakably with frustration; and the sound seemed to break Eisenstadt out of his stunned paralysis. "Adams! —break contact!" he barked.

"No!" I snapped. If we lost this chance— "Thunderhead! —if the alien ships die, so will you. *Listen* to me—please."

Kutzko had manhandled Adams halfway back onto the cot. "You have no power ov . . . er us," the thunderhead spat toward me. "Your rulers will destroy . . . the Invaders."

"Yes, they will," I shot back. "And then those same rulers will destroy *you*."

"You lie—"

"Do I?" I cut him off. "Have they asked you what will become of the Cloud once the Invaders are dead?"

The glazed eyes stared at me, and I could sense the sudden uncertainty there. "No. They have not."

"Any mention of the Cloud at all?" I pressed him. "Any discussion of travel in and out of Solitaire system? Any questions about the Deadman Switch and your role in its operation?"

"There's been nothing of the kind," Lord Kelsey-Ramos murmured from behind me; and I could hear in his voice that he, too, had suddenly recognized the significance of that.

I nodded. "Surely you realize, thunderhead, how difficult it is for us to sacrifice a life every time we wish to enter or leave this system. Don't you think the commission negotiating such things with you would have suggested the Cloud's removal as the price for our dealing with the Invaders?"

Lord Kelsey-Ramos touched my arm warningly. "Gilead, if what you're implying is true, talking about it here could be extremely dangerous."

How well I knew that . . . but it was too late to back out now. If the thunderheads were incapable of rational thought and decision, we were already dead. "It doesn't matter," I told Lord Kelsey-Ramos, putting as much confidence into my voice as I could on the chance that the thunderheads had learned to read such nuances of human speech. "They can't stop it now. Certainly not alone. Their only chance is to cooperate with me."

He grimaced, eyes drifting over my shoulder to Adams. For the first time, I could tell, he was truly seeing what it was he'd committed himself to, and it was more than he'd bargained for. *And indeed, which of you here, intending to build a tower, would not first sit down and work out the cost to see if he had enough to complete it?* "If you'd like, sir," I told him quietly, "you and the others can leave. I can handle this part alone."

For a moment he was tempted. But only for a moment . . . and when he brought his gaze back to me, it was alive with the cold fire I'd seen there through a hundred corporate battles back on Portslava. "We're wasting time," he said firmly.

I nodded and turned back to Adams. Kutzko had released his wrists now, but still hovered nearby, ready for trouble. "They made no such request, thunderhead, did they?" I asked. "Would you like to know why not?"

For a moment the glazed eyes stared into space, a look I'd come to associate with a quick consultation among the thunderheads. Then the eyes refocused on me. "It is impossible," he whispered flatly.

"Why?" I countered. "Once the Invaders are gone, our rulers have no need for the Cloud—and since you yourselves are obviously the source of it, it follows immediately that they'll have no more use for *you*."

"We will fight," the thunderhead hissed.

"And you will lose," I told him bluntly. "Even if you could somehow destroy all of us here—which you can't—the mechanism for your destruction is already in place, and already triggered. When the Invaders are destroyed, it will automatically activate."

Eisenstadt took a step forward to where he could look into my face. "What are you talking about?" he demanded. "What mechanism?"

"I'm talking about a group of compressed air bombs," I explained, mentally crossing my fingers that the scheme I'd dreamed up would sound reasonable to him. If it wasn't—and if he called me on it—the whole structure I was trying to build here would come crashing down around my head. Too late, I wished I'd made him stay back in his office. "The Pravilo has scattered them around Spall in the major weather corridors. They're filled with algae that's been specially tailored to alter the local soil acidity. *Drastically* alter it." I looked back at Adams. "Within a year—two at the most—there won't be a single native plant or animal alive here."

I held my breath; but if the plan had any glaring flaws Eisenstadt didn't spot them. "You mean . . . we're talking *genocide* here," he breathed. "No. No—that's simply *unthinkable*."

"I've seen the records of the deliveries," Lord Kelsey-Ramos said heavily—and so sincerely even I could barely hear the lie there. "They're already in place—and they're equipped with automatic timers."

"Probably already set," I nodded, picking up on the cue. "Give the Pravilo a couple more weeks to get ready, a day or two to destroy the Invaders and confirm they're all gone, and maybe two more weeks to quietly get all the top people out of the system in case you decided to retaliate. Four or five weeks—no more—and it'll begin."

There was hatred in Adams's eyes. Blistering, alien hatred . . . but for the first time, there was also fear. "They will not escape," he whispered.

I shook my head. "It doesn't matter. Even if you could kill everyone on Solitaire, it's a price the rulers of the Patri would be willing to pay to finally have free access to the system. Human pride alone would dictate that you be punished for the way you've manipulated us all these years."

There was a strange pain—a very alien pain—in Adams's face. "What alternative do . . . you offer?" the thunderhead asked.

I took a deep breath, almost afraid to believe it. The first, most critical piece was now in my hands. "I've told you already," I said. "I offer life for all. It *has* to be for all—you see that, don't you? As long as the Invaders are alive, the Pravilo can't touch you, because with the Cloud gone they would be facing a war fleet with full Mjollnir capabilities."

The thunderhead seemed to consider that. "Yet if the Invaders . . . live, they will soon be here," he pointed out.

I nodded, consciously relaxing my jaw. It was a thought that had frequently occurred to me. "We'll have seventeen years," I reminded them. "Enough time for us to talk to them, perhaps work out a deal between you."

Beside me, I felt Lord Kelsey-Ramos stir uncomfortably, and it wasn't hard to guess what he was thinking. The Patri had already rejected the idea of talking to the aliens; if I forced them to do so anyway, they would not be pleased. Another thought that had frequently occurred to me . . . "Well?" I prompted the thunderhead. "Will you cooperate, or not?"

Again, Adams stared into space . . . and when his eyes came back there was no defiance left in them. "We will," the thunderhead whispered.

My knees felt a bit weak. We'd already seen thunderhead adaptability; now, we knew them to be rational, as well. I could only hope the aliens were equal to them in both qualities. "Good," I said, trying to sound brisk and businesslike. "I'll be contacting you again; and when I do, you'll need to do whatever I ask. Agreed?"

A slight pause. "We will," the thunderhead hissed again, an aura of distaste about the words. The manipulators agreeing to be manipulated, and not liking it at all.

"All right," I nodded. "It'll be in a few days at the most, and from out in space. Oh, and by the way . . . you *do* know how to talk to the Invaders, don't you?"

Another pause, slightly longer. "Yes."

"Good," I nodded again. "We'll leave the details for later; I don't want to push this contact any longer than necessary." In fact, Shepherd Adams was doing fine; but the thunderheads wouldn't know I knew that. "Thank you, and good-bye. Shepherd Adams?—you can break contact now."

Adams stiffened, then slumped back onto the cot, gasping for breath. "You all right?" I asked as Kutzko leaned over with a supporting hand.

"Yes," he said hoarsely. "Hard on the throat, though."

"Not to mention the heart and brain," Eisenstadt reminded him, stepping toward him. "No—don't try to get up."

He reached under Adams's jaw, checking the other's pulse, and I felt Lord Kelsey-Ramos move closer to me. "You really think the Patri plans to destroy the thunderheads?" he asked quietly.

I felt my stomach muscles tighten at the thought. "You said it yourself, sir—none of the commission has even mentioned the Cloud in their talks with the thunderheads. I can't see something that obvious being overlooked by accident."

He shook his head in disbelief. "Incredible. Just incredible they'd even consider something that cold-blooded. But what if . . . ?"

"The thunderheads call our bluff?" I shrugged, a tight hunching of my shoulders. "They can't afford to, and I'm pretty sure they know it. Remember that they have no way of knowing whether or not there really *are* algae bombs sitting out there with timers already set. Besides which, a first strike against us would leave them with no way at all to stop the aliens."

"Point," he admitted. "I don't know, though—this whole thing still seems awfully loose. The communication itself, for one thing—you should have nailed down the method and language right here and now."

I nodded. "Agreed. And I would have, too . . . except that I was reasonably sure the thunderheads would have lied or otherwise clouded the issue."

He cocked an eyebrow. "I hope you're not counting on them rolling over like pet dogs and meekly giving you anything you ask for once you're out in space. Because if you are . . ." He left the sentence unfinished.

"I believe," I said carefully, "that I have a way to force them to give me the cooperation I need, when I need it. I'd rather not say any more right now."

He frowned at me, doubt and worry and trust swirling around and through each other like battling tornadoes. "I don't like not knowing what you're planning," he said at last. "But I suppose . . . so far you've always been worth trusting. I just hope that that religious naivete of yours isn't playing you false."

Look, I am sending you out like sheep among wolves; so be cunning as snakes and yet innocent as doves . . .

"Yes, sir," I told him, an involuntary shiver running up my back. "I hope not, too."

He pursed his lips. "So . . . what now?"

I glanced past him to where Eisenstadt was still

checking Adams over. "Now I'm going to need transport out to the aliens."

"Just like that?" Lord Kelsey-Ramos asked. "No other
preparation needed first?"

"No, sir. Well," I amended, "I *will* need some reasonably portable long-range communications gear—the
more sophisticated, the better. But I'm sure we can
scrape that up somewhere on reasonably short notice.
Transport will be the tricky part."

His sense changed subtly. "Do you want to take the
Bellwether?" he asked.

I'd seen the offer coming, but that didn't make it any
less impressive. For him to offer up his beloved ship to
an unknown fate . . . "I appreciate the offer, sir," I told
him, and meant it. "But I don't think we need to go
quite to *that* extreme. I was thinking more along the
lines of one of the rocheoids that've been fitted with
Mjollnir drives."

I'd spoken softly, but obviously not softly enough.
Crouching beside Adams and Eisenstadt, Kutzko's head
swung up, a startled look in his eyes. Straightening up,
he left the others and stepped over to join us.

Lord Kelsey-Ramos glanced at him, turned back to
me. "The *Bellwether* would be considerably easier," he
reminded me. "For starters, it's right here—crewed
and ready to go—instead of being three days away at
Collet. *And* it already has the comm gear you want."

"Yes, sir," I nodded, thinking furiously. "Unfortunately, it's also very strongly linked with you. I really
don't want any of you associated more with this than
necessary."

Lord Kelsey-Ramos snorted. "I'm already up to my
eyelids here, and you know it. Try again—and this time
let's have some of that honesty you religious people
prize so highly, eh?"

I looked him square in the eye. "What I have in
mind is going to be dangerous," I told him flatly. "I
don't want to risk any more people than absolutely
necessary. The *Bellwether* crew isn't absolutely necessary."

For a long minute he gazed at me. "When will you need the rocheoid?" he finally asked.

"Sir?" Kutzko interrupted before I could answer. "Request permission to accompany him, at least until he's aboard the rocheoid."

I looked at Kutzko . . . read his sense and intentions. "Thanks, Mikha, but I really don't want you along."

"You'll need me," he said, eyes steady on me.

"No, I don't," I told him with equal firmness. "Shepherd Adams and I can do it alone." I focused past him, to find Adams looking at me. "That is, if you're willing," I added to him.

"Do I have a choice?" he countered calmly. "You need someone through whom you can talk to the thunderheads—if not me, then another Seeker."

"It's going to be dangerous," I warned him, his quick acceptance giving my conscience a twinge. "I really can't *ask* you to—"

"Come now, Gilead," he smiled, a trace of irony coloring his determination. "The reason I came to Spall in the first place was to seek the kingdom of God, remember? If I die . . . then I've found it."

I looked at him closely . . . and in his sense I could see that, somehow, he indeed recognized the full magnitude of the risk we were facing. And was indeed prepared to accept it. "Thank you," I said quietly. I paused, listening to the awkward silence from the others, and took a deep breath. "Well, then," I said briskly, bringing the mood back to less uncomfortable ground. "That's it, Lord Kelsey-Ramos. If you and the *Bellwether* could give us transport out to the rings—"

"That's not quite it," Kutzko interrupted me. "If you're going out to meet the Invaders you're going to need to get hold of a zombi."

Lord Kelsey-Ramos looked at me, my feelings about the Deadman Switch running visibly through his mind. "He's right, you know," he agreed carefully. "Depending on how long you'll need to stay out there, you may even need more than one."

"And you'll need someone to guard them," Kutzko

added. "As well as to . . . use the hypo on them. Which is why you need me along."

"Thank you—again—for your offer," I told him. "But I don't think we're going to need any zombis." I nodded past him toward Adams.

He glanced over his shoulder. "What do you mean?" he frowned.

"He means," Eisenstadt said, "that the thunderheads have just confirmed something we've suspected for quite a while: that they can physically operate a Halloa in a trance as fully as they can a regular zombi."

Kutzko muttered something startled under his breath, and Adams's eyes widened. His thoughts busy with the dangers and uncertainties ahead, that aspect of his communication hadn't yet occurred to him. "God save us all," he whispered.

Lord Kelsey-Ramos looked at Eisenstadt. "I believe Shepherd Adams is still officially assigned here," he said. "We'll need your formal permission to take him with us."

Eisenstadt nodded. "Yes, I'll need to record something for you. Let's go back to my office—all the proper protocols are there."

It took them nearly half an hour to get the permission recording done exactly according to standard format . . . and in their concentration neither man noticed that I slipped out for a few minutes to one of the labs down the hall. By the time Lord Kelsey-Ramos had what he needed, I was back . . . with what *I* needed safely hidden away in an inner pocket.

An hour later we were back aboard the *Bellwether*, heading at top acceleration for the rings of Collet. Where we would find out whether the inspiration that had come to me in my Pravilo prison cell was actually going to work.

And where I would very probably die.

CHAPTER 35

The Pravilo commodore read the page through twice before finally raising his eyes to look at us. "You put me in a rather awkward position, Lord Kelsey-Ramos," he said. I listened carefully, but though there was considerable annoyance beneath the courtesy in his voice, I could hear nothing that sounded like suspicion. "I respect your position here; at the same time, I'm sure you're aware of how close to the wire Project Avalanche is running. Handling guided tours is pretty far down the worklist."

"I understand that, Commodore," Lord Kelsey-Ramos said, his tone managing to combine understanding sympathy and firm resolve. "I'm sure *you* understand in turn that when I put my name on a recommendation, I like to know how well the orders are being carried out."

He had not, in fact, signed the commission's official recommendation, but the commodore probably didn't know that. "Yes, sir," he nodded, "and I'd really like to accommodate you. But as I said, we simply don't have the people to spare."

"Not even a clerk or desk worker?" Lord Kelsey-Ramos persisted. "Come, now, Commodore, I'm not

334

asking for a full Pravilo honor guard or anything like that. I have my own launch and my own pilot—all I'm asking is for you to give me a security clearance and someone to point out the high points as we go along."

The commodore grimaced and reached for his control stick. "Lord Kelsey-Ramos, I really don't have time for this. You want a clearance?—fine; I'll have one made out for you. But you and your launch had better stay out of our way. We've got thirty tugs buzzing around out there, and you so much as near-miss one of them and you're out."

"I understand," Lord Kelsey-Ramos nodded. "Don't worry; we don't intend to spend much time in the current work areas. My primary interest is with the rocheoids that have already been fitted with Mjollnir drives."

The officer's forehead creased slightly at that, but there were too many other matters clamoring for his attention for him to bother with an odd comment from a civilian. "Fine," he grunted, tapping a few keys and pulling a red-stripped cyl from its slot. "Replace your launch's ID beacon with this," he instructed, handing it across the desk, "and don't pull it out until you're ready to leave the area—if you do, it'll erase."

"Thank you," Lord Kelsey-Ramos said, taking the cyl. "What about a guide, now?"

I held my breath. We didn't really want a guide— didn't want *any* witnesses around when I hijacked the rocheoid—but Lord Kelsey-Ramos had persuaded me that it would be strongly out of character for someone in his position not to demand some kind of official escort. He'd toned down the request as far as he reasonably could, and I could tell the Pravilo commodore had noted that. Now if the latter would just push the protocol a little from his direction . . .

He did. "Again, sir, I'm sorry," he said, "but the best I can do is offer you my aide for a couple of hours."

Lord Kelsey-Ramos nodded. "That'll be quite satisfactory, Commodore," he told the other. "Is he available right now?"

"If you want him to be," the other shrugged, waving his control stick at the intercom. "Grashchik? Finish up whatever listing you're on and pull the overview file. Got some visitors here for you to give a *brief* tour to." He got an acknowledgment and waved the intercom off. "It'll be just a couple of minutes."

"Thank you." Lord Kelsey-Ramos glanced behind the commodore, to a real-time schematic of the entire Project Avalanche area. "Tell me, how close to schedule are you running?"

"Dead on, sir," the other said, an obvious note of pride in his voice. "The original plan was for the rocheoids to be able to fly six days from now; we figure we'll be ready in a little over five."

I felt my stomach tighten. Five days—just five days. Deep down, I'd hoped that the project would be behind schedule, that there would be a little more time for us to prepare ourselves before we had to do this. But that hadn't happened. Today—right now—was the time.

I glanced over to find Lord Kelsey-Ramos's eyes on me. I nodded fractionally, got an acknowledging nod in return, and he turned back to the Pravilo officer. "Since time is of the essence, Commodore," he suggested, "why don't we go on back to the *Bellwether* and get the launch ready to go? Your man can meet us there."

The other nodded, almost absently, his mind already on more important matters. "Whatever you want to do, sir," he said. "Grashchik will be there in a few minutes."

Lord Kelsey-Ramos nodded. "Thank you, sir," he said . . . and I could hear the grim determination lurking beneath the words. "We'll be ready for him."

Visually, Project Avalanche was a disappointment.

Not surprisingly, I suppose. The image I'd started with—two hundred mountain-sized rocheoids floating in formation with a hundred workships darting around between them—that picture had pretty well disappeared from my mind as soon as it occurred to me that it would be far more efficient to leave the rocheoids wherever they originally were in orbit and to simply move the Mjollnir-lacing equipment back and forth through the rings as needed. Still, traces of the image had lingered, reinforced perhaps by the fact that the last fifteen rocheoids were being fitted simultaneously from this one orbital station.

But even those fifteen rocheoids turned out to be scattered over a thousand cubic kilometers of space; and the tugs and workships attending them flew for the most part on cold nitrogen maneuvering jets. Even in the middle of it, it was hard to imagine anything at all unusual was happening out here.

Which was, I suspected, exactly the way the Pravilo wanted it to look.

"That's the one, over there," Lieutenant Grashchik pointed through the launch's viewplate toward our target rocheoid. "If you look carefully, you can see the attached tug just below center, on the dark side of the terminator line."

Beside him, Lord Kelsey-Ramos nodded. "Yes, I think I see it. Will we be able to go aboard?"

"I suppose so, sir, if you really want to," Grashchik said, an expected lack of enthusiasm in his voice. "Let me see if it's been left pressurized . . ." He reached past the pilot and tapped in a telemetry code. "Yes, sir, it has," he nodded. "I can tell you right now, though, that there's really nothing there to see. Just an old, stripped-down tug fitted with a Deadman Switch and not much else."

"Has it got pseudograv capabilities?" I put in.

The lieutenant twisted around to throw me a surprised look. "I don't really know. I doubt it'll matter one way or the other to the zombi."

"I'd like to know for sure," I told him, my heart thudding in my ears. The lieutenant's boredom had subtly altered; not yet a real suspicion, but definitely a recognition that something here was just a shade off-key. The sense seemed to be universal: beside me, I felt the shifting of Kutzko's muscles as his hand drifted a few centimeters closer to his needler; behind me, I heard the rhythm of Shepherd Adams's breathing change slightly.

Grashchik studied me. "Why?" he countered.

"Because it could be important," Lord Kelsey-Ramos came to my rescue. "I'm sure you know that flights in and out of Solitaire system routinely leave their pseudogravs on, on the bridge as well as elsewhere. The thunderheads who guide the zombis are used to it by now; it's even possible they wouldn't be able to manage the pinpoint accuracy we'll need without it."

The thought, I saw, had never even occurred to Grashchik. "Ah . . . yes, sir, I see your point," he said, his doubts evaporating. "Well, let me check the specs."

"I'd prefer seeing directly if the pseugograv generator is operational," I said as he slid one of his cyls into the slot.

Lord Kelsey-Ramos threw me a puzzled glance. "It's just something that occurred to me," I told him, unable to explain further with Grashchik sitting there.

The puzzled look remained, but he nodded his recognition that I wasn't just making conversation. "Well, Lieutenant?" he asked. "We're going in there anyway— surely we can flip on the current for a second and see if it's functioning."

The other hesitated, and I could see the muscles of his jaw tighten. Uncertainty, this time, not suspicion. "I don't know, sir. I'd have to open-code the board to do that, and these ships are supposed to stay dead until they're all ready to fly."

I felt my heart pick up its pace. An unexpected bonus—I'd wondered how in the world we were going to persuade him to open-code the tug's control systems. Unwittingly, I'd given Lord Kelsey-Ramos an ideal lever to use.

And he knew it. "Then you'd better call the commodore and get permission," he said firmly. "Mr. Benedar is right—now is *not* the time to start experimenting with techniques and parameters."

"Yes, sir," the lieutenant sighed. Another type of officer would probably have simply given in; but this one knew his job better than that. Reaching for the microphone, he flipped on the comm board.

The commodore was thoroughly annoyed—even from the single carefully guarded side of the conversation we could hear that much was evident. The entire discussion took most of the rest of our trip to the rocheoid, and it was only as we locked tubes with the dormant tug that the commodore finally relented.

"All right," Grashchik said as we unbuckled from our seats, not even trying to hide his own irritation at having been put in the middle of this. "The commodore's authorized me to run the pseudograv *once*, just long enough to make sure it's working. I hope that'll be satisfactory because, frankly, that's all you're going to get."

"Quite satisfactory," Lord Kelsey-Ramos nodded. "Lead on . . . ?"

The lieutenant eased past us, far more graceful in zero-gee than the rest of us would ever hope to be. A quick but thorough check of the seal indicators, and he popped the lock door. A wave of cold air swept into the launch as he opened the tug and floated in. Shivering, from nervous anticipation as much as from the cold, I followed him.

The tug was dark, the only light coming from the small viewports and from a set of firefly indicator lights. A darker shadow—Grashchik—floated at the main panel. A faint glint of light from the edge of his cyl as he inserted it—

There was an audible click of relays, and abruptly the main lights came dimly on. Grashchik turned them up a bit, then moved to the other side of the helm chair. "You ready, Lord Kelsey-Ramos?" he asked over his shoulder. "Listen for the hum . . ."

He flipped a switch, and in the silence the faint drone of high-frequency oscillating current filled the tug. In Mjollnir space that current—or, rather, the flickering electric field it was generating—would take on the character of a gravitational field; right now, in normal space, about all it was doing was radiating a highly distinctive electromagnetic signal all over this part of the ring system.

The lieutenant was thinking about that, too. "That's all I can do," he said, switching it off after perhaps two seconds. "We'd just as soon not broadcast the fact that there are ships out here that aren't registering on the traffic displays. Well. This is it, Lord Kelsey-Ramos. If you have any questions, I'll try and answer them."

Lord Kelsey-Ramos sent me a questioning glance, and I floated over to the board for a quick look. The controls seemed simple enough, certainly compared with the simulated helm Captain Bartholomy had set up aboard the *Bellwether* for my two-day piloting crashcourse. Set in place over the center of the helm board was the by-now familiar black Deadman Switch keyboard. "Looks all right, sir," I told Lord Kelsey-Ramos, the words coming out with difficulty in my nervousness. This was it; time for Lord Kelsey-Ramos and Kutzko to ease Grashchik back into the launch.

Lord Kelsey-Ramos nodded his understanding. "Good. Now, Lieutenant, if you'll come back into the launch for a moment—"

"All of you just stay where you are," Kutzko's voice came quietly from the lock. Quietly enough that the click of his needler's safety was clearly audible . . .

I turned slowly, peripherally noting Lord Kelsey-Ramos's stunned expression as I did so. So this was now Kutzko's play entirely. "Kutzko—"

"Quiet, Benedar," Kutzko cut me off. "Leave the cyl where it is, Lieutenant, and move this way. Slowly."

"Whatever you think you're doing," Grashchik growled, "you're not going to get away with it. Security could *walk* over here faster than you can fly this monstrosity."

"I appreciate your concern," Kutzko said calmly. "Now do like I told you—I don't really want to have to shoot you. You, too, Lord Kelsey-Ramos, if you please."

I looked behind Lord Kelsey-Ramos to where Adams was quietly floating . . . and in his face I saw that he, alone of all of us, hadn't been caught unawares by Kutzko's move. Something they'd cooked up together, probably while I was occupied with my flying lessons, in an obvious attempt to push Lord Kelsey-Ramos as far as possible out of direct implication in this. A scheme I'd been too wrapped up in my own worries to even notice . . .

"Not you," Kutzko said into my thoughts. I focused on his face, saw the calm determination there as he looked at me. "You stay aboard with me. You too," he added, glancing briefly at Adams.

Grashchik, halfway to the lock, suddenly stiffened, and I saw the impotent anger in his sense turn to horror as he abruptly realized that Kutzko wasn't planning to fly the tug away through normal space . . . and recognized what the implications of that were to Adams and me. "Wait a minute—wait a minute," he said, his voice beginning to shake. "You can't—look, blaze it, that's premeditated *murder*. This tug can't possibly be worth *that* much to you—"

"You let *me* decide that, all right?" Kutzko cut him off coldly. "You just be a good boy and get into the launch."

A sort of enraged panic flooded Grashchik's sense—a panic built of duty, pride, and anger—and for that single moment I thought he would decide to fight back, after all. I clenched my hands into fists . . . but as he hesitated, the panic subsided, and with returning sanity he saw that resistance would accomplish nothing but the useless sacrifice of his own life. Clenching his teeth, muscles tight with bitter fury, he silently continued on into the lock.

Some of the tension went out of Kutzko's face; he, too, had sensed Grashchik teetering on the brink. "Now you, sir," he said.

Lord Kelsey-Ramos pursed his lips, followed Grashchik off the tug without comment. "Now—you, Benedar," Kutzko gestured to me. "There's a satchel just inside the lock. Get it—and don't forget that I'll be covering you."

He winked reassuringly as I moved toward the lock. An unnecessary gesture; I already knew the threat had been solely for Grashchik's benefit.

Another unnecessary gesture, as it turned out. Grashchik was nowhere in sight as I collected the massive satchel and carefully maneuvered it through the zero-gee onto the tug. "He's gone forward," I told Kutzko as I pushed the satchel over into a corner and eased it toward the deck. "Probably calling in the alert. Get going—we'll seal the lock from here."

"Don't bother," he said calmly, swinging the lock closed.

I stared at him, feeling a horrible tingle run through me. How had I failed to notice—? "Kutzko, get out of here," I snapped.

"Get the engines fired up," he said, ignoring the order. "I trust you remember how?"

"Mikha—"

"And you'd better get busy—like you said, Grashchik's up there calling for help. Be a waste of a good hijacking if they get us while we're sitting here arguing."

I glared at him; but it was a useless gesture. If he was determined to come along, there was nothing I could do to stop him. And we both knew it.

Tight-lipped, I went over to the board, where Adams had already seated himself in the helm chair. By the time I had the power indicators reading operational, he was ready.

"Thunderhead?" I called. "Are you there?"

For what seemed like a small eternity there was no reply. Heart pounding in my ears, I watched Adams's slack face, thoughts of treachery and betrayal spinning through my mind—

"I am here," Adams whispered.

I swallowed, the worst of the tension draining from my muscles. "We're ready to go. Do you know exactly where the Invaders are at the moment?"

"I do. But where is the zombi . . . for me to use?"

There was a totally uncaring attitude toward human life hidden beneath the words. "There will be no zombi," I gritted. "Shepherd Adams—the man you're speaking through—will act as your hands."

For a long moment Adams just stared at me, an alien

yet unmistakably surprised look on his face. Apparently that implication of their Seeker contacts hadn't yet occurred to the thunderheads, either. "I don't know if it will . . . be possible to—"

"So try it," Kutzko broke in brusquely, nodding toward the displays. "We've got company coming."

Adams's face twisted, his hands reaching tentatively for the black Deadman Switch. I held my breath . . . and abruptly fell a few centimeters to the deck below me as the Mjollnir drive came on and the pseudograv began to function.

I exhaled raggedly, swaying a bit as my circulatory system adjusted to weight again. A moment, and my vision cleared . . . and I turned to find Kutzko looking at me. "Well," I said to him. "It worked."

He nodded, a quiet grimness to his sense. "So far, anyway," he agreed. "Now what?"

"We see how long he can handle it," I said evenly. "If he can get us all the way to the alien fleet in one jump, fine. If not . . . we see how long he needs to rest between contacts."

"And once we're there?" Kutzko persisted. "You can't have him fading in and out on you while you're trying to hold a conversation with the Invaders."

"Let's just see what happens, all right?" I snapped, my mouth dry. Beneath his casual words I knew what it was he was offering.

For a moment Kutzko studied me. Then he nodded, once, and turned back to the satchel in the corner. "Sure," he said over his shoulder. "There's no rush. Come on—give me a hand and we'll get this comm gear of yours set up."

I stared at his back, my muscles trembling with anger and dread. No, there was no rush; and if we were lucky, there might be no need to go through with it at all.

But I could tell Kutzko didn't believe that. And down deep, neither did I.

CHAPTER 36

We were forty-five minutes out from Solitaire, three-quarters of the way to the alien fleet, when our luck ran out.

There was no warning at all that I could see—nothing in Adams's face or body language that preceded it. One minute he was sitting at the Deadman Switch, glazed eyes staring tautly into space; the next minute, there was the crack of circuit breakers, gravity abruptly vanished, and Adams was gasping frantically for breath.

We reached him at the same time, Kutzko jamming the oxygen inhaler we'd brought over his nose and mouth as I searched his face for other symptoms.

It didn't look good.

"I'm all . . . all right," Adams managed after a couple of tense minutes under pure oxygen. "Just let . . . me catch my . . . breath, okay?"

Kutzko turned to me. "How is he?"

I took a careful breath of my own. "Not in any immediate danger, I don't think," I said. Before Aaron Balaam darMaupine and the paranoia that had followed in his wake, Watchers had sometimes been employed by hospitals as complements to the standard medical sensors.

Fleetingly, I wished some of that specialized training had been available to me. "Heartbeat's stabilizing, and blood pressure seems all right. Brain functions . . ." I peered into Adams's eyes. "Pupils are responding normally, and . . . I don't see any evidence of pain."

"Nothing hurts," Adams confirmed, still somewhat short of breath. "Just give me a few . . . more minutes to rest."

I looked up to find Kutzko's eyes on me . . . and I knew what he was thinking. "We can do the rest of the trip in shorter stages," I told him firmly. "We're only fifteen minutes or so from the alien fleet—we can let him rest up and then go on."

"What about your talk with the Invaders?" he countered. "You going to confine *that* to fifteen-minute chunks, too?"

"If need be, yes," I said, keeping my voice steady. The lie was an unnecessary caution, perhaps, with the thunderheads presumably no longer listening in . . . but with so much hanging in the balance, I preferred unnecessary caution to unnecesary chances.

How easily I'd learned, and learned to rationalize, the art of lying. *There are ways that some think straight, but they lead in the end to death* . . . "Besides," I added to Kutzko, hurrying to get my mind off that thought, "any talking I do with the aliens will nooooosarily be chopped into short segments. They'll be shooting past us at twelve percent lightspeed, remember?"

He grimaced, but for the moment at least he seemed willing to trust me. "All right," he said at last. "We'll give him some time—maybe give him another shot of Dr. Eisenstadt's fancy mixture. See how quickly he recovers."

I glanced at Adams; but if he'd heard the unspoken *and if not* in Kutzko's tone, he gave no indication of it. "Agreed," I nodded, my stomach tightening. *And if not* . . . then either Kutzko or I wouldn't be returning to Solitaire.

We waited a little more than an hour . . . an hour that will forever remain etched on my memory.

Not for anything in particular that happened. On the contrary, the most dominant feature of that time was its extreme boredom. Wrapped in our own individual thoughts and fears about what lay ahead, none of us really felt like talking; and with our equipment already set up there was absolutely nothing for any of us to do. I don't know how many times I floated past the board, studying the never-changing indicators, or how many minutes I spent at the viewport, looking out at the stars and straining my eyes to try and follow the contours of our tethered rocheoid in their dim light.

But what I did mainly was fight against terror.

Not fear. Fear I'd expected, and had been more or less prepared for. But as the minutes ticked by, and I ran out of other things with which to occupy my mind, I began to focus more and more on the image of the alien ships rushing inexorably down on us. It did no good to remind myself that they were two years away at their normal-space speed—my gut instincts had already latched firmly onto the fact that, as far as we were concerned, they were a bare fifteen *minutes* away. It was a totally irrational terror, but reminding myself of that did nothing except make me too ashamed of myself to try and talk it out with the others. More than once I told myself that the thunderheads might be behind at least some of the emotion, amplifying my feelings as they had back in the Pravilo cell on Solitaire. But this time, even that knowledge didn't help.

And so, for an hour, I suffered; alone, bored, terrified, and ashamed. It was like a foretaste of hell . . . and as close as I ever again want to be.

Which probably also explains why, when Adams finally decided he was ready, I immediately agreed to let him do so. I've often wondered whether things would have worked out differently if I'd been more cautious.

"You will reach the Inva . . . ders in three minutes," the thunderhead whispered through Adams's lips. "What are your instructions?"

My throat was dry enough to hurt. Against all odds—

against all opposition—we'd made it. Now it was in my hands alone. "Stop us here," I ordered, "as close to being in the path of the lead ship as possible. If you can control our position that accurately, that is."

"I can," the thunderhead hissed, and I got the distinct impression I'd just stepped on his pride. I'd rather thought he would take it that way; hopefully, that would translate into the pinpoint accuracy I needed. Holding my breath, I watched as Adams's hands moved to make a slight correction in the course; then, with a crack of circuit breakers, gravity vanished and the stars once again appeared in the viewport.

We were there.

"All right," I said, fighting to keep my voice from trembling. "Now. Pay attention to this, thunderhead, because this part is crucial." I pulled myself over to Adams and indicated an instrument Kutzko and I had wired into the main board. "This device is measuring the magnetic field strength outside the tug," I explained. "Magnetic fields are what the Invaders are using to scoop hydrogen into their ships' engines, and fields of that strength can be dangerous to our species. You understand?"

"Yes," he whispered.

"Good. Now, this has been set to give you a short—a very short—warning before the strength gets to dangerous levels. When the red light here goes on—" I touched the test button to demonstrate—"you must immediately take us back into Mjollnir space. Understand? —immediately."

"I understand," the thunderhead said.

I desperately hoped so; Lord Kelsey-Ramos's best estimate was that the red light would give us barely three seconds to get out of the aliens' way. A tape-thin margin for error; though at the speed the fleet was making, I suppose we were lucky to get even that much warning. "Good," I told the thunderhead, trying to sound confident in his abilities. "You watch the light while I get this transmitter ready to go."

I moved to the comm gear we'd set up, watching

Adams out of the corner of my eye . . . and I had no trouble catching the thunderhead's sudden surprise. "You are already pre . . . pared to signal the In . . . vaders?" he asked.

"Well, of course I've got to tune this thing first," I said off-handedly. "After that, I'll need you to tell me exactly what to say. You *did* tell me you could communicate with them, didn't you?"

Some of the thunderhead's nervousness left Adams's body. "Yes," he whispered. "We have promised to give . . . you whatever aid is . . . necessary."

I nodded, as if I really believed the face value of the words, and turned to the comm. "Okay, now. Let's see . . ."

I had asked Lord Kelsey-Ramos for the most sophisticated equipment he could get, and he'd taken me doubly at my word. The comm gear, for all its compact size, was a virtual catalog of dials, setting switches, readouts, and adjustments. I fiddled busily with them, keeping a careful eye on Adams and the red light sitting in front of him. If the warning came and the thunderhead didn't notice—

Abruptly the light flicked on. "Thun—" I started to shout; and then gravity returned and we were once again safe in Mjollnir space.

I took a shuddering breath, fighting to banish the vivid image of flaming death hurtling down on me. "That was very good, thunderhead," I managed. "Well. That came sooner than I expected, somehow. Where are we headed?"

"Outward," Adams whispered. "Beyond the Invaders."

"Come back around, please," I instructed him. "Put us back in front of the lead ship, again three to four minutes ahead of them."

"Why in front of them?" Kutzko asked. "Why can't we sit off to the side where we won't have to worry about them slamming into us?"

My stomach knotted; sternly, I willed it to relax. "Because that would generate too many complicated Doppler effects," I explained with the casual sincerity

I'd learned so well how to wrap my lies in. "From here in front, there's just one constant effect for them to unscramble. Or there will be, anyway," I amended, "once I get this thing working."

"Let me help," Kutzko offered, stepping forward. The step became a lazy arc as the circuit breakers again snapped and the Mjollnir drive kicked off. He cursed under his breath, flailing for something to grab onto. "Can we at least turn off that blazing pseudograv?" he growled. "This flip-flop stuff is going to get one of us a broken neck."

"No!" I snapped as Adams's hand moved to obey. "I want it left on."

"Why?" Kutzko frowned.

I bit down hard on my lip, searching furiously for a reason he couldn't argue with . . . and finding one. "Because the story that we spun for Lieutenant Grashchik wasn't just froth, that's why," I told him. "We *don't* know how the thunderhead control would be affected by zero-gee, and I'd rather fight some extra nausea than risk losing position. Speaking of which, thunderhead, where are we?"

"Approximately two . . . minutes in front of the . . . Invaders," he whispered.

I'd asked for three or four. So much for pinpoint accuracy. "Okay," I said. "Don't forget to keep watching that light."

"I will. Are you ready for our . . . assistance yet?"

I hissed between my teeth. "Not even close. Hang on—let me figure out how to do this . . ."

In my peripheral vision I saw Kutzko raise an astonished eyebrow. "Are you telling me you spent four days on the *Bellwether* learning how to run that thing and *still* haven't got it down?"

"Look, just shut up and let me work, all right?" I snarled at him. "I know what I'm doing—it's just going to take a little time."

Kutzko glanced at Adams, back at me. Still more or less willing to trust me; but that trust was eroding fast. "You know, if it's going to take this long," he pointed out, "we could skip this three-minute stuff and pull back a decent distance—say, an hour or so—and do it there. I'd hate to have the thunderhead miss his cue before you even get that blazing thing working."

"It's *not* going to take that long," I shot back, tension adding more snap to my voice than was probably called for. Without knowing it, Kutzko was skating perilously close to the truth, and the last thing I could afford was for the thunderheads to catch on to what I was really up to. "It'll take just another minute to get this going, okay?"

"Fine," Kutzko said, his patience starting to go the way of his trust. "I just hope it won't take you this blazing long to find the right frequency to send on. *Or* to figure out what you're going to say to them."

"I hopefully won't have to find a specific frequency," I growled. "This is a multispectrum transmitter—that's one of the reasons the adjustments are so tricky. And as for what I'm going to say, I'm going to transmit a simple greeting from the Patri and then repeat it in the language the thunderheads will give us. Then we'll pull back and wait for a reply. You happy now?"

His reply was cut off by the sudden return of gravity. "Right," Kutzko nodded, his voice hard. "Just another minute, huh?"

Deliberately, I turned my back on him. "Sorry, thunderhead, but I guess we'll have to do this again. Same thing, all right?"

"Very . . . well," he sighed. His voice—

I spun around, muscles tensing. A single glance was all it took to confirm what my ears had already told me: Adams was starting to lose it. We would have to get off the aliens' course right away, give him time to recover. "Thunderhead—"

But it was too late. The circuit breakers snapped and gravity vanished . . . and Adams gasped for breath.

Kutzko shot past me toward Adams, braking himself with a hand on the helm chair as the other hand snatched the oxygen inhaler from its grip and jammed it against

Adams's face. "How far?" he snapped. "Come on, Adams—how far are we ahead of them?"

"Th—three mi . . . min . . . utes," Adams panted.

Kutzko looked over the helm chair at me . . . and for the first time since I'd known him, there was genuine fear in his eyes. Fear . . . and resignation. "Three minutes," he murmured. "Three minutes . . . and we're all dead."

CHAPTER 37

So it had come: the moment I'd hoped and prayed could be avoided. *If it is possible, let this cup pass me by* . . . "Check the course reading," I told Kutzko, my heart pounding in my ears as I fought against the sudden nausea of fear. "Make sure we really are in the aliens' path."

He twisted his head around, eyes searching out the proper readout . . . and with his attention away from me I moved quietly toward him, fingers dipping into my side pocket. The hypo I'd stolen from the lab on Spall was there, hard and cold and lethal. "Help me get Shepherd Adams out of the helm chair," I said to Kutzko, pulling the hypo out and palming it in my right hand.

I don't know why I expected to get away with it. In a single smooth motion Kutzko turned back toward me, his left hand taking over the grip on Adams's oxygen inhaler as his right drew his needler from its holster. "Don't try it, Gilead," he said quietly. "Slapshot clip—I can knock that hypo out of your hand without even drawing blood."

I took a deep breath. "It has to be done, Mikha."

"I know." Releasing the needler, he left it floating before him in midair as he reached into his own pocket. "But you're not going to do it," he said, holding up a hypo of his own. "*I* am."

I clenched my teeth, frustration and anger and despair welling up within me. Another moment I'd seen coming, as far back as Kutzko's last-minute insistance on coming along. I could have confronted him then, or any time since. But I'd put it off, irrationally hoping it wouldn't have to be dealt with . . . and now, with less than three minutes remaining to us, I had lost forever the opportunity of doing this gently.

Now, in my last moments of life, I was going to have to hurt him. "This isn't for you to do, Mikha," I told him.

"Since when?" he countered. Retrieving the needler, he holstered it again. "*I'm* the professional shield, remember? It's my job to risk death for other people."

"I know," I nodded. "But it's a job you never should have taken . . . because you're doing it for the wrong reasons."

He snorted: derision, with a shading of nervousness beneath. "I thought you religious types believed that dying for your friends is the highest form of martyrdom," he said sardonically.

"Yes, I do," I said. "And so did your parents. But *you* don't. Not really."

His face tightened. "My parents have nothing to do with it—"

"They have everything to do with it," I snapped. Two minutes to go . . . and it would take one of those minutes for the drug in my hypo to kill me. "You were raised in a religious household," I told him. "Don't try to deny it—the signs are all there. In the process you absorbed a lot of your parents' principles . . . but it's all just going through the motions. You don't really believe in God, or even in a set of absolute standards that your actions will be measured against. You risk your life for Lord Kelsey-Ramos and others because your parents taught you it was noble to do so; that's the *only* reason you came aboard this tug with a hypo in your pocket." I locked eyes with him. "You're living a lie, Mikha. I can't let you die one, too."

His face might have been carved from stone. "My past is none of your business," he bit out; and for an instant I could see an echo of Aikman in his eyes. "And neither is why I do what I do."

I looked at his face, read the determination there. A minute and a half to go . . . and I had run out of time. "In that case," I sighed—

And without warning I grabbed at the safety cap of my hypo, twisting it off. *To your hands I commit my spirit* . . . Locating the vein in my wrist, I jabbed.

I should have known it wouldn't work. The hypo wasn't even within five centimeters of the vein when the slapshot pellets slammed into my hand, sending the instrument spinning across the tug and leaving my fingers numb and tingling. "Mikha!—no!"

"Sorry, Gilead," he said, his voice trembling but with that same iron firmness beneath it. "Right reasons or wrong, it's still *my* job . . . and I'm going to do it." Visibly setting his teeth, he released his grip on the needler and reached for his own hypo's safety cap.

I don't know why I jumped at him. It was a futile gesture—even if I could possibly have covered the distance between us in time, I knew full well there was no way I could overpower him. But the frustration flooding my soul would simply not allow me to stand passively by without one last attempt.

Or so I thought . . . but even as I flew through the air toward him—as he hesitated, then paused to raise a hand against my attack—a small fact that my back-brain had perhaps already noticed burst abruptly into conscious awareness. "Mikha—stop—" I all but screamed—

And broke off as the deck slammed up into my face and chest.

For a long moment I just lay there, temporarily paralyzed from the shock and from having had the wind knocked out of me. The butt of Kutzko's needler lay within my view, as did his still untriggered hypo. Above me, I could hear the sounds of skin against cloth as Kutzko fought to regain his equilibrium in the suddenly returned gravity; the sounds of his breathing, and of his whispered curses.

From Adams, still in the helm chair, there was nothing. No gasping; no movement.

No breathing.

Slowly, carefully, I got my hands under me and pushed myself up off the deck. Another pair of hands slid under my armpits, helping me the rest of the way to my feet. "Adams," Kutzko said, his voice a mixture of shock and horror.

I nodded, my head aching furiously from the fall. "I know. He'd stopped gasping—I didn't even notice when." Steeling myself, I turned to look.

He was dead, of course. The empty look on his face—the slackness of his muscles and eyes—it brought me back with a rush to the *Bellwether* and the man whose death I'd witnessed there. More than once I'd noted the way Adams and Zagorin had seemed to take on alien characteristics when in contact with the thunderheads; now, for the first time, I could see how those characteristics remained when everything that was human was gone. It was eerie and abhorrent, and it made me want to be sick.

And to cry.

Beside me, Kutzko took a shuddering breath. "How about you? You okay?"

"I think so. You?"

"Yeah," he said, a quiet bitterness in his voice. His willingness to die, preempted . . . and once again the professional shield was forced to contemplate the limits of his power. "What now?—we go home?"

I blinked tears from my eyes. I had talked Adams into this trip—had talked him, for that matter, into involving himself with the thunderheads in the first place. My project, my ambitions, my errors. His cost. "We stay," I told Kutzko with a sigh. "Thunderhead, if you can still hear me, please continue with what we've been doing: bring us around to a position three to four minutes further back toward Solitaire."

There was a moment of hesitation, a noticeably slower reaction to the command than the living Adams/thunderhead combination had displayed. Perhaps it was merely surprise on the thunderhead's part that we were going to keep on with it.

Surprise, or disappointment.

I turned back to Kutzko, to see the question on his face. "We have to keep trying," I told him. "Otherwise his sacrifice will be for nothing."

He held my eyes another moment, the question fading into accusation: that if I'd been ready to transmit when we first arrived, that sacrifice might not have been necessary. I braced myself for a fresh argument; but the emotional strain of the past few minutes had left him as weary as it had me, and he merely nodded and turned away. Wiping one last tear from my cheek, I walked back to the transmitter and resumed my tinkering.

The gravity vanished a few seconds later, and I was still making adjustments three and a half minutes after that when the red light flashed on and the thunderhead controlling Adams's body—I couldn't bring myself to think of it as a zombi—took us back onto Mjollnir drive. Across the tug Kutzko watched me, a dull bitterness slowly growing through his sense at my continued failure to finish what he still believed were serious preparations for talking with the aliens. "I think I'll have it in another run," I announced. "If you'll just take us in one more time, thunderhead—?"

My sentence was cut off by the now-familiar crack of circuit breakers, and we were once again in zero-gee. I licked my lips, started to turn back to my transmitter—

And without any emotional sense whatsoever, Adams's body rose from the helm chair and turned to face me. "You—Benedar," he whispered.

A shiver of horror went up my back at the sound of that voice. There was nothing even remotely human about it, despite the fact that it came from a human throat. With the passing of Adams's soul all the human elements were gone . . . and what was left was the closest thing to a pure thunderhead voice we were ever likely to hear. "Yes, thunderhead, what is it?" I managed to say.

The dead eyes gazed emotionlessly into my face. "Betrayer," the thunderhead whispered. "You will die."

And, moving awkwardly in the zero-gee, he started toward me.

CHAPTER 38

"**D**on't fire!" I snapped, holding a warning hand palm-outward toward Kutzko. Out of the corner of my eye I saw him hesitate, his needler still trained on Adams's body, the fingers holding it bone-white at the knuckles. Never in eight years had I seen him as thoroughly rattled as he was now—and I could hardly blame him. "Don't fire," I repeated, fighting hard to keep down my own horror at the sight. "What are you going to do, kill him?"

His answer was a hiss between clenched teeth.

"I know," I agreed. "Just stay cool—I'll handle it."

"Oh, good," he breathed. "Mind telling me what's going on that you need to handle?"

I cocked an eyebrow at Adams's dead face. "You want to tell him, thunderhead, or should I?"

"You have lied to us," the alien whisper came again. The body, still slow and clumsy, was nevertheless getting too close for comfort, and I found myself moving backwards in response. "You have betrayed us. You will die."

"How could I have betrayed you?" I asked. "Haven't I done exactly what I said I'd do?"

358

The thunderhead ignored the question, as I'd rather expected him to. Logic and prior agreements were clearly not in the forefront of his mind at the moment. "You will die," he repeated.

I clenched my teeth, fighting to stir up some emotional energy. The battle was over, and I'd won—the thunderheads' fury was all the proof I needed of that—and with the victory all the drive of the past week had drained into deep fatigue. For the moment I honestly didn't care whether the thunderheads killed me or not.

But if I died now, Kutzko would die with me. For his sake, I had to see this through to the very end. "Has what I've accomplished made things any worse for you?" I demanded, forcing myself to look directly at the dead eyes. "Or have you forgotten that your existence as a race is directly dependent on the Invaders' own survival?"

"You will die—"

"Enough of that!" I snapped. "Answer my question—or else admit that you never meant to cooperate with me in the first place. That you intended all along to sabotage my efforts."

"There was no sabotage."

"Not *yet*, no," I growled. "But there would have been, wouldn't there, just as soon as I asked you what I should say to them?"

There was no answer. "Get it moving, Gilead," Kutzko said, his voice tight. "If you don't talk him back to the helm in a couple more minutes we'll be smashed into powder."

"We've got all the time in the world," I told him evenly. "The fleet's not behind us anymore—they're angling away from Solitaire."

He stared at me. "They're *what*?"

"They've chosen to live," I said, my eyes steady on Adams's face. "The only question now is whether or not the thunderheads will be smart enough to do the same."

The thunderhead hissed. "You bargain for your life?"

"Bargain?" I shook my head. "No. The bargain's already been made and is being carried out. I simply point out that killing us won't gain you anything at all."

"It will gain revenge."

"Revenge for what?" I snarled, suddenly tired of thunderhead singlemindedness. "For the failure of your grand scheme to have us destroy your enemies? It would never have worked—you should have known that *years* ago. Human beings aren't brainless insects you can manipulate without consequences—we hate and we resent and we fear, and no matter what you did with us, sooner or later we would have wiped Spall clean of you."

I broke off, hearing my voice ringing through the tug and abruptly realizing I'd been shouting. I took a ragged breath, forcing calmness over the frustration and anger and weariness. "You have just two choices left," I said quietly. "You can have us as mediators and, perhaps, as willing allies *if* you can persuade us that your side is in the right . . . or you can have us join the Invaders as your enemies. There are no other possibilities."

For a long minute Adams's body floated motionless in the middle of the tug. Totally dead, now, with even its alien life gone from it. "What's happening?" Kutzko asked.

"He's gone to discuss it with the others, I'd guess," I said. I focused on his face . . . "You've figured it out."

He gave me a lopsided smile; and from his sense I could see that one of my worries, at least, could be laid to rest: that he didn't resent me for having kept him ignorant of my plans. "I may be slow, but I'm not totally stupid," he said wryly. "Cute—and nicely devious, in all directions. I'd have thought that kind of thing beyond your talents."

I grimaced, feeling a curious sadness growing within me. "We all have the potential for deceit," I sighed. "Even Watchers."

He snorted gently. "As Aaron Balaam darMaupine so graphically proved."

Aaron Balaam darMaupine. "It's funny, you know," I said, the words sounding distant in my ears. "Every Watcher for the past twenty years has had to suffer because of darMaupine—the parents' sins bringing punishment indeed on the children and grandchildren. His name's a curse and an insult everywhere in the Patri and colonies—for years I despised the sound of it, and even now I can't hear it without cringing. And yet, it was that name that gave me the key to what we've just done."

Kutzko's forehead furrowed. "I don't understand."

"His humility name. Balaam." I blinked sudden moisture from my eyes. "You remember the story of Balaam, don't you?"

"Sure—he was a prophet sent by someone to curse the Israelites. The one whose donkey talked to him."

I nodded. "The one whose donkey revealed what was waiting for him in the road ahead—"

I broke off as Adams's body subtly reanimated. "Well?" I asked the thunderhead. "What have you decided?"

There was no answer; but the dead hands groped for position on the ceiling handholds, turning Adams's body back toward the helm chair. Visibly steeling himself, Kutzko moved to assist . . . and a couple of minutes later, the stars vanished and gravity returned.

I watched Kutzko lean over Adams's shoulder to study the heading indicators; and even before he spoke, I could tell from his posture what the thunderheads had decided. "We're heading back to Solitaire," he announced quietly.

I closed my eyes. *God then opened Balaam's eyes and he saw the angel of God standing in the road with a drawn sword in his hand; and he bowed his head and threw himself on his face . . .* "I guess," I murmured, mostly to myself, "even thunderheads know the angel of death when it stands before them."

Kutzko looked back over his shoulder. "The Invaders?"

I shook my head. "Us."

CHAPTER 39

The wind had picked up over the past half hour, cutting between the Butte City cliffs like frigid stirring spoons intent on whipping up the snow into as many miniature spinstorms as possible. Sitting a few meters up the sloping ridge Calandra and I had climbed so long ago, I listened to the wind whistling past the visor of my insulalls and watched as Lord Kelsey-Ramos gestured Kutzko to remain below and then crunched his way up to meet me. "Lord Kelsey-Ramos," I nodded as he came within earshot. "This is a surprise—I would have expected you to call."

"I'd have expected that, too," he grunted, sitting down carefully beside me. A few snowflakes landed on his shoulder and quickly melted; for all the extra cost of his expensive insulalls, they weren't quite as good as my plain Pravilo-issue ones. "But then it occurred to me you'd probably have found the quietest and most private place around, and that I might as well take advantage of that. The encampment still has a lot of madhouse about it."

I nodded. "I take it you have news of my fate?"

"Actually, I'm more here just to talk," he shook his

362

head. "Officially, the Pravilo's still batting your case back and forth between departments; though unofficially, Admiral Yoshida has pretty well conceded that they really don't have any choice but to turn you loose. Much as he'd love to nail you to a wall somewhere for preempting his strike, he's smart enough to know that if he brings *you* up on charges, he'll have to do the same to Eisenstadt and me."

"And both of you have too many friends in high places?"

He nodded without embarrassment. "That, plus the truism that sailfish attract more attention than guppies. They put us on trial—especially on charges of treason—and the security cover they've so carefully woven around Solitaire would be gone within two weeks. The Patri's not ready for all this to become public knowledge; not yet, anyway." He made a sound that was half chuckle, half snort. "Besides which, the scheme *worked*. Awfully hard to argue against success, you know."

I grimaced. "So I get off scot-free."

Lord Kelsey-Ramos cocked his head to peer at me. "You *wanted* to go to prison?"

Quietly, at my sides, I clenched my hands into fists, my eyes drifting to the snow-dusted thunderheads below. Each of them had developed a crisscrossing of thin black lines across their bodies in the past few days—a seasonal occurrence, I'd been told, that had to do with their hormonal response to cold weather. For a moment I watched the subtle changes in the tall white shapes as the souls within them flitted back and forth, and wondered that I'd ever seen them as nothing more than plants. "Have the thunderheads accepted the situation yet?" I asked.

Lord Kelsey-Ramos threw me another look, and I could sense the underlying concern there. "Like the Pravilo, they don't have much choice," he said. "As you so elegantly established, their lives are pretty well entwined with both ours and the Invaders' at the moment. Even if that triangle is no longer exactly equilateral," he added.

The doubt in his voice was impossible to miss. "I gather the commission still isn't convinced of that last point?"

He sighed, the blast of warm air momentarily fogging a spot on his visor. "Afraid not," he conceded. "For that matter, I'm not entirely convinced myself. I don't argue your reasoning, but I also see no guarantee that the Invaders will follow the logic the same way we do."

"They were logical enough to understand the implications of a rocheoid that kept appearing and disappearing from in front of them," I reminded him.

"It was hardly an implication they could miss," he returned dryly. "Especially with you broadcasting the whole time on pseudograv-generator radio frequencies. Even the most fanatical admiral would think twice before taking on a defense force whose Mjollnir drive worked where his wouldn't."

I nodded. "The point remains that they know we could have killed them all—or even just destroyed a couple of ships as a demonstration—but that we deliberately avoided doing so."

"True enough," he shrugged. "On the other hand, though, we *did* make them abort a campaign that they've already invested nearly a century in. That could put a considerable damper on whatever gratitude they're feeling toward us."

"I suppose that's possible," I admitted. "Still, everything that they've done indicates beings who take a long-term view of things. I really think that our balance sheet with them will work out all right when we're finally able to talk with them."

"Perhaps. Not much we can do at the moment but hope you're right about that, too." He shook his head. "That was still an awful chance you took out there, Gilead."

I looked down the slope to where Kutzko was standing his usual casual-looking guard. "I know. You'll remember, sir, that I tried to keep it down to just Shepherd Adams and me."

He nodded. "Which means that you knew right from

the start that the thunderheads might leave you out there to die."

The question in his voice was unobtrusive but obvious. "I deliberately glissed over that point during the debriefing, sir," I told him. "Our relationship with the thunderheads is strained enough; I didn't want to add to that tension by explaining why they were so angry with me."

"Because you'd lied to them?"

I shook my head. "Because they had an alternative scheme in mind. One which depended on them making sure I *didn't* contact the Invaders."

He frowned. "But you'd already proved to them that the Invaders had to live."

"No, sir," I told him, some of the bitterness in my soul seeping out into my voice. "All I'd proved was that *some* of them had to live."

For a long moment he was silent . . . and then he swore, quietly. "You're right," he said, his voice grim. "Absolutely right. And all they really had to do was pretend to cooperate with us; guide all the rocheoids out there, right on schedule . . . and then allow one of them to miss its target."

I nodded, the image sending a shiver up my back. "And there wouldn't have been a single thing we could have done about it afterwards. As long as any of the Invaders were alive we'd still have had to leave the Cloud in place—otherwise the survivors would escape home on Mjollnir drive with the news of what had happened."

"And before we knew it we'd have had a full-scale war on our hands." Lord Kelsey-Ramos swore again, viciously this time. "A war we ourselves would have effectively started."

His anger was like an almost physical wave of heat. "I'd appreciate it, sir, if you'd keep all this to yourself," I said. "There's no proof, after all, that that's really what they had in mind."

He sent me a hard-edged look. "Besides which, you

don't believe in emotions like anger and hatred?" he bit out. "Even honest ones?"

If your enemy is hungry, give him something to eat . . . "We still have to work with them," I reminded him quietly. "Unless you're prepared to abandon Solitaire. Try to remember, too, that we still don't know what the quarrel is between the thunderheads and the Invaders . . . or what the consequences would have been for the thunderheads if they'd lost."

Slowly, almost reluctantly, the anger faded from his sense. Not all of it, but enough. "Well . . ." he said at last, "I don't suppose any single example of thunderhead deceit would make the Patri any less vigilant in their dealings with them. Besides, it may not hurt to have something we can hold over their heads again."

"Thank you, sir."

"Don't thank *me*," he snorted. "I'm considering it an extremely temporary secret, one I expect I'll be using against them somewhere along the line." Moving carefully on the slippery rock, he got to his feet. "Anyway; break time's over. I'd better get back before some blazing fire-eater talks Yoshida into bringing you up on charges and never mind the consequences. You want a lift back to the encampment?"

"With your permission, sir," I said, avoiding his eyes, "I think I'll stay here a little longer."

For a second he didn't move, and I didn't have to see his face to know he was frowning down at me. "If you'd like," he said, his voice overly casual. "I'll keep you advised of developments."

"Thank you, sir," I said again. "I appreciate all you're doing."

"No problem," he grunted. "All I want is to clear up all the loose ends and get back to Portslava. Preferably without having to leave my Watcher behind."

Nodding, he turned and made his way down the ridge. At the bottom he paused and conferred briefly with Kutzko. A moment later he was walking back across the Butte City toward where he'd left the car, and Kutzko was heading up toward me. "Aren't you derelicting your duty or some such?" I asked as he approached. "Letting him go off by himself that way?"

"Daiv Ifversn's waiting in the car," he said equably, sitting down where his employer had been a minute earlier. "Besides, he ordered me up here—thought I might want to talk to you."

"I had the impression that coming up here was *your* idea," I told him mildly.

He shrugged, unconcerned at my once again being able to read straight through him. "Well, he concurred with it, anyway," he said easily, glancing around at the sea of thunderheads below. "Nice view. You just waiting around to see if Ninevah gets destroyed?"

I blinked. "Excuse me?"

"The story of Jonah," he amplified. "Prophet told to preach doom to Ninevah, ran off and got swallowed by a fish, then did as he'd been told and got mad when the city was let off the hook."

"I remember the story, thank you," I said. "I hardly think it applies here—if you'll recall, I'm the one who was ready to risk his life so that the thunderheads *wouldn't* be destroyed."

"That wasn't what I was referring to, exactly," he said. "I was thinking more about the part that goes, 'Next, when the sun rose, God ordained that there should be a scorching east wind; the sun beat down so hard on Jonah's head that he was overcome and begged for death, saying, I might as well be dead as go on living.' Sound like anyone you know?"

"I see you've been reacquainting yourself with your personal heritage," I commented sourly.

"A little," he nodded. "So you going to loosen up and tell me why you're sitting out here hoping the thunderheads will decide to blaze you?"

"That's not why I'm here," I growled. "Anyway . . . whatever they think of me, if they were going to do something like that they would have done it days ago."

"Uh-*huh*," he said, entirely too knowingly. "So the thought *had* crossed your mind." His sense softened. "Because of Calandra?"

My stomach tightened into a knot. "Not really," I told him. "I see you know all about it."

"Most of it," he admitted, his own discomfort deepening a little. "I helped Lord Kelsey-Ramos sift through the transcripts of her first trial. Look . . . it still wasn't murder, you know—once she'd fingered the saboteur and gotten his bomb away from him, tossing it out a window was probably the only way she could think of to get it out of the building. Just because her throw didn't make it all the way across the street doesn't change that."

"She said she was innocent," I told him. "No mention of extenuating circumstances, no niceties of distinction between manslaughter and murder. Innocent."

Kutzko took a deep breath. "Let me tell you something, Gilead. Two things, really. One: when she told you all that, she thought she'd be dead within two weeks. That would have been the end of it . . . except that she'd have had a friend for those last few days." He shrugged. "She didn't exactly expect you to jump on a white horse and go charging off into the middle of it like you did."

There was authority in his words; in his words, and in the way he said them. Not speculation, but certain knowledge. "I'm glad to see she was willing to talk to *someone* before leaving for Outbound."

"You blame her for not wanting to face you?" he asked pointedly. "Especially feeling the way you are right now?"

"Do you blame *me* for wanting honesty instead of lies?" I countered.

He cocked an eyebrow. "Oh, is that how it goes? All right, then, here's some honesty for you. One, she thought she'd be dead in two weeks; and, two, you *wanted* to believe she didn't do it."

"If you mean I was willing to give her the benefit of the doubt—"

"Oh, come off it," he snapped. "I was *there*, remember? Even *I* could see how much it bothered you to think that a Watcher could have fallen off the golden ladder—and if *I* could see it, *she* sure as blazing could, too. All she did was tell you what you wanted to hear."

I sighed, the flash of anger fading into heartache. What I wanted to hear. After all of Aikman's hatred and paranoia—after all the Patri's suspicions and fears—it turned out that I was just as capable of prejudice and willing self-blindness as anyone else. Somehow, down deep, I suppose I'd wanted to believe that as Watchers she and I were somehow different from the rest of humanity—I'd been raised, in fact, to believe that, and it was one of the few solid handholds I'd always been able to hold onto in Lord Kelsey-Ramos's soul-numbing world.

Only now I knew better. Just one more example of willing self-blindness.

"It's not just Calandra," I told Kutzko, shaking my head. "It's the way that this . . ." I waved a hand helplessly, trying to find the right words. "Well, the way that nothing has worked out the way it should have."

He gave me an odd look. "We got contact with an alien race, we *didn't* get into a war, and Calandra's going to get a new trial. How *should* it have worked out?"

"You don't understand."

"So explain it to me."

I took a deep breath. "I started this whole thing, Mikha. I lied and stole and betrayed people's trust right and left—I shredded half of my ethical standards, first for Calandra and then for the Invaders."

"And, what, you want more of the credit?"

"You're missing the point," I said bitterly. "Lord Kelsey-Ramos and Dr. Eisenstadt are up to their chins in trouble with the Pravilo, the Halo of God has been pretty well destroyed as a religious community, Shepherd Adams *died* out there, for heaven's sake . . . and I'm not even going to get a slap on the hand." Tears rose to my eyes; angrily, I blinked them back. "In every case, someone else has had to pay for my actions."

I expected a quick and possibly glib reply. I got,

instead, a long silence. "You know," Kutzko said at last, his voice unusually reflective, "my parents used to talk like that. Used to say that we were here in life to suffer. Oh, not in those words—they talked about it as building character and patience and stuff like that. But that's what it all came down to in the end: that suffering was how you proved you were doing what you were supposed to." He nodded toward the thunderheads. "Now, the way *I* like to look at things is to count up what got accomplished and then compare it to whatever extra it cost. And I'll tell you right now, Gilead, that except for Adams, you accomplished a blazing lot for practically nothing."

I glared at him. "You don't consider Lord Kelsey-Ramos and the Halo of God worth all that much, do you?"

"I said whatever *extra* it cost," he reminded me with strained patience. "You know full well that Lord Kelsey-Ramos and Eisenstadt are too important for any of this to stick to them; and if you weren't so bent on feeling sorry for yourself, you'd admit you didn't do anything to the Halloas the thunderheads wouldn't have done by themselves in a few months. They *had* to make contact with us pretty blazing soon if they wanted us to tackle the Invaders for them—they were probably waiting until we'd just have enough time to do the job but not enough to stop and think about it."

I gritted my teeth in irritation. Irritation, and the slightly galling knowledge that he was in fact right. "It still doesn't seem fair," I said, just for something to say.

"It's not," he agreed easily. "But since when do you care about fair?"

I blinked in surprise. "Since always."

"Since never," he retorted. "You don't want fair, Gilead—you've *never* wanted it. *Any*one can get fair—the Patri judiciary can usually manage *that* much."

"Oh, really," I said sarcastically. "Well, in that case, perhaps you'd be kind enough to tell me what it is I *do* want."

He shrugged. "You're the religious one. You tell *me* what you're supposed to be giving out."

I glared at him again; but it was a glare without any power at all behind it. He had me, and we both knew it. "Compassion," I muttered. "Mercy. Forgiveness."

He spread his hands. "There we go," he nodded. "Nothing like a little heathen argument to sharpen your focus."

"Oh, thank you," I growled. "Thank you very much."

He grinned, then sobered. "You know, I think I've finally figured it out. Remember that stuff about being the salt of the earth?"

You are salt for the earth . . . "Yes," I said.

"Well, you're not salt—you aren't, anyway. You're more like a catalyst."

I snorted. " 'You are catalysts for the earth.' It loses a little in the translation."

"No, I'm serious," Kutzko insisted. "Sure, you got through this thing pretty clean; but look at all the people who wound up doing things for others along the way." He held up gloved fingers, began ticking them off. "I mean, there was Adams; there were Lord Kelsey-Ramos and Eisenstadt; there's the Halloas. Not to even mention what all this is going to do to the Deadman Switch."

I stared at him. "What about the Deadman Switch?"

"I mean the Halloas taking over for the zombis, of course," he snorted. "Or didn't you think the Patri would notice that Adams did as well out there as any zombi could have?"

"They *did* notice it, and he didn't do nearly well enough," I retorted bitterly. It was one of my own secret hopes, too . . . or rather, it *had* been, before I'd seen the commission's reaction to it. "The commission made it perfectly clear that no one's going to be interested in hauling ten or fifteen people on runs into Solitaire when they can do it with two prisoners instead."

"Yeah, but you're assuming Adams's forty-five-minute limit is all you can get," Kutzko reminded me. "Don't forget that he had some medical problems to begin

with—*and* he didn't have all that many contacts on his
scorecard. You may not know it, but Zagorin's already
done two hours at a stretch without getting into trouble, and there's no reason why that's the end of the
line, either."

I sighed. "Except that the commission isn't interested, no matter *where* the end of the line is. Replacing
the Deadman Switch would mean putting Solitaire
navigation—or at least the navigator training—into the
hands of people they consider to be religious fanatics.
They won't accept that; I know, I saw their faces after
my testimony."

He grinned. "Yeah, but you didn't see their faces
after *my* testimony."

I frowned. "And just what did you testify to?" I asked
cautiously.

"Oh, nothing special," he said, his sense all smug
innocence. "I just made sure they got a description—a
blazing *good* description—of how the thunderheads
picked up Adams's body and tried to attack you with
it."

And even as the memory sent a cold shiver up my
back I saw that he was right. A zombi sitting peacefully
and obediently at the Deadman Switch was one thing; a
zombi moving about the bridge was something else
entirely. A ghastly horror, straight out of mankind's
deepest and darkest fears. "Yes," I agreed, taking a
shuddering breath and trying to force the image away.
"I can understand why that would . . . bother them."

"*Bother* them?" He snorted. "Try terrified them out
of their minds. By the time I was through they were
falling all over each other getting study groups set up.
It might take a year or two, but the Deadman Switch is
finished—count on it."

Death, where is your victory? "I guess it's not a bad
list, at that," I murmured, almost reluctantly.

"Awfully generous of you," Kutzko said dryly. "I'd
say *not a bad list* covers it pretty well. Sort of give you
a different angle on things, doesn't it?—unless, that is,

you're the type that's stuck on being a candidate for martyr."

Martyr. I listened to the sound of that word as it echoed through my mind. *Martyr.* A noble, honorable way to serve humanity . . . or a hypocritical and cowardly way to escape from that same service. Which motivation, I wondered, had been behind my willingness to give my life aboard the tug?

I still had no answer for that question . . . but now, I saw with sudden clarity that I didn't need to. Kutzko was right: my job was not to concentrate on the suffering or the sacrifices, but on my service to those around me.

And with Lord Kelsey-Ramos busy pulling strings with the Pravilo to keep me out of prison, it was pretty clear who those people would be. At least for now.

"Martyr, huh?" I commented to Kutzko as I stood up. "Anyone ever tell you that tact isn't your strong point?"

"Oh, all the time," he admitted cheerfully, getting to his feet with me. "Why do you think I picked a job where I get to carry a weapon around? That was a pretty fast trip out of the doldrums, if I do say so myself."

"It sure was," I agreed. "You don't make a bad catalyst yourself."

"Don't start that," he said, mock-warningly. "I gave up religion a long time ago, remember?"

"Sure," I said. And smiled to myself as, together, we headed down the ridge.

TIMOTHY ZAHN

CREATOR OF NEW WORLDS

"Timothy Zahn's specialty is technological intrigue—international and interstellar," says *The Christian Science Monitor*. Amen! For novels involving hard-edged conflict with alien races, world-building with a strong scientific basis, and storytelling excitement, turn to Hugo Award Winner Timothy Zahn!

Here is an excerpt from the new novel by Timothy Zahn, coming from Baen Books in August 1987:

TIMOTHY ZAHN

TRIPLET

The way house had been quiet for over an hour by the time Karyx's moon rose that night, its fingernail-clipping crescent adding only token assistance to the dim starlight already illuminating the grounds. Sitting on the mansion's garret-floor widow's walk, his back against the door, Ravagin watched the moon drift above the trees to the east and listened to the silence of the night. And tried to decide what in blazes he was going to do.

There actually *were* precedents for this kind of situation: loose precedents, to be sure, and hushed up like crazy by the people upstairs in the Crosspoint Building, but precedents nonetheless. Every so often a Courier and his group would have such a mutual falling out that continuing on together was out of the question ... and when that happened the Courier would often simply give notice and quit, leaving the responsibility for getting the party back to Threshold in the hands of the nearest way house staff. Triplet management ground their collective teeth when it happened, but they'd long ago come to the reluctant conclusion that clients were better off alone than with a Courier who no longer gave a damn about their safety.

And Ravagin wouldn't even have to endure the

usual froth-mouthed lecture that would be waiting when he got back. He was finished with the Corps, and those who'd bent his fingers into taking this trip had only themselves to blame for the results. He could leave a note with Melentha, grab a horse, and be at the Cairn Mounds well before daylight. By the time Danae had finished sputtering, he'd have alerted the way house master in Feymar Protectorate on Shamsheer and be on a sky-plane over the Ordarl Mountains ... and by the time she made it back through to Threshold and screamed for vengeance, he'd have picked up his last paychit, said bye-and-luck to Corah, and boarded a starship for points unknown. Ravagin, the great veteran Courier, actually deserting a client. Genuinely one for the record books.

Yes. He would do it. He would. Right now. He'd get up, go downstairs, and get the hell out of here.

Standing up, he gazed out at the moon ... and slammed his fist in impotent fury on the low railing in front of him.

He couldn't do it.

"Damn," he muttered under his breath, clenching his jaw hard enough to hurt. "Damn, damn, *damn*."

He hit the railing again and inhaled deeply, exhaling in a hissing sigh of anger and resignation. He couldn't do it. No matter what the justification—no matter that the punishment would be light or nonexistent—no matter even that others had done it without lasting stigma. He was a *professional*, damn it, and it was his job to stay with his clients no matter what happened.

Danae had wounded his pride. Deserting her, unfortunately, would hurt it far more deeply then she ever could.

In other words, a classic no-win situation. With him on the short end.

And it left him just two alternatives: continue his silent treatment toward Danae for the rest of the trip or work through his anger enough to at least ge back on civil terms with her. At the moment, neither choice was especially attractive.

Out in the grounds, a flicker of green caught his eye. He looked down, frowning, trying to locate the source. Nothing was moving; nothing seemed out of place. Could there be something skulking in the clumps of trees, or perhaps even the shadows thrown by the bushes?

Or could something have tried to break through the post line?

Nothing was visible near the section of post line he could see. Cautiously, he began easing his way around the widow's walk, muttering a spirit-protection spell just to be on the safe side.

Still nothing. He'd reached the front of the house and was starting to continue past when a movement through the gap in the tree hedge across the grounds to the south caught his attention. He peered toward it . . . and a few seconds later it was repeated further east.

A horseman on the road toward Besak, most likely . . . except that Besak had long since been sealed up for the night by the village lar. And Karyx was not a place to casually indulge in nighttime travel. Whoever it was, he was either on an errand of dire emergency or else—

Or else hurrying away from an aborted attempt to break in?

Ravagin pursed his lips. *"Haklarast,"* he said. It was at least worth checking out.

The glow-fire of the sprite appeared before him. "I am here, as you summoned," it squeaked.

"There's a horse and human traveling on the road toward Besak just south of here," he told it. "Go to the human and ask why he rides so late. Return to me with his answer."

The sprite flared and was gone. Ravagin watched it dart off across the darkened landscape and then, for lack of anything better to do while he waited, continued his long-range inspection of the post line. Again he found nothing; and he was coming around to the front of the house again when the sprite returned. "What answer?" he asked it.

"None. The human is not awake."

"Are you sure?" Ravagin asked, frowning. He'd once learned the hard way about the hazards of sleeping on horseback—most Karyx natives weren't stupid enough to try it. "Really asleep, not injured?"

"I do not know."

Of course it wouldn't—spirits didn't see the world the way humans did. "Well . . . is he riding alone, or is there a spirit with him protecting him from falls?"

"There is a djinn present, though it is not keeping the human from falling. There is no danger of that."

And with a djinn along to— "What do you mean? Why isn't he going to fall?"

"The human is upright, in full control of the animal—"

"Wait a second," Ravagin cut it off. "You just told me he was asleep. How can he be controlling the horse?"

"The human is asleep," the sprite repeated, and Ravagin thought he could detect a touch of vexation in the squeaky voice. "It is in control of its animal."

"That's impossible," Ravagin growled. "He'd have to be—"

Sleepwalking.

"*Damn!*" he snarled, eyes darting toward the place where the rider had vanished, thoughts skidding with shock, chagrin, and a full-bellied rush of fear. *Danae*—

His mental wheels caught. "Follow the rider," he ordered the sprite. "Stay back where you won't be spotted by any other humans, but don't let her out of your sight. First give me your name, so I can locate you later. Come on, give—I haven't got time for games."

"I am Psskapsst," the sprite said reluctantly.

"Psskapsst, right. Now get after it—and *don't* communicate with that djinn."

The glow-fire flared and skittered off. Racing along the widow's walk, Ravagin reached the door and hurried inside. Danae's room was two flights down, on the second floor; on a hunch, he stopped first on the third floor and let himself into Melentha's sanctum.

The place had made Ravagin's skin crawl even with good lighting, and the dark shadows stretching around the room now didn't improve it a bit. Shivering reflexively, he stepped carefully around the central pentagram and over to the table where Melentha had put the bow and Coven robe when she'd finished her spirit search.

The robe was gone.

Swearing under his breath, he turned and hurried back to the door—and nearly ran into Melentha as she suddenly appeared outside in the hallway. "What are you doing in there?" she demanded, holding her robe closed with one hand and clutching a glowing dagger in the other.

"The Coven robe's gone," he told her, "and I think Danae's gone with it."

"What?" She backed up hastily to let him pass, then hurried to catch up with him "When?"

"Just a little while ago—I think I saw her leaving on horseback from the roof. I just want to make sure—"

They reached Danae's room and Ravagin pushed open the door . . . and she was indeed gone.

August 1987 • 384 pp. • 65341-5 • $3.50

To order any Baen Book, send the cover price plus 75¢ for first-class postage and handling to: Baen Books, Dept. BB, 260 Fifth Avenue, New York, N.Y. 10001.